Black Roses

by Christine Morgan

Published by:

Sabledrake Enterprises
PO Box 30751
Seattle, WA 98103
http://www.sabledrake.com
sabledrake@sabledrake.com

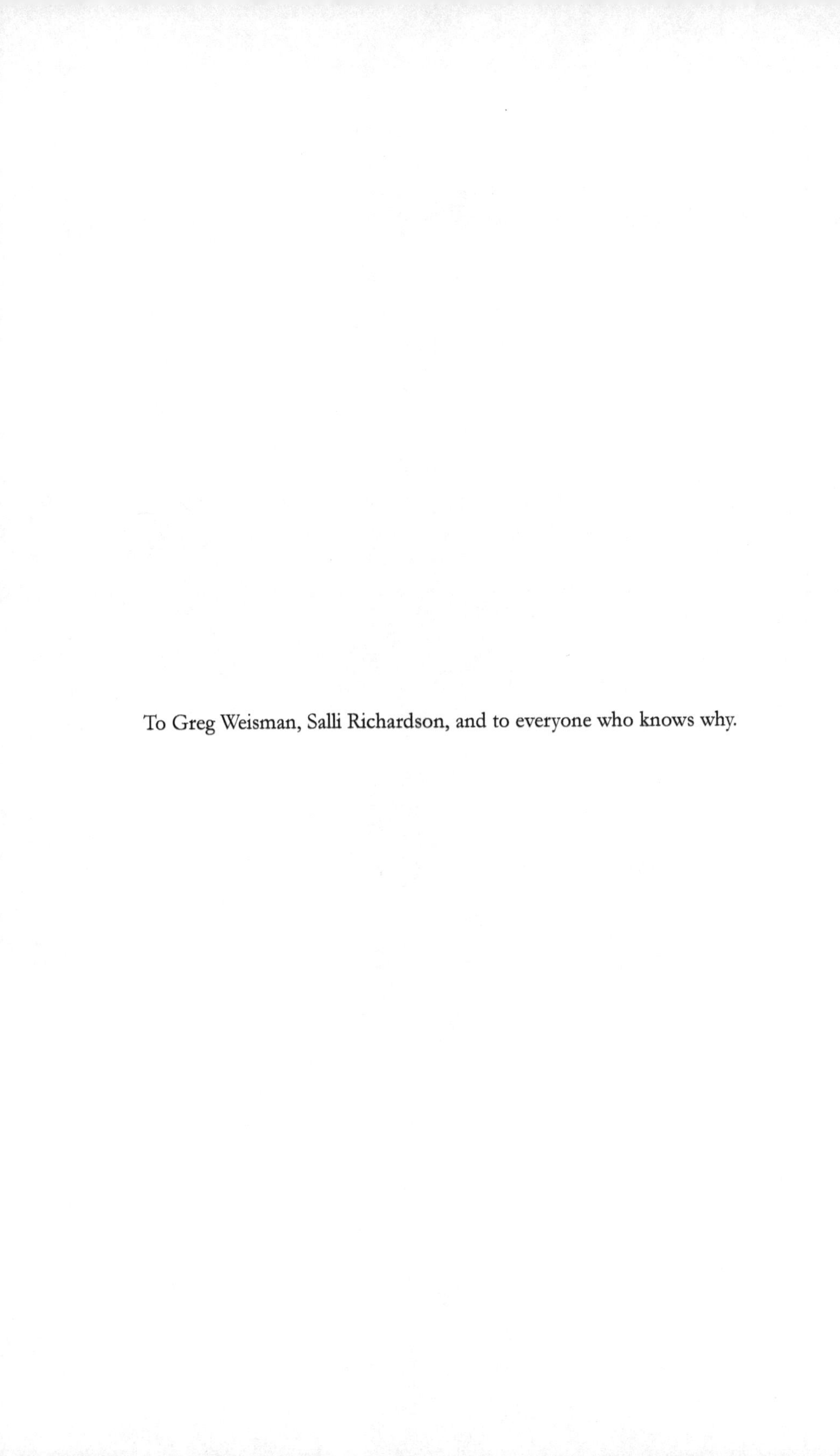

To Greg Weisman, Salli Richardson, and to everyone who knows why.

"Theresa Zane! You've just flushed your marriage and career down the drain; what are you going to do now?"

Her voice rang horridly cheerful, as if she was an announcer asking the all-important question in front of thousands of screaming fans.

The only one to hear her was Jack. He looked up in acute feline disinterest before returning his attention to grooming. He was almost a year old now, how the time does fly. She'd gotten him in October of last year, when the lonely emptiness of the apartment became too much to bear.

Jack'O'Lantern. She'd named him after coming home one day to find the orange kitten curled up inside the pumpkin she'd carved for no reason other than because Lora always loved to have a pumpkin.

That was last year, though, and this was this year. August was past, September was passing, and the holiday season was looming like a juggernaut on the horizon. The world was speeding along out of control, carrying Theresa with it.

"Can't afford to go to Disneyland," she answered herself, and was unnerved at how frayed and shaky her voice was.

For a moment, she trembled on the threshold of tears, then got hold of herself. She hadn't cried when Steven said he thought divorce was their only option, hadn't cried when the judge gave him custody of Lora, so damned if she was going to cry over a cartoon show!

The phone rang, interrupted by the machine and her own recorded voice. "Hi, this is Theresa Zane. I'm happy with my long-distance carrier, I don't participate in surveys, and when I want to make a donation, *I'll* contact *you*. Anyone else, here's the beep."

Beep.

"Terri, hi, Suze here."

Theresa picked up. "Hi, Suze."

She hated being called Terri, but Susan Marsh called all her clients by a nickname, and if some unwary person rejected the first one she chose, the next was apt to be particularly unpleasant. For example, Louis Corey, who wrote delightful books of children's poetry, would forever be known as Melon-Head. So Theresa put up with Terri, if not gladly, at least gratefully, considering the possible alternatives.

"You've heard the bad news?"

"They called this morning." Theresa sighed. "So much for *Lora and Ruff*."

"That producer has the brains of a gerbil, I swear to God. Never mind giving kids something to watch that's educational as well as fun; let's fill their wee little heads with singsong mush that has good marketing potential. If I ever see one of those cutesy-ass puppets of his in a toy store, I'll buy one just to roast it with a flamethrower."

Suze could usually get a smile from her, but today, Theresa's smiler seemed to be out of order. She managed a half-hearted sound that was meant to be a chuckle.

"So you listen to me, Terri, don't let that s.o.b. get you down. This isn't over yet."

She mumbled in all the right places as Susan went on, alternating between outlining plans for their next move and promising gaudy revenge on anyone who got in their way.

All the while, she searched her heart for enthusiasm and found zilch. The proposed show was dead in the water. She knew it, and Suze knew it too.

Ten books in four years, starting with *Lora and Ruff Go to the Circus* and ending with *Lora and Ruff Go to the Moon*. There would not be an eleventh book, and that was something Suze *didn't* know but Theresa did.

How could there be an eleventh book? Lora, her inspiration, was living with Steven and his new wife in Phoenix, and Theresa hadn't been able to write a word since.

The most ironic thing was that they'd broken up because of *Lora and Ruff*. It hadn't been the money. Of which there wasn't much, as her bank account could attest. It hadn't been the fame. See money, above. It had been the move. He wasn't willing to move to L.A., and she wasn't willing to give up her chance.

"Earth to Terri! Hey! You still there?"

"Here, sorry. I was woolgathering."

"You were moping."

"I was moping."

"Steven?"

"Lora. She starts first grade tomorrow."

There wasn't much Suze could say, and Theresa knew it. The Marsh kids were all grown, out of the house, and had as little to do with their flamboyant mother as they could.

It depressed Theresa even more to think of it. She ran through her female acquaintances in her head, trying to think of one, just one, that had a good relationship with her mother. She came up empty. Was it something all mothers and daughters had to face? Was it going to be like that for her and Lora? They were already off to a good start – her daughter's soft, heartbroken "Oh, okay," when Theresa had told her no, she wouldn't be able to come to the bus stop with her on her first day at the big kid's school, had cut deep and close to the bone.

She'd vowed countless times over the years that she was never going to turn out like her own mother, but now she realized she didn't have to. She could lose Lora just as effectively through distance and perceived indifference as she could through criticism and harsh words.

After making the necessary conversational noises and hanging up, Theresa looked around her apartment and heaved another sigh. She'd been too busy to clean and then too stressed to clean. The evidence of her state of mind was everywhere. Ben and Jerry were her two best friends, and who ever believed that there were supposed to be four servings in one of those little tubs?

The frantic schedule of the past few months had made her drop several pounds, the comfort food of the past few weeks had put it all back on, so she was right back where she started. Lose and gain, gain and lose, like a merry go round and no matter how many times you went around, you never got anyplace.

"Story of my life," she muttered.

Jack's ear twitched at her as if to say, *hey, Theresa, I'm trying to catch a nap here, do you mind?*

She was sinking into a mire of self-pity. Justifiable, sure, here she was washed up at twenty-eight, didn't she have some right to feel sorry for herself?

But if there was one thing her mother had harped on that made sense, it was that there was no point in whining about what had happened. The question was, what was she going to do about it?

She suddenly knew that if she stayed indoors another minute, she was going to go bonkers.

Grabbing her purse, she was out the door and into the muggy slap of heat that passed for late summer in L.A. before she could talk herself out of it. There was a little park a few blocks away, squeezed between a junior high that could pass for a detention center and an office block that looked like an abstract sculpture. She headed for the park, stopping at the mini-mart on the corner to pick up a bottle of soda and a package of cookies.

Some of the schools had started already, but most – *like Lora's*, the nagging mother-voice spoke up in the back of her head – would start tomorrow. The playground was full of kids playing with desperate intensity, the last day of summer, the last day of freedom.

Theresa sat on a bench beneath a tree whose leaves were already curling into arthritic brown husks. She loved L.A., loved the gritty sprawling buzz of it, loved the variety and the mingled cultures and the busy energy of it all. Everyone seemed like they were going someplace fast. Up or down, becoming successes or nobodies, but they were going there fast. It was like a hub between all possible worlds. A drive of a few hours could take you to sunwashed beaches or ski slopes or panoramic high desert vistas where Joshua trees poked their bristly arms at the sky.

She loved it, but she felt a surprisingly strong hunger for the cool green of home.

Not Phoenix. That wasn't home now, hadn't been since the door of Steven's house had closed behind her for the last time. Even when she'd lived there, it had never really been *her* home; he had inherited it from his grandparents and she'd always felt their presence, if not disapproving, *waiting* to disapprove.

Strange to think of Trinity Bay as home. She'd only lived there until she was nine. But it, more than any of the other places she'd stayed since her mother walked out on her father and dragged Theresa along for the ride, was what she thought of now as she watched the children laugh and yell under the hazy sunshine. Home.

She realized with bitter rueful amusement that this was what the whole Gen X hoopla was about. Here she was, twenty-eight, done with college and having no luck in either the job or marriage departments, heading home to live with her folks.

"Good God, I've become a statistic," she said, and laughed. Some of the nearest kids gave her wary looks much too adult – couldn't be too careful, those young/old eyes proclaimed, couldn't be too careful, there were psychos everywhere.

Would Lora's eyes look like that in a few years? Was that the fate of the kids of today, the heirs of the new millennium? Now, *there* was a cheery thought.

Home and Trinity Bay. Images like cozy slippers for the soul. Maybe what she needed was a fresh start, and what better place to do it than one of the few places she had been truly happy?

Her father had offered. When he'd first heard of her split-up from Steven, he'd made the offer and she knew it was sincere. If you need a place, honey, remember your old dad. Not made for form's sake or as a veiled barb, the way her mother would have said it. An offer made as if he really did want her there.

At the very least, she decided, she would give Dad a call. He might have changed his mind; it had been fifteen months and even in Trinity Bay, things changed.

It wasn't even inconceivable that he might have a new woman in his life and not need his style cramped by his grown daughter hanging around the house. After all, Travis Zane was still a good-looking fellow at age 60. His Native American ancestry gave him rugged, noble features and striking dark eyes. Women had always been drawn to him, which had been one of the things Theresa's mother complained about the most.

That and the house. Lois had hated the house from the word go.

Theresa sat up straighter on the bench, her eyes, which had drifted into a pleasant daydream half-close, now widening. A big beaming smile curved her lips, and a man who was walking past with an Irish Setter on a leash turned to walk backwards and return it with interest. Theresa barely noticed. Her mind was riffling through the pages of memory, looking for a name.

Glory. Yes, it *had* been Glory! And years later, she would name her own daughter Lora, never consciously seeing the connection until now.

Glory. Lora. Close enough for government work.

If Steven, practical Steven, knew that she had named their daughter after the imaginary friend of her own childhood, he would just about choke.

The more she thought about Trinity Bay, the more she convinced herself it was the answer. Drive up, stay with Dad for a while, get her head on straight and her life back in order. The change of pace, the change of surroundings, would be just what she needed to figure out what came next. The break might even jump-start her creativity. Could be there were more books in her; if not the continuing adventures of *Lora and Ruff,* maybe a novel.

She didn't want her last cookie. She was hungry for real food, something nutritious. A chef's salad, crisp veggies and lean ham and hard-boiled eggs. A big glass of iced tea with lemon.

Theresa brushed crumbs from her jeans and walked briskly back to the apartment, pausing to wave up at Jack on the windowsill before she backed her car onto the street and drove to the market. Fresh fruit, roast beef and Swiss for sandwich makings, milk, cat food, some yogurt, the salad fixings, and Hershey's Kisses because she was afraid her body might go into shock if she went cold-turkey from the junk and sweets.

Humming to herself, she wrestled the bags up the stairs and balanced them with one arm while she groped for her keys. Jack twined meowing around her ankles, adding a further obstacle as she tried to make her way to the kitchenette without a disaster. Mission accomplished, at the cost of one accidental tread on a declawed paw.

"Sorry, Jack!" She mollified him with a helping of cat food, holding her breath as she did so. She loved Jack, but she was never going to get used to the rank odor of his chow, or the gelatinous smack it made coming out of the can.

It had been a long time since she'd taken pleasure in cooking. A long time since she'd taken much pleasure in anything. Even the television show – she now saw that she'd thrown herself into it with such gung-ho energy not because she loved the idea (though she did) but because while she was focused on *Lora and Ruff*, she wasn't thinking about the real Lora, or Steven.

There was a framed photo of Lora on the table, and Theresa gazed at it while she ate. It had been taken the summer before last, just before she and Steven broke up. Lora in the backyard of the Phoenix house, by the pool. She had Theresa's hair, black as polished ebony, but she had Steven's clear green eyes.

Those eyes had been what first drew Theresa to him. She was sure they were contacts, wondering at that conceit in a guy who seemed otherwise modest. Steven Taylor, sandy-brown hair, a nice face, a decent body, soft-spoken. Unremarkable, except for those eyes. They'd dated for four months before she found out the color was true.

Steven had been good for her. She'd been a teen rebel, wild to break away from her mother and stepfather's strict, stifling rules. Steven had been the one to make her see how she'd been ruining her own future trying to get back at her mother. Looking back, she could hardly believe she had been that girl.

"What a difference ten years makes," she said to the picture, to Lora's bright smile.

What a difference, indeed! From feast to famine! She'd had exactly one date since the divorce became final, and that was with Susan's brother-in-law. A perfect gentleman until they were alone, and then he grew six more arms. She wasn't eager to jump back into her old habits; her self-respect had gone up too many levels for that.

Still, she missed having a man in her life. For that matter, she missed having a life! She'd thought earlier that the world was rushing along and carrying her with it, but the truth was, the world was rushing along and she was sitting like a lump watching it go.

* * *

Over the next week, *she* rushed along and dragged the world in her wake.

Her father had been delighted at the prospect of her visiting, even staying for as long as she liked. She sensed a bigger relief in his tone than the occasion warranted, making her wonder if there was more going on than Travis was telling.

Suze had been aghast at the thought of one of her clients, even a suddenly less-than-profitable client, moving to a backwater town in the middle of nowhere. Of course, to the people of L.A., the Bay Area was Northern California, and anything beyond that was the great uncharted wilderness.

"What are you going to *do* there anyway?" Suze demanded. "Grow pot? Shoot film of Bigfoot? Chain yourself to a redwood to save the spotted owl?"

"Those aren't the only regional pastimes," Theresa said.

"Name another," Suze challenged.

"Um . . ."

Her agent's objections aside, the rest of the planning had gone swiftly and easily. Her furniture all fit into one medium-sized storage unit. She took her clothes, her computer, what books she couldn't bear to do without, all her pictures of Lora, and of course a very indignant Jack in a plastic cat-carrier.

Driving at night would let her avoid traffic and the heat. Straight up I-5 – literally straight; if she had cruise control, she could have just pointed the car north and let it drive itself.

She wasn't ready yet to explain to her ex-husband how the show that had been worth wrecking their marriage over had gone to TV Heaven. After she got settled, she could get in touch and maybe even convince him to let her have Lora up for Christmas.

But that was still a few months away. Who knew, it might not work out. She and Dad might get under each other's skin in no time, and then she'd be back in freefall. For now, the thing to concentrate on was getting to Trinity Bay, getting the new start she needed.

I-5 north, long black ribbons of asphalt unspooling in the glow of the headlights. Big rigs droned along at seventy miles per hour. A few other cars, other travelers like herself. The moon sailed its slow, steady course toward the sea. Jack's unhappy yowling finally became silence as he curled up and went to sleep.

Although she'd slept late that morning and loaded up on convenience-store coffee, the tedium of the drive worked a hypnotic spell. Soon Theresa was rolling down the window to scoop night air onto her face, cranking the radio in hopes of warding off the sandman. No good. The jaw-cracking yawns continued, and by the time she reached Redding, she was gritty-eyed and shaky. In no condition for the trek across Highway 299, a winding course through the mountains.

She pulled into a rest stop, let Jack out of the carrier so he could use the cardboard box of litter on the floor, reclined her seat as far as it would go, and pulled her jacket over herself like a blanket. She was dimly aware of the warm soft weight of a cat on her lap, and then she was out.

The blare of a horn jolted her awake, and for an adrenaline-shrieking moment she was sure she had fallen asleep at the wheel and dreamed parking at the rest stop. She uttered a little scream in the close confines of the car and jerked upright, spilling

Jack down by the pedals.

It was still dark. No blazing twin suns of an oncoming semi. Her car wasn't about to be flattened or run off the road. Theresa waited until her heart resumed a normal rhythm, then got out and winced at the stiff tingling in her limbs.

She hurried to the ladies' room, peed for what seemed like forever – all that coffee – and checked her watch. Quarter past four in the morning. She'd been napping for over an hour.

Not nearly enough, but she was wide awake now and might as well keep going.

The last time she'd gone across 299 was as a child of nine, terrified that her mother was going to crash them right through a guardrail and into the rocky river below. A child with tears of fear and confused grief streaming down her face.

Thank God I didn't put Lora through anything like that, she thought. *At least Steven and I parted on decent terms.*

Her mother had been married three times, divorced three times. In the great courtroom of life, the jury might still be out on whether or not men were shit, but as far as Lois Abbey-Marriott-Zane-Kowalski was concerned, the verdict was, "Guilty!"

That didn't stop her, however, from blaming Theresa for letting her own marriage fail. All men were shit, Steven was a man, therefore, Theresa must have been a bad wife. Logical. Sure. All the way.

Twisty mountain road. Close-hugging trees on one side, a steep drop on the other. Oncoming headlights were sudden and eye-wateringly bright, all the worse because they were so few and far between that her eyes readjusted to the dimness before the next set came beaming out of the darkness.

She drove with even more caution than normal, so much caution that she had to use the turn-outs several times to allow other vehicles to pass. It was as if she had an unseen passenger, a little girl clinging to her seatbelt with white-knuckled hands, crying because she already missed her father, her friends, her home.

The world lightened as the miles went by. The sky went from black to indigo to slate, and then to a soft pearl-grey. Now Theresa could see the towering redwoods, their shaggy rust-colored bark rising above the ferns and underbrush. Fog wreathed the tops of the trees, ghosted between the trunks in eddies and swirls.

Theresa rolled down her window and breathed the cool moist air tinged with sea spray. It revitalized her in a way the coffee couldn't have done. To smell the sea was to smell the unknown, the mysterious, the uplifting.

The sun rose as a bright spot in the uniform silver of the cloudbank. It shed a light at once alien and peaceful. Like being on Venus, if Venus were the misty paradise of imaginings instead of the steam-cooked hell it really was.

By the time she had descended toward the coast, the sky had gone a milky blue, and she knew the last of the clouds would burn off by noon. It would be one of those postcard-perfect days that belied the rumor that there was nothing but dreary, soggy weather behind the Redwood Curtain.

From 299, she got onto 101 north, past McKinleyville and Trinidad and Patrick's Point State Park. It was the overlap between the end of the tourist season and the beginning of the student season at Humboldt State University in Arcata, a few miles south, but at this hour, she still had the highway mostly to herself.

Trinity Bay Next Right, read the sign, and Theresa's spirits lifted. She took the off-ramp, noted a sign directing her to the North Valley Shopping Center – that was new, to her at least – and buttonhooked back under the freeway onto the rather too grandly named Trinity Bay Boulevard.

At once, the groves closed around her. Dense green in a thousand shades. If not for the gravel driveways disappearing through the treetrunks, and the mailboxes in clusters along the roadside, she could almost have believed she had been transported to the forest primeval.

Then she topped a rise, and the view opened up like a long-awaited gift.

To her right, a tumble of rocky islands clustered around a mammoth bulk of stone. Some were still partly connected by natural bridges shaped over the millennia by the ceaseless waves. That portion of the land curved inward, sheltering the bay, while on the far side the waves crashed and sometimes kicked sprays of foam high into the air.

From there, Theresa let her eye follow the gravel beach past the campground, which now featured cabins and a brand new motel. A small but modern-looking medical center stood at the edge of the town proper – quite a change from the days when Doc Kensington's large brick home had doubled as the office of Trinity Bay's only resident physician.

Agate Way, the old trestle bridge still standing, presumably now extended past Mill Road and led to the North Valley Shopping Center. The sawmill was out of sight of the town except for the sickly sweet-sour plumes from the stacks, which blew their nauseating miasma out to sea, or over town when the wind was wrong.

She recognized the combined elementary/high school, and the town square around the grassy plaza complete with a statue of some forgotten mariner. The business district clustered around the plaza, and from there homes spread out like ripples in a pond. Little had changed from the pictures she carried in her memory, though it all looked smaller. Which she should have suspected; it had been almost twenty years since she lived here, and her brief visits in the interim had not updated her mental image.

On the left, the south end of town, the land rose again into a bluff, and overlooking the town like some smug Midas was Seacliff. Theresa had once done a report on the house, the last assignment she'd turned in before her mother whisked her away.

Built in 1870 by redwood baron Jacob Cliffwood, Seacliff had gone through ups and downs in harmony with the prosperity of the town and the logging industry. It had begun as a six-room house, grand by the standards of the day, but ten years later in honor of the birth of his first child, Jacob had expanded and improved upon it. Each successive generation had made their own changes, and now it loomed with a proud majesty that nearly equaled that of the Carson Mansion in Eureka.

Theresa drove through town, around the series of one-way streets that framed the plaza, taking in the sights. The town-hall-slash-library was just as ugly as it had ever been; most of the shops seemed to have enjoyed a face lift in recent years. While the town didn't give the feeling of great prosperity, it seemed to be thriving in a quiet, companionable sort of way.

She turned onto Cliffwood Road, which had originally been the driveway leading up to Seacliff. Her father's house had once been a guest cottage on the main estate, but the Cliffwoods had been forced to sell off many of their outbuildings and land during the Depression. Her grandparents had bought the house then, though Myra Cliffwood, maiden-aunt matriarch of the manor, hadn't been thrilled at the prospect of having the Zanes for neighbors. Thaddeus Zane had, after all, married an Indian woman.

There was a stubborn streak running through the Zane family, though, as Theresa could personally attest. They weren't going to let one woman's disdain drive them out of their home.

And in a way, Theresa supposed, her family got the last laugh. There might be no more Cliffwoods in town, but now another Zane was back in Trinity Bay.

* * *

So beautiful!

He watched intently as the woman got out of the car and stretched. The wind lifted her long black hair like a banner. Her shirt pulled taut across her breasts, her jeans molded the lovely outline of her hips and buttocks.

Oh, yes, very beautiful!

He wanted to go to her, touch her, but the distance between them was too great. His only choice was to watch. For now, at least. Soon, though, he knew there would be an opportunity for them to get to know one another. Intimately.

The door to the old guest house opened, and Zane came out. He greeted the woman gladly. Even from here, the observer could see the resemblance between them. Zane's daughter, then.

Jealousy twisted through him as they embraced, as Zane led her into the house and out of his sight.

He wanted her.

He wanted to know her every thought, her every secret desire. He would prove himself worthy of her love, and then she would be his.

Forever.

* * *

Theresa tried not to show how shocked she was at her father's appearance, but he nodded at her as if he knew just what was on her mind.

"Don't worry," he said, setting one of her suitcases at the foot of the stairs. "I haven't been sleeping well, that's all. I've already been to Doc Kensington – wait until you see the truckload of vitamins I'm on!"

"Isn't he retired yet?" Theresa asked, unlatching the cat carrier. Jack, who had pitched a literal hairy cat fit every time she put him in it, now crouched at the back and refused to come out, staring with suspicious green eyes.

"Oh, Lord, no, wouldn't hear of it. He'll work 'til he drops. By the way, his Danielle, your school chum, is still in town. She's got my old job now."

"What about you, Dad? What have you been up to?"

His dark eyes slid away from hers. "You've had a long drive. Let's get your things inside. Once you're settled, and have had a good nap, we can talk."

Theresa considered pushing it.

Not sleeping well, he'd said. Okay. Was that all of it? No. Since she'd seen him last, just after Lora was born, his hair had gone from solid iron-grey to nearly pure white. His face was deeply lined, his skin an unhealthy color. He'd lost weight, too, and not in a good way. Always trim and muscular before, now his flesh seemed to hang slack on prominent bones.

She could have demanded answers, but she knew her father too well, and she was too tired. He was right. They could talk after her nap, and right now she felt she could nap for about eighteen hours straight.

"I had Mrs. Davis fix the big room up for you," Travis said. "She comes in a couple of times a week to do the cleaning."

"Your room? Dad, I can't take your room!"

"I'm in there now." He pointed through the long living room to the small door beside the kitchen. "Where your grandma used to sleep. It's warmer, right by the fireplace."

Theresa studied him, then looked at the stairs. Travis' face was set in the familiar determined lines – hadn't she just been thinking as she pulled up how stubborn the Zanes were? Possibly he couldn't handle the stairs anymore, but wasn't going to admit it. And it probably *was* warmer in the little room downstairs.

"Besides," he went on, as if feeling he needed to add more, "I think you've outgrown the furniture in yours. Who knows, maybe Lora will come visit."

"I hope so," Theresa said. "She'd love it. I always did."

"You used to play in there for hours," Travis recalled, smiling. "Talking to your invisible friend."

"Glory."

"That was the one." He chuckled. "You know, sometimes I think she's still around, waiting for you."

"If I've outgrown the furniture, I've probably outgrown my invisible friends, too," she said, adding her laughter to his until her laughter turned into a yawn.

"Go on, Theresa. Get some sleep. I'll have dinner ready –"

"Since when can you cook?"

"Since I had to learn," he replied dryly. "I make a great salmon casserole."

"Sorry, Dad, I didn't mean –"

"I know." He kissed her on the forehead, an unusual show of affection that silenced her with surprise.

She lugged most of her stuff inside, but only took her overnight bag and Jack upstairs. He still hadn't ventured out, and his fur was puffed up like it did when he caught scent of a strange cat.

The master suite was at the end of the hall. The curtains were drawn back, exposing windows with a stunning view of Seacliff, the bluff, and the bay. The ceiling was made of peeled logs, the floor was hardwood with a braided rug. Prints of horses adorned the walls – her father had never ridden a horse in his life, but loved them all the same.

She put the carrier down, figuring that Jack would come out when he was good and ready. Maybe giving him the run of the house wasn't such a good idea just yet. Let him get used to this room first, and then maybe he'd be up for some investigating.

There was a bathroom attached, small, but it had a jetted whirlpool tub and Theresa sighed in anticipation. She unpacked her overnight bag, brushed teeth that felt coated with fuzz after fourteen hours on the road, changed into the oversized flannel shirt that served as her pajamas, and crawled into the large bed.

She was asleep almost as soon as she pulled the goosedown comforter to bunch warmly around her shoulders.

* * *

Beautiful.

He hadn't seen such a magnificent creature in a long time. Far too long.

Watching her as she moved around the bedroom, as she undressed, only fueled the fire that burned within him.

He ached to see her up close, how she burrowed into the pillow and how her expression reflected the dreams of her sleeping mind.

Not yet. Not yet.

But soon.

He consoled himself with that thought. Soon.

She would be his.

* * *

Theresa woke once with the certainty that someone was in the room. Looking at her. Leering at her. She sat up with a gasp, clutching the sheets, and saw only Jack.

He wasn't sleeping, wasn't even sprawled in his customary lounging position, but was hunched at the foot of the bed, his eyes wide and fixed unblinkingly on the window. When he saw her, he twitched, sprang to the floor, then raced in a circle, leapt at the drapes, fell back down because he had no claws with which to grip, and scooted under the chair.

"Weird cat," she murmured affectionately, then rolled over and went back to sleep.

She woke much later, aware that whatever weirdness had gotten into the cat was now out. He was by the door, sniffing along the base, and Theresa could smell dinner. Salmon casserole, as promised.

Stiffness had settled into her bones. She sat up, feeling like everything was creaking. A twist of her back sent a series of crackles down her spine, and Theresa groaned in mixed pleasure and squeamishness.

Halfway to the bathroom, shrugging out of her flannel shirt, she paused. Her skin was creeping into gooseflesh. It had gotten dark outside, not the dusty orange-tinted dark of LA but a soft velvety grey-black that pressed against the window. It was dark in her room too, only the rosy glow of a single corner lamp providing light, yet Theresa felt as exposed as if she'd been standing naked in the middle of a shopping mall.

Silly. There was no one to see her. The only house within sight was Seacliff, and Seacliff was dark. Dark, and empty. Had been for years. The last Cliffwoods had moved away even before Theresa and her mother left Trinity Bay.

Jack uttered an inquisitive mew from the door, as if to ask how long she was going to make him wait before letting him check out that fascinating aroma.

"Okay, okay." Theresa closed the drapes and got in the shower.

* * *

He would have to be more careful. She was observant, her senses keen. Like the prey, stepping lightly through the underbrush, that instinctively knows it has been scented by the predator.

There was plenty of time. She'd only just arrived.

Let her settle in, get comfortable. Let her feel welcome in Trinity Bay. She would stay. It was where she belonged. Here, with her father, with her unseen and as-yet-unmet lover.

The father might pose a problem. Travis Zane was a strong-minded man. He might be inclined to be protective of his only child.

If it came to that, if the old man was the only thing standing in the way . . . well, he could be dealt with.

* * *

Theresa now knew the truth of long-distance relationships. No matter how often letters were exchanged, no matter how many phone calls were made, you couldn't really know what went on in a person's life when you were most of a state away.

She was in the uneasy state of feeling both more at home and more guilty than she ever had before.

The first shock – the second shock, if you counted the haggard way her father looked, fifteen years older than his actual age – was when a minibus pulled up in front of the house bright and early Wednesday morning and tooted its horn.

Theresa was in the cozy brick kitchen hunting for sugar when the bus arrived. She looked out the window, read "Silver Grove" on the side, and frowned.

"There's my ride," Travis said, coming in with his empty breakfast plate.

"Your ride? To where? What's Silver Grove?"

"It's over by the hospital." He ran water over his plate and dried his hands. "I'll be back by three."

"Dad . . . what's going on?"

He replaced the dish towel and smiled disarmingly.

"Dad." She tapped her foot meaningfully.

"There's a day program at the old folk's home," he admitted. "Keeps me off the streets. After the heart attack –"

"*Heart* attack!"

"Kel McGuire and Doc Kensington teamed up on me," he continued, as if he hadn't noticed her outburst. "They wanted me to move in permanently, but I talked them out of it. On the condition I'd go play cribbage and Scrabble with the other old farts four or five days a week."

"Heart attack, Jesus, Dad, when?"

"About a year ago," he said indifferently.

Theresa leaned against the counter and dragged a stunned hand down the side of her face. A year ago, she'd been on the phone to her dad almost constantly, alternately giddy about the show and distraught about her divorce, and he'd said not a word. Guilt washed over her like dull heat. "Why didn't you *tell* me?"

"You had your own things going on, honey. I didn't want to burden you with mine." He patted her arm. "No wild parties while I'm gone, okay?"

An automatic smile, more of a grimace, twisted her mouth. It was the same way he used to say good-bye when she was eight years old and he was off to work.

"Dad . . ."

The horn beeped again.

"Got to go. If I'm late, Elsie takes my favorite chair."

She stayed by the window, watching him emerge into the pale fog. He pulled his jacket on and settled it on his shoulders with the same flip-and-shrug she remembered from her childhood, but then he'd been on his way to Nate's where he worked as a bartender. Not on his way to spend the day in some threadbare dayroom where the tube was always set to game shows and the bookcase was filled with large-print versions of Reader's Digest.

As the minibus pulled away, Theresa pressed her forehead against the glass like she'd always done as a little girl. Bitter tears stung her eyes. She wasn't sure if she was more upset at her father's stoic, stiff-necked, old-fashioned pride – women and kids don't need to know the troubles a man is facing – or her own lack of perceptiveness.

She recalled thinking how tired he'd sounded during some of their conversations. Tired. That was all. Now to learn he'd had a heart attack, that the Reaper's cloak had brushed against him, and she hadn't even known!

Guilt and shame, racing around and around like mechanical rabbits on the track of her mind. She hadn't known, and when she finally did come to see her father, it hadn't been to take care of him, but to flee her own problems and let him take care of her.

Selfish, thankless child! If the show hadn't been canceled, she would still be in L.A., still chatting with him every so often on the phone, with no idea! Now she understood the relief with which he'd greeted her tentative request to move back to Trinity Bay. He would have never asked, not wanting to be a burden to her.

Her chest hitched once, and then she drew upon that same stiff-necked pride that she'd inherited along with her dark hair and eyes. She was here now, that was what mattered. She would be here for her father and herself, and things would work out fine for both of them.

With that resolve firmly in place, she did the breakfast dishes and tidied the kitchen, then lugged the rest of her things in from the car and started unpacking.

There was an old desk in the corner of the long living room, tucked back in a windowless corner by the stairs. It was away from the distractions of television and windows, a good place to write. Travis had assured her he used it for nothing more than a place to stack things he was procrastinating on putting away, so the desk was hers to use if she wanted it.

She cleared away the clutter, finding homes for most of it and putting the rest on the table so she wouldn't be able to forget to ask where it went. The desk itself was in good shape, a mammoth old fossil from the days before most furniture was made of pressboard.

One drawer stuck fast, one opened with a protesting squeal, and all the others worked just fine. In the bottommost one, she was startled to find a thick packet with her name on it, full of test papers and art projects from her school days.

From the kitchen windows, she saw a path winding into the redwoods that butted up against the property, bringing back more childhood memories. The shortcut to school, past the former gatehouse of the Seacliff estate.

She wondered if Mrs. Douring, the high school English teacher feared by generations of Trinity Bay teens, still lived there. April Cliffwood and her friends had lived in utter terror of the woman, and as April frequently baby-sat young Theresa before her family moved away, she had transmitted that fear.

But in the fertile mind of a child, Mrs. Douring with her dyed-orange hair and her pursed lips became a witch, and every day Theresa would scoot along the path with her heart in her throat until the house had come and gone.

She smiled a little at her own foolishness. Old, yes, and scary-looking, but not a witch.

After she set up her computer, she switched it on and pulled up a word processing program just to make sure everything worked. She sat and stared sourly at it, fearing that she would never use it for anything other than writing letters, then turned it off and decided to go for a walk.

A light sweater was all she needed. The morning chill was already lessening, though the day did not promise to be the blue-sky knockout of yesterday. Still, sunbeams slanted through the clouds and made shifting patterns of light and shadow in the woods.

She closed the door but didn't lock it and felt a qualm, making a mental note to herself to get a copy of Dad's key. True, this was Trinity Bay, not L.A., but even that didn't make her rest easy leaving the door unlocked.

Although the path beckoned, first she decided to go around the house and look at Seacliff. She hadn't really gotten a chance to admire it yesterday, so tired from her drive, and she'd often daydreamed as a child about living there, in the grand manor, having servants and money and cars.

There had once been a gravel walkway leading from the guest cottage to the mansion, but all that remained of it now was a long skinny depression in the grass. On the Zane property, things had been allowed to go back to their natural state decades ago.

She followed the former walkway, wondering what old Myra would think if she could see her family's pride and joy now. Those thoughts, though, derailed in a hurry as she rounded a hydrangea bush half again her own height, exploding with bouquet-sized lavender blossoms, and got her first good, attentive look at Seacliff.

The place was far from abandoned. Her first impression was that someone must have hired a good caretaker to look after the place, but she gave up that line of reasoning quickly. The house just didn't have the desolate, unoccupied look she would have expected. Someone was living there.

Who would be living in Seacliff? The last of the Cliffwoods had moved away in early 1979 after Edward's nervous breakdown and his sister Barbara's death. The local kids, as well as their parents, speculated hungrily over which had come first — did her death make him crazy, or did his hidden insanity lead to her Christmastime overdose on sleeping pills?

April, Edward's daughter, had been seventeen at the time. She and her mother moved out. The last words April had had to say on the matter was that she was glad. She hated the house, and would be just as happy if she never saw it again.

But someone was living there now. Had the place been sold? Her father hadn't mentioned it, but then, Travis had never been one to pass around gossip. Or maybe he had mentioned it, and Theresa had forgotten. Possible. Especially if it had been recent.

That line of thinking brought back the guilt and shame. What else might he have said, that she might have missed? She was upset at him for keeping his health a secret; what if he'd tried to tell her, but she'd been so wrapped up in the misery of her own life that she hadn't heard?

She stood, wallowing in bleak emotions, staring blankly at Seacliff. *Who would want such a giant monstrosity anyway?* the part of her that wasn't occupied with making herself feel about *yea* big said to itself.

Seacliff was a mansion in every sense of the word. It was positioned to command a sweeping view of the town and the bay, and also so that the town could look up admiringly at its gables and chimneys and windows.

The central part of the house was three stories tall, topped with a domelike bubble of blue and green stained glass. Two-story wings angled back from the central section, giving the house the shape of a wide V. Theresa knew that a wrought-iron fence stretched from the ends of the wings to enclose the rear garden, which had once been featured in a magazine that couldn't say enough good things about its terraced pools and artful design.

Half of the stable had been converted to a six-car garage, and as she looked at it, one of the doors swung up. An engine roared once, then purred contentedly as a sleek black sports car backed out. Theresa could read the license plate: MYDLITE.

"Your delight, huh?" she murmured, raising an eyebrow.

The car started down the long, curved drive, then slowed as the driver saw her. A tinted window slid down and a man looked out at her.

"Well, hello," he said, smiling. Million-dollar smile, perfectly capped, bleached, and cultivated. God's gift to woman, from the tips of his toes to the top of his full, wavy blond hair.

Theresa scolded herself. Just because the man was forty-something and drove a car that was the epitome of "what are you trying to prove?" with a cutesy-ass — thank you, Suze, for that piquant turn of phrase – license plate, just because he had gone to great pains to take care of his looks, didn't necessarily mean he was shallow and vain.

"Hi," she said. "I didn't know anybody lived here."

"Don't worry, I won't bust you for trespassing." His smile widened, and she felt herself give one in response, unwillingly.

Next he's going to say he hasn't seen me around here before . . .

"I haven't seen you around here before." He stuck his hand out the window. "Brad Thornton."

"Theresa Zane." She shook quickly, then let go. For some reason, maybe because he reminded her of too many slick people she'd known in the entertainment industry, the vibes he gave off seemed thinly coated with slime.

"Travis' daughter! I should have known! So we're neighbors. Your dad's quite a guy."

"He didn't tell me Seacliff had been sold."

An expression of sorrow so ersatz and schmaltzy that Theresa almost recoiled replaced Brad's winning smile. She resisted the urge to wipe her palm on her sweater.

"It belonged to my wife, April. She passed away three years ago."

"Oh, I'm sorry!" Theresa said, and she was. Not for him, but for April, who had always been so bright and full of hope. April, who had wanted to be a professional dancer, who had dreamed of a life beyond Trinity Bay even before tragedy struck her family. "She used to baby-sit me."

"Ironic, isn't it?" He got out of the car – six feet and a little, a good bod that was only just beginning to get a little too cushy in the tushy – again, thanks, Suze – and around the middle. He looked up at Seacliff with undisguised pleasure. "She never told me about this place. I didn't find out until after she died. All she ever said was that she hated her family home. I don't see how anyone could hate a place as great as this."

"Well, you know," Theresa offered lamely.

"Yeah." He laughed. "I wasn't too wild about my hometown either. It's all a matter of what you're used to."

"I guess so." She stuffed her hands in the pockets of her jeans. "It's a pretty house, though."

"I've been getting it fixed up. Thinking of turning it into a hotel."

"A hotel?"

"Sure, why not?" He spread his arms expansively. "Trinity Bay already thrives on tourism. Seacliff has its own indoor pool, plenty of guest rooms, a huge kitchen, riding and hiking trails right on the property. Can't you see it as a resort?"

"Yeah . . ."

"Come on in, I'll give you the tour, show you what I want to do. It's always good to get a fresh perspective."

"Oh, I can't," she said, not too hastily, trying to sound regretful. "I was just taking a break from unpacking, and everything's a shambles. I really should get back and finish up before Dad comes home."

"Rain check, then." He winked. "Dinner, maybe."

"Maybe," her mouth agreed, while her brain added something about Satan going for a sleigh ride.

Brad folded himself back into the car, waved, and drove off. Theresa watched him go, now allowing herself the moue of distaste she hadn't dared show before.

She turned and went back to the house.

* * *

A spirit, an angel, a goddess upon the earth!

Up close, she was even more than he'd hoped. Her eyes, so dark the pupil was barely distinguished from the iris, making her look eternally wide-eyed and innocent. Her hair, the shade of black that gave blue highlights in the sun. Her cheekbones high and striking, her mouth lush, her neck as graceful as a doe.

Beautiful.

He was more sure than ever that he had to have her. She made all the other women look shabby and drab by comparison. There was a vitality in her, too. She was alive and awake in a way that so many of the others hadn't been.

He would have her. She was the one.

First, a gift to prove his love.

* * *

Few things were creepier than an underground parking structure at three in the morning.

Rows of cars stood with an abandoned air, their colors washed to weird dream hues by the orange glow of the overhead lights. Shadows collected in deep pools. The painted lines on the cracked concrete were a scabrous, peeling yellow.

The only sounds were magnified, a steady drip becoming a somber drum beat, the hum and rumble of street noises becoming the drone of a giant hive. The man's footsteps clacked and rasped.

The garage smelled as depressing as it looked and sounded. Ghosts of old exhaust, faint but discernible urine odors, rust and corrosion, with a sickly patina of gas and oil overlaying it all.

Not another soul in sight. The man was alone as he walked between the ranks of cars. He passed beneath a light that spat and flickered irregularly, and it turned his shadow into a jittering hanged man.

Normally, he wouldn't be bothered by the eerie solitude. Normally, he would stride carelessly to his car, toss his briefcase into the passenger seat, pop in a CD, and be on his way.

Tonight, he paused. He could see and hear nothing out of the ordinary. But something, some ill-defined sense, told him that he was no longer alone in the night.

He scanned the garage, listened intently. He wasn't afraid, not yet, but he was concerned.

He was a fit man, priding himself on eating well and going to the gym four times a week. He was confident that he could handle any physical challenge. The problem was that more and more criminals these days, some of them kids no older than twelve, carried guns and used them with impunity. A bullet killed a man just as dead no matter how often he used the Stairmaster.

Kids couldn't stay quiet this long. Even one kid, going it alone, would have moved or shifted by now. There was no hint of anyone nearby.

Still, that sense of being watched wouldn't go away. Worse, it quickly gave way to a sense of being hunted. That his life was in danger.

He had no enemies that he knew of.

The skin crept on the back of his neck. His gut and groin tightened apprehensively. He realized he was sweating, a cold fearful sweat. His mouth filled with bitter saliva.

He could see his car. Less than twenty steps away. A maroon Acura, only a year old, with all the extras. Safe haven.

He tried to take a step toward the car, but his feet did not want to move. The impulse of the prey was too strong.

His eyes began to ache from staring unblinking into the shadows, darting from one car to the next, not knowing which concealed the stalker but knowing that someone was there, perhaps even moving closer with uncanny silence.

Perhaps even behind him already. So that if he turned, he would find himself face to face with something out of his worst nightmare, nothing so simple as a man with a gun, something inhuman and horrifying.

A small whine, almost a whimper, escaped his throat. He heard it and understood that he had passed well beyond fear now, into the realms of keen terror.

The sound released him. He sucked in a huge gasp and ran for his car, briefcase slamming against his leg, groping for the keys.

Ten steps away. He triggered the remote that would deactivate the alarm and unlock the door.

Five steps. He heard a low, malicious chuckle.

Two steps, reaching for the door handle.

And he was yanked off his feet, one of them flailing to connect with the driver's side mirror hard enough to snap it off. His briefcase flew onto the car's roof and slid off the other side, snapping open and shedding a drift of papers.

He was thrust upward, his head slamming into the low ceiling, and then hurled to the ground. A scream died unvoiced when he was struck in the stomach. His right arm was pulled around behind his back, shoulder on fire with agony before it popped enormously and went numb.

Thrown again, this time into the side of a Blazer. He dented the door and rebounded. He caught the briefest glimpse of his attacker, a large dark form, before he was picked up by the ankles and swung into one of the concrete support posts. He was able to get his left arm over his face but still his nose exploded and his jaw sprung loose.

He landed on a smeary oil stain and a faded number 41. He couldn't scream, couldn't get up, couldn't even crawl. Blood was pouring down his chin.

"Please," the man said, or tried to, the word garbled by his ruined mouth.

A shadow fell over him.

* * *

Within every proud father beats the devious heart of a matchmaker, Kel McGuire thought, hiding a smile.

"... as you've been such a help, with the shopping and the day program and all, I just wanted to show my thanks," Travis Zane concluded. "Tomorrow at seven?"

Travis looked better already, healthier and happier than he'd been in months. In just a few days, his daughter had worked wonders. Kel was interested, but that interest was colored with the same exasperated chagrin he imagined many unattached men felt.

Especially in a town as small as Trinity Bay. When everybody knew everybody else, gossip and speculation had a way of getting around.

He knew that he was the object of much talk. Good-looking in an artistic and vaguely aquiline way that had been the bane of his school years, habitually neat, living alone — was he or wasn't he? His name hadn't been linked with any of the eligible women in town. His secretary, Nancy Ellsworth, was a blonde with the figure of a silver screen goddess, but she reported that he'd never once put a move on her. Was he or wasn't he?

Kel wasn't. He liked women just fine, thank you. He'd never put a move on Nancy, that was true, but she always neglected to mention her boyfriend. See a guy like that in the woods at night, and you'd be inclined to believe in Bigfoot. Kel was straight, but he wasn't stupid. Rand Kostas was the sort who wouldn't think twice about yanking off someone's arm and beating him to death with it.

He regarded Travis Zane, knowing what the clever old fox was up to. Travis usually kept his own matters to himself and expected everyone else to do the same, even when his stiffnecked independence and refusal to admit to symptoms had very nearly killed him.

But Kel didn't put it past Travis to try and fix him up with the daughter. Theresa.

According to the pictures, she was a knockout. Smart and talented, too, judging by her books. Two days a week, Kel worked as a counselor at the elementary school, so he was familiar with the adventures of *Lora and Ruff*.

Still, Theresa Zane was recently divorced, and Kel wasn't sure he was ready to get involved with someone who had so many issues. It would be a little too much like work for comfort.

Then again, where was he going to find someone who *didn't* have issues? He was never going to have a relationship untouched by his work, because he was a psychologist and social worker, and despite some persuasive arguments to the contrary, all people did have minds and personalities.

Then again again — over-analysis was one of his less endearing character flaws, something of which he was well aware but seemingly hopeless to change — it could be that Travis was just honestly trying to thank Kel for helping get his life in order.

All of this had gone through his head in a quick second. He grinned at Travis. "Sure, tomorrow's great. What can I bring?"

* * *

"Dammit, Jack!" Theresa groaned.

She'd heard of cats expressing themselves like this, but that didn't mean she had to like it. She got a handful of paper towels and cleaned up the mess, then went looking for the temperamental feline.

He'd awakened her from a dead sleep this morning by leaping onto her chest, fur standing on end, hissing. Too sluggish to react swiftly, she'd only just opened her eyes when his paw whipped out hard across her cheek. If he'd had claws, he would have laid her face open.

"Crazy cat," she said now.

The first day or two, he'd seemed okay, a little skittish getting used to his new environment. He had his litter box in the enclosed porch off the kitchen, a little privacy to take care of his kitty business, and he hadn't had any difficulty learning where it was. But this . . . this was no accident.

She went looking, but Jack must have known she was annoyed and had hidden himself too well. Either that, or he'd gotten outside somehow. All the windows were shut against the damp and the drafts, but he could have slipped out when Travis left for his day program.

Before checking, she ran the can opener. Although Jack's canned food came with a pop-top, and he'd never eaten from a regular tin can, that never failed to bring him running. Probably genetic.

She heard a rustling in the pantry, and opened the door.

A box of cereal fell right in front of her, loud as a guillotine.

Theresa jumped back and uttered a screamy gasp, instantly ashamed of herself. She'd slept strange, been woken badly, and hadn't cleared the cobwebs from her brain yet. But that was no excuse to go carrying on like some dippy schoolgirl.

Jack was on the highest shelf, peering down at her with glinting green eyes.

"What's the matter with you today?" She reached up.

He slunk backward, opened his jaws wide, and hissed through a mouthful of fangs.

"Jack!" Reproachful.

A dog would have had the decency to look guilty, but not so a cat. Jack swatted her fingers, then turned and bolted along the shelf, his furry haunches knocking over a row of boxes. More cereal, crackers, Malt-O-Meal, and a stack of raisin snack-packs went down like dominoes. The Malt-O-Meal opened and sprayed golden-brown across the brick floor.

Jack sprang from the shelf, feinted right, then shot around Theresa's legs on the left. He vanished into the living room, trailing back one plaintive, eerie yowl.

Theresa's pulse was racing. She was fully awake now, having shaken off the last of the lethargy that had followed her out of sleep. "What's gotten into you?" she called after Jack.

Another wavering yowl sent shivers up her spine.

"Crazy cat," she repeated, and set about cleaning up this mess too. "If someone doesn't straighten up and fly right, guess who's going to spend the night in his carrier."

No answer. When she went back into the living room, there was no sign of Jack. None too eager for a repeat performance, Theresa decided to ignore him. He'd come around.

She set out for another walk. It was already becoming a daily ritual. She hadn't done much walking in L.A.; few people did. In Phoenix, everybody with an ounce of sense stayed inside where it was cool. But walking here, beneath the redwoods, made her feel good. Cleansed. Healed.

She circled the house and started down the path through the forest. Time to see if she remembered the way to town, and if Mrs. Douring's place looked as scary as in her memories.

Just as the shadows closed around her, she paused. A feeling of watchedness slipped over her like an eddy of icy water. She turned in a slow circle and saw no one.

Maybe it was only Jack, watching her from one of the windows . . .

Her breath caught in her throat.

A pale shape was at the upper curved window.

Theresa stepped closer, and the angle shifted.

Only the light dancing strangely on the glass.

Chagrined relief made her chuckle at herself. The quiet of Trinity Bay was getting to her. She was accustomed to noise and bustle, and the lack thereof was making her jumpy. That was all. She'd get used to it soon.

Come to think of it, that was probably what was the matter with Jack, too. The apartment hadn't been right near a freeway, but there had still been the constant pervasive drone of city-sounds. Traffic, voices, sirens, the occasional gunshot. By comparison, the windy whisper of the trees and the low rhythm of the distant surf was a little spooky.

She continued on. Soon the old gatehouse came into view, and it didn't look like half the haunted house she remembered. It was far smaller – again, that trick of childhood's perception – and much less ramshackle.

A whimsical fence made of irregular pieces of driftwood bound together with woven hemp ambled agreeably around the house. The front path, of crushed stone that matched the river-rock fireplace, wound under an archway formed by two stumps that had been carved into totem-like shapes: an eagle on one side, a standing bear on the other. Balanced across the heads of the eagle and the bear was a gorgeously-polished slice of redwood burl with "The Forresters" burnt into it.

The yard was a hodgepodge of weeds, herbs, and wildflowers, the sort of thing Theresa had once heard Steven describe as a "Victorian garden." More wooden objects – a windmill, a skillfully-made bench, a birdhouse, others – decorated the yard.

A large shed had been added to the side of the house. Judging by the sawdust and chunks of wood laying around, it was the source of the creations. The door was open, and she could hear faint music coming from within.

Might as well introduce myself to the neighbors, Theresa thought, and went through the arch. Her shoes gritted on the gravel, announcing her presence to a gangly half-grown mongrel pup that came bounding in her direction. It was all big feet and lolling tongue, with one ear that stuck up and one that folded down, giving it a permanently inquisitive expression. It yapped once, then frisked happily around her legs.

A little girl looked out of the shed. She was nine or ten, with soft brown hair and big blue eyes, a pretty child except for the red speckles that marred her face. "Don't come closer; I've got chicken pox!" she announced.

"I've already had them," Theresa said.

"Who's that, peanut?" a man's voice asked.

"It's Mr. Zane's daughter."

Theresa grinned. "Word gets around, I see! Hi, I'm Theresa Zane."

"I'm Jenny Forrester, and that's Bingo. And this is my dad."

Like the puppy, Mr. Forrester was gangly and mongrelish, with big feet, though he lacked the lolling tongue. His hair was long, clean but unkempt, and a greying goatee lengthened his Ichabod Crane face. His jeans, flannel shirt, and Birkenstocks were flecked with sawdust and woodchips; his hands were overlarge, callused and nicked with old scars.

"Hey, good to meet you," he said.

She shook his hand, instinctively liking him. Forrester struck her, even on first glimpse, as being the sort of man who wandered through life in an amiable sort of daze.

"Moo-oom!" Jenny hollered. "Company!"

"I was just passing by," Theresa said. "I was admiring the woodcrafts, and heard the music."

"You like them?" Forrester beamed. "I make them. Sell them, during the summer."

The door opened, and an aproned woman came out. Pleasantly plump, honey-colored hair, a wide smile. Theresa recognized her at once.

"Sandy? Sandy Wright?"

"Theresa Zane!" Sandy hurried forward and gave her a hug that smelled of brown sugar and chocolate. "It's Forrester now; this is my husband Charlie. I was going to come up and see you tomorrow on my day off, and I was just making some cookies to bring for you and your dad. Come in, come in! It's been years! Oh . . . Jen's got the –"

"She told me. It's okay. I had them when I was two."

Sandy ushered Theresa into the kitchen, which was tiny but bright. Almost too bright. The yellow paint was just short of neon, softened by the potted plants that crammed every available surface. There were more examples of Charlie's work, from the handcrafted knobs on the cabinets up to the table, which was made from a slice of redwood balanced upon a gnarled stump.

Bingo followed them in and promptly tried to get at the cookies that were cooling on the countertop. Jen shooed him outside.

"Coffee?" Sandy offered.

"Please. I didn't know you were living here. What ever happened to going the long way around from Seacliff so you didn't have to pass this house?"

Sandy giggled, still sounding very much like the teenager Theresa had known. "Once Mrs. Douring retired and moved to Florida – yes, it's true, will wonders never cease! – there was nothing to be afraid of!"

"I'm going back out to the workshop," Charlie said, kissing Sandy on the top of the head, helping himself to a cookie, and meandering out in a way that suggested he only missed running into the doorjamb by pure luck.

"Can I watch TV?" Jenny wheedled. "Please?"

"What about that stack of homework Jerry brought for you?"

"I can do it later. Pleeeease?"

Sandy flapped a hand at her. "Go on, but I don't want you watching any of those talk shows." She sat down and looked at Theresa. "I swear, it's nothing but 'I Slept With My Wife's Gynecologist' and 'Eleven-Year-Olds Who Dress Like Whores' on television these days. I don't want to raise my kids in a bubble, but it gets harder and harder to keep that trash away from them."

Theresa began to laugh. "I remember when you and April and Claudia Haverley first got ahold of *Forever*, by Judy Blume."

"That wasn't trash!" Sandy protested, laughing too. Then she sobered. "Have you heard about April?"

"I met her husband," Theresa said, nodding. "Up at Seacliff."

"Him." Sandy snorted. "I never would have expected April to marry someone like that. He thinks he's hot stuff, all right. Half the women in town are nuts over him. He's got the mill going again, you know. Bringing in high-powered legal types from San Francisco to step on the environmentalists. He's even got plans for an offshore oil rig."

"Aw, no." Theresa tried to imagine that, and didn't like the picture.

Sandy fanned her flushed face with the hem of her apron. "Whew, I didn't realize how hot it was in here. Like I said, not April's type at all. But I guess she wanted someone more dependable, after the musician she was living with ran out on her when the baby was born."

"Baby?"

"Her daughter, Angela." Sandy's face darkened, and she dabbed at the corners of her eyes. "Such a terrible thing."

"What happened?"

"After April died, Brad and Angela moved here. She was my son Jerry's age. She was so pretty, too. Dark red hair, just like April. She was always so quiet. It must have been hard for her, losing her mom like that. We tried to bring her out of her shell, but last year, she . . . she . . ."

"Suicide?" Theresa asked softly.

"Why would a sixteen year old kid go and do something like that?" Sandy spoke with the futile tone of one who'd been over it a thousand times in her own mind and knew there was no good answer. "I know what they say, that teenagers make attempts to get attention. But this wasn't like that. She didn't tell anyone. Just did it."

"Oh, my God, Sandy, that must have been terrible for you!"

"It was worst for Jerry. He saw it happen. He was down on the beach that night. A bunch of the kids were having a party. He saw her running . . . running along the bluff. Then he saw her jump off."

"It couldn't have been an accident?"

She shook her head, fished a tissue out of the gaily-patterned box on the counter, and blew her nose. "He says she stopped, looked down, like she was trying to find the best place to do it. Then she just . . . jumped."

* * *

Before going to bed, Theresa stood at her window, staring over at Seacliff. Brad Thornton hadn't seemed like a man who'd lost his wife three years ago, and he certainly hadn't seemed like a man whose stepdaughter had taken her own life less than one. Either he was doing a damn good job of concealing his grief, or he wasn't bothered at all.

Her skin crept over her flesh again, as if the window was a large eye, a giant's eye, peering in at her even as she looked out. She closed the curtains with a shudder.

There had been no new outbursts from Jack. He'd emerged from hiding about an hour after Theresa had gotten back from her walk, acting for all the world as if nothing unusual had gone on. Later, he'd even claimed her lap as she was trying to read. She was convinced all cats were members of FALL, the Feline Anti-Literacy League, because nothing proved more tempting to them as a napping-place than an open book, magazine, or newspaper.

Her father had come back in good spirits, all but springing off the minibus when it dropped him off. She wasn't sure what to make of his rather smugly-delivered news that they were having a dinner guest on Saturday.

That night, Theresa dreamed of a red-haired girl running across Seacliff's lawn, running in terror from a pursuing, malevolent, unseen presence. The thorny fingers of a rosebush, its blooms as dark as the sky above, clawed at her silken nightgown, snagging it. She pulled free with a desperate wail, slapping at the velvety roses.

The girl spun away from the rosebush and ran blindly until she reached the edge of the bluff, where flickering light leaped against the rock face from a bonfire on the beach below. Rock music – the dream was so vivid Theresa could even identify the song – and young laughter bounced up the bluff.

With tears pouring down her face, she threw a panicked glance over her shoulder, then dashed along the bluff until she was over a place where the sea had undercut the stone. No beach, just crashing waves driving with echoing, booming force. The girl paused, cast her eyes heavenward as if in prayer, and leaped.

"NO!" Theresa shouted herself awake in the dead of night, soaked with clammy sweat. The smell of sea spray and woodsmoke and roasting marshmallows filled her lungs. For a moment, she still heard the rock music, the laughter of teens turning into horrified shrieks.

Gasping, she fell back against the pillows. From downstairs, her father's voice called out in alarm.

She scrambled out of bed and met him at the bottom of the stairs. "It's okay, Dad. Just a dream. I'm sorry."

He looked like she had almost sent him straight into another heart attack. "Must have been a bad one. Want to talk about it?"

"No, that's all right. I don't remember now," she lied. "Are you okay?"

"Fine, fine," he said, patting her reassuringly on the shoulder. "I'd forgotten how you used to scream at night."

"What?" Theresa frowned. "I used to what?"

"When you were about five. Nightmares. It made your mother crazy."

"What didn't?" she mumbled. More clearly, she asked, "Nightmares about what?"

"That's the funny thing. Your little invisible friend. During the day, you'd have tea parties with her, and at night you'd be crying and saying someone was hurting her and locking her up in the dark."

She shivered as a faint half-memory came to her, then was gone. "This wasn't like that."

"Thought you said you didn't remember," he pointed out cannily.

"Enough to know it wasn't about Glory," she evaded.

"You want some cocoa?"

"No, thanks, Dad. I'm just going to try and get back to sleep. You should too. I'm sorry for waking you up like that." She kissed him on the cheek, then climbed the stairs and waited on the landing until she heard his door close.

Movement caught her eye. Jack, padding along the hallway. When he saw her, he hunkered down and hissed, then yawned and followed her into her room. She got into bed and he hopped up to stand on her chest, pushing with his paws.

"You're schizo," she said, petting him. He responded with an affectionate head-butt that squashed his cold nose into her eye.

"Okay, okay, I love you too." She convinced him to curl up on the other pillow, and drifted into a dreamless sleep.

*　*　*

Sandy Forrester tossed and turned until Charlie, normally the most placid of men, dug his elbow into her amply-padded ribs and growled something into his pillow.

She kicked off the sheet. Normally, she slept with pajamas, socks, and the quilt. But tonight she was nude, and even the single sheet was too hot, stifling, scratchy. The only reason she had pulled it over herself was because she couldn't stand lying there with nothing at all covering her.

The fever was back. She could tell that much just by pressing the inside of her wrist against her forehead the way she did when one of the kids was sick. A weird sort of fever, too. No chills, no other symptoms. Just a burning restlessness.

If it was chicken pox, she was going to kill Dr. Kensington. She'd had the full range of childhood diseases when she was little, and he had assured her that nobody could get re-infected.

She got out of bed, pulling on a loose robe. No sleep tonight.

The house was quiet and dark, except for a faint line of light and low music from Jerry's door. Sandy tiptoed that way, knowing what she would find – he had fallen asleep reading again, studying his lines. Jerry was the star of the school drama club and had even played minor parts in college productions down at the university.

Meaning to turn off the light, she silently pushed the door open.

Surprise froze her in place and prevented her from making a sound.

Her son was in bed, but he wasn't sleeping. He was on his back with his eyes closed, caressing himself.

A sheen of perspiration broke over Sandy's skin. She wanted to turn away, but was held captivated by the sight. The thought that he might at any moment open his eyes and see her should have filled her with embarrassment, but it only made her breath quicken.

Drawn by some terrible compulsion, she stepped into the room. Her gaze fixed briefly on a poster above his bed, some rock band or another. What caught her eye was a rose, floating in the foreground of the usual clutter of crazy-clothed musicians. A rose, black as midnight, with a red jewel gleaming at its center.

For some reason, the rose made her think of the most secret part of a woman's body. A flush spread upward from her loins.

Jerry's hand was moving faster now, the bedclothes rustling beneath him as his hips rocked in counterpoint. He was very close.

A noise escaped Sandy, a small whimper. Quiet as it was, Jerry heard.

"Mom! Jesus!" He scrambled to cover himself, turning beet red.

"You don't have to stop," Sandy said in a husky voice unlike her usual one.

The fever was racing, racing through her veins. She understood the heat now. It would burn her up unless she found a way to get rid of it. She dropped her robe, showing her body to her son without a twinge of shame.

"Mom!"

"Shh, honey," she crooned, approaching the bed. "Mama make it all better."

He gaped at her, but she could tell that his mortified horror was mixed with lust. His gaze traveled avidly over her breasts and the plump, blonde-furred mound between her thighs. Had he ever seen a naked woman before outside of a magazine? Had any of his schoolmates given him more than a peek and a promise? She didn't know, didn't care. All she knew was what she wanted.

She went to her knees on the bed, pulling the covers away. Jerry recoiled, but she reached out and took hold of him.

"God! Mom!" He threw his head back, his erection lurching at her touch.

Sandy ran her tongue over her lips. "Do you want me to?"

An inarticulate moan was her only answer. He was helpless, could only lay there as she lowered her head, her hair falling across his thighs and belly. She could smell his excitement. First smell, and then taste it on his skin.

She took him deep in her mouth. His back arched, his limbs stiffened, his fingers fisted in the sheets. Sandy slid her hand between her legs, amazed at how damp and ready she was.

It was over in a matter of seconds. They climaxed together, her busy stroking hand bringing her to the brink just as Jerry tensed, then shuddered in release and filled her mouth nearly to overflowing. She kept at it until he was drained, exhausted, then raised her head and gave him a slow, Cheshire-Cat smile as she licked her lips.

* * *

Theresa woke Saturday morning to the secret sound of rain.

"Ugh."

She flopped onto her back and stared at the ceiling. The mattress was far softer than the one she had in the apartment. Maybe that was why she kept waking feeling as if she'd just done a triathlon. Or maybe it was the change in climate, or a combination thereof.

All she knew was that if things didn't improve, she'd be paying a visit to old Doc Kensington. Which reminded her, she meant to call Danielle and set up a meeting.

They hadn't seen each other since they were nine years old, probably had nothing in common. Her father said Dani had his old job, which meant she was tending bar down at Nate's.

Tomorrow. Today, she had to help Dad get ready for their dinner date. Kel McGuire. The name sounded like it belonged to a ruddy-cheeked, beaming, twinkle-eyed Leprechaun of a man.

She rolled over and looked at the clock.

Ten-forty. Oof. No wonder she felt so dragged out. That was three hours more sleep than she was used to, even allowing for midnight wake-up calls like the one she'd had last night.

"No more of that," she told herself.

She tried to overcome the lethargy with a stingingly cold shower and plenty of caffeine, and it was at least partly effective. An hour later, she and Travis were headed for North Valley Shopping Center, where Tom's Market was surrounded by a bunch of smaller shops, including a pet store, Hallmark, and a cafe. Across the optimistically-named Mall Road, a new complex of apartments was advertising for renters.

"Pretty nice," she said.

"I guess the college kids don't mind the drive. Town's growing."

"You don't sound all that happy about it."

He shrugged and got out of the car. "You know what they say, change is bad except from a vending machine."

Theresa laughed and tied a scarf over her hair to ward off the worst of the rain, which by now was more of a heavy, constant mist that hung in the air.

"That Thornton, he's got some idea about turning Seacliff into a hotel. It's his land, his money, and if he wants to throw it down a hole, it's his business. I'm just worried he's going to get everybody's hopes up, then let them down and leave them in debt."

"Don't you think he can pull it off?"

Travis shrugged again and snared a cart from the corral in front of the market. "He's turned the mill around, I'll give him that. Whether it's a good idea or not . . . that's another thing. The foreman, Big Al Haverley, he raves about Thornton no end. Lots of men have jobs now that didn't before – women, too," he added hastily, giving her a sidelong amused glance.

"Oink, oink, Dad," she grinned.

"But the hotel . . . I have a feeling Thornton's going to be sorry. Seacliff isn't a good place."

"What do you mean? It's big enough, it's gorgeous . . ."

"Something's wrong with that house. Always has been. Everyone who's lived there has had more than their share of bad luck."

She stopped just inside the doors and looked at him. "That doesn't sound like the hard-headed Travis Zane I remember. Haunted houses, Dad? Come on!"

"Did I say haunted?" He paused, as if replaying their conversation in his mind just to assure himself he hadn't. "I said no such thing. Bad luck, that's all."

"Excuse me!" Sandy Forrester trilled brightly from behind them. "If you don't move, I'm going to run you right over!"

They turned and saw their neighbor, vivacious and sparkle-eyed under a jaunty red rain hat that made Theresa want to ask if she was on her way to Grandma's house.

"Sandy!" Travis said warmly. "Wonderful cookies, as always."

"Thank you, Travis." She dimpled at him like a coquette of sixteen instead of a woman of forty.

"How are the kids?" he asked.

A strange expression flitted across her face, and for a moment Theresa thought Sandy Forrester might turn and flee with all the devils of hell on her heels. But then it cleared, and she smiled, though it seemed a trifle forced.

"Jen's still a little spotty and itchy, getting underfoot and making me crazy. Jerry's . . . fine." She groped in her purse and found a grocery list. "How about you? Theresa, settling in okay? You look tired."

"I am. What's your secret, Sandy? You look great."

Again, that strange expression, gone so quick Theresa wondered if it had been a trick of shadows. "Yesterday, I thought I was coming down with a fever or something, but whatever it was is gone now. I guess I just needed a good night's sleep."

She twiddled her fingers at them and steered her way toward the produce department.

"A good night's sleep," Theresa murmured longingly. "That would be nice."

Travis, who had been watching Sandy go on her way with a perplexed frown, now turned it on his daughter. "I thought I was the insomniac around here."

"Oh, I'm sleeping," she told him. "Just wake up feeling like a herd of buffalo trampled over me."

"Not used to the bed yet, that's my guess," Travis said.

"Not used to my whole new life yet," she amended with a smile.

"You and that cat of yours. He tore the holy hell out of a throw pillow last night."

"Oh, Dad, I'm sorry!"

He winked at her. "That's okay . . . it was that one your mother made . . . I never quite had the nerve to throw it away."

"Jack is nothing if not helpful," Theresa said, giggling into her hands as she hadn't done since she was a child.

She remembered that pillow all too well. Sewing had never been one of Lois' strong points, and she'd made it worse by selecting lemon yellow and blinding turquoise to pick out her idea of a Native American eagle. Even at the tender age of seven, Theresa couldn't help but suspect that maybe her mother had made the horrible thing on purpose, knowing Travis would hate it but never dare say a word if he wanted to keep harmony in the household.

Still, even if Jack had done a public service by destroying the damn thing, it wasn't like him. Not used to his new life, sure, that was the probable reason, but a kitty check-up might be in order if he didn't mellow out soon.

"I'll broil the steaks," Travis said. "You're in charge of the salad."

"Your secret sauce? The ingredients of which you promised to reveal to your only daughter one day?"

"I guess today's that day," he chuckled. "Might as well pass it on while I still remember."

* * *

Kel McGuire, Trinity Bay's one-man social services department, showed up promptly at five after seven, with a bottle of wine and a Dutch apple pie. The way he and Travis greeted each other told Theresa that there was genuine friendship between them, though they'd only met when Travis' heart attack and subsequent ill health had brought him to the attention of the Elder Care program.

Not the sort of man she might have expected her father to want her to meet. Evidently, the years had mellowed Travis from the days when he would have dismissed someone like McGuire as a sissy.

Kel was taller than Travis by an inch or two. He would have been gawky as a teenager, all shins and elbows and long bony legs, but now he was lean and carried himself with quiet agility. His hair was red, but coppery rather than the carrot-orange Theresa had envisioned. His eyes did not twinkle; they were the dark blue-grey of late twilight. His face had a foxlike handsomeness, his grin quick and infectious.

Certainly no Leprechaun, she thought. But then, no deliberate Ken-doll imitation like Brad Thornton either. She hid a grin.

"I'm so pleased to finally meet you," he said, taking one of her hands in both of his after Travis had divested him of wine and piebox and coat. "Your father's told me all about you."

"I wish I could say the same." She threw a rueful look Travis' way. "I had no idea he was attending any programs until I got here on Tuesday."

"I didn't want to worry you," Travis said.

At the same moment, Kel said, "He didn't want to worry you," and they both laughed.

"He wanted to go over my head, call you himself," Travis went on.

"At least one of you wasn't being stubborn," Theresa said. While she tried to match their bantering tone, she looked over at Kel and hoped that he could see the mix of contrition, concern, and thankfulness for his help behind her words.

His barely-perceptible nod told her that he did see, and that he understood. "Now that you're here, though, I've finally badgered him into signing a release. So we can talk about him all you'd like."

"Hey, now," Travis protested. "I invited you over for dinner, not a consultation. I'm sure you can come up with better things to discuss than me."

"He'd rather we talked behind his back," Kel confided. "It's all a ploy to get me to ask you out. Shall we humor him? Lunch next week? Jordano's, on the Bay?"

"I'd like that." Theresa glanced at her father, saw him making a show of indignance but unable to mask his pleased smirk.

The steaks came out just right. She now knew the recipe for the Zane secret sauce, promising herself she wouldn't wait until she was sixty to share it with Lora. The salad was crisp and delicious, and the wine was very good.

Theresa was content to let them carry most of the conversation, but didn't feel excluded even when they talked about people she didn't know. It was a peek into her father's life, a glimpse beyond the front he felt compelled to put up around family.

After dinner, they took their pie into the living room and sank into the deep chairs around the fireplace. Jack appeared and made a few tentative sniffs at Kel, then apparently decided he passed inspection and jumped into his lap.

"They always know," Kel said, shaking his head. "They always know who's allergic."

"I'll get him –" Theresa offered, starting to stand.

"I don't mind. I *like* cats, that's the curse of it. Much better than dogs. And don't even get me started on birds. My big sister had birds, and to this day, even a cuckoo clock makes me shiver." He petted Jack, who took that as an invitation to crawl onto Kel's chest, drape his forepaws over Kel's shoulder, and bury his nose in the hollow under Kel's ear.

"He'll drool," Theresa warned. "And if he had claws, he'd be filling your neck with pinholes."

"I can feel him kneading, all right." He raised his hand and a drift of orange and white hairs floated onto his slacks. "Shedding, too." At Theresa's look of dismay, he smiled. "Really, it's okay. What's a little sneezing among friends?"

"Think I'll head off to bed," Travis said.

Theresa suspected this sudden pleading of weariness was a ruse – hadn't her father just this morning mentioned insomnia? He'd always been a night owl, which was one reason why the six-to-two shift at Nate's had suited him so well.

If ploy it was, this time it failed. Kel checked his watch, started at how late it was, and disengaged Jack. True to form, beads of saliva stood like jewels in Jack's whiskers, and there was a sizable damp patch on the back of Kel's sweater. Not to mention a wide swath of cat hair down the front.

"I'm really sorry," Theresa said, brushing ineffectually at him.

"Like I said –" was as far as Kel got before he sneezed, three in quick succession, not window-rattling bellows but severe enough to cause his body to jerk and his coppery hair to tumble over his forehead. It gave him a boyish look that would have been appealing if he hadn't at the same time been wiping his red-rimmed eyes.

"Might have to call in sick tomorrow," Travis teased.

"Never." Kel blew his nose.

"Never is right. You know, Theresa, the man has not missed a day of work in five years? They gave him an award."

"A paid day off," Kel said. "How's that for ironic?"

"No vacations?" Theresa asked.

"I live in paradise – where would I go for vacation?" He retrieved his coat from the pegs by the door. "Thank you for dinner. I think that's the most relaxing meal I've had in months."

They walked him onto the porch. Theresa could see a single light burning on the second floor of Seacliff, diffused by sheer curtains.

"I'll see you Monday," Travis said, and shook Kel's hand firmly.

"Bright and early," Kel confirmed. He turned to Theresa, shook her hand too. "Lunch, don't forget. Shall I call you?"

"Please do. My schedule is pretty flexible. Unless Dad expects me to get a job.

That's what he used to tell me when I was little. Nobody over the age of eighteen was going to live under his roof without earning their keep."

"You didn't think I really meant that, did you?" Travis winked. "Besides, it sounds like you're doing pretty well." He grinned at Kel. "Been here almost a whole week and she hasn't hit me up for spending money yet."

"I can last a while," she said. "That is, provided this Jordano's place isn't too expensive. Is it the one down by the marina?"

"Wait, wait!" Kel protested, smiling. "I may not be chivalrous enough to open doors for a woman, but I'm not a barbarian! When I ask a woman out, I don't expect her to pay her own way."

"What *do* you expect?" She hadn't meant it to come out so flirtatious, but there it was, hanging between them.

He laughed warmly. "Just the joy of her company, I assure you. And that she'll pick up the check, if she asks me out the next time."

* * *

Sandy Forrester lay wakeful.

It wasn't from fever this time, at least not fever with any physical cause. This was a burning in her blood born not of lust but of guilt and shame.

How could she have done what she'd done last night?

She didn't even *like* oral sex!

Didn't she?

Always before, it had seemed like something tedious, a selfish request on the part of a self-centered man. That was one reason why she'd married Charlie. When it came to sex, he could take it or leave it, and never made any demands.

No, Charlie wasn't like any of the boys she'd dated in high school. Boys who felt that a kiss was an entitlement to the whole package, ready or not. Their reasons and arguments, always sounding so petty and pouty, but making a girl feel obligated. *If you loved me . . . a way to prove our love . . .*

It wasn't that she objected to sex. Not at all. It could be quite pleasant. But she just didn't hold with the idea that it was a man's right. Especially not when it came to using a woman's mouth.

So what the hell had she done?

And with Jerry! Her own son!

She could still taste him. She must have brushed her teeth half a dozen times today, chewed a whole roll of mints. Even now, under that cool tingly sensation, she could taste the salty sweetness of him. Could still feel her lips sliding, up and down. Her tongue circling. Her throat opening to accommodate, though she'd never been able to do that before without gagging.

Sandy moaned in anguish, pressing her closed fists against her eyes. Red starbursts bloomed in that interior darkness, but it wasn't enough to blot out the image of Jerry, his face contorted in mixed shock and ecstasy as he stared unbelievingly down at her.

Her own son!

They hadn't spoken. When it was done, when she rose from his narrow bed with her smug smile, she'd just turned and silently gone back to bed. There, lying in the darkness beside Charlie, she had caressed herself until the soft explosion shivered through her again, making her flesh clench in delicious spasms.

Then, exhausted, she'd fallen asleep, and awakened to find the fever gone. Awakened brimming with energy, so much so that she nearly bounded out of bed.

Energy? Mania, more like.

She'd been in the kitchen cooking long before anyone else woke. Usually, her job waiting tables at Jordano's left her not caring if she ever served another meal, so Charlie often did most of the cooking, bringing his absent-minded but somehow thorough skill to it. Breakfasts in particular were typically of the cold cereal and toast variety, which the kids made themselves. Baking, such as the cookies she'd been making when Theresa Zane visited, was about the only culinary task Sandy really enjoyed.

It had been different today. Her usual morning ritual of sitting by the window with a cup of coffee, staring absently out at the fog and the forest and the occasional wandering wildlife until the caffeine kicked in, did not appeal. She felt that if she sat still too long, the manic energy that filled her would release itself in sparks jumping from her skin.

By the time the rest of her family appeared at the table, she'd whipped up a platter of waffles, fried ham, and a heap of scrambled eggs.

Seeing Jerry, though, broke through her like lightning. He shuffled into the kitchen same as always, wearing sweatpants and a T-shirt advertising the Shakespearean Festival in Ashland, Oregon. His brown hair stuck up in unruly sleep-spikes, his eyes were bleary, he was smacking his mouth like a hound dog with a jawful of chewing gum . . .

. . . and he was the most gorgeous thing she had ever seen.

Sandy's hands had started shaking so badly that she spilled coffee, then knocked the cup on the floor as she went to wipe it up. Her son seemed to walk in light, an angelic radiance.

He'd looked at her, and she tensed, knowing that now it would begin. The shocked accusations and questions. The horrified tears. Ruination. Downfall.

But he'd only said, "Morning, Mom," and fallen upon the breakfast like a starved thing.

Not a word.

Not one word.

Like it had never happened.

Like it had been a dream.

Then again, Jerry was an actor, with a rare talent that would someday make him a star. If anyone could hide his feelings, it was her son. That had to be it. Hiding it, for the sake of family peace, maybe unable himself to believe it had happened.

She'd turned from the sink, and caught him looking at her. Looking at her with a knowing, lascivious smile. At that, Sandy had cried out, dropped a plate. Shards of crockery sprayed across the floor, cutting her ankles.

And Jerry had been all innocence once again. Concerned. "Jeez, Mom, did you hurt yourself?" Kneeling to pick up the broken plate, to dab her wounds with a dishcloth, his head bobbing just in front of her thighs.

It had been all Sandy could do to keep from screaming. She was sure she was going crazy. After breakfast, Jerry had gone out, thank God. Every time she set eyes on him, that same awful mix of lust and shame and dread whipsawed through her.

Charlie and Jenny hadn't noticed anything out of the ordinary, except to compliment her on the food. Then Charlie wandered out to his workshop, and Jenny settled in front of the television to watch cartoons, leaving Sandy alone with her churning emotions.

The mania hadn't left her. She began with cleaning the kitchen, but from there went on a spree that took her through the entire house. By the time she left for the grocery store, she was feeling bubblier and giddier than she had since high school. The way she'd felt when she'd developed a crush on some new boy.

She'd spent the day in a flurry of anticipation and fear, waiting for Jerry to come home. She had to see him again, never wanted to see him again. They could not go on as if nothing had happened. They had to at least talk about it.

Talk about it? What to say? Ask him if he liked it? Ask him if he wanted seconds? No! Horrible idea! Revolting!

Yet it sent a pulse twanging along her nerve endings.

The entire day had gone like that. Jerry brought Gary Haverley home for dinner, and she could tell just by looking at them that he'd told his best friend all about it. Those sly, sly grins. Evil and strange.

It had been a relief to escape to bed, or so she'd thought. But here it was, nearly midnight, the hour of the rose. Nearly midnight and she couldn't sleep.

She considered waking Charlie, but rejected it right away. It wasn't him she hungered for.

God help her, she wanted Jerry. Not just to taste him this time but to get astride him, pump her hips, feel him thrusting up into her.

Sandy rose from her bed, hearing her own helpless, trapped whines as she made her way through the darkened room and down the hall. She paused outside of Jerry's door.

This was wrong. This was evil.

She couldn't let herself do this.

There had to be another way. A way to free herself from this torment.

* * *

Sunday morning, Theresa scrawled a quick note for her father and left it by the coffee maker, then walked down the hill into Trinity Bay in search of a donut shop.

She had the grassy square mostly to herself, except for a good-looking uniformed black man and an old wino with a mossy overcoat. Having seen similar scenes enacted in L.A., she was pleasantly surprised when the young cop gently ushered the wino into the Trinity Square Bar and Grill and bought him breakfast.

Nice to see that people were as friendly as she remembered. Also nice to see that she and Travis weren't the only ones whose ancestry wasn't one-hundred-percent pure white. All those pale faces, made paler by the infrequent sunshine, had been quite a shock after the Southern California mix she was used to.

The donut shop was right where it had always been, a little seedier now but still open all night and still with its display window full of sugary, fatty treats.

The man behind the counter stared at her without raising his eyes above her collarbones as he put her choices in a paper bag and made change.

She strolled around the plaza, looking in store windows. Red's Salon, an arcade and ice-cream shop called Galaxy West, a folksy clothes boutique, the combined library and town hall. Which included the sheriff's office, she noticed, as the young cop tipped her a friendly wave as he went up the wide front steps.

On one corner, in the bottom storefront of the eternally-defunct Bay Towers Hotel, was Agate River Books and Coffee. Theresa paused in surprise. The front window display featured children's books, with a complete set of *Lora and Ruff* occupying center stage. Above the books was suspended a blowup of her jacket photo, and careful lettering – *Local Author!*

Bemused, she started toward the door, meaning to check their hours. Before she reached it, it swung open and a tall black man emerged carrying a broom. He was about her father's age, with skin like dark chocolate and hair beginning to powder to white.

The man started, then grinned broadly as he saw her. "Why, Theresa Zane!"

"Good morning . . . ?" she made it a question, hinting.

He laughed a low, mellow laugh, revealing strong, even teeth. "No, you don't know me, but I know you. Your father's shown me your picture so often it would be engraved on my mind, even without *that*." He indicated the poster in the window. "I'm Malachi Edwards."

"You're a friend of my dad?"

"Oh, yes. Come on in and have a cuppa. On the house." He winked at her. "Though I may try and get a few autographs out of you."

"My pleasure." She followed him into the store and knew right away that she would be spending a lot of time here. It was divided into two sunken areas by an airy, raised hallway tiled in toffee-brown and covered with green and gold throw rugs.

The left half of the space was filled with bookshelves in a chin-high maze, the tops of the stacks and the upper walls showcasing a collection of polished brasswork – animal statuettes, trays, urns full of dried autumn grasses – and woven mats in African designs.

The children's section, by the windows, had lower shelves, white wood painted with whimsical characters from African mythology. Theresa didn't know much about it, but she recognized Anansi the Spider, trickster and storyteller, prominent among them. Childrens' books were spread invitingly on low tables, and a box brimmed with puppets and toys.

The other half of the store was the coffee shop, with more gleaming brass and glossy wood, and windows that looked out on the square and the park. Leather-topped stools ran along a curving bar, cozy booths and little round tables cluttered but did not crowd the floorspace.

The wall behind the bar was lined with shelves, this time holding ranks of tall bottles with colored liquid – flavors for coffee and Italian sodas – and a spice rack of cinnamon, nutmeg, shaved chocolate, and other sprinklings. The menu was written out on a large chalkboard, and a well-worn copy of "The Latte-Lover's Dictionary" was attached to the base by a length of cord.

The air was fragrant with the aromas of coffee and spice. Theresa breathed deeply and sighed in contentment. Spying a glass dome covering a silver tray of pastries, she held up her bag of donuts with a chagrined smile.

"Guess I should have waited!"

"Well, now, we wouldn't want to run them out of business." Malachi Edwards went behind the bar and regarded her for a moment. "You look like a mocha lady. Maybe with a shot of something . . . peppermint, or raspberry."

"Surprise me!" She eased onto a stool, hooked her feet on the brass rail beneath the bar. "This is a great place, Mr. Edwards."

"Malachi," he corrected. "So, how are you liking Trinity Bay? Think you might stay a while?"

"I love it here," she said honestly. "It's like coming home. I should have done it years ago."

"Ah, here comes my Ruthie." Malachi placed a generous mug in front of her, then went to the door to greet an elegant black lady in her late forties, with a face that could have been carved on an idol of a pagan goddess of beauty. She wore a loose shift of sunset hues and held a boy of about eight by the hand.

"The early bird finally caught a worm, I see!" the lady said, smiling at Theresa. "I kept telling him nobody in this town was ready to stir before ten on a Sunday, but now you've made me wrong!"

"Ruth, Toby, this is Theresa Zane. Travis' girl. Theresa, my wife Ruth, and our son. Toby loves your books. Which one's your favorite, son? *Lora and Ruff Go to the Moon?*"

He nodded shyly. "I like the rocketship."

"So do I," Theresa said warmly.

Ruth Edwards took the stool next to her. "We're so glad to finally meet you. We've heard so much about you, it's like you're our long-lost niece."

"My dad really talks about me that much?" It was something of a foreign idea; she'd always known he was proud of her, but he rarely said it in so many words. The thought of Travis bending the ears of others with stories about her was at once amusing and comforting.

"Whoo, Malachi, my love, you've got the heat turned up too high again," Ruth chided, fanning herself with a long slim hand that would have been equally well-suited to a concert pianist or an artist.

"Sorry, sweet one." He adjusted the dial on the wall.

"Can I have a cookie, Momma?" Toby asked, in the politest tone Theresa had ever heard from a child.

"No, dear. No cookies before lunchtime." She accepted a glass of ice water from Malachi

"Okay." Without a single pout, Toby went over to the book half of the store to plop down on the child-sized sofa with one of the adventures of *Lora and Ruff*.

"I was just telling your husband what a great place this is," Theresa said.

"You should visit my shop too," Ruth replied. "Though I open at a more civilized hour, and not at all on Sundays." She pointed across the square to the folksy boutique Theresa had noticed earlier, whose sign read For Me.

"I certainly will!"

"Good gracious, Malachi, did you turn *up* the heat by mistake?"

"It's at sixty-five," he said.

Ruth fanned herself again and rolled her glass of ice water across her brow. "Maybe it's the Change," she said half-jokingly. "That, or I'm coming down with something. Because it feels like it's ninety degrees in here."

* * *

By the time Theresa left Malachi's shop, the coffee had warmed her blood and shaken loose the last of the lethargy with which she'd awakened. Maybe a good jolt of caffeine was all she needed. Maybe Dad was slipping her decaf.

Or, and here was a devious thought, maybe he was supposed to cut down on the real stuff himself, doctor's orders, but was too stubborn to comply so Kel McGuire or Shauna Davis, who had been doing the shopping for him, were up to something sneaky.

The rising sun had taken the damp cool edge off the day. Trinity Bay was coming slowly to life. More people were on the streets, not a lot, but more than there had been an hour ago.

She left the town behind and began the climb along the wooded path, the bag of now-slightly-squashed donuts swinging from her hand.

All in all, it was turning out to be a great day, and it wasn't even nine o'clock yet. She'd had her walk, had her coffee, met some new friends, and a familiar but long-absent feeling was stirring down deep in her mind.

Quickening, that was how she thought of it. Like the first flutters of movement when she'd been pregnant with Lora. But this was a quickening of the mind. She wanted to *write* again. It had been months since she'd felt that soul-hunger, and only when it returned did she realize just how much she'd missed it.

She even dared to think that this time she might be up for a different, ambitious challenge. A novel. Aimed at older kids, maybe. They were into ghost stories these days. Or even something for adults. She'd never before thought she had the stick-to-it-edness to complete a novel. Writing and illustrating the short *Lora and Ruff* books had been daunting enough. But now she thought she might just be able to give it a try.

"One word at a time," she said, and laughed softly to herself.

A chipmunk chattered indignantly in response, and Theresa pinched off a piece of glazed donut and tossed it onto the thick mossy root at the base of the tree.

"There you go, wise guy, have some cholesterol."

One word at a time. And why the hell not? Her whole life was undergoing a fresh start. Why not her writing too?

Voices ahead made her pulse spike briefly in an unpleasant surge of fear. Young male voices, accompanied by rock music. Her fingers closed reflexively over the small canister of pepper-spray attached to her key ring.

"Dude, you're shitting me."

"No way. She really did."

"Whoa, must've freaked you out."

"Freaked? Scared the hell out of me!"

As she came around the bend and saw the Forresters' house and nothing more alarming than Jerry and another kid tossing a basketball back and forth, she chided herself for her conditioned response. This was Trinity Bay, for God's sake. The idea of gangs or roving packs of teenage rapists prowling the woods was just plain ridiculous.

"Heya, Ms. Zane," Jerry called. Mizzane, it came out.

His companion looked at her with undisguised interest. He was shorter than Jerry, wiry, with a mop of curly darkish hair and vaguely rodentlike features – quick, sly, clever. He was dressed in a way that made Theresa smile. She hadn't seen parachute pants with that many zippers since the late '80's.

"Hi, Jerry." She set down her donuts on the hood of a bile-green Mustang that had to belong to the other kid, and opened her hands for the ball.

Parachute-Pants passed it to her with a moderately sinister grin. It thwacked hard into her palms, stinging them briefly, but she didn't let it drop. She bounced it a couple of times, eyeing the distance to the hoop haphazardly nailed to a post, and let it fly.

"Hey! Two points!" Jerry crowed as the ball whooshed through.

"Not bad," the other admitted, the *for an old chick* going unspoken.

"Guess I've still got it," Theresa said, instantly realizing that wasn't the sort of thing one should say to seventeen-year-olds who ran on high-octane hormones. They each dipped down for a quick ogle, and both blushed when they realized she'd seen them do it.

"Mizzane, this is Gary, Gary Haverley," Jerry said. "Another weirdo from the drama club."

"Yeah." Gary drew his brows together and curled his lip. "For some reason, they always cast me as the bad guy and Romeo here as the hero. He's Peter Pan this year and I gotta be Hook."

"At least you don't have to wear tights!" Jerry protested.

"You love it and you know it. Your Robin Hood tunic last year was so short you shoulda been arrested for indecent-fucking-exposure. Sorry, Mizzane."

"No problem, Gary. Believe it or not I've heard the word before." She retrieved her bag. "Jerry, is your mom home?"

The boys exchanged a peculiar, wary look. "She's asleep," Jerry said in an odd voice.

"Is she okay?"

"Uh . . . yeah . . . I guess."

Now she understood that look. *Don't tell her, she's one of them, a grownup, she won't understand.* It made her feel old and glum for the second time in under ten minutes.

"Well, I won't bug her then," she said. "See you guys later."

As she continued on, she heard them whisper to each other.

"You gotta tell somebody, dude!"

"What am I going to say? That my mom's started sleepwalking?"

"Jeez, Jerry, she had a *knife!*"

"So she was making a sandwich or something."

"In her sleep?"

For that, Jerry had no comeback, at least none that Theresa heard.

* * *

"What are you doing, hon?" Travis asked, coming into the living room with a sandwich in hand and Jack prowling around his ankles.

Theresa looked away from the screen. "Writing."

"You sound like it's not going so well."

"Oh, no . . . it's going fine."

"You often cuss when you write?"

"Dad!" she gasped, then giggled. "Okay, you caught me. I can't seem to get started. It's frustrating. This blank screen – it's staring at me. Reproachful. I want to write, but I don't know what to write about."

He chuckled. "How about your little invisible friend? You used to make up stories about her."

"About Glory? Really?"

"Didn't we have this conversation a few days ago?"

"That was about dreams, not stories. What kind of stories?"

"Here, read some of them yourself." He slid open the bottommost desk drawer and took out the packet of her old school papers. There was a thin folder stuck inside the packet.

The folder held sheets of stationery that brought back long-ago Christmases to Theresa in a wave of nostalgia. Her aunt Dorry, Travis' older sister, had sent her the same thing every year. Notepaper with her name scrolled across the top and bordered by hearts and flowers, a set of matching pencils, and a rubber stamp of an ornate capital T with an ink pad to go with it.

"This is strange," she murmured. "I don't remember ever writing about Glory. Or dreaming about her. Or waking up screaming from nightmares. Are you sure, Dad?"

"Oh, I see, it's easier to believe the old man is getting forgetful," he huffed in mock offense. He tapped the faded stationery. "How do you explain this, then?"

Theresa shook her head. "I don't know."

"I'll let you figure it out. Would the TV bother you if I watched the game?"

"Only if you still yell at the players."

"I'll yell quietly."

"Deal."

He turned away, toward the television, but Jack stayed where he was, staring up at Theresa.

"What?" she mouthed.

Those wide, unblinking, inhuman eyes.

Jack stood on his hind feet, braced one forepaw on her knee, and used the other to swat at the papers she held.

"These aren't for you, fuzzball." She bapped him on the head with them.

He twitched first one ear and then the other, swatted again, then scooted up the stairs with that eerie, silent, liquid speed cats had.

She forgot about her weird pet and started looking through the papers. One was nothing but ink-stamped letter T's, this way, that way, upside down, sideways, making patterns. But the next was covered with her own small, precise childhood handwriting, so different from her current scrawl.

* * *

Once upon a time, there was a garden in the back of the big house. A garden in the back, and a secret in the attic where Glory couldn't go.

Her Nana said it was full of mice and spiders and other nasty things. Her Nana said the floor was broke and Glory might fall through. She had her promise to never go in the attic.

Glory promised. She didn't like mice. She didn't like spiders.

She didn't know about the bad man.

Glory liked her new house. It was lots better than the one in Chicago. Her Mama and Papa were happy here too. They were all happy. Nana was happy because she wasn't all by herself now.

There was going to be a horse. Glory was going to call it Sunshine, unless it was black. Papa was going to show her how to ride it. Nana was going to have parties for her. Mama was sewing and making pretty clothes, and was doing things for the new baby when it came.

One day Nana gave Glory a present. A necklace. A special necklace with a rose on it. Glory felt special like a princess and the necklace was magic too.

Theresa frowned. "I don't remember this at all."

She picked up a pencil and absently sketched a rose, its petals surrounding a faceted gem. Then a necklace of linked leaves and thorns. She shaded the petals dark.

The next piece of paper was blank, until she turned it over.

Theresa went cold.

There, on the unlined back, was a crayoned drawing of a necklace. Waxy black petals. A blood red jewel. Silver-grey leaves and thorns.

She held it next to the one she'd just done.

They were practically identical.

* * *

"Spank me," Ruth Edwards said.

Malachi stopped mid-thrust and looked down at her. "What?"

She writhed catlike beneath him and raked her long fingernails over the smooth flesh of his back. A rose, pure black, was painted on each nail. "Spank me! Play rough with me, Malachi!"

He grinned uncertainly. "Are you sure that's what you want?"

"Do it!" she snarled.

Malachi swatted her lightly on the hip, a playful pat. "Has my Ruthie been a bad girl?"

"Not like that! Like this!" Her palm connected searingly with his buttock, and he yelped in surprise.

"Damn, woman, what are you doing?" He withdrew and knelt on the bed, his confusion beginning to take its toll on his erection.

Ruth whirled into a crouch, presenting her rear to him while looking over her shoulder. "Spank me, I said! Do it hard!" Her voice was a savage growl.

A gleam lit Malachi's eyes. "If that's what you want . . ."

* * *

Sandy Forrester sat at her kitchen table, which was bare except for the shining deadly wedge of a knife.

She remembered standing by Jerry's door last night, alternately wanting and hating. Wanting and hating. Him and herself.

That seething emotional stew had finally boiled over into physical nausea. She'd fled down the hall, into the kitchen, and thrown up into the sink. Straightening up, her gaze had fallen upon the block of knives. She'd drawn one, the handle sucking the sweat from her palm and the chaos from her mind.

It all became so clear to her then!

It wasn't *her*, it was *Jerry*!

She'd always known he was gifted. His abilities weren't limited to the stage, that was it. He had powers. Psychic powers. He was getting into her head, sending her these tormenting, tormented thoughts.

His was the sick, twisted, evil lust.

Not hers.

His.

How many times had she and Charlie marveled to each other over their luck? Their children were the closest thing to perfect any parent could expect. Not like Al and Celeste Haverley, whose three kids despised them. Not like kids who stole, drank, got into fights.

Their perfect children.

Now she knew better.

All along, it had been a lie.

Her perfect son, her sweet, funny, talented Jerry, was really a demented monster. Using his perverse mind powers, he had reached into her head and made her do things to him. Made her like it. Made her act the slut. His own mother!

She'd realized last night that she could put an end to it by putting an end to him. That thought had come to her as cleanly and sharply as the knife in her hand. All she had to do was put the blade in his wormy, treacherous heart and it would be over. She would be free. No one would ever find out the things he had made her do.

It seemed the only way, so she'd taken the knife, gone to his room. He was asleep, but even in sleep there had been a knowing sneer on his face. She'd raised the knife . . .

. . . and then got ahold of herself. If she did it, people would demand to know why. What could drive a mother to murder her own son? They would find out the truth. They would blame her.

The knife had lowered while she considered this new possibility. Nobody would believe what he'd done. If he was dead, there was no way to prove he'd been sending those thoughts into her head. They would think she was crazy. Lock her up. She would lose Charlie, lose Jenny.

They'd call *her* the monster. Her, not him. Who would believe she was defending herself against horrible psychic mind control?

She'd sobbed then, only once, softly, but it was enough to wake Jerry. Confused, befuddled — or acting like it exceedingly well! A bright flash of hate had shot through her as she suddenly knew he'd been awake the whole time, watching her debate and suffer. She'd come very close to just doing it then, just ramming the knife into him . . .

But the image wasn't of the knife ramming into *him*. It was of something else ramming into *her*. Lust undid her knees and nearly spilled her to the floor. She staggered/stumbled out before Jerry could manage more than a sleep-fuzzed mumble.

If he could play his games, so could she. She could pretend it had never happened. She could resist his evil tricks.

So she thought, but once again, sleep had abandoned her as soon as darkness cast its velvety cape over the bedroom. With the night came the image of the rose, opening in front of her, beckoning, begging to be touched, the gem at its heart flashing like a beacon, beating in time with her own longing pulse.

Only the knife banished the rose. She sat and stared at it, stared at the shine of its honed blade. Sat and stared, waiting for the sky to begin to lighten. Waiting for the black petals of the rose to draw in upon themselves once more.

* * *

6

He had to make her notice him.

As the lines worry and stress had carved into her face began to smooth, she became even more beautiful. Trinity Bay brought her to life. The vitality he had noticed before now blazed in her like a bonfire. She wasn't sleeping well, and that left its mark, but he knew that would pass in time.

She'd sleep better if she didn't sleep alone.

What would it be like to cover that tawny-toffee flesh with his own? To part her softest lips and enter her warmth?

He shivered just to imagine it. Of the countless women he'd possessed, he knew she would be the ultimate conquest. The ultimate seduction, triumph, prize.

She might even be worthy to bear his seed.

Watching her was bliss, but soon watching her would not be enough. He would have to touch. To kiss, caress, lick, nuzzle, suckle, taste, devour. She would have to be his completely, body and soul, before he would be satisfied.

He wasn't strong enough to approach her yet.

The other women meant nothing to him. The merest flicker of his notice. Enough to entice them, he was sure, for how could they resist his heat? But they were of no consequence. He only did what he did out of habit as far as they were concerned. It was Theresa who captured his attention. Theresa he wanted, and would have.

He hadn't yet sufficiently proven his worth. She set quite a task before him. Quite a past to overcome.

It would be done. He had always enjoyed a challenge.

The task would weaken him, but Theresa gave him strength.

Beautiful Theresa.

She would be his.

* * *

There was a sealed can of coffee in the pantry, and it wasn't decaf. So much for *that* theory.

Theresa yawned and scrubbed a weary palm up the side of her face. Her mouth felt coated with sludge, and leaden denseness seemed to have settled into her bones overnight.

Small wonder. She hadn't slept well at all. Jack had gone berserk about one in the morning, leaping at the wall until his noisy cavorting roused her enough to get out of bed and unceremoniously toss him into the hall. He'd bounded down to the door to her old room, feet hardly touching the floor, and crouched there mewling pathetically.

Now he came trotting into the kitchen, tail held high, and went expectantly to his dish.

She fed him, hearing her bones creak as she leaned over. "Ohh, I'm getting old," she groaned.

"That's my line," Travis said. "Still having trouble sleeping?"

She stretched. "I'm all stiff."

"Hunched over the computer half the night, I'm not surprised. Maybe I'll get you one of those trendy posture chairs. You know, the ones with knee braces and no backs?"

"No, thanks," Theresa said. "I tried one of those once. It made my feet fall asleep, and I always felt like I was going to fall on my face. Do you go to your program today?"

"Need me to give a message to anyone?" he asked. "About a certain lunch date?"

"If the opportunity presents itself," she said. "I was going down to the square today. Ruth wants to show me her shop."

"Good people, Ruth and Malachi. Told them we'd have them over for dinner sometime."

"You are just turning into the party king, Dad," she said fondly.

"Ah, well, people were telling me I was becoming a recluse anyway. Might as well prove them wrong."

They had breakfast, chatting about the town that had already firmly asserted itself as home in Theresa's mind. She could almost believe she had never left, that the years between were all some strange and unimportant dream. Except for Lora. If Lora could be here, life couldn't be better.

"I ought to call Steven," she mused. "I'd like to get Lora's holiday plans settled."

"It's your turn, isn't it? Last year, Steven had her for Christmas."

"Yeah . . . but this'll be his and Cheryl's first Christmas together. They might want to make a big family thing of it."

"We're her family too," Travis reminded her gently. "Our first Christmas together in almost twenty years."

"And you haven't seen Lora since she was a baby. I'll call him tonight."

The minibus arrived then to chauffeur Travis to Silver Grove. Theresa waved good-bye, then tidied up and sat down to review what she'd written the night before.

In some of the writing classes she'd taken in college, she'd listened with envy as other students described how it was to *blaze*. To have the words not come dragged painfully one by one *from* them but to flow *through* them. She'd never experienced it herself, though she had always nodded in understanding like everyone else in the class.

Last night, she had *blazed.*

It exhilarated her and scared her green.

She'd never written anything like it before. A ghost story for kids, she'd thought. But as soon as she'd started, she'd realized this was not going to be for kids. Not by any stretch.

Mourning Glory
a novel by Theresa Zane

Before the wicked girls and the window, there had only been the room and the mirror.

*The window had been covered for as long as he could remember, and he'd never thought of disturbing it. A world beyond the room? The room **was** the world, and the door in the floor was the gate to the Underworld. The Underworld, the old woman's lair.*

There was nothing else . . .

. . . until the day that a board slipped. A thin line of light pierced the room. At first, he cowered, afraid. Eventually, his curiosity overcame his fear and he crept over for a closer look.

He gasped as he saw the towering trees, shrouded in high pearly mist. Water formed a flat expanse of slate beyond wide mud flats. A sloped, shingled roof was below him, and beyond that was a green lawn bordered with flowers.

Dim memories came to him of playing on the grass, of running under the trees. But these memories brought a sickening feeling to his head, so he replaced the board and returned to his narrow bed, clutching the blanket to his chest.

The mirror glared like a murky blind eye from the wall above him. He carefully worked it loose of the nail that held it, and regarded himself. As always, the face he expected to see was gone, hidden beneath a tangled growth of itchy hair. A scary face, a troll's face.

He much preferred looking at his wicked girls. He'd found them hidden beneath the bottom of a chest. A stack of pictures, yellow and grainy. Now he kept them under the bed, and only dared take them out when he sensed it was a long time yet until the old woman brought the food.

They were nothing like the old woman in her shapeless dress, with her pinched face and glittering rings. These were young, pretty. Their legs, and sometimes more, showed through their clothes.

The first time, he'd been frightened at the change that had overtaken him. The thing in his pants, the thing he made water with, had grown hard and swollen. He'd choked back a scream, his fear of the old woman's wrath overpowering even this new terror.

Nastybad, he'd recalled suddenly. A voice like thunder, telling him it was nastybad, that he should never, never touch it unless he was making water or washing, and even then, he should never look at it.

Now, though, he liked it. He liked to feel his nastybad thing get big. He liked to touch it while he looked at the wicked girls. It felt good.

The wickedest girl of all was wearing nothing but high stockings. Her hand was draped across the place where her nastybad thing would be.

Except girls didn't have nastybad things. He remembered that much from a little girl he used to know, before he went to live in the room. They'd taken off their clothes, looked at each other. Up in a high place that was filled with straw and lazy drifting motes in shafts of light.

Little wicked girls had bare places split open like peaches. Maybe big wicked girls did too.

He slowly rubbed his hand up and down. Small moans caught in his throat. He imagined he was right there in the picture with the wicked girl. She was smiling at him. She would move her hand, show him if she had a split-open peach under it. Maybe he would touch it, and she would touch him.

His curled fist moved faster. His breath hitched. A gathering, drawing sensation tightened at the root of his loins.

He did not hear the creak of the stairs and the rattle of the latch, until it was too late. The door slammed open and he was caught in the harsh glare of lamplight.

He scrambled to hide himself, hide the picture

Too late. She'd seen, she knew.

Her single harsh gasp came back out as an outraged howl. She nearly dropped the lantern, the oil within it sloshing and threatening to spill. One of her black shoes tottered backward over the door to the Underworld.

His mind gibbered in hopes that she would fall, that her punishment would never come to pass. Such luck was not with him. She regained her balance, shoved the lantern heedlessly at the table, and her hand snapped out in a witch's claw.

She tore the wicked girl from his grasp. He uttered a silent squeal and pulled the blanket over his head, reasoning in some dim way that if she couldn't see him, he'd be spared.

He heard the thick rip of paper. The picture, gone, destroyed. Then the blanket was yanked off of him, and the old woman's fury descended in a terrible storm of shrieks and blows.

It didn't end until he was curled on the floor under the bed with his arms wrapped around his head, his nastybad thing shriveled away to nearly nothing, sobbing soundlessly. He stared helplessly as she seized up the rest of the pictures, shredded them, scattered the pieces into the glassy throat of the lamp. They flared and curled and turned to ash.

She stood over him, shaking, her normally white face crimson in anger. Her black eyes glittered like spider's eyes, full of loathing.

Then she was gone in a dry rustly swirl of skirt. The door slammed, plunging him into darkness and silence.

He stayed there a long time, hunger driving him to catch and eat the insects and mice that shared the room with him. Even that wasn't enough;

soon he could feel his bones standing out like boards.

At last, when he was too weak to do more than lie on his bed, she began to bring him food again. His strength gradually returned, and in time he regained the will to creep over to the window, slide the board aside, and gaze out at the green and pearly grey paradise that he would never get to experience.

Then came the day that he looked, and saw the people. The carriage. The trunks and boxes being carried into the house. The old woman, smiling, happy, embracing the man and the woman and the little girl.

The little girl, blond and laughing.

Blond and laughing, like the wicked girl who had undressed with him in the hayloft so long ago.

She had come back.

She would be his.

"Jesus," Theresa said softly as she finished reading over the first part.

She'd set out to write something whimsical about her childhood invisible friend, but it had taken a dark and definitely creepy turn. All thanks to one bit from her old scribblings.

Those papers were still in the drawer. Theresa found the one she was thinking of, after pausing again to marvel at the similarities between the necklaces she'd drawn so many years apart.

The one that had disturbed her read:

The bad man came from the attic.

The scary man came from the attic.

Nana couldn't stop him, so Glory ran away. But the bad man chased her. He chased her out of the house and down the lane. She tried to hide but he found her.

He hurt her.

He put her in a dark box and closed it up.

Theresa shivered. She was lucky her folks hadn't carted her off to a child psychologist after reading that. But then, on second thought, Travis wouldn't do something like that and Lois probably hadn't bothered to read any of it. As long as Theresa brought home papers with good grades on them, Lois didn't care what the content was.

"No wonder I woke up screaming," she said to Jack. "Good God!"

Easy to see, therefore, what had inspired the *blaze*. She just didn't know what came next. A walk would help her get her thoughts in order, and she had promised Ruth she'd stop by.

Moments later, she was on her way to town. For Me, Ruth's shop, was open and the lady herself was chatting animatedly on the phone. Ruth looked radiant, her eyes shining like stars. As Theresa walked in, Ruth was apparently relating something juicy that Malachi had done the night before, because when she saw Theresa, she got an embarrassed look and changed the subject quickly.

Theresa waved at her to continue her conversation, and browsed the merchandise. A small neon question mark was burning in the back of her mind as she tried to envision Malachi Edwards doing the raunchy things Ruth had been describing. She just could not make that knowledge fit with the genteel man she'd met yesterday. Still, Ruth his wife would know him far better. Everyone had their secret kinks and quirks, after all.

The clothes for sale in For Me were a mix of items handmade by local folk artists or imported from faraway lands. Lots of granny dresses, scarves, garments with an Eastern or African flair. Theresa was admiring a bold top in shades of cinnamon, ivory, and violet when Ruth finished her call and came over to her.

"Sorry about that," she said. "Once my sister and I get talking, it's hard to make us quit."

"You didn't need to stop because of me," Theresa said.

"I needed an excuse anyway." She peered closely at Theresa. "Are you feeling all right? Forgive me for saying so, but you look like you've been up all night."

"Feel like it too. I asked Sandy Forrester and I'll ask you too – what's your secret?"

"Knowing her husband Charlie, it can't be the same as mine!" Ruth's laugh was throaty and sexy, but she hushed herself quickly, looking abashed.

"Oh, *that's* your secret?" Theresa teased. And that, the teasing, seemed to make everything okay in Ruth's mind, elevating Theresa from the daughter-of-a-friend status to one-of-the-girls.

"Honey, Malachi Edwards was one of the best-kept secrets in the state. Last night, though . . . whoo! I'd been thinking I wouldn't be in the mood; I'd had a fever all day. Nothing like a love-cure, let me tell you! Poor Malachi, though . . . I must've wore him out, because he says he doesn't remember a thing! Either that, or he's too shy to talk about it."

* * *

Monday evening, Theresa called Steven in Phoenix and had another of those stiff, stilted exchanges that had been all they'd managed since the Big Fight and the subsequent divorce. Talking to Lora was much more pleasant, hearing all about her new school and teacher and friends.

Steven agreed to send Lora for all of Christmas break with what Theresa thought was unseemly eagerness. But who was she to criticize? He'd been there for Lora every day, while Theresa had thrown away home and family to chase after her career. She still couldn't bring herself to tell him that the show had been canceled; in a deceit unlike her usual self, she let Steven believe she had come to Trinity Bay purposefully to take care of her aged, ailing father.

When she went up to bed, she saw Jack prowling around the door to her old room. The room that would, in a few weeks, be Lora's. For a brief time, anyway.

She went to it. Jack came to her, purring and rubbing, as she opened the door. The moment he could slip through, he did.

Travis was right. The room hadn't changed. Mrs. Davis, Seacliff's housekeeper who also cleaned for Travis once a week, had kept it dusted and reasonably fresh, but there was still an air of desertion, abandonment, loss, sorrow.

"Kooky-bear," Theresa murmured in amazement. She crossed to the bed and picked up the floppy panda she'd thought lost long ago. "Dad found you!"

A cold wind stirred her hair, whispered across the back of her neck.

Theresa turned. The pale green curtains weren't moving, but the draft had to be coming from the window.

That had been her favorite spot in the whole house. The window, which bowed outward in a half-moon curve. There was a window seat, big enough for even a full-grown woman to curl up comfortably. The once-white cushions had gotten a bit dingy, a bit threadbare, and the wooden mock-cabinet beneath groaned mildly under her weight.

She smiled to herself, hugging Kooky-bear and thinking of all the time she'd spent searching for the catch that she knew had to be somewhere in the windowseat. The mock-cabinet couldn't really be just wood made to look like little doors. She'd been sure, as a child, that if she could only do it right, she would be able to open the secret compartment and find a long-hidden treasure.

Jack, purring like a fiend, crowded onto her lap and started kneading at Kooky-bear. Dust puffed up – Kooky was in dire need of a trip through the washing machine, but she worried he might simply disintegrate if she did so.

The window glazing seemed solid. No draft. Only an errant eddy from the hall.

Outside, night pressed against the glass. She could see the path winding through the woods, and a hint of lights where the Forrester place was. She remembered the start she'd given herself last week, imagining that she saw a pale shape at one of the windows.

This window, as a matter of fact.

Silly.

She caught herself getting drowsy. The last thing she needed was to spend the night scrunched into the window seat. If she thought she was having trouble sleeping now . . .

Kooky-bear went back in his place of honor on the bed. Lora would love him. *After that trip through the wash*, she reminded herself.

Jack did not want to leave, making her engage in an undignified chase-and-shoo to get him out of the room. She closed the door firmly. None of his temper tantrums in there, thank you very much.

* * *

"Mom? Dad?" Ricky appeared in the doorway, clutching his teddy. "There's a monster outside my window!"

Maria Navarro glanced at her husband, but he was snoozing on the couch with the remote resting on his chest. Two hundred channels and there was still nothing good on Monday nights.

She set down her book. "What, honey?"

"A monster!" Ricky insisted. His lip began to tremble. "I seen it looking in!"

Sweetly, patiently, Maria began, "Ricky, we've talked about this before. There are no such things as –”

Raptor, their German Shepherd, sprang up from his spot in front of the television and let loose a torrent of barks and snarls that jolted Jim from his doze. Ricky ran to his mother, bursting into terrified tears.

“What the hell –?” Jim said.

Raptor streaked into the kitchen. The family cat, Mister Grinch, shot past going the other way, puffed to twice his normal size. Even over the barking, they could hear Raptor’s claws scratching madly at the door.

“The monster, the monster!” Ricky sobbed, pressing his face against Maria’s stomach.

Getting scared herself, Maria looked at her husband. “He says he saw something . . .”

“I’ll check it out. You two stay put.” Jim tied his robe and headed for the kitchen.

“Maybe we should call the police,” Maria suggested.

“If that damn dog doesn’t shut up, I bet the neighbors will.” He made sure Ricky wasn’t looking, and reached onto the high shelf to get the gun from its hiding place.

Maria hugged her son nervously. “You think it’s a . . . b-u-r-g-l-a-r?”

“Could be,” he said grimly. “The Lansings were robbed two weeks ago. But don’t worry. Raptor’s probably already scared them off. I’ll just make sure.”

He vanished from her sight and she stayed put, moving only far enough to hitch the phone closer, ready to dial 911. She heard the back door open, and Raptor’s volley of barks as the dog plunged into the yard.

The barks cut off with shocking finality.

“Raptor?” she heard Jim call, his voice unsure.

Don’t go out there, she wanted to say.

“Raptor! Hey, boy!”

No answering bark. Not so much as a yip or a whine.

“The monster got Raptor,” Ricky wept, his words muffled.

Maria stroked his hair. “I’m sure Raptor’s fine.”

She heard Jim again, farther away, and realized that he had gone outside despite her silent plea. “Who’s out there?”

And then a cry of alarm, a gunshot, and a series of breaking and crashing noises.

Maria grabbed the phone. Ricky began to shriek for his daddy.

Something heavy thumped on the roof, and then all was still.

* * *

Buried alive.

She was alone in the dark, buried alive.

The walls crowded in on all sides. Bare wooden walls. Encasing her, trapping her.

Panic roared like a beast in her mind. She remembered her grandfather, his strict and severe face slackened into waxy dough by death, hands folded on his breast. They made her touch him, made her kiss his cold cheek as she'd never done when he was alive.

When the funeral was done, they had closed the lid, shut him off from the light forever. The carriage, drawn by horses with black plumes atop their heads, bore his coffin to the graveyard, where a gaping hole awaited.

She remembered standing beside her grief-stricken mother and somber father, her black dress and hat weighing her down. Watching as ropes and men lowered the coffin into the earth. The white marble headstone, with his name carved into it. She could only read a little bit, but she knew what it said. Her grandfather's name, his birthday, and the day he'd died. Three days ago.

He was dead and gone, dead and gone, his days of ruling with stern tyranny over forever. His days of arguing with her father, scorning and criticizing her mother, and ignoring the girl herself all over forever.

She knew she was supposed to be sad. Her mother was sad. But she couldn't find it in her heart to shed an honest tear for her grandfather.

Was that why she was buried alive? Because she had not loved her grandfather, she would spend eternity in a grave of her own? Was that her punishment?

Pain battered every part of her body, so many pains that she couldn't tell where one left off and the next began. Except for her legs, drawn up, curled up, because the coffin was no bigger than that a doll might use.

No lining of satin, no pillow for her head. Her grandfather had been buried in his finest suit; she was half-naked and cold and covered with sticky wetness.

Buried alive.

It hurt so much.

Where were her parents? Why had they let this happen? Didn't they love her any more? Or was it just that they couldn't stand in the way of her punishment?

So cold. So alone.

She screamed. Couldn't help it. Children should be seen and not heard, and not even seen unless absolutely necessary. That had been her grandfather's rule. But everything had changed. Hadn't it? Hadn't it? She had gone to a new place, where she was allowed to run and laugh and play.

And scream.

She hammered at the wooden walls, not caring that the impacts sent jarring bolts through her agonized limbs.

Why? Why?

She hadn't done anything wrong!

Had she?

It didn't matter what she'd done. She wanted out! Out! An end to the hurting!

Please! Somebody!

Shrieking and pounding.

Shrieking and pounding.

Shrieking and . . .

. . . pounding.

Theresa Zane bolted upright, her breath slashing in and out of her lungs.

Nightmare.

Whew.

Except . . . the shrieking and pounding were still going on.

The sounds had followed her out of sleep.

No. They were real.

Wakefulness like ice water splashed over her as she realized the sounds were coming from the front door. The child's screams of her nightmare.

"Please! Somebody! Help me!"

Theresa leaped out of bed and ran downstairs. She nearly collided with her father, who had just come out of his room, belting his robe on inside-out in his rush.

They tore the door open together, and Jenny Forrester fell inside.

"Jenny!" Theresa flipped on the light, saw that the soaked, shuddering girl was barefoot and wearing a nightgown filthy with mud and muck. "Jenny, what's wrong?"

Sobbing and hysterical, Jenny threw herself into Theresa's arms, clawing and clambering at her as if she was a tree to climb. Theresa picked her up, feeling the frantic trembling all through the child's body.

"Help, please, you gotta help!" Jenny wailed. "My mommy . . . my mommy . . ."

Travis was already at the phone. "Somebody must've broke into their house –"

"No!" Jenny said. "My mommy! She's got a knife . . . she cut Jerry . . . Daddy told me to run . . ."

"Call," Theresa told her father. "Jenny, hon, tell me what happened."

"You gotta help Daddy! They're fighting! And Jerry's got bad owies!" In the extremity of her emotion, Jenny's voice and words were becoming more and more childlike.

"It's okay, honey, it's okay," Theresa said. "We're calling people right now. Everything's going to be just fine."

"Chief Blake? Travis Zane here." He turned away, cupping his hand over his mouth, speaking quietly but urgently.

"She cut him," Jenny said.

"Shh, shh."

"He's bweedin'. Jerry's bweedin'." She dissolved into a tempest of wracking weeping.

Theresa bundled her onto the couch and held her.

Travis hung up. "Maybe I should go down there."

"No, Dad!"

"They might need help. I'll get my rifle —"

"Let the police handle it, Dad!"

"I'm not too old to do what's right, Theresa!"

"It's dark, it's raining, and if the cops gets there and sees a man with a gun, they'll blow you away first and ask questions later. We don't know what's going on."

"She said Sandy . . ." he said, shaking his head.

"I don't know what to believe. Maybe you're right, someone broke in, and Jenny got mixed up."

"No, no," she mumbled through her tears. "Mommy gots a knife."

"We just —" Theresa began, then stopped dead. In her mind, she heard Gary Haverley's voice — *Jeez, Jerry, she had a knife!*

When had that been? Sunday morning.

Sleepwalking? Had Jerry said something about sleepwalking?

But Sandy had been fine on Saturday when they'd run into her at the market. Fine, happy, cheerful, bouyant.

She hugged the child, stared up at her father.

"Somebody's got to go down there," Travis said. He went to the closet, got out the long locked box that held his rifle.

"I'll go, Dad." Theresa disengaged Jenny's arms from her neck.

"Theresa —"

"Stay here with her. Call the hospital, too, have them send an ambulance."

She took the rifle, looked at it, realized she hadn't fired a gun since the time she and Travis had gone target-shooting when she was eight, looked at him, and saw in his eyes that he hadn't fired it since then either. Wordlessly, she handed it back and grabbed her pepper spray out of her purse. That, she was sorry to say, she *had* used on two occasions, once in a darkened parking lot and once on the street outside of a comedy club, of all things.

Travis sat down beside Jenny and put his free arm around her, holding the phone with the other. "Be careful, Theresa."

She had left her hiking boots by the front door on a ribbed rubber mat to catch the mud; now she stepped into them and laced them tight, thankful that she'd gone to bed in thick sweats instead of just a T-shirt and panties. She threw on her jacket, found a flashlight on the pantry shelf, and let herself out into the steady rain.

The light bobbed and danced, making shadows that seemed to be lunging at her. Adrenaline rollercoastered along her nerves. Her hand clenched and fidgeted on the pepper spray, revolving it and revolving it until she made herself stop, worried that she might need it and find she'd reversed it so that she tagged herself instead of any potential enemy.

A siren keened through the night. Another good thing about a town this size. Nothing was more than five minutes away, and it was extremely unlikely that rescue vehicles would get caught in traffic.

The Forrester house was just ahead. Several lights were on, the kitchen door stood open, Bingo barked wildly at the end of the rope tethering him to his cunningly-made doghouse.

She approached cautiously, thinking wryly to herself that stuff like this was just what she hated most about horror movies. Here she was, alone in the woods in the middle of a rainstorm just past midnight, inadequately armed, with possible psychos galloping gaily on a mission of slaughter. Didn't she always, watching such a movie, criticize the idiot protagonists for doing just what she was doing now?

It didn't stop her, though. She continued up the path and peered through the open door.

Sandy Forrester's neon-yellow kitchen was garishly decorated in blood.

Theresa froze, only her eyes moving as they ticked over the hideous scene. Puddles and streaks on the floor. A handprint perfectly outlined on a cabinet. A fine spray of droplets making scarlet constellations on the wall. A knife, a butcher knife roughly the size of a bayonet, had spun to a rest beneath a chair.

Cookies were scattered everywhere. The heavy ceramic jar that had held them, a jar whimsically shaped like a smiling pig in a yellow apron, was cracked into pieces. It lay near the head of Sandy Forrester, whose hair was matted with blood. She was wearing a sleepshirt with a row of raised-tail cat rumps across the back.

The door between the kitchen and the living room swung open. A gangling scarecrow-form loomed. Theresa came within a heartbeat of letting Charlie Forrester have it full in the face with her pepper spray, and he almost clouted her with a baton.

Not a policeman's nightstick, a majorette's baton. Silver with trailing spangly ribbons from the rubber nubbins at either end. It added the final unreal touch.

Theresa sprang back, slamming into the corner of the table hard enough to leave a fist-sized bruise that she wouldn't notice until the next day. "Charlie! It's me!"

He was covered with blood and bits of broken crockery, and a ladder of cuts marched up his forearms. Defense wounds, the medical shows called them. His eyes were blank and aghast, but recognition finally came and he lowered the baton.

"T-theresa?"

"Charlie, what happened, are you okay? Did someone break in?"

"We need a doctor."

"My dad already called. Where's Jerry?"

"Out there. He's hurt." Charlie waved vaguely in the direction of the living room, then slumped into a chair and stared at his wife with such a befuddled and uncomprehending expression that Theresa suddenly knew Jenny was right. No intruders. Sandy with a knife.

"I'll go check on him," she said.

Jerry was stretched out on the floor, on his back with his feet propped on a pillow and an afghan over him. His boyishly handsome face looked ancient, sallow, warpainted with his own blood.

She knelt beside him, saw that he was still breathing. Like his father, he had defense wounds, seeping sluggishly. Theresa gently drew back the afghan and sucked in air between her teeth.

Charlie, for all his seeming state of habitual dazedness, had done what he could for his son. Dishcloths were folded and pressed to the wounds, held in place with masking tape. The cloths were already dark and wet. It looked like Sandy had stabbed him at least four times, maybe more.

An unwilling picture formed in her mind. Sandy, her normally pretty face twisted into a witch's mask, attacking her son. Charlie struggling with her, earning a few cuts of his own before seizing up the cookie jar and crashing it down on her head. Jenny a witness to some or all of it before fleeing into the night.

Red and blue lights revolved across the front of the house. The siren warbled to a stop, but Theresa could hear more in the distance.

Jerry opened his eyes and looked up at her, bleary and suffering. Her mind made a quick insane cross-connection and she found herself thinking of the time her stepfather's dog had been struck by a car. Duke's eyes had looked just like that. Not understanding, only pleading for someone to make it all better.

Glory's eyes looked like that too, she thought suddenly and for no reason.

Bang-bang-bang on the front door. "Charlie? Sandy?"

"In here!" Theresa called.

The door opened. Unlocked. She still couldn't get used to that, and judging by the look on the face of the handsome black cop, he was thinking that it was overdue for Trinity Bay's *laissez-faire* attitude regarding home security to claim a victim.

He leveled his gun at her and Theresa recoiled. She was unarmed, didn't even have the pepper spray because she'd dropped it to examine Jerry. Thank God she hadn't brought the rifle!

As fast as he'd drawn down on her, the cop raised his gun to that ready beside-the-head stance familiar to her from action movies.

"I'm a friend," she said once her pulse stopped hammering from the fright of looking at the bad end of the gun, realizing how stupid *that* must sound in a house where the mom had apparently gone berserk. If a mom could do that, who knew what a friend might do? "Theresa Zane."

He gave Jerry a quick once-over, then popped into the kitchen to survey that unholy mess. Judging by the disconnected, drifting tone of Charlie's answers, the cop wasn't going to get any information that way. He reappeared, the gun now holstered.

"The ambulance is on the way," he said. His voice was rich and deep, striking. "I'm Damon Blake."

She nodded, then told him what had happened, starting with Jenny's arrival. She hesitated, then mentioned the overheard exchange between Jerry and Gary on Sunday.

By the time she finished, the paramedics had arrived.

* * *

The next few hours were chaos personified.

Theresa called her dad, telling him what she'd found in as mild of terms as possible. Although her nerves felt stretched to the breaking point and she would have given a lot to be someplace else, she was glad she had insisted on coming down herself. Travis didn't need a shock like this one. Nobody did. He promised to keep an eye on Jenny, who had listlessly agreed to get cleaned up and then fallen into a restless sleep.

Things like this just didn't *happen* in Trinity Bay! She wasn't the only one to think so; the paramedics kept exchanging astonished looks even as they worked swiftly and professionally. Accidents, yeah, those were inevitable . . . but this sort of violence was unheard of in such a sleepy little town.

The only one who kept his cool was Damon Blake, Trinity Bay's chief of police, though a couple of times Theresa saw him pause briefly and close his eyes as if to ward off the horror.

The sirens had alerted half the town, so soon Blake's men had a flock of looky-loos to contend with. As if the weather itself were conspiring with them, the rain had slackened to a heavy mist, not nearly enough to deter curiosity.

Theresa could hear them whispering as they crowded around the house, the tale growing in wildness as it leaped from one person to the next.

Heads nodded sagely; Sandy had always been a little . . . a little high-strung, hadn't she, the poor thing; or maybe Charlie had been growing something stronger than wacky tobaccy out behind the shed, something of the . . . shall we say . . . fungoid variety?

It hurt Theresa's heart even though she knew it was the nature of the human beast. Crocodile tears for the family rent asunder, then go for the throat with malicious cutting cruelty. Neighbor against neighbor, friend against friend.

There was only one ambulance, necessitating two trips. Jerry and Charlie went first, while one of the paramedics remained to tend Sandy, who remained unconscious.

"I hoped I'd never see anything like this again," Blake murmured.

"You've seen something like this before?" Theresa asked.

"Not here," he said. "I came here to get *away* from this kind of thing. Came eyeball to eyeball with it once too often in New York."

She nodded in understanding, thinking of the L.A. papers and newscasts that never seemed to be without at least one mention of senseless attack, while the *Trinity Bay Gazette* got by on weekly doses of local gossip and events.

Speaking of which . . . she saw Lan Scribner come in, blanch at the sight that greeted him, and drop his notepad and jaw at the same time. The owner, editor, and sole reporter for the *Gazette*, Scribner used to boast that his name predestined him to be a journalist. His family had been among the original settlers, and while their fortunes would never come close to the Cliffwoods – though at least one Scribner had married into the Cliffwood clan, if Theresa's memory served – it was enough to let him run his paper without worrying about profits.

Theresa recognized him at once, for he hadn't changed in the past twenty years except to grow a little portlier, a little jowlier.

"The press has arrived," Blake observed, moving to intercept.

Close on Scribner's heels was the *real* source of information for Trinity Bay, Celeste Haverley. The only parts of her that looked as Theresa remembered were her eyes, bright and avaricious and somehow spongelike. Taking it all in. Missing nothing.

She started toward the kitchen, and Theresa, already regretting it, blocked her path.

"I don't think they want anyone in there," she said.

Celeste looked down on her in both a figurative and literal sense; a tall woman thin to the point of emaciation, she had a good six inches on Theresa. "Don't be silly, Theresa. I'm one of Sandy's best friends. I should be with her in her time of need."

"Right now, she just needs a doctor."

"A doctor?" Celeste practically pounced. "Is she hurt? How badly? Or do you mean the *other* kind of doctor?"

"I wouldn't know," Theresa said coolly.

"I heard you got here first," Celeste said, leaning close. "Was it bad?"

"Of course it was bad!" Theresa snapped. "What would you expect? My God, Celeste, don't you have anything better to do than carry all the lurid details to every ear in town?"

Her voice had raised considerably, and she became aware that she had the attention of everyone in the room. Most of them, though, looked as if she'd just said something each of them had been wanting to say for years.

Celeste's eyes flashed angrily. "I am trying to help," she said with great indignation. "We're a community here, Theresa. We look out for each other. We take care of each other. Whatever affects one of us, affects us all."

Damon Blake approached. "Sorry, ladies, but I'm going to have to ask you to take your discussion outside. The ambulance is back, and we need to move Mrs. Forrester."

"I think we're done," Celeste informed him, as if she were a grande dame permitting a waiter to remove her plate. "We'll just wait over here."

"Outside, if you please, ma'am."

Theresa had to bite back a sudden grin despite the grimness of the situation. It was all in the "ma'am." Joe Friday it was not; Blake sounded like a sheriff in a Western flick. Except those dusty cowboys could say it sincere; this time, it carried a freight of exasperation and annoyance.

Celeste seemed about to argue, then it must have occurred to her that they would bring the stretcher out the back and from in here she wouldn't have a good view. "Of course, officer," she said sweetly. "It's much too hot in here anyway."

Hot? Theresa was almost shivering despite her jacket; the open doors and chilly night made for a damp draft sweeping through the house. Celeste did look flushed, but it was probably more due to irritation than anything temperature-related.

Celeste swept grandly out, and in her wake Theresa and Blake shared a look that nearly got her grinning again.

"I better throw you out too," he said, "or she'll accuse me of playing favorites."

"I imagine you wouldn't want her as an enemy."

He waved it away, the corners of his coffee-brown eyes crinkling in amusement. "After how you told her off, I'd say the place of honor goes to you."

"I'll manage. When I was a kid, she thought I was a brat; why break a pattern?"

"Sorry you had to see all this," he said, suddenly sincere, "but I'm glad you were on the scene. Kept your head. A lot wouldn't."

One of his officers, a short but very muscular man, approached while Theresa was trying to decide if there was something more than admiration in his tone. Unlikely. Here she was in jammies, coat, and boots, her eyes starey from shock, her hair a Medusa-snarl. The stress of the night had her imagining things.

"We ran a quick search of the place," the officer reported. "No pot, no mushies, no syringes or pills or any sort of paraphenalia."

"Do me a favor," Blake said, "and go out the back, come around the front to meet me, and tell me that again. In a good loud voice so Busy Bee Haverley hears it."

This time, Theresa did grin.

* * *

Theresa let herself in and heard her father say, "Of course she can. Tonight, tomorrow, as long as she needs."

She passed Jenny Forrester, who was asleep on the couch with a plaid blanket over her and her thumb in her mouth. Even in the dim light, she could see how puffy Jen's eyes were, and the glistening snail-trails of tears that had dried on her cheeks. She paused in passing to tuck the blanket around the girl's shoulders, and stroke her hair.

The kitchen light was on, and it was there she found Travis, along with Kel McGuire. Though there probably should have been an officer present, too, Theresa knew, the entire Trinity Bay police department – all, what? three of them? – was out in force tonight already.

"Theresa," Kel said, with a smile that came out rather strained.

"Hi, honey," Travis said. "Tea? It's chamomile."

A faint grin tugged at her lips. Travis and his tea. He had picked up the habit from his mother, who believed a cup of tea was a cure for all the world's ills, and that there were countless benefits to be had depending on what went into the cup. Of course, Grandma Tashi had grown, dried, and mixed all of her own herbs, while her son made do with the variety pack from the supermarket.

She helped herself to tea, curling her hands around the cup for warmth and breathing the fragrant steam. "So, tonight it's child protective services?" she asked Kel.

"Another of my many hats. Your dad has agreed to let Jenny stay here tonight. Charlie's being admitted to the hospital, and the Forresters don't have family in town."

"We'd be happy to help," Theresa assured him.

"What if Charlie can't take care of her?" Travis asked bluntly. "He's a nice guy and all, but without Sandy, he's going to have trouble enough taking care of himself."

"If it comes to that, we can arrange a foster home placement."

Theresa suppressed a shudder and with it suppressed her own memories of a brief stay in a foster home at age fourteen, following a botched attempt at running away from home. "Are there any in town?"

"She'd probably have to go down to McKinleyville," Kel said.

"Like I told you, she can stay here," Travis said. "Sandy and Charlie have always been good friends of mine."

"Well, we'll worry about that when the time comes." Kel rose, picking up his notebook. "I'll be back first thing in the morning. Try to get some sleep, both of you. If you need me, call and I'll be right over." His gaze found and held Theresa's. "What about you? It must have been terrible for you."

"It still is," she admitted. "But I'm okay. Dad raised me up tough."

"Yeah," Kel said, smiling. "I can see that he did."

* * *

The phone woke Theresa, and as she jerked upright, a spike of stiff pain lanced down her neck. Gasping through clenched teeth, she craned and twisted her head while groping for the phone with one hand. She saw the clock – nine thirty, but for a moment she couldn't remember what day it was, and whether it was morning or evening.

Just as she lifted the receiver, her cervical vertebrae made one of those hideous pops that always left her fearing she would suddenly go numb from the neck down.

It was Ruth Edwards, sounding like she'd been up and about for hours while Theresa slept crooked in one of the living room chairs. No wonder she ached! But she hadn't wanted Jenny to awaken and find herself alone in the dark.

Ruth was saying something about a cleaning party, and Theresa mumbled responses while trying to clear the cobwebs from her brain.

"Not all of us are vicious do-nothings like Celeste Haverley," Ruth concluded. "She begged off anyway with a fever. Must be going around. So, meet us there at one?"

"Meet you where?" Theresa asked foggily.

"The Forresters' place," Ruth said patiently.

"Oh. Okay. Sure." She looked at the couch, and the sight of the blanket on the floor and the cushions empty of a little girl brought her fully out of her lingering sleep-haze. "Ruth, I've got to go. I'll see you then, okay?"

She hung up, and called softly. "Jenny? Jen, hon?"

No answer.

The chain was still in place on the front door. Last night, she suspected, the Zanes weren't the only ones in Trinity Bay to lock up. Even though what had happened at the Forrester's hadn't been the work of an outside intruder, people locked up, for all of a sudden the world wasn't as safe and innocuous a place as it had been before.

If someone as outgoing and friendly as Sandy Forrester could snap and go on a violent rampage, it could happen to anybody.

But since the chain was still on, Jenny couldn't have gone out. Theresa checked the kitchen – empty. The bathroom – likewise empty. From behind her father's door came Travis' raspy snores, and when she peeked in there was no sign of Jenny.

The windows were all closed and latched, so Theresa headed upstairs.

The door to her old room stood half-open, and Jenny Forrester was on the bed with Kooky-Bear in her arms and Jack sharing the pillow. She looked very small and defenseless in one of Travis' T-shirts that reached past her knees.

Theresa pulled the covers to Jenny's shoulders and settled herself on the window seat, trying to remember her conversation with Ruth.

A cleaning party. At the Forresters' place.

Then she understood. Ruth, Shauna Davis, and some of the others were going to clean up.

Thoughts of biohazards flickered through her mind, along with wonderings about who usually *did* clean up when something like this happened. The police came, the emergency medical people came, sometimes the coroner came. But of course none of them brought mops and Pine-Sol.

These musings distracted her for a while, and then the shakes set in. The shock of the previous night had worn off, leaving her nauseated and trembling with reaction.

Then a calm assurance washed over her like a cool breath of air. It hadn't been Sandy's fault. Sandy was just as much a victim in this as the rest of her family. A victim to some strangeness that had touched down in their loving home like a capricious tornado.

She had no idea why she should think that, figuring it was probably her mind's attempt to deny and deal with the tragedy. Certainly, it was easier than believing that Sandy had been harboring a buried insanity for months, even years.

Jack regarded her with a steady green gaze, as if privy to her innermost thoughts. He winked one eye, as he often did when they got into a staring contest, as if he knew it would make her laugh and therefore make her lose.

All she could manage was a wan smile, but it seemed to satisfy the cat. He rose, stretched in that spine-curving body wave that looked like it felt so damn good, and then walked over Jenny to hop to the floor.

The girl mumbled and rolled over, Kooky-Bear dangling from one hand. A deep sigh escaped her, and then her eyes opened. For a moment, she looked around blankly, disoriented, and then she saw Theresa.

"It's gonna be okay," Jenny declared.

Puzzled, having expected to see the grief and fear come flooding back into the child's eyes, Theresa sat on the edge of the bed. "What?"

"It's gonna be okay. Mommy didn't mean to hurt Jerry. Somebody made her do it."

Theresa was silent, wishing that Kel was here. Perhaps he'd know the magic words, know what to say to this little girl who had watched her whole life come apart. Jenny's assurance went so well with the thoughts she herself had just been having that she couldn't really muster an argument. How would one tell a child, anyway, that her mother suffered a breakdown? She decided to leave that to the professionals.

"I know she didn't mean to, honey."

"Are they gonna lock her up?"

"Well . . . I don't know."

"They can't lock her up," Jenny said, anguished. "They can't put her in jail or in the looney bin. She didn't mean to! She couldn't help it! Someone made her do it! I know!" Now she began to sob, and Theresa hugged her.

"Shh, shh," she whispered, as she used to do when Lora was upset.

"Did . . . did Jerry die?"

Why hadn't she called the hospital first? But no, surely they would have contacted her if the worst had happened.

"They took him to the hospital, honey. The doctors are going to do everything they can to help him. We'll call them in a little while and find out, okay?"

"Where's my daddy?"

"He went with Jerry. Did you ever have stitches?"

Jenny nodded and pointed to her head. "I tripped on the steps and had to get seven stitches," she said almost proudly.

"Well, your daddy needs some stitches too, but I'm sure you'll be able to see him soon."

"Is he going to take me home?"

"Uhm . . . home's kind of messy right now . . . some of us ladies are going to go clean it up for you first. Until it's ready, you might be staying here a while. I'll bring you some clothes and things from your room, okay?"

"Will you feed Bingo?"

"Sure." She glanced at Jack. "Maybe Bingo will come stay here too."

Jack's ear twitched, but he carried on nonchalantly grooming his forepaws.

* * *

"They say bad things happen in threes," Shauna Davis said.

Theresa was piling rags into the washing machine in the laundry room just off the Forresters' sunny kitchen, wearing thick rubber gloves and wincing like she did when she had to pull the innards out of a turkey.

In the kitchen, Ruth and Shauna and a few other people were scrubbing at the last of the bloodstains. The shattered cookie jar had been swept up and thrown away, Bingo had been fed, and the house was almost back to normal.

"What are you talking about?" Ruth asked. "What threes? This is one thing, a terrible thing, granted, but only one."

"Yes, but what about last year? First Lenny James dying in that accident at the mill, and then that fellow from Frisco who smashed up his car, and then the poor Cliffwood girl. One-two-three, all in a row. This could be the start of a new set."

"None of those had anything to do with each other," Nancy Ellsworth said.

"Oh, don't they?" Shauna asked archly. "What about Seacliff?"

"What *about* Seacliff?" Ruth said.

"All of those things happened right after Mr. Thornton moved in, that's what.

Bad things always happen at Seacliff. Remember Edward, and Barbara? That house has a history, that's all I'm saying."

Ruth's sigh was rich with exasperation. "The accident at the mill was at the *mill*, Shauna —"

"Which Thornton started up again, and he lives at Seacliff."

"The lawyer from Frisco went off the trestle —"

"But he was Thornton's lawyer, and had just come from Seacliff."

Another woman laughed meanly. "Maybe it's Thornton, then! Angela was his stepdaughter."

"And she lived in Seacliff," Shauna said, as if that settled everything.

Theresa came back into the kitchen, stripping off her gloves. "And I suppose," she said, knowing she was being a smartass but as fed up as Ruth sounded, "that since this used to be the gatehouse for Seacliff, that's why it happened."

"Exactly," Shauna said, pleased.

"So, why do you keep working there?" Ruth demanded. "And how come nothing bad has happened to you?"

"Wellnow!" Shauna went from pleased to miffed. "My family has worked there since 1900, I'll have you know. Here I'm trying to bring a rational explanation to these things —"

"Rational!" Nancy rolled her eyes.

When Theresa had been introduced to Kel McGuire's blond bombshell of an assistant, she'd gone through a series of responses ranging from astonishment that she and Kel weren't an item, catty assumption that Nancy had the brains of a hamster, admission that Nancy was as bright as she was beautiful, and then a resurgence of the astonishment.

But then, an hour into the cleaning party, Nancy's gigantic bearded hunk-of-muscle boyfriend showed up, and Theresa realized that lean, foxlike Kel didn't match Nancy's critera.

Leaving them to the argument, not wanting to get drawn further into it since Shauna Davis seemed to think Theresa was on her side, she went into Jen's room to pack a bag.

News had traveled fast and accurately through town. Only thirteen hours after Theresa had awakened to Jenny's frantic screams, it seemed like everybody in Trinity Bay knew the whole score.

Jerry Forrester was in critical condition, having spent six hours in surgery. One wound had missed his aorta by a half-inch, another had punctured a lung; the rest were less serious. But it would be a long time before Trinity School's star drama student was ready to go back on stage.

Charlie Forrester had fared considerably better, having only sustained defense wounds, but he was still deeply in shock. A pacifistic man who would sooner capture a spider and release it outside than squash it, he would probably be years coming to terms with the fact that he had given his beloved wife, to whom he had never even offered a harsh word in eighteen years of marriage, a skull fracture.

Sandy Forrester was in a cookie-jar-induced coma, and already there was talk that she would be evaluated and possibly committed to the mental hospital near Blue

Lake. As she hadn't regained consciousness, nobody had been able to question her. So speculation as to *why* still ran high as spring meltoff.

Despite Damon Blake's best efforts at debunking it, the reason of popular choice remained drugs. Sandy, one of the sweetest and kindest women in Trinity Bay, had freaked out on drugs and tried to kill her family.

Devil worship was the runner-up reason, not because anyone really took it seriously but because the sensationalism of it was fun to talk about.

Mental illness came in third, though plenty of people seemed willing to back that one up with claims that they'd known Sandy to act oddly in the past. Claims that Theresa felt were more fancy than fact.

Theresa was still, weirdly, inclined to agree with Jenny. Coming into the house this morning, she just couldn't accept any of the reasons. It was something else, something strange.

"Listen to you," she chided herself. "Soon you'll be out there siding with Shauna for real."

She filled a suitcase with clothes and a few toys that Jenny had asked for, then grabbed Jenny's bookbag – which she had not asked for.

She also went into Jerry's room to retrieve Jen's radio, which apparently Jerry had borrowed to make duplicate tapes of some of his cassettes. It was standing on top of a worn sketchbook, and when she picked it up and saw the drawing on the front, she blinked.

It was a rose necklace, the petals shaded dark. Done with a far more skillful hand than her own (either as a child or adult), but unmistakably the same one she'd drawn at her desk last week.

She picked up the sketchbook and flipped through it. The first pages were unremarkable, landscapes and portraits drawn by that same skillful hand. There was a stark ink picture of Seacliff, depicting it as somber and moody as any haunted house, followed by one of a mermaid surfacing in Agate River, and then the roses began to appear.

At first just doodled into the corners, like something the hand did while the brain was trying to decide what to do next in the main picture. A bloom here, a rosebush there, then a bouquet extended in an unseen man's hand.

But then the necklace, in a charcoal sketch of a little girl. And then the necklace itself, in minute detail. The ornate swirls of the setting, a faceted jewel at the heart of the dark petals.

Chilled and at the same time filled with wonder, Theresa closed the sketchbook and tucked it into Jenny's bookbag. Then, on impulse, she pulled it out again and looked inside the front cover.

A name was written there, faded but still perfectly legible.

Angela Cliffwood.

* * *

Brad Thornton set down his empty glass and looked around approvingly.

The bar, Nate's, was just right. Dark wood paneling, a lot of brass, a few vaguely nautical decorations. No annoying theme. Just a nice regular bar where a working man could relax and tip a few with his buddies after a long day. Or, where the boss could make like he was one of the regular guys.

And the bartender, Dani Kensington, had legs clear up to her chin and showed them off in short skirts that stopped a bare few inches below paradise.

"Just the thing," he said to Al Haverley.

Big Al, as he had been known since his glory days on the high school football field, was head foreman. Now pushing fifty, he was building a layer of fat over his thick, muscular frame. His crewcut was West Point grey, but that was all of the military there was about him.

"Nothing like some suds to settle the day," Al agreed, draining the last of his own beer. He stifled a belch against the back of his hand. "So, I hear the quarterly inspection report came back . . . how's the mill?"

"Doing fine and dandy," Brad said. "Sure you don't want to take that management spot?"

Big Al laughed. "Not very damn likely. Too much paperwork and ass-kissing. No offense. I'm happy just being a foreman. The wife'll bitch about it, though. The extra money and all."

"You don't let her push you around, I hope," Brad said.

"Hell, no. She's pretty well-trained. Knows about how far she can take it. Oh, she comes across all pushy, but no matter what people think, she doesn't have me by the short hairs and never has."

"That's good to hear. That's the way it should be. Wife should know her place." He fell silent for a while, thinking of April and Angela, his mouth curling into a dour frown. "Kids, too."

"Yeah, well, don't talk to me about kids," Al sneered. "Oldest is up the college, studying socio-fucking-ology. Damn waste of money. The daughter's married. Two kids of her own already. Youngest is a lazy, no-good little shit."

Brad shook his head sympathetically. "My stepdaughter, she was the mousy type. Reading all the time. Drawing. Thought she was going to be an artist. At least now I don't have to worry about her getting in trouble with some boy."

He was aware of Big Al giving him a sidelong troubled look, and manufactured a strained smile. "I should know better than to talk about Angela when I've been drinking. Poor kid. Losing her mother like that . . . I guess I wasn't much help to her. I thought she was getting better, and then . . ." He shook his head as if to shake away unpleasant memories. "I try not to let it get to me, but it comes out sounding like I didn't give a damn."

Al grunted and signaled Dani Kensington for another round, his gaze wandering to the large television bolted in the corner. "You hear about the Forresters?"

Brad nodded. "Hell of a thing."

"I always knew that boy of theirs would come to no good. He runs with my youngest. Drama club pansies, both of them. Spoiled brats. Wouldn't surprise me if they found out he was the one who gave his mom drugs."

"Wouldn't surprise me, either," Brad said. "Actors. As bad as dancers, and I know all about dancers."

Dani, approaching with their beers, laughed scornfully and tossed her braid of tawny gold hair from one shoulder to the other. "Jerry Forrester, a druggie? Are you kidding?"

"You got a better explanation?" Al demanded.

"Sandy had a breakdown. It happens." She shrugged. "And having everyone in town talking about it won't make it any easier for her to get better."

"Well, Charlie shoulda kept her in line. She was always a little crazy, needed a firm hand to help her along."

Dani's grin was tight and humorless, but she knew better than to piss off her paying customers by getting into a debate. Instead, she just took their money, left their change, and retreated to the end of the bar.

"Her, too," Big Al confided to Brad with a subtle nod in Dani's direction. "Full of ideas. Uppity broad. World's full of them these days. That's why I was so glad to see the mill open back up. This town was built on hard work and traditional values. Good to be getting back to that."

"She doesn't seem so bad to me." Brad flashed his pearly whites at Dani, hoping to hint that he was only putting up with Big Al, didn't share the man's viewpoint but couldn't afford to antagonize the man who kept the mill running. She considered him for a moment, then conveyed by a slight smile and a shift of her shoulders that she sympathized with him for having to listen to such crap.

"She's a looker, all right. No Nancy Ellsworth, but a damn sight better than most. No boyfriend, either." Al drank deeply, then added, "prolly a lesbian."

"What?"

"Oh, she says she's got some guy in Eureka, goes down there every couple of weeks, but if you ask me, her guy is a gal and that's why no one around here has ever seen him."

Brad listened with half an ear, drinking his beer and munching pretzels, the rest of his mind occupied once more with thoughts of April.

April and her dance students, her musician friends, the whole hippie brood that used to fill the downstairs rec room of the Oakland house with music and booze and smoke – sure, they said it was just cigarettes or cloves, but there had been plenty of times when Brad had detected a certain other type of smoke. For all he knew, they were carrying on orgies down there while he was out working.

Fine role model for Angela, her mother had been. No wonder the girl had turned out the way she did. No morals, no realistic goals.

He'd tried. Lord God, but he had tried. Tried to reform April, provide guidance for Angela. Tried to give them both a good home, all the things money could buy.

He'd supported them, taken care of them, and all the while April had been sitting on a mansion and a fortune, without saying a word. If she hadn't tripped on the stairs after one of her nights out with her friends, he never would have found out. He'd still be busting his ass in the advertising firm.

And Angela would still be alive. Alive, but not free of her mother's influence. Even moving to the quiet of Trinity Bay hadn't helped. Now he knew why.

That boy.

That Forrester kid. Dream-chaser. Not a serious bone in his body. He'd picked right up where April had left off, filling Angela's head with fluff.

Maybe Angela was better off now.

Maybe the Forrester kid would be too. Maybe his mom had done him a favor. Whatever else, there was one punk teenager who was never going to see the world the same way again.

Brad ordered another beer, and contentedly let his thoughts wander to more pleasant things. Like Dani Kensington's legs, the state of his bank account, and the smug satisfaction with which he'd received the news that the final results of the investigation were back . . . and the death of his lawyer had been ruled an accident.

He'd gotten away with it . . . again.

* * *

Kooky-Bear had not disintegrated in the wash, but emerged fresh and huggable as a pile of towels from a fabric softener commercial. Except that he'd sprung one seam, and one of his eyes had popped loose to dangle by a string.

Theresa performed those minor repairs, then placed him on the windowseat. The bed was cluttered enough with Jenny's personal menagerie of plushies, mostly characters that Theresa recognized from animated films.

She could hear the murmur of voices downstairs. Kel McGuire and Jenny. Still wearing his CPS hat but also working with the police, he was simultaneously comforting and questioning the little girl, trying to help her and help everyone else make sense of what had happened last night.

Underlying the voices were the sounds of Travis in the kitchen, whipping together one of his famous "surprise stews." That had been the only thing Theresa ever remembered him cooking when she was a child, throwing together all the leftovers and anything from the cupboards that caught his eye, simmering it into a thick soup, and serving it with crusty fresh bread.

Surprise stew was therefore never the same twice, but helping Travis rummage and suggesting silly ingredients had boosted Jenny out of the miserable lethargy that had lain over her all day.

Theresa went back to her room and took Angela Cliffwood's sketchbook from where she'd hidden it in her dresser. She carried it downstairs to the desk, meaning to compare the images.

As she'd thought earlier. The same necklace. The only differences were in the talent of the artwork. Details only suggested in her two were vividly clear in Angela's.

Even if she had subconsciously remembered something she'd drawn twenty years ago, that couldn't explain the weird coincidence that a girl she'd never met would draw the same thing.

"Theresa?"

She started, and Jenny Forrester jumped.

"I'm sorry!" they said together, and then laughed. It was the first time Jenny had laughed all day, and even if it was brief and weak, it made Theresa's heart lift happily.

She glanced around, and saw that Kel was helping her father set the table. An outsider peering in might think they were getting ready for a family dinner. The grandfather, the young couple, and their little girl. Except, of course, for the complete lack of resemblance Jenny bore to either her or Kel. All the same, she felt a melancholy homesick yearning for just such a comforting scene.

"What's that?"

With a twinge of shame, Theresa held it so she could see. "I . . . I found this in your brother's room . . . I shouldn't have taken it . . . but I was curious about these pictures."

"Angela made those." Jenny touched the rose, and Theresa fought the sudden urge to slap the girl's hand away as she might slap it from a hot stove. "It looks real, doesn't it?"

"Do you know why she drew it?" Theresa asked, trying to keep her voice even and unconcerned.

"She dreamed about it," Jenny said, dropping into a whisper. "I heard her telling Jerry. She dreamed about a little girl, a crying little girl wearing a necklace just like this."

Theresa shuffled papers until she found the one she sought.

One day Nana gave Glory a present. A necklace. A special necklace with a rose on it. Glory felt special like a princess and the necklace was magic too.

Reading over it without letting Jenny look, she asked softly, "Did Angela know the little girl's name?"

"Glory," Jenny replied promptly. "Isn't that a pretty name? Jerry even wondered . . . don't laugh," she added solemnly, "that maybe Glory might be a ghost. He even saw her once."

"They saw a ghost?"

"Well . . . that's what he *said*," she amended with the expression of a girl who'd had pranks played on her before by her dramatic, imaginative big brother.

"Glory's ghost?" Her voice wanted to shake, but she kept it even. "Where? Here?"

"Nuh-unh. Up in back of Seacliff, by the rosebush."

"Rosebush?" That time, her voice did quaver, ever so slightly. "What rosebush?"

"The black one," Jenny said in a matter-of-fact tone.

Jack leapt onto the desk, scattering papers, and Theresa couldn't keep from screaming.

* * *

"I shouldn't be here, I shouldn't be doing this," Celeste Haverley moaned to herself as she pulled into the parking lot.

Her words did nothing to stop the churn of anticipation inside of her. If anything, her words only made it worse. Wasn't that part of the attraction? Part of the dirty sneaking slinking appeal?

She parked her car by a small restaurant. Before getting out, she got a pair of cats-eye sunglasses out of her purse and put them on. It was a dumb thing to do, she knew that. Anyone seeing her would be more inclined to wonder why she was wearing shades on an overcast day such as this.

For that matter, why hadn't she dressed more sedately? Why her usual flamboyant style? Her flame-red knit dress clung to her thin, angular body, making her look like a fashion model. Damned if she was going to dress like an old frump. She was still a sexy woman.

But still . . . she should have given it more thought. She would have been less recognizeable, even here in Eureka where she hardly knew anybody, if she'd worn something plainer.

That, though, would be just as suspect as the sunglasses. If someone she knew did happen to drive by and saw her wearing drab clothes, that would make her only stand out more.

She finally decided it didn't matter. She was here. She wasn't going to drive all the way back to Trinity Bay to change, then come back. Not when she was already five minutes late.

Celeste circled the restaurant, passed between it and a gas station, and cut across the tarmac toward the motel. She walked briskly, head held high, as if she had every right in the world to be here.

Room 11. Again, that churning thrill went through her. She was here, she was going to go through with it.

She paused at the door, then rapped softly and tried the knob. Locked, but she could hear movement on the other side.

Now fear spiked through the churning. What if Al opened that door, demanding answers, hurling accusations? What if he'd known all along, set this up to trap her?

She was on the verge of turning and hurrying away when the door opened, and Brad Thornton smiled welcomingly.

His hair was appealingly tousled, and he had removed his jacket and his tie. The collar of his shirt gaped to reveal dark blond curls on his chest. He was barefoot, and held a tumbler of Scotch in one hand.

"I was starting to think you'd changed your mind," he said, devouring her with his stormy blue eyes.

She stepped inside and he closed the door. One of the bedside lamps was on but dialled down low, spilling a golden glow across the bed. The bedspread, deep green with a pattern of black roses, bore the imprint of his body where he'd been reclining to wait for her.

"I almost did." The husky whisper sounded foreign to her own ears. "If Al finds out . . ."

"He won't," Brad said confidently. "He's got his hands full at the mill. As far as he knows, I'm at a business meeting."

"And I left a note saying I was shopping."

"So he won't find out." Brad gently removed her sunglasses. "Let me see those pretty eyes."

She slicked her tongue across her red-tinted lips, her mouth going dry as he moved close to her. His hands, so different from Al's callused ones, descended onto her shoulders and he pulled her into his arms.

An inner voice screamed one last time that she shouldn't be doing this, that she should think of her husband, her children, the field day the town would have if it ever got out. But that was the last she heard from her inner voice as Brad began undressing her, began doing things to her that she had only imagined.

His mouth was everywhere, kissing places Al had never kissed, bringing wave after wave of unbelievable sensation. They fell across the bedspread's roses in a half-naked tangle, gasping and sighing as they eagerly explored each other's bodies.

Soon Celeste was wailing like a siren, her hands grasping Brad's sweat-slippery back, urging him to even greater efforts. It had never been like this, never! Al had been her first and only, and still approached sex the same way he had approached football — no fancy moves, just get it into the endzone fast as possible, risking penalties for unnecessary roughness.

No, it had never been like this, never been so good . . . and she knew that this was only the beginning.

* * *

It wasn't enough.
He wasn't strong enough.

The other women could warm him for a while, but couldn't give him what he craved.

He needed her.

Theresa Zane.

She haunted his thoughts. The sweep of her hair as she moved. The golden light of her bedroom garbing her in goddess-like radiance. The way she, thinking herself unobserved, chewed the end of a pencil as she stared thoughtfully into the space above her computer.

He couldn't see the words on the screen, wondered idly what it was that so held her fascination. What dreams, what longings? It was in part that spark, that lively and creative spark, that drew him to her. How rich her dream world must be! How textured and sensuous!

At first, he hadn't been able to see her there, and just the thought of being cut off from her where she spent so much of her time was maddening, infuriating. Imagining her wasn't satisfying. Only by stretching his senses to the limit could he finally manage to do it, to watch her as she wrote. How alive she came as her fingers flew over the keys! How her eyes danced!

That, he knew, was how Theresa Zane looked when she was doing something fulfilling. He also knew that she hadn't looked that way often. Her life had been empty, lacking.

All her life spent searching. He knew that now. Searching unsuccessfully, not even knowing what she was missing.

Yearning for him, unaware that he existed. Trying to fill that yearning with lover after lover. Each of them only took from her, never gave.

What they had taken, he would give back.

Every parcel of her soul stolen away by those blind and foolish men who hadn't seen what a treasure she was. Yes. He would return those pieces to her, one by one. And then she would know the true depth and power of his love.

She would know, and she would be his.

* * *

The city that never sleeps, Detective Derrek Blake thought as he wove his way through the crowded precinct office toward the back-to-back desks he shared with his partner. *Good old New York. Never a dull moment.*

Even at this early hour, the place was busy and bustling. Muggings, robberies, and the ever-popular homicide. Sometimes he wondered if maybe his brother had had the right idea. At the time, he'd about busted a gut laughing. Move to the West Coast? Not even to L.A. but to some tree-hugging backwater? Yet there were times that he caught himself thinking that Damon's quiet job had a certain appeal.

Times like now, when the gleefully morbid grin on his partner's face told him that he was in for a long day.

"Morning!" Mark Gladstone hailed as Derrek approached. "Got a juicy one this morning! Real messy. Richards was first on the scene, and even he lost his cookies."

"Richards?" Derrek echoed. "Old Iron-Guts? That's a first. What was it? Car wreck? Industrial?"

"Looks like murder, but I talked to Skippy at the coroner's office, and he says they don't have clue one about what the weapon was. His best guess was power tools."

Derrek wrinkled his nose. "Nice."

"Yeah. Richards said the scene looked like an explosion at a spaghetti sauce factory, on a day they were making a batch of extra thick and chunky."

He sat down and took the pictures Mark handed his way. He tapped one. "What's that?"

"That, believe it or not, is the guy's torso. And see this? A single black rose, placed right over where his heart used to be."

"A black rose?" he frowned.

"I know what you're thinking. It's got trademark serial killer written all over it," Mark said excitedly. "I've got feelers out to other departments to see if they've got anything similar. Maybe we're lucky enough to get the first one, stop him before he really gets going, but I don't have that feeling. I'm betting we're going to turn up a few more."

"Have the papers got ahold of it yet?"

"No, but that leech Marshall Trent is sniffing around."

"Figures. So, who's the stiff?"

Mark showed him another picture. "This is his head. As you can see, we're having some trouble getting a positive I.D."

Eight years on the force, eight years of grim and horrible sights, couldn't keep Derrek's stomach from rolling. "Is that the front or the back?"

"Front. Lady walking her dog found it forty yards away from the rest of him. We've been going over missing persons reports but so far, nothing. We also found a rental-car tag nearby, might have belonged to John Doe here, and I should be getting a call-back on that any minute."

"Gladstone!" came a shout from across the room.

"That's the captain." Mark jumped up. "Back in a flash."

"Yeah," he said distractedly, flipping through the photos. One in particular kept drawing him. The black rose, resting carefully, almost delicately, above a gaping hole lined with jagged broken rib-ends.

He was glad the department used high-quality black-and-white film instead of color.

Mark came back with a sheaf of papers, waving them almost triumphantly. "Pay dirt! We've got two other cases, both with the same M.O., both with the black rose."

"Serial killer," Derrek repeated dolorously. "Another worm in the Big Apple."

"Yeah, but they're not all here. We got one in Sacramento, one in El Paso —" Mark's phone rang and he swept it up. "Gladstone. Oh, yeah. You do? Great." He held the phone between shoulder and ear and waved for a pen. Derrek tossed him one and he scribbled a few words. "Yeah. Thank you very much. No, no. When we find the car, we'll be in contact." He hung up.

"Rental company?"

"Yep. Car was rented to a Benjamin Spencer, from Boston. In town on business."

"Three guys," Derrek said, sifting through the reports. "Three different parts of the country. They're all about the same age, but other than that . . . what's the link?"

"Random psycho, that's the link."

"Well-traveled random psycho. Fast, too . . . these all happened in the last week."

Gladstone ticked off on his fingers. "First guy, Wayne Allen. Editorial assistant, alone in a parking garage. Security guard nearly ran over what was left of him. Second guy, Jim Navarro. P.E. teacher. Wife said he went out back to look for a prowler, wound up on the roof of his house. Family dog was killed too, a big German Shepherd, neck broken."

"And now Ben Spencer. All with a rose."

"All with a rose. And just like our boy, they all died of extreme trauma, by weapons unknown."

"What the hell does that mean, weapons unknown? Their job is figuring out stuff like that." He took another look at Spencer's savaged corpse and reluctantly had to admit that he could see why. In his career, he'd seen murder by gunshot, by knife, by baseball bat, and in one memorable case by woodchipper – *not gonna forget that one anytime soon*. But this looked nothing like any of those. It looked like . . . it almost looked like . . .

"Claws?" he ventured.

"That's what they thought in the Navarro case. Panther maybe escaped from the zoo or something. But the wounds are inconsistent. The dog wasn't so much as scratched, just had a snapped neck. And look at these guys. Someone . . . or some*thing* . . . tore them apart like an overdone roast chicken."

"Some*thing?*" Derrek repeated, giving Mark 'The Look'. Gladstone was a good partner, but he watched too many shows of the inexplicable, and occasionally got carried away.

Undeterred by 'The Look,' Gladstone's grin widened and became ghoulish. "And they all happened at night."

"Oh, man." Derrek rolled his eyes. "Don't even start."

"Okay, then, Detective, how do you want to handle it?"

He picked up the torso shot again. "How about with the black rose? Let's go visit some florists."

"New York's finest," Gladstone said dryly as he put on his coat. "Hot on the trail of a murder investigation. Off to the flower shop."

* * *

Jenny Forrester chattered brightly all the way up to Seacliff.

Theresa did her best to keep up her end of the conversation, but she had awakened feeling like a speed bump, and it was all she could do to keep track as Jenny hopscotched from one topic to another.

At first, she was pleased despite her weariness. Jenny seemed to be getting over her shock of the other night, bouncing back with the resiliency that only children could show.

The prospect of seeing her father, who was due to be released from the hospital this afternoon, and the news that her brother's condition was improving and that her mother had come out of her coma, had helped to lift her mood.

Theresa saw no reason to tell her about the rambling, worried call she'd gotten from Charlie Forrester that morning, the call that had roused her from her like-the-dead yet oddly unrefreshing sleep. She'd leave that to Charlie, or to Kel McGuire.

Maybe Kel would know a better way – there was no good way – to explain to a nine-year-old girl that her mother had apparently gone crazy.

Delusional. Paranoid ideations. Thought transference. Late-onset schizophrenic break.

Theresa knew enough to know she didn't like the sound of it. All she could do was offer empty words of hope and comfort to Charlie. The poor man sounded even more lost and befuddled. His whole family had come apart. And it saddened Theresa to know that she, only in town a couple of weeks, was the only person Charlie felt he could talk to.

Although going for a walk after breakfast was the last thing Theresa wanted to do, she couldn't break her promise to Jenny. They had a mystery to solve. Intrepid girl detectives off on a case. Off on an adventure.

"I dreamed about her last night," Jenny said. "About Glory. She was in my room."

"What did she do?" Theresa asked.

"She was sitting by the window. She was wearing a piffanore."

"A what?"

"A piffanore. You know, one of those old-fashioned dresses."

"A pinafore?"

"Yeah, okay. And that necklace, like in Angela's book."

"Did she say anything?"

Jenny bobbed her head. "I remember. She said 'it has to stop, please, it has to stop,' and then she was crying. Do you think . . . do you think she really *is* a ghost? My teacher said there's no such thing, but . . ."

"Well," Theresa said carefully, "I used to think there wasn't, but it kind of makes sense, doesn't it? When I was little, I used to dream about her, and write about her, and think she was my imaginary friend. But I never even met Angela, so how could she know the very same things?"

"A real ghost," Jenny said in an awed, hushed voice that made Theresa smile despite the overpowering sense of chill and weirdness. Oh, for the wonder of a child's view!

They circled around behind Seacliff, keeping just within the fringe of the woods so as to avoid being seen. Walt Davis was trundling over the lawn in a riding mower, a taciturn man who was never without a 49ers cap pushed far back on his weathered pate. He rode around the corner of the house to do the vast front lawn.

Seacliff's gardens were even finer than Theresa remembered. Much as she disliked Brad Thornton, she had to admit he'd done a good job with the place. It could easily be the resort he envisioned. But, impressive as the place was, it still had an air of brooding secrecy.

Or was that just her imagining? Seacliff was just a house . . . a house in the real world, not a Shirley Jackson or Stephen King story. It carried the weight of the past in its halls and walls, sure. Misfortune had visited on the family from time to time, sure. But those things were a part of any old house.

Her thoughts sailed lazily back and forth like a balloon batted across a volleyball net. On the one side was the rational team – Seacliff was just a house, the stuff about Glory and the roses and the necklace were suggestion and coincidence, there was no connection between herself and Angela Cliffwood, no connection between Seacliff and Sandy Forrester.

On the other side, though, was the team fantastic. Their argument was much less logical, more visceral, and persuasive. *Coincidence?* that team cried. *Coincidence, my ass! What about the drawings? What about Jack? What about the way you've been sleeping . . . or* **not** *sleeping? What about the dreams? What about the book? You really think that's* **you** *writing it? It's coming* **through** *you, Zane, you were right the first time!*

Since she was here, traipsing through the woods looking for a rosebush, she had a pretty fair notion which team was winning.

"Whatever walked in Seacliff, walked alone," she murmured.

"There it is!" Jenny ran ahead, and a nasty needle of fear sank into Theresa.

"Jenny, wait!" She broke into a run though her aching bones protested, but the girl stopped well away from the rosebush.

Theresa stopped too.

She'd expected a tidy plant of the sort her mother grew in the garden of her brother's house. Trellises, raked white rocks around the beds, the bushes checked daily for bugs and dead leaves, everything in order. Garden-neat. Not so.

The rosebush was a gnarled twist of deep green the size of a shrub. The leaves were broad-bladed and serrated, oddly resembling holly. The thorns curving out from the thick twigs were long and sharp as cat claws. A profusion of buds dotted the plant, dark as dollops of midnight. A few blooms were open, spreading their velvety petals to reveal reddish hearts.

Dread settled onto Theresa like a cloak. The roses were beautiful, hideous, unnatural, powerful.

She felt a strong, almost overwhelming urge to run to Walt Davis, throw him from the seat of the riding mower, bring it around, and drive it right over the rosebush. In her mind she could see the shredded petals and leaves spraying out from under the machine, hear the thudding and squealing of twigs getting sheared apart by the whirling blades.

"It's kinda creepy, huh?" Jenny said, hushed.

"Yeah . . . your brother saw something here?"

Jenny nodded. "It was just before Angela . . . before Angela died. He came up to see her, but he had to sneak because her stepdad wouldn't let him visit. I heard him telling Gary on the phone. And when he came back, he was all scared. I thought maybe Mr. Thornton saw him and yelled at him, but then he was calling Gary again and telling him about the ghost."

Theresa took a few more steps, closer now. She could smell the flowers. Not the usual perfume she associated with roses. Not light and sweet. This was as if the night wind had a scent all its own. Dark. Mysterious. Alluring and strange.

The ground beneath the rosebush was strewn with fallen petals and leaves. It was in the center of a small clearing, a place where the ground sunk a little.

She reached out despite Jenny's worried warning, and caressed one petal. That touch triggered a strange association in her mind. Soft skin, Lora's soft skin when she had been a baby, the sensitive smoothness of her own inner thighs.

A shudder traveled in a ripple along her spine.

A stab of pain made her pull back her hand with an indrawn hiss. Blood was welling from the tip of her forefinger, growing into a swollen ruby bead. She instinctively started to put it in her mouth, then caught herself and blotted it on her jeans.

"Are you okay?" Jenny inched closer.

"I wasn't even near a thorn," Theresa said. She dug a tissue out of her jacket pocket and wrapped her finger, then leaned in to examine the rosebush. "I wasn't near one at all!"

Jenny's laugh was shaky. "Maybe it bit you."

"Maybe it did," she said absently. "Look . . . do you see that?"

"What?"

"That stem. It's been cut. And that one too."

"There's another one over there." Jenny pointed, keeping her hands at a prudent distance.

"It was probably Mrs. Davis," Theresa said, not believing the words even as she heard them leave her lips. The three snipped stems, the three missing roses, troubled her for reasons even the fantastic team in her mental volleyball match couldn't explain.

"Can we go back now?" Jenny asked, wrapping her arms around herself and shivering although the day was warming up nicely. "I don't think I like it here."

"I don't think I do either."

But as they left, her gaze was drawn repeatedly back, until the rosebush was out of sight.

* * *

"I was thinking . . ." Celeste Haverley began.

"Good for you," her husband grunted from behind the newspaper. "You want a medal?"

Gary, the only one of their kids still living at home, snickered and then sobered as his father's stern eye fell upon him.

"Don't laugh at your mother," Big Al said.

"Whatever," Gary mumbled, gathering his schoolbooks and going into the kitchen.

"Wouldn't it be nice," Celeste went on as if the interruptions had never occurred, "if we had your boss over for dinner Sunday night?"

"Brad? Yeah, that'd be good." He turned a page and changed the television channel.

Celeste had heard of "multitasking," but she sure didn't think that was it. Leaving Al to his entertainments – the sports section and one of those "Most Gross Stuff Caught on Video" shows, she hurried into the kitchen to plan the meal.

Something special, she thought, opening cupboards. Something fancy. Humming, she sat down to make a list and only then realized that her son was watching her with a funny look.

"Ma? You okay?"

Celeste flushed and dropped her pen. Her laugh as she bent to retrieve it was high, brittle, false. "Fine, dear. Just fine."

He didn't buy it, going back to his homework with that suspicious expression still in place.

This was a mistake. She shouldn't be seeing him again. Certainly shouldn't be inviting him into her very house, to sit at the supper table with her husband. What if helpless heated glances passed between her and Brad? Heated glances, weighted remarks? Al wasn't a very perceptive man, but what if he noticed?

But she had to see him again! This was far more than a casual affair! This was the sort of passion that only characters on her afternoon programs seemed to find, the sort that never happened to real people.

She closed her eyes and savored the memory, her breath coming faster, her pulse speeding up.

"Ma?"

"Quit staring at me!" she snapped, opening her eyes. "What's the matter with you?"

He recoiled, then his lip curled. "Jeez, Ma, I didn't do anything!"

"Then go do something, and leave me alone!"

"Fine! Jeez!" He grabbed up his books again. "Are all the moms in town going nuts, or is it just you and Mrs. Forrester?"

"Gary!" She jerked as if slapped. "What a thing to say!"

"Okay, forget it, just don't come at me with a knife, okay?" He stalked out, grumbling.

Celeste rubbed her forehead and temples, where it felt like a tension headache was grinding into the soft meat of her brain.

She knew she shouldn't take out her stress on Gary, but having him staring at her like that, staring at her the way everyone in town would stare if they found out her secret . . . all those years of ferreting out the latest dirt had made her more enemies than friends, and they would just love to have their payback day.

They'd drag her down. Laugh at her.

She couldn't let them find out. Nobody would find out. Nobody would know.

All she had to do was act as if everything was normal. All of Gary's acting talent must have come from somewhere, and it certainly hadn't come from Al's side of the family.

Yes, that was what she would do. Act as if everything was normal. Give no one a reason to think otherwise. They would have their dinner, she would be perfectly polite, everything would go smoothly.

Oh. She should also get some fresh flowers for the table.

Maybe some roses.

* * *

10

Jordano's was a restaurant of the dark timbers and brass fixtures variety, its walls adorned with oil paintings of seascapes. All along one wall, picture windows overlooked a weathered pier where gulls perched on posts and the occasional sea lion could be glimpsed in the bay beyond.

The tables were covered with crisp white linen, the napkins navy-blue cloth folded into little boat shapes, and the staff all wore blue aprons over white shirts and black slacks.

Theresa and Kel were shown to one of the window tables. At three in the afternoon on a Friday, they had the place mostly to themselves.

"This is nice," Theresa said, as Kel gallantly held her chair. She'd practically been living in jeans since her arrival, but for their late lunch date, she'd dressed in a wine-colored wool skirt and a soft sweater.

Kel sat opposite her and smiled, but even his smile couldn't hide how tired he looked. He looked, in fact, almost as dragged-out as she felt, but in his case, it was probably more due to overwork than simple lack of quality sleep. Or both. He just seemed like the type who would lie awake in bed, unable to shut down his brain, re-hashing the day and wondering what could have been done differently, trying to anticipate the problems of tomorrow.

"I recommend the clam chowder," he said, passing her a menu. "Best in the county."

The waiter brought a basket of fresh, hot, sourdough bread and glasses of ice water. He recited the specials of the day, then retreated to let them decide.

They talked of light and inconsequential things over the chowder, which really was excellent. They shared similar tastes in books, agreed that television was largely a waste of time, didn't concern themselves much with politics or scandals of the stars, and both had the same secret passion for bad movies – campus comedies for him, high-speed action thrillers for her. His only family in town was a younger sister, Megan, who worked as a nurse's aide in the hospital.

Over the shrimp, which was stuffed with shredded crabmeat and mellow cheese, then breaded and deep-fried, Theresa asked him something that had been on her mind ever since she'd taken the sketchbook from Jerry Forrester's room on Tuesday.

"Did you know Angela Cliffwood?"

"Not well enough. I met with her when she transferred into the high school. I do counseling out there a couple of times a week. She was fitting in okay, but having some trouble dealing with the death of her mother. Blaming herself for something that wasn't her fault."

"This might sound weird . . ."

He chuckled ruefully. "If I had a nickel for every time I heard that, I could take you for a spin in my new Mercedes."

"Did she ever say anything about . . . dreams? Or roses?"

"Dreams, yes, roses, no. Why?"

"What kind of dreams? If you can tell me, I mean."

He poked his fork at a piece of crabmeat, pushing it around his plate. "Her mother died in a fall, down a flight of stairs. Angela used to dream about it, trying to warn her, catch her, the whole trapped-in-slow-motion helplessness. She also mentioned a few anxiety dreams, the falling kind. Not at all unusual, given what had happened. She never seemed suicidal. Shy, lonely, confused . . . but even that seemed to be improving. She made some new friends, was doing fine in school, so we stopped meeting. And then . . ."

Theresa shuddered slightly as she recalled her own dream of the red-haired girl leaping from the bluff. "No one saw it coming?"

"No one. I spent a lot of time at the school in the weeks after it happened, talking to the kids, but nothing."

"Did you talk to Jerry Forrester?"

"Several times. They were almost going together, Jerry and Angela. The only thing he'd say was that he knew she was afraid, but he wouldn't tell me of what. He never thought she would hurt herself. After, though, the more I thought about it, the more I got the idea he was hiding something. Even when he's not on stage, Jerry's a damn fine actor."

"What about her stepfather?"

A flicker of distaste passed across Kel's face so swiftly Theresa wasn't sure he was aware of it. "He said she'd always been 'high-strung,' looking for attention, getting wild and out of control. They'd had an argument the night she died because he wouldn't let her go to the beach party with the rest of the kids. So his opinion was that she'd jumped to get back at him."

"That's dumb," Theresa flared.

"It was like we were talking about two different people. The Angela I knew was nothing like that. She wasn't one of those kids who slash their wrists to get attention. She didn't do drugs, didn't run around with boys, none of what he was saying."

"More like he was a control freak, trying to run her life," Theresa said bitterly. "Never let her have any freedom, never let her have any fun. Pretend like it's just guidance, when it's really all about control. Until the kid gets to thinking that running away is the only way out. Not to get back at them, just to escape, just to escape." She shut herself up in a hurry, but it was too late.

"That sounds like the voice of experience talking."

"I wish it wasn't. Did Dad tell you much about my mother?"

"He didn't have to; it was all in what he *didn't* say and how he didn't say it."

"I've always been a terrible disappointment to her," Theresa said with a tight grin that was more of a clenching of the teeth. "She lives in Portland now with my older half-brother, George. I don't even call her anymore because I am so sick of hearing about what a good son he is. She doesn't come right out and bash on me, but I hear it . . . like you said, in how she *doesn't* say it."

He nodded encouragingly. "I'm the middle child of three, my older sister's the star of the family, so I know that drill all right."

"*George* is happily married," Theresa mimicked. "*George* has a real job. George this and George that until I just about want to push him in the pool so I can watch him walk on water."

"Your mother must be a very unhappy woman. It can't have been easy growing up with her."

"That's why I split when I was seventeen. One reason, anyway." Her face darkened. "My stepfather was as bad as she was. Always after me, nagging on my clothes, my friends, searching my room for dope, all of it."

"You ran away?"

"Dad bought me a car for graduation." Her grin this time was far more genuine. "Pepto-Bismal pink. Ugliest thing you ever saw. I think he must've done it just because he knew it would drive my mother absolutely bonkers. That summer, I packed my stuff and took off. I wound up in Arizona, and that's when I started getting my life back on track."

"You're lucky things worked out."

"I know. When I look back now, I think I was just as crazy as they were."

They fell silent for a while, eating shrimp and watching the gulls wheel and shriek outside.

"We've wandered a bit," he said, "but why did you ask me about Angela Cliffwood?"

"I found her sketchbook," Theresa said, then explained the similarities between the drawings, the rosebush out back of Seacliff. She didn't yet go into the matter of Glory or all the other things that had struck her as increasingly weird – Jack's behavior, her own dreams, the effortless but bizarre progress on her novel.

"If the rosebush is as large as you say, it must be pretty old," Kel said. "Maybe you saw it when you were younger and remembered it."

"But I never –" she broke off, for as far as she knew, she might have seen it and then forgotten it as she'd apparently forgotten nearly everything else about Glory. "What about the necklaces, then?"

He spread his hands and shrugged. "Maybe Angela saw your drawing?"

"It's been sitting in that desk drawer for twenty years." Then, before she knew she was going to, the rest of the story came tumbling out.

Kel's russet eyebrows climbed ever higher on his brow, and when she was done, he slowly shook his head. "Theresa . . ."

"Let me guess," she said, angry at herself but taking it out on him; it had sounded perfectly reasonable when she laid it all out for a nine-year-old girl. "A couple quick calls and you can get me the room next door to Sandy Forrester."

"After what happened to Sandy, it's understandable that you would be in a great deal of emotional distress. All of this about roses, you probably picked up from her ravings."

"What?"

"The night of the incident. You were too upset to notice it consciously at the time, but what she was saying must have burrowed down into your subconscious."

"Kel, she was already out cold by the time I got there! Are you telling me she was talking about roses? Black roses?

"Just part of her delusional system."

"How could I have known about that?"

"She must have seen the sketchbook," he decided, visibly relieved that he'd come up with an explanation that made sense. "It was in her house, after all."

"What did she say?" Theresa asked, leaning forward, twisting her napkin around her fingers.

"Like I said, it was all delusional, and I really shouldn't be discussing it."

"Confidentiality," she said.

"Confidentiality," he agreed. "You could try asking her husband, since he isn't bound by the same rules as me."

"I'll do that." She sat back and began buttering another slice of sourdough, more to have something to do with her hands than out of hunger. "In the meantime, though, you promised to fill me in on my dad."

"He's doing a lot better now," Kel said. "I don't think there's anything to worry about. He's looking after his health, taking his medications, and his spirits are higher than they've been all year."

"He says he doesn't sleep well."

"He says you don't either."

Theresa groaned. "Oh, great, now he's telling you my woes?"

Kel winked impishly at her. "No confidentiality laws there."

"That seems unfair somehow. Because, I bet if I pressed you for details, you could claim that as he's your client, you aren't at liberty to discuss it without his permission."

"Just how much of a weasel do you think I am?" he said with feigned indignation.

"That remains to be seen," she replied archly, and they laughed together as the waiter approached with the dessert menu.

* * *

"I always used to believe in the poem," Detective Derrek Blake said.

His partner didn't turn away from the computer, but indicated that he was listening by a tilt of his head. "What poem?"

"*A rose is a rose is a rose.* Wasn't it Shakespeare? You know, in *Romeo and Juliet?*"

"That, Mr. Culture, was *a rose by any other name would smell as sweet.* What are you talking about, anyway?"

Derrek sank into his chair and poked at the stack of floral catalogs they'd collected. "Before all of this, I used to think a rose was a rose. Long-stemmed red ones go fifty bucks a dozen and make the women happy. That was all I knew, all I needed to know."

"Ah," Mark Gladstone said. "But now your eyes have been opened to the reality of roses. All of the hundreds of varieties, the exclusive clubs and companies that provide them, and so forth?"

"Exactly. We have talked to half the florists in Manhattan, been through all of these catalogs, visited every website your savvy skills could find. And nobody has seen anything that even comes close to our Exhibit A."

"Which has led me to conclude that it's a new variety," Mark said. "Trust me, partner, we find out who's growing these black roses, we've got a link to our killer."

* * *

The whistle died on Brad Thornton's lips as he opened his office door and saw a package on his desk. A small box, wrapped in white paper and tied with a red satin bow.

He had locked the door when he'd left early that afternoon, knowing that his lunch meeting with a trio of Eureka businessmen followed by a visit to the golf course with the vice president of a bank looking to open a branch in Trinity Bay would keep him out of the office the rest of the day.

He had no secretary and got along just fine without one thanks to the miracle of voice mail, and the only other person with a key to his door was Big Al Haverley.

So what was up with the gift? It looked like a Valentine, but February was still long months away. Wasn't anywhere close to his birthday, either. What was it, how had it gotten here, who was it from?

Figuring that he could put answer to at least one and possibly two of those questions by opening it, he picked it up. Inside, nestled in tissue paper, was a pair of tiny white briefs with red kiss marks all over.

"What the hell?" Brad said, holding them up, half-expecting a bunch of people to leap out and shot "Surprise!" and inform him he was on Candid Camera.

A square of paper seesawed to land on his desk blotter.

Next time, it read, *wear these, and I'll wear something to match. I can't stop thinking about you.*

"What the —" he started to say again, and then he realized who the gift was from, and his puzzled frown widened into a knowing smile.

* * *

Theresa stopped by the Forrester house Saturday afternoon to see if they needed anything at the market, and possibly to take Kel's advice and see if Charlie would tell her what confidentiality prevented Kel from saying.

Charlie had been released from the hospital on Thursday, the day after she and Jenny had gone on their little nature walk. Now he was home, back in the house from which all traces of the terrible night had been scrubbed.

There had been a tremendous sympathetic outpouring from the community. Poor Charlie, the town's consensus seemed to be, couldn't take care of himself let alone his daughter. People dropped by with casseroles and pies, offered to help with the shopping and the laundry.

Most of all, nearly every home in Trinity Bay now boasted a new Charlie Forrester wood creation as everybody made a point of stopping by his workshop to offer their support.

Charlie himself continued his haphazard style of drifting through life, but his eyes had a hurt, shocked look. He seemed more lost than ever, going purely on autopilot.

"Some of the kids have been teasing me," Jenny confided to Theresa as they conducted an inventory of the fridge. "About my mom being crazy and stuff."

"That sounds rough."

"Yeah. I tell 'em to shut up, and my friends do too. Why are people so mean?" She looked so forlorn that Theresa hugged her.

"I wish I knew. Sometimes they just are, and all we can do is try to ignore it or do what you did, and tell them to shut up."

"But . . . but she *is* crazy, isn't she?" Jenny whispered. "She went crazy, and they locked her up."

"She needs special help," Theresa said, stroking Jen's hair. "It's like being sick. It's nobody's fault. Listen, kiddo, I've got to talk to your dad a little, but if you need anything, or someone to talk to, you think of me, okay?"

Jenny managed a brave smile and went off to play with Bingo, who seemed to sense in his own befuddled doggy way that things weren't right around the house and was trying to make up for it by being extra cute and frisky.

Theresa watched the two of them run in the yard, and was overcome with a rush of longing for Lora so strong she had to blink away tears. Having Jenny staying with them, even just for a few days and even under such distressing circumstances, had reminded Theresa how much she missed her own daughter.

When she'd gotten her emotions under control, she went around back to the workshop and found Charlie Forrester sitting on a stool, staring blankly at a chunk of redwood burl.

"Charlie?" she said, hushed.

"I think this one wants to be a clock," he said.

"That would be nice."

He reached for his toolbox, then just sort of sagged in place with a sigh that came right from the tips of his toes. "Maybe tomorrow."

"Charlie . . . I know it's none of my business, and I know I shouldn't even bring it up, but I need to ask you something about Sandy."

His head came up with a startling speed and when his eyes fixed on hers, they were fiercely bright. "I don't want to *not* talk about her!" he cried, rocking Theresa back on her heels. "I don't want to pretend nothing's happened, nothing's changed!

Everything's changed! How can it be worse to talk about it?"

"I . . . uh . . ." Theresa stammered.

The energy that had filled him drained away as suddenly as it had come. "Sorry," he mumbled.

"Charlie, what did she say about roses?" she asked in a rush.

Listless again, he poked his long bony finger through the sawdust. "That's what she was saying in the hospital. They let me see her a couple of times, but it didn't help." A tear rolled slowly down his prominent cheekbone, catching in his beard. "How she'd gotten it in her head that Jerry . . . that Jerry was making her do things . . . it doesn't make any sense. And then she was talking about a black rose, and when it opened, she could see all the bad things inside people, and the thorns were in her head. I don't know what she meant. I wish I did. Then maybe I'd understand."

Theresa tried to come up with the right words, but they failed her, so she rested her hand on his shoulder. Finally, she ventured another question. "Would it be okay if I went and visited Jerry?"

"I think he'd like that," Charlie said. "They're moving him into a semi-private room tomorrow."

She left him to his work – or, rather, left him to his private grief. Her own thoughts were dark and troubled.

Delusional, Kel McGuire had said.

Maybe so, but Theresa knew there had to be more to it than that. It *was* connected, all of it. If she could only figure out how!

* * *

Malachi Edwards knew he was in the doghouse, but damned if he knew why.

He could hear Ruth in the kitchen, where she normally sang show tunes or danced along with the radio. Toby would often join her, one of the few times the boy would overcome his innate quietness and groove with his mama.

But today, the kitchen was silent except for the clatter and occasional decisive bang of pots and pans. Toby had wandered in once, then emerged in a hurry with an apple and a worried look. He'd gone straight to his room, and from that end of the house came the sounds of one of his video games.

Ruth's mood had been off all week, but at first he'd attributed it to the touch of fever, and then to reaction over that awful business at the Forresters'. Now he'd come to realize that his wife was in a state of high queenly piss-off at him, for no reason he could figure.

That wasn't right.

That wasn't like his Ruthie. She'd never been much of a one for hiding her feelings. When she was happy, the whole world knew it and why, and when she was mad, ditto. This silent glaring, this was new.

He closed his book and set it on the table by the lamp, thinking he should go to her and at the same time thinking he'd do well to just steer clear. She was putting off the sort of vibes that many husbands knew all too well. The kind of vibes that said he was supposed to be doing something, but was too dumb to know what it was he was supposed to be doing, but she wasn't going to tell him because he should be able to figure it out on his own.

It reminded Malachi of his own parents, both long since in their graves. His mother would be storming and stomping around – just as Ruthie was now – and Will Edwards would go on, oblivious, until steam was just about curling out of his wife's ears. Then he'd ask, "Something the matter, Yvonne?" and his wife would reply with a scathing, "Nothing!" Which the Edwards kids knew really meant, "Plenty and lots of it and it's all your fault," but Will would nod to himself as if that settled things, and go back to what he'd been doing.

He didn't want to see that happen between him and Ruthie. So, gritting his teeth and preparing to face the lion in its den, he went into the kitchen.

She was standing at the butcher block cutting board, her back to him, shoulders rigid, hacking up vegetables into shards and slivers instead of her usual neat slices.

Malachi paused by the table, a flicker of something that was almost fear gnawing at him. He knew the feeling right away for what it was. After Sandy Forrester's crazy attack on her own son, there weren't many people in town who wouldn't suffer a qualm at the sight of a knife in the hands of an angry woman.

"Ruthie –" his father's words, something the matter, caught in his throat. None of that. He might as well get right to the point. "What'd I do, Ruthie?"

"Are you ashamed of it, Mal Edwards?" she asked without looking around. Honed steel sheared through crisp celery and thunked into the cutting board.

"Ashamed of what?"

"Or do you really not remember?"

"I must not, because I don't know what you're talking about."

"Oh, don't you?" She sounded so eerily like his mother that when she did turn, he was half-braced to see Yvonne's features instead of Ruth's. "Don't you?"

"God's honest truth, honey." Seeing that she still had the knife clenched in her fist, Mal felt that squirm of almost-fear again and actually found himself glancing around for a means with which to defend himself, should it come to that.

Ruth's sewing box was open and spread all over the kitchen table. She'd been embroidering small black flowers onto a length of green linen, a light scarf. Mal judged her scissors to be within easy reach, even as the very notion filled him with incredulous dismay. Could he be standing here in his own house, contemplating fending off a knife attack from his beloved Ruthie with a pair of sewing scissors?

"I don't see how you could *not* remember," Ruth said. "You enjoyed it as much as I did, admit it! So you must be ashamed. That's it. Ashamed. Or maybe you think I'm sick to even want something like that. Is that it?"

"Ruth, honey, I swear I don't have the faintest idea what this is about!"

"I'm talking about Sunday night," she said in a scornful tone that suggested he was losing his grip. "You remember Sunday night, don't you?"

He cast his mind back, and nodded. "What about it?"

"I *liked* it, Mal!" she shouted. "So did you! What's so bad about that? I thought you could take a hint after that first time, but I guess I was wrong! I don't want to have to ask straight out every time! I've been waiting all week, hoping you'd get the hint, but you act like it never happened!" She drove the knife point-down into the cutting board – *chunk!*

"Ruthie –"

"So I guess I do have to make the first move." Her hands went to the front of her blouse and buttons began springing open one by one.

Malachi gaped at her as she stripped off her clothes, right there in the kitchen with the curtains open and anyone passing by able to look right into the well-lit room.

Proud, naked, and beautiful, she strode toward him. She swept her sewing off of the table, skeins of embroidery floss scattering over the tile floor, spools of thread rolling under the refrigerator, the scissors he had only half a minute ago been eyeing as a possible weapon whirling away like a silver propellor to fetch up against the leg of a chair.

Ruth snatched up the half-finished scarf as she hoisted herself onto the table. She looped it around his neck and for an instant he thought she meant to throttle him with the thing, but she used it to pull him closer, pull him down.

She hiked her legs up so that her ankles were resting on his shoulders and her butt was halfway lifted off the table, stretched with amazing fluidity to seize his wrist, and used it to bring his palm *smack* against her ass.

Even as his brain was reeling, Malachi felt his body respond eagerly. So this was what she wanted? Bold, wild, risky, right in full view of the windows?

He slapped her on the butt again, and although it was a fairly tentative blow, she writhed and uttered a gutteral sound that was half-snarl and half-gasp. She tugged on the scarf and Mal could feel the raised nubbins that formed the flowers rubbing against his skin.

"Harder!" she demanded. "Go on, do it!"

Malachi drew back his hand, ready to give her a stinging swat that would turn her bottom maroon. At the last minute, he froze, coming to his senses as if he'd been doused in cold water.

"Good God, Ruthie!" he blurted, backing away from her. "Not like this! What if Toby walked in? What about the neighbors?"

She coiled sinuously into a crouch, still on the table, her hair hanging ferally around her face, the scarf clenched in her fist. "Fuck the neighbors," she spat, and Mal reeled again. "I want it, Mal, I want it like before!"

He took another step back. "Not like this, Ruthie. We're not like this."

She glared at him so hotly that he wouldn't have been surprised to feel himself blister. Then Ruth abruptly burst into tears. She scrambled from the table and fled the kitchen, her sobs trailing behind her, leaving her clothes where they lay.

Mal, stunned, sank into a chair and tried to make sense of what had just happened in here.

"Like before?" he murmured, echoing what Ruthie had said. "Like *before?*"

* * *

The concert was over, the post-concert party was over, and the post-party fucking was over.

"It's Miller Time," Nick Diamond said.

The girl beside him, some little blonde whose name he couldn't remember, didn't answer. Didn't even move. She slept with a dreamy smile, and why shouldn't she? Hadn't she just been nailed by Nick Diamond, lead singer of Scarlet Angel, next big star in the rock and roll cosmos?

He'd seen her, third row and a bit left of center, one of a gaggle of high-school girls dressed as skimpily and made up as outrageously as possible. But even from the stage, he'd noticed something in her the hopeful tilt of her eyes, the innocence of her heart-shaped face.

A good girl. Damned if he could resist bagging a good girl.

So he'd had her brought backstage for the party, and after a few drinks and some smooth patter on his part, had her convinced that True Love had come her way. Then it was off to his room for a sexual adventure. Her giggly protestations of virginity hadn't taken long to overcome, and her awe at being in bed with *the* Nick Diamond had let him coax her into doing things that she'd probably never even imagined.

He got out of bed, grinning smugly. Pulling a pair of black jeans over his naked hips, he went into the sitting room half of the suite, flipping on one lamp.

Let the little honey sleep, he thought. Poor thing was all worn out. She would have a hell of a story to tell her girlfriends and write in her diary the next day.

He was more right than he knew.

As Nick bent over to snort a line of high-quality glistening coke, a pair of huge hands grabbed him from behind.

His surprised cry gusted coke in a powdery mess onto the floor, but Nick didn't care. All of his attention was focused on the pain lancing from what felt like two rows of short knives digging into his ribs.

Nick tried to whirl, meaning to pummel his fist into the face of whatever asshole thought he could break into Nick Diamond's room. As he began to move, he was picked up as if his 190 pounds of chick-pleasing handsomeness weighed nothing at all.

The next thing Nick, knew, he was flying. He had a terrifying glimpse of the window coming toward him, with its ten-floor drop on the other side. But he smashed into the wall beside it instead of going through, rebounding and crashing a round-topped table into kindling.

Dazed, groaning, aware of blood oozing down his sides and pooling in the waistband of his jeans, Nick Diamond raised his head.

What he saw was enough to make him wish he *had* gone through the glass.

Out in the hall, two doors popped open simultaneously, followed by a third. Johnny Harlowe, Scarlet Angel's guitarist, burst from his room and nearly collided with the band's wild-haired drummer, a stocky young woman named Pagan.

"The damn bastard is at it again!" Johnny exclaimed as they both looked toward Nick's room, which was the source of high-pitched shrieks.

"I'll rip his balls off!" Pagan said, leaping toward the door.

Aquarius, their tall and lanky 60's refugee keyboardist, took her by the shoulder. His movements were slow and languid, chronically laid-back, while hers were full of explosive energy, yet he intercepted and stopped her.

"Don't do it, girl," he said. His wide, fearful eyes belied his easygoing tone. "There's some serious bad shit going down here."

"He can't keep doing this!" Johnny shouted, furious. "Last time, he put a girl in the hospital! When's it gonna stop? When he kills someone?"

Just then, the shrieks cut off with suddenness and finality.

A long tense moment of utter silence followed, a moment during which the three of them looked at each other in knowing dread. But then a new scream split the night, a horrified scream interrupted by the sounds of violent retching.

Johnny tried the door, found it locked, and threw himself against it. It rattled in the frame but did not give. Pagan, with a snarl of impatience, shoved him aside and pistoned her foot at the door. The lock popped free, the door swung open.

A nude blonde teenager, hair in frightful disarray and vomit splashed halfway up her shins, raced out and collapsed, weeping and shaking, against the far wall. Johnny scanned her to see what that son-of-a-bitch had done to her, but there wasn't a single mark on her.

"Oh, man," Aquarius moaned, staring into the room.

Pagan looked, and her face went paste-white beneath her garish tufts of green and purple hair.

Johnny saw their expressions, and a crazy urge came to him. He could close his eyes, shut the door, go back to his room, and forget all about it.

But he looked. The beer and food he'd put away during the party rose like a thick bubble in the column of his throat. He staggered to one side and bumped into Aquarius, and both of them leaned like drunks against the doorjamb.

If not for the tattoo of the red-robed angel on what was left of a tanned bicep, they wouldn't have been able to tell that the body was Nick's. They would have barely been able to tell that it was human.

Resting atop the wreckage of his chest was a single black rose.

* * *

Theresa Zane found Jerry Forrester in remarkably good spirits, or else putting on one heck of an act.

The other bed in his room was empty, so he had it all to himself. His was the bed by the window, the sill crowded with get-well cards, the table loaded with flowers. No roses, thankfully; if there had been, Theresa might have run screaming down the hall.

The television bolted to the wall was tuned to VH-1, and as Theresa came in, a music video by the Bee Gees was playing. But the music was overlaid by a weird little *bloop!* sound that she at first thought was some sort of medical monitor, until she realized that Jerry wasn't hooked up to anything.

"Mizzane!" he hailed cheerily.

"Hi, Jerry. Mind some company?"

He waved at a chair. "You'll have to move the zoo."

She grinned, for the chair was full of stuffed animals. Puppies, teddy bears, a red dinosaur holding a little bouquet of cloth daisies, a floppy bunny rabbit, more. "Quite a collection."

Jerry tipped his eyes toward the ceiling. "Well, you know . . ."

"Let me guess. Girls from school."

"Yeah. They think I'm cute."

She scooped the animals into her arms and deposited them on the other bed. Jerry's tone was one of mingled amusement and wry resignation, and she suddenly understood that while he had plenty of female friends, they were all just that – friends. He was the sort of guy she remembered well enough from her own school days. Nice Guy Syndrome. All the girls would like him, but in a brotherly puppy-dog kind of way. He was safe, the kind of boy all their mothers adored, while the girls themselves reserved their crushes for the jocks and hoody rebels.

Some things never changed.

Jerry looked good for someone who had been in the critical care unit until yesterday. He wore blue pajamas instead of a hospital johnny, covering the bulky bandages that wrapped his chest. His face was still a little pale, a little waxy, and there were hollows beneath his warm hazel eyes, but his hair was freshly washed and neatly combed. His smile was a bit less sunny, but it was there.

Bloop!

It came from the television, she realized, and glanced up to see an oval of white with black lettering, like a thought bubble in a comic strip. It was gone so fast she wasn't sure she'd read what she thought she'd read, something about tight pants causing low sperm count, and she turned to raise her eyebrows at Jerry.

"What are you watching?"

"*Pop-Up Video*," he said. "It's the coolest. They pop up all these factoids and crazy stuff about the video and the artist and everything. It's really neat."

"I brought you something," she said, reaching into the scruffy leather tote that served as her purse and all-purpose carry-all.

"If it's a stuffed animal, I might puke," he warned good-naturedly.

"Actually, I smuggled you in some junk food," she said, taking out a couple of cans of Pepsi and a bag of Cheetos. "Jen thought you might appreciate it."

"Oh, man, do I!" He grabbed a can. "Four days of eating through a tube, I thought I was gonna go nuts. Then they move me to this room, and you know how everybody jokes about hospital food and you think it can't really be that bad? It is!"

"Just don't tell on me, okay?"

"No prob, Mizzane!" He drank deeply, then leaned his head back against the raised pillows with a blissful sigh. "I may live after all!"

"How's it been going?"

For a split second, his cheerful facade cracked and she saw through to the boy beneath, a boy who was scared and aware of his own mortality in a way that few teens ever were. A boy who knew his whole life had come apart and nothing would ever be the same.

"Good as it can, I guess. You want all the boring medical stuff?"

She shook her head. "Your dad says they patched you up pretty well."

"Yeah, they might even let me out in another week."

"Have you . . . talked to anyone?"

"You mean Mr. McGuire, the school shrink? He's been here, yeah."

Theresa started to speak, changed her mind, and lapsed into an awkward silence. On the television, pop-ups were telling her all sorts of quirky things about Elton John, making her wonder just who came up with these informational blurbs.

"What's on your mind, Mizzane?" Jerry asked, his voice having lost its bantering edge.

"Jerry . . . I know I haven't been here long, not even two weeks yet, so it's really all none of my business . . ."

"Hey, you're our neighbor. You helped out, taking care of Jen."

"I just don't want to make things worse for you by asking you nosy questions."

He shrugged. "Like what?"

"Well . . . about your mother . . ."

Jerry looked away, looked out the window. "Yeah. Mom. That was pretty hairy, huh?" He sounded okay, and Theresa would have been fooled if not for the shine in his eyes.

"I'd like to hear what happened, if you can tell me."

"Oh, jeez." Jerry ran a shaking hand through his hair. "Why? It's all over now, right? The men in the white coats hauled her away and that's that."

Theresa took in a deep breath and exhaled in a slow rush. "There's something strange going on, and I think what happened to your mom is part of it. I think Angela Cliffwood was, too. I know it's not easy to talk about, but I really need to know. It's important. I need to know about the roses, Jerry. Jen showed me the rosebush."

"The . . . the roses?"

She showed him the sketchbook, told him everything she'd told Jenny. "Then I heard that your mother said something about roses too. I need to know, Jerry. What did she say?"

He finished his soda, seemed to gather his strength. Theresa waited, giving him the time he needed.

"I lied to Mr. McGuire," he admitted in a low whisper. "I lied to the doctors and everybody. Even Dad. So you've got to promise not to tell. It's too weird, too gross."

"I promise," she said solemnly.

"She'd been getting kind of strange, and Saturday night I woke up and she was in my room with a knife." He swallowed, and there was an audible click in his throat. Theresa opened the other soda for him and he nodded in thanks. "The same knife. I thought she was sleepwalking, you know, because her eyes looked all weird. It really freaked me out."

"I heard you and Gary talking about it on Sunday," Theresa said.

"And she'd keep looking at me. A creepy kind of look. When Dad or Jen were around, she ignored me but then I'd catch her looking at me in that creepy way again. A couple times, she'd mumble stuff. Mostly I couldn't understand it, but she said, 'you think once that rose opens, you can do whatever you want.' I remember that."

"Once that rose opens . . ." Theresa repeated musingly.

"She thought I was making her do stuff," he said. "Uh . . . sex stuff." He blushed hotly, looked ill, but the words poured out of him in a torrent anyway. "Like I was using mind control or something. And, I mean, I *never* . . . I *would* never . . . with my own mom? Jesus! Who'd even think something like that? She was talking like she caught me jack – uh . . ." He floundered and his face went an even darker red, nearly magenta.

"But she didn't," Theresa said as mildly as she could.

"No!"

"Delusional."

"Yeah, but still . . ." he shuddered, then swallowed convulsively as if to steel himself to tell the rest. "Then, Tuesday night, I got up to get a drink, went into the kitchen, and she was sitting there, just sitting there in the dark. And she said she knew what I wanted, that I wasn't going to get it, that I couldn't make her do those things anymore. That she was going to get the evil out of me if she had to cut it out. That was when she held up the knife – she'd had it under a dishtowel on the table." He had gone from deep red to ashy pale as he related it, his eyes grown wide and haunted. "After that, it all gets kind of hazy. The docs say I might not ever remember exactly what happened, and I don't want to anyway."

Theresa laid her hand on his forearm and squeezed gently. "I'm sorry."

"She was yelling, though. While she . . . while she stuck me. Yelling about black roses and how she was seeing them everywhere, flowers of evil, proof of what I was doing to her. That she knew I saw them too, and if anyone else did, they'd know, and they'd kill her even though it wasn't her fault. So she was going to kill me first, it was the only way to save herself and her family. Like I wasn't her son anymore, like I'd been possessed or taken over by aliens or something."

"It's all so hard to believe," Theresa murmured.

"Tell me about it." He looked out the window again, watching the sweep and dive of gulls over the bay, then looked back at Theresa. "It's even weirder with all the other stuff you told me. And Angela. Shit. I knew about her sketchbook and everything, but didn't even connect it until now. What is all this? What's going on?"

"I wish I knew . . . no, I wish I didn't. I wish I didn't know about any of this." She bent over and propped her knees on her elbows, sinking her head into her hands. "It just doesn't make any sense. Why would Angela and I draw the same necklace? I've thought maybe it was something I picked up from her mother, a story April used to tell . . . that would explain why both I, who she used to babysit, and her own daughter would know about it. But it doesn't *feel* right, dammit!"

"I *saw* that little girl," Jerry said firmly. "I know what I saw. I wasn't dreaming, I wasn't high, I wasn't losing my grip. I *saw* her. And two days later, Angela was dead."

"Why did she do it?" Theresa asked.

He stared at his hands, which were knotted together on the blanket. "I don't know if I should say."

"Jerry, I've dreamed of her. Whatever's going on here, what happened to Angela is a part of it. If I'm going to figure this out, I need to know everything."

"I think her stepdad . . . Mr. Thornton . . ." Jerry's fists closed on each other so tightly that his knuckles cracked. "I think he was after her, the son of a bitch. You know what I mean?"

"More than you know," Theresa said grimly.

"But he's rich, owns the mill, wants to turn Seacliff into a hotel, bringing new jobs, everybody loves him, everybody thinks he's such a goddam great guy. If I said anything, nobody would believe me." There was more bitterness in his voice than Theresa had ever heard before. Bitterness didn't belong that strong in someone so young. "Everybody knows I'm too dramatic, too imaginative. Or maybe I'd just say bad things about him because he wouldn't let Angela go out with me."

Theresa thought about Brad Thornton as she'd met him last week. Brad Thornton with his sports car – MYDLITE – and his winning smile and his charm. "I believe you."

"Good to know someone does." He smiled, weak and relieved. Then his eyes clouded again. "Angela wouldn't have killed herself for some stupid reason like her folks wouldn't let her go to a concert or get her nose pierced or something dumb like that. She was trying to get away from something so awful she felt like she'd never be okay again."

A tremendous wave of sorrow and infuriation swept over Theresa. "I wish I'd known her. I wish I'd been able to talk to her. To tell her that someone understands, that it doesn't have to be the end of the world."

Jerry's eyes widened. "Mizzane . . . ?"

"Never mind," she said. "It was a long time ago, Jerry. But let's just say I know what Angela might have been going through." She spotted him looking at her wrist, realized she was absently rubbing at the white scrawl of scar there. She cleared her throat self-consciously and tugged the sleeve of her shirt down, rotating her wrist in toward her waist to hide it.

"What I don't get," Jerry said, picking up on her very clear desire to move away from that subject, "is how the roses fit into it, and the little girl. And my mom."

"I'm pretty sure that I know what happened to the little girl. To Glory." Theresa thought of her manuscript, which she now suspected hadn't been created by her own mind at all but really *had* come through her. Through her from somewhere else, using her as the conduit and the computer as a high-tech Ouija board. "But I wonder what will happen next. Because this isn't over. Whatever is going on, I know it isn't over."

* * *

"Jesus H. Christ!" Al Haverley swore, swinging toward his wife with the department store receipt crumpled in his hand. "Two hundred bucks? For a dress?"

"And a pair of shoes," she said, holding up the bag with the shoebox in it. "They were on sale."

"What the hell were you thinking? We can't afford this!" His eyes narrowed. "Did you have your hair done too? It looks different."

Celeste exhaled in a short, sharp huff. "Is that all you can say? I was in the beauty shop for three hours, a complete makeover, and all you can say is that I look *different?*"

"How much?" he asked, his voice dropping to a near growl.

"Ninety dollars." She held her head proudly, catching the reflection of her new hairdo in the mirror over the mantle.

"Ninety –" Al sputtered.

"I wanted to look nice for the party tonight." She smiled and stroked the garment bag that held her new dress. It was the loveliest shade of crimson, swirled through with a black pattern that resembled floral silhouettes. The new shoes were sexy strappy high heels. She didn't bother telling Al that she'd also bought a pair of silk hose sewn with little roses climbing the back seam. He wouldn't understand.

"Party? It's just Brad coming over for dinner."

"He's your boss, Al. It's important that we make a good impression."

"*This* is going to make a good impression? Showing him that you throw away my hard-earned money on this kind of crap?"

"It's not crap! I want to look nice, that's all!"

Gary, who had been slouched in front of the television with his headphones on, glanced up with a snide grin. "Hey, Dad, I think Mom's got the hots for your boss."

Al started to turn toward him, ready to tell him to shut up, but Celeste was there first. She tore the headphones from his ears and slapped him across the face.

"How dare you!" she snapped.

Gary shot to his feet, one hand pressed to his cheek. "You bitch!" The words clearly surprised him as much as they did her.

Al planted his big hand in the center of his son's chest and shoved Gary back onto the couch. "Don't you talk to your mother that way!"

"She hit me!"

"You had it coming," Al said. "Now get to your room before I dish you out a second helping."

Gary rose again, and glared at his father. "You hit me, you better make sure the first one kills me, because that's the only one you're going to land."

"Are you threatening me, you little shit?"

"I'm just telling you how it's going to be."

"I don't have to put up with this shit from you, mister. You're under my roof —"

"Yeah, yeah, blah-de-blah," Gary mocked. "Like living here is some big treat."

"The door's right over there," Al said.

"Stop it! Both of you, stop it!" Celeste got between them, her eyes blazing fiercely. "Nobody's leaving, nobody's getting hit. Gary, I think you owe me an apology, and then we can all get ready for a nice dinner. Br – Mr. Thornton will be here at seven."

"Apologize to your mother," Al ordered.

"Sorry I called you a bitch," Gary said sullenly, gaze fixed on the floor.

"Good. Now go get cleaned up."

He gave his father a wide berth and headed for his bedroom, muttering to himself as he went, "How come nobody ever apologizes to *me*?" and then he was gone. Moments later, he turned his music up loud.

Al sank into his chair and opened a magazine. "So what's for dinner?"

"Filet mignon," Celeste chirped, then added worriedly, "I hope the wine is all right. I had to go all the way to Eureka; they just don't have a very good selection at Tom's Market."

Sports Illustrated dipped and he regarded her over the top. "Filet mignon? How much was that?"

"Don't *worry*, Al," she said, exasperated. "It's only money. I just wish I could have found the right kind of flowers. Must be the wrong time of year."

"Why are you making such a big deal about this? It's not like he's never been to dinner before. Remember the barbecue?"

"This is hardly the same as a backyard barbecue! I want everything to be perfect. To be just perfect."

Al snorted in bullish amusement. "Maybe the kid is right. Maybe you do have the hots for him."

Her laugh was a brittle trill. "Don't be silly. You know I'd never do anything like that."

"Damn straight. I'd beat the snot out of you if you even thought about it." He disappeared behind his magazine again.

Her lips drew up in a strained grimace that was meant to be a smile, and it was a good thing that Al's attention was elsewhere, or even he might have recognized guilt for what it was. Before she betrayed herself, Celeste hurried from the room. But the moment Al was out of sight, her smile relaxed into one of thrilling anticipation and she hurried to make herself beautiful.

Under her dress, she wore tiny white panties which laced up the front with thin red ribbon, and a lacy bra that had a red silk rose nestled in the valley between the cups.

Somehow, just the thought of knowing that Brad would be wearing the gift she'd sent under his clothes too was even more enticing than actually seeing him in them. She knew she would spend the entire meal imagining, and so would he.

* * *

"Get down from there, you fuzzy nuisance!" Travis Zane scolded.

When he'd gotten up a couple of minutes ago to fetch a sandwich from the kitchen, Theresa's cat Jack had been sprawled atop the television with his hind leg and tail dangling to partly obscure the screen. Travis was watching the British version of C-Span, in the House of Parliament or the House of Lords or someplace, because it made him grin to hear those proper stuffy Englishmen refer to each other as "the right honorable gentleman" before claiming so-and-so was full of what makes the grass grow green.

Now, though, Jack stood stiff-legged and puffed up atop Theresa's computer. He hissed at Travis, then made an eerie low yodeling sound.

"I said –" Travis started that way, meaning to deliver a well-earned smack to a certain feline's hindquarters, when he heard sobbing from upstairs.

Sobbing. A little girl.

"Jenny?" he called, though there was no way she could have gotten into the house without him knowing, and she wouldn't have anyway, not without knocking.

The sobbing ceased. Jack leapt from the top of the monitor onto a stack of printed pages with Theresa's illegibly scrawled corrections in the margins. The papers shot out from under Jack, making him slide off the desk, landing on his feet as cats did.

Before the last of the knocked-over pages had finished see-sawing through the air to land on Travis' shoes, Jack had pelted up the stairs.

Travis uttered an oath and set down his sandwich. He bent to gather the pages, then stopped as the words caught his eye.

Theresa hadn't told him much about the book-in-progress, hadn't offered to let him read it. As a child, she would never let her parents read her assignments until they were complete, and he didn't think she had changed much since then as far as privacy of her writing went.

But this . . .

What the hell was this?

He crouched on the wet grass like an animal. His hand trickled blood from cuts he'd gotten breaking through the window. The stinging pain was nothing compared to the fear that gripped him.

How was he going to get back?

The room, the prison from which he'd so yearned to escape, was now his idea of paradise. He looked up at the roof. The eaves were too high to reach, the slope too steep. He couldn't jump, couldn't climb. He was as trapped out here as he had been in there.

He cowered against the wall and peered at the house. A shape passed behind the curtains at one of the windows, striking sparks of fear from his heart.

He had to get back to the attic! Before she found him! Before she punished him! She could stop the food from coming, or do even worse things.

Were there worse things? He was sure that if there were, the old woman could think of them.

But how?

A small, pitiful noise escaped him. He clapped a hand across his mouth and hurried toward the front door. If he was quick and quiet, he could go in and the old woman wouldn't see him. He could sneak past her and be safe again. So he told himself, and only that spurred him into moving.

Up. The attic was at the top, so he had to go up. Quietly as he could through this clean and warm place of light. No dust-covered, shroud-draped furniture here. He climbed the stairs as fast as he dared, freezing in horror each time they creaked beneath his muddy feet.

From ahead of him, he heard something. Singing. Not the old woman. This voice was pretty, pretty enough to push the worst of his fear down in his mind and make room for wonder. Nobody who sang so sweetly could be cruel.

It came from behind a door. He stopped and listened. There was a tiny hole in the door, just under the handle, so he stooped and put his eye to it.

It was the little girl.

He stifled a gasp as he saw her.

She had her clothes off like his woman pictures!

He felt his nastybad thing grow at once, hot and pulsing and eager. He hadn't been wicked in a long time, a very long time.

She must be wicked too, going around with no clothes. No, now he saw she had underthings on, which were so pale they looked like nothing at all. Underthings, and a black flower on a necklace of silver.

A ruffled white dress was on the bed, but the little girl didn't put it on, just sat and combed her hair and sang to herself in the mirror. It was yellow as sunshine, soft as a cloud.

He wondered if the girl liked being wicked too. She was smiling. If she smiled, she must like it.

A new thought occured to him. Bare places split open like peaches. His pictures had never showed him, and he wasn't sure if what he remembered from so long ago was true. Maybe this wicked girl would show him.

He opened the door, wanting to go in and be her friend, as he'd been friends with the little girl from long ago, before the old woman made her go away, and made him go live in the room all by himself.

She saw him in the mirror and turned quickly, screaming. It was loud and hurt his ears.

The old woman would hear now for certain, and punish him. The girl wasn't his friend at all. She was just a bad wicked girl.

She should be punished, not him. She was the one who had screamed.

He grabbed her.

The little girl screamed even louder and hit at him, and he recoiled. His shock and fear gave way to anger. He reached for her again but she ran past him. He caught her in the doorway, swept her into his arms and clamped a hand over her mouth.

Her body struggled against his, rubbing his swollen nastybad thing, making it lurch and pound with even more delicious wickedness. And then he knew, he suddenly knew, just what it was for and why girls had peach-places instead of things.

He'd show her. She would see how fun it was, how good it felt. Even if it was wicked.

His arms relaxed a little, sure now that everything would be all right. But the little girl kicked at him, and he dropped her. She ran for the stairs.

Down and down, and then straight across the room and out the door, still screaming. He chased after, the grass cold and wet on his legs.

The little girl ran to a house and started banging on the door. No more screaming, she had stopped screaming and was trying to catch her breath.

No one came to the door. As he got closer, she pushed it open and ran inside. She tried to slam it, but he was too fast.

It was not going to be for nothing. If he was going to be punished, then he was going to earn it. He was going to enjoy his wickedness fully.

She went upstairs looking for help, but he was right behind her, and there was no one to answer her cries. No one was in the house. No one but them.

"This house," Travis said without hearing himself speak aloud. "My God, it happened in *this* house!"

The pages fell from his hand. He mounted the stairs like a sleepwalker, his sandwich forgotten. At the door to the room that had once been Theresa's and more recently Jenny Forrester's, Jack was crouched low to the floor, his green eyes shining at Travis.

"It's here, isn't it?" he asked the cat.

Jack meowed as if in assent. When Travis opened the door, Jack streaked into the room and sprang onto the windowseat. He stretched high in that spine-lengthening way cats have to paw at the window, then hopped down and began scritching at the wooden base.

"No can do," Travis said. "That's fake. It just looks like a cabinet."

And then he knew. A clammy sweat broke out all over his brow, a dull heat spread across his shoulders, a faint pressure like indigestion tightened his chest. He ignored the symptoms, striding to the windowseat with the brisk movements of a man half his age. He hooked his fingers under the lip of the board that held the cushions, and pulled upward with all his strength.

Jack jumped down, head tilted inquisitively.

Wood squalled against wood. Hidden hinges squealed. The top of the windowseat creaked open – one inch, two, four, ten. Then, with ridiculous ease, it flew open the rest of the way and whammed against the windowsill hard enough to make the panes rattle.

Travis didn't care about the windows. His whole attention was focused on what lay in the dark, concealed space below.

Then the pain rammed into his chest like a hammerblow. He staggered backward, letting go of the lid, letting it slam back down.

Gasping air in shallow sips, he tottered down the hall to Theresa's room and reached for the phone.

* * *

"Jer! Did you hear?"

He'd been about dozing off, cruising on his afternoon dose of painkillers, thinking that a nap would be just the thing before what passed for dinner around here. A nap, hopefully a dreamless one to take the edge off of the nutty, scary things that had been going through his head ever since Theresa Zane's visit.

But there was no chance of a nap now, not with Gary Haverley making one of his usual whirlwind entrances. He blurred around the room, shutting the door, throwing back the curtain that Jerry had pulled to close off the view of the hall, hooking a chair with his foot to drag it beside the bed, and grabbing for the remote. In that last action, he also managed to bean Jerry in the side of the head with a warm, grease-spotted bag emblazoned with the Golden Arches.

"There better be a Big Mac and fries for me, or I'm having the nurse throw you out," Jerry said groggily.

"I'm glad to see you too, hoser."

"Nobody uses that word anymore."

"I do."

"My point exactly."

"My ass and your face, Forrester. So, hey, didja hear?"

"Hear what?" He tried to wrestle either the remote or the McDonald's bag away from Gary, failing in both endeavors thanks to his sludgy reflexes.

"Here, greedy guts." Gary dropped the bag on his chest and turned on the television, flipping expertly to a news channel.

"The news?" Jerry said, raising his eyebrows. He dug into the bag, pulled out a

Big Mac, and breathed deep of the fragrant aromas of all-beef patties and special sauce. "What's up?"

"Dude, Nick Diamond is dead."

"What?" Jerry said through a mouthful of burger, spraying shredded lettuce and sesame seeds onto his pajama shirt. "Nick Diamond? Don't screw with me, Scarlet Angel is my favorite group!"

"Mine too! I kid you not! Somebody killed him last night. Mashed him to jelly, that's what I heard."

"No way."

"Way!"

They had to wait through the sports and weather, and then an image off the back cover of the latest Scarlet Angel CD appeared in the corner above the anchorman's shoulder. Jerry stared, the Big Mac forgotten, as the sketchy report was delivered, interspersed with a clip from the previous night's concert and a live shot of the San Diego hotel where Diamond had been found "apparently beaten to death." Certain details were being withheld to aid the investigation. The anchorman went on to say that an unidentified jailbait bedmate of Diamond's had been hospitalized for shock and had not yet been questioned.

"Goddam," Jerry said softly. "He's really dead."

"Dead as a bologna sandwich. I would have called you, but I was glad to get out of the house. My dad's big-shot boss is coming over for dinner, and my mom's all, like, it's God himself." Gary rubbed at his face, his eyes narrowing. "I'll be glad when I'm out of there."

"Brad Thornton's going to dinner at your place? Don't blame you for wanting to get out."

"Yeah, my mom's really got a hair up her butt about it too. She spent *beaucoup* bucks on a new 'do and a new dress. Dad just about hit the roof. And yesterday, I asked her to drive me to the mall, and she dragged me to every flower shop between here and about fuckin' Garberville trying to find black roses. Can you believe it?"

Jerry sucked in a shocked breath, and also sucked in a hunk of patty and bun. It lodged halfway down his windpipe. A series of explosive coughs wracked his chest, until his head swam and his luings burned. He spat the chewed mess into his hand and began gasping.

He thought he was going to hurl, but his stomach elected to stay steady for the time being. He sagged back onto his bed, wincing. Every part of him felt bruised and abused. Especially sharp discomfort throbbed beneath his bandages.

A nurse, drawn by the noise, hurried in and assessed the situation with one razor-keen glance. She lingered accusingly on Gary, who usually made a point of dressing as disreputably as possible. Today he was wearing a t-shirt with a picture of a monstrous squid-faced thing hulking over a podium, in front of a banner that read: *Cthulhu for President – this time, vote for the GREATER of two evils.* He also had a bandanna knotted around his head like a ganger wanna-be, and a dog's choke chain looped around the instep of one boot. Gary's folks just about barfed hairballs looking at him, which was just the way he liked it.

"You'll need to leave," the nurse informed Gary as she bent over Jerry and opened his pajama shirt. Now, there was the stuff schoolboy fantasies could have been made of, if he hadn't been in such pain and if she hadn't been a nurse of the forty-something drill sargeant variety.

"No, wait, I need to talk to him," Jerry rasped, barely noticing that splotches of blood were growing on two of his bandages.

"Later," the nurse said. "You've broken some of your stitches. We need to get you patched back up."

"It's important!" Jerry tried, but it was no use. She shooed Gary out, and he went with a hangdog look, knowing that sooner or later, probably sooner, he'd get in trouble for sneaking in the hamburger in the first place.

Black roses, Jerry thought dismally. He had to warn Gary. Mizzane was right. It wasn't over.

* * *

She was driving up Cliffwood Road, lost in her own dark thoughts about roses and ghosts and sex and death, and at first she didn't assign any special significance to the wailing siren coming up behind her. In L.A., such things were dismayingly commonplace. She automatically pulled onto the right shoulder and stopped while the ambulance flew past.

It was only when she started moving again that she was smacked with realization. This was Trinity Bay, not L.A.. There were only three houses this far out Cliffwood Road – Seacliff itself, her father's place, and the Forresters'.

She tromped on the gas, suddenly sure that she would find the ambulance in the driveway of the Forrester house. That it would be Charlie this time, Charlie having either gone berserk and hurt Jenny, or, more likely, killed himself out of despondance over his wife.

But when she reached their driveway, she saw both Charlie and Jenny standing in the front yard, peering worriedly up the road.

Theresa had been slowing; now she stepped on it again. A very uncharitable part of her brain whispered *please let it be Brad Thornton*, but then she rounded the curve and saw Damon Blake's police car and the ambulance parked in front of her father's house.

She almost ran her car into the mailbox, sprang out leaving the keys in it, and raced in. Just inside the front door, she collided full-tilt with Damon Blake. He rocked back but caught her and for a moment they swayed like dancers.

"My dad!" she said.

"It's okay." He set her steady on her feet. "They're taking care of him right now."

"What happened?" She could hear voices and activity coming from upstairs.

"Looks like another heart attack," he said. "He made it to the phone, called for help."

"Oh, God!" Theresa moaned, her hand closing convulsively on Blake's arm. "Is he all right?"

"He was conscious when I got here, stubborn as ever, wanted me to just fetch him his medicine. I begged to differ. Like it or not, he's going for a ride, probably spend a few nights in the hospital."

"I shouldn't have left him," Theresa said, awash in guilt. "I should have come right back instead of stopping in town."

He grinned with half his mouth. "Hey, you can't watchdog him every minute."

"But if I'm gone when it matters, what good am I?"

"If you start beating yourself up over this, I'll haul you in for domestic violence."

She looked at him, astonished, and then her overwrought tension broke and she managed a weak laugh. "Okay, okay. I guess you wouldn't be cracking jokes if it was too serious."

"That's right."

The paramedics – the same two she'd seen Tuesday night; Trinity Bay's emergency response team was small and close-knit – began levering a stretcher down the stairs. She met them at the bottom and her heart twisted when she saw her father. He looked like a mummy unearthed from a tomb beneath the sands, his greyish skin stretched tight over the ridges of his cheekbones, his eyes so sunken and dark that they almost seemed to have fallen in, leaving only empty sockets behind.

"Oh, Dad," she breathed.

One wavering clawlike hand rose from the blanket that covered him. She grasped it, felt his fingers squeeze hers with some of his familiar strength.

"The windowseat . . ." he whispered harshly.

"What did he say?" one of the paramedics asked.

Some strange instinct made Theresa reply, "I couldn't tell," even as she squeezed back and made a slight nod to show Travis that she did.

"Don't . . ." he added. "Don't look."

She blinked, puzzled, and stood back as they took him outside and put him in the back of the ambulance. By now, Jenny Forrester had appeared at the head of the path that shortcut through the woods, and Shauna and Walt Davis both stood on the porch of Seacliff.

"Want to ride with me?" Damon Blake offered.

"Thanks," she said. "Just let me lock up first." She went back inside.

Jack was skulking along the wall with his tail all puffed up. When she called him, he turned his fey green eyes on her for a moment and then disappeared into the pantry. She heard the clink of his license against the edge of his dish.

Theresa paused at the bottom of the stairs, her father's words echoing in her ears. *The windowseat . . . don't look.*

"Dammit, Dad," she said. "Pandora's Box, Bluebeard's little door . . . don't look."

She set one foot on the lowest riser and her hand on the rail.

Had he seen something? Had something frightened him into a heart attack? Glory's ghost, perhaps? She'd tried to keep all her crazy speculations from him; if Kel McGuire didn't believe her, then her hard-headed father who looked for the logical explanation for everything would have really thought she'd highsided it.

After all, who could she get to back up her story? Jerry and Jenny Forrester, both good smart kids but kids nonetheless. That wouldn't do much for credibility. Easy to blame it on a shared reaction to Sandy Forrester's breakdown.

Why had her father gone upstairs, though? He hardly ever did anymore; it played merry hell with the arthritis that he steadfastly wouldn't admit to, and she knew he was worried about taking a fall and breaking a bone.

Whatever was up there, she decided, could wait. Her dad was on the way to the hospital, and that was where she needed to be. Not standing here scaring herself silly with ghost stories.

She locked the doors, made sure the appliances were off, and grabbed her jacket from the hook by the door. It had been a lovely, warm, late fall day, but the sun was kissing the horizon and soon it would be dark, cool, the fog rolling in from the sea to cloak Trinity Bay in the hanging mist that made the redwoods grow.

When she got back outside, she saw Damon Blake talking to Jenny Forrester, assuring her that Mr. Zane was going to be fine. He straightened up when he saw Theresa. "Ready to go?"

"I'm sorry your daddy's sick," Jenny said somberly.

"Me too, hon. I'll tell him you said hi, all right?" She hugged the little girl, then watched as Jenny headed down the path. "Back to the hospital. I was just there this afternoon. Stopped to have a cup of coffee at Malachi Edwards' place." She frowned, remembering the distracted, upset mood Malachi had been in. "I'd better give him a call once I know something. He's one of Dad's best friends."

Then it was too much for her. All at once, it was too much for her. She leaned against the side of the car and covered her face with her hands, trembling and sure that she was going to start weeping like a banshee. The whole past year and a half seemed to come crashing down on her like an avalanche. The divorce, the move to L.A., the struggles with the show, the stress, the failure . . . and then to have the escape that had seemed like a wonderful chance for a fresh start turn into two weeks of tragedy and insanity . . .

She drew in a long, shuddering breath and willed herself to find that Zane toughness. She was used to having no one to rely on but herself. It had never bothered her before. Why now?

As she struggled, she felt a gentle but firm touch on her shoulder. Damon Blake turned her toward him, put his arms around her. His easy strength, the scent of aftershave, and the crispness of his uniform shirt against her cheek worked a calming spell.

A spell with an unexpected side effect – it had been so damn long since she'd been held by a man! Even when it was just for comfort.

"You're not alone, you know," Blake said. "People here look out for each other. You've got the whole town here to help, whatever you need."

She stepped back and smiled up at him. "I forgot that for a little while. Thank you."

He opened the door for her. "Anytime . . ." and then with a wink that told her he knew just what she'd been thinking last week, he added, "Ma'am."

Theresa burst out laughing. "Oh, no. No you don't. Please. Call me Theresa."

"If you'll call me Damon."

"You've got a deal."

* * *

Rage roared through him like a forest fire.

How could she?

How could she look at another man like that?

She was his! Didn't she understand? His!

Blake had nothing to offer her. Nothing compared to the gifts he could give.

Soon she would begin to realize. He would make her most hidden wishes come true, show her how much he adored her. And then, she would see.

What a pair they would make! She was the one, the one he'd waited for. Such a long time, such a long wait. None of the others had come close to her beauty, her vitality.

He'd thought once or twice before that he'd found the perfect one. Each time, though, he'd been disappointed. Now he knew why. He'd been consoling himself with poor substitutes, waiting for her to enter his world.

Theresa Zane.

She would be his.

* * *

Malachi Edwards pulled out the sofa bed, his back already muttering in protest. Whoever had designed these things, he was convinced, had been a professional torturer in a past life. His back was already muttering in protest, recalling all too clearly how he'd spent the previous night. Shifting around on the thin mattress, trying to find a comfortable spot where the iron bar didn't dig in.

Still, he tried to console himself, it could be worse. He could be in a hospital bed right now like Travis Zane.

But as he listened to Ruth's steps passing the den without even slowing, he found himself thinking that maybe Travis wasn't so bad off.

He'd gone down to the hospital after dinner, but Doc Kensington wasn't letting Travis have visitors yet. Not even his daughter. Theresa had been in the waiting room, looking awfully chummy with Police Chief Blake. That lifted Mal's spirits a little. He knew Travis had a bee in his bonnet about fixing up his daughter with that social worker McGuire, but he personally would put his money on Blake if it came down to a betting situation.

Toby was finally asleep, his bewildered crying having worn him out.

Sunday was usually their special family day, even though Mal still opened the shop. He would go in early, and then when Ruth and Toby were ready, they'd walk over and all three of them would enjoy a leisurely day together, reading, chatting with the customers, enjoying each other's company. Then, at three when Mal closed up, they would go to the park if the weather was fair, or maybe to a movie if it was not. Then they'd all come home together, Ruth would whip up a batch of chili or chowder or hearty stew, and they would eat in the living room and play a card game or a board game.

Today hadn't gone at all like that. Malachi had headed down to the shop as usual, but Ruth and Toby never showed. He'd come home at three and found Toby sitting on his swingset, moping because Mama was mad at everybody.

Mama, Mal knew, wasn't mad at everybody. Just him. Just him over what had happened the night before. She had never been like that, not in all their years together. They'd always been perfectly compatible, in bed and out.

He couldn't just let it go on like this. He loved his Ruthie, but this was like living with a stranger. A frightening stranger.

Steeling himself for another shouting match, he went to the bedroom. The door was closed against him, forcing him to knock. Knock, like an intruder in his own house.

That made him a little mad, especially when she didn't answer. He opened the door.

"Ruth?"

She was in the bathroom, staring at herself in the mirror as if trying to make sense of what she saw. The fear and sadness reflected in her eyes drained off what little anger Mal had felt, replacing it with concern.

"What is it, Ruthie? What's been eating you up?"

"I don't know," she said listlessly.

"Maybe you should make an appointment with the doctor . . . could it be the change?" he ventured, having never been at ease discussing female problems.

"It's not the *change*, Malachi." Annoyance rippled through her voice.

"It's something. You haven't been right all week."

"Whose fault is that?"

"If you want me to say it's mine, you've got to tell me what I did."

"It's not what you did, it's what you didn't do. Don't tell me you didn't like it, Mal Edwards, because I know you did."

"Ruthie, love, I still don't know what you're talking about!" he protested. "Last night, you came at me like a wild woman, what was all that?"

"I'd been hinting all week," she snapped. "But you weren't taking the hint. So I thought it would be best to take the direct route. And you walked out. You *are* ashamed, admit it!"

"You wanted me to slap on you," he said.

"Like Sunday night, Mal! I wanted it just like last Sunday!"

He shook his head, perplexed. "Ruth . . . last Sunday wasn't like that."

"The hell it wasn't!" she flared.

"We made love, sure, but not like that!"

"Oh, so now you're telling me I'm crazy?"

"I'm not saying that! But I think I'd know if I'd been roughing you around!"

"I think I'd know, too! What, I suppose it was a dream?"

Before he could reply, a horrible look came across her face. Her mouth dropped open and she clapped her hands to her temples as if to keep her head from exploding. Her knees buckled and dumped her gracelessly onto the floor. She made a haunting sound, part wail and part moan and all soul-wrenching.

"A dream! God! Mal! It *was* a dream!" The words burst out as if yanked, and then she collapsed on the rug, fingers fisted in her hair, her body wracked with silent convulsive sobs.

"Ruth!" He knelt beside her and tried to put his arms around her, but she rolled away from him.

"Don't touch me!" she blurted in a tone so full of self-loathing that Mal could hardly stand it. He hugged her anyway, feeling her face work against his chest as she tried to give voice to those terrible sobs and couldn't.

"Hey, hey," he said. "Come on now, it's okay."

"No, it isn't! I've been mad at you all week over something that was only a dream!"

"Must've seemed pretty real."

"Mal, I am so sorry! It did, it seemed so real, I thought it was." Tears, a hot and sudden flood of them, soaked his shirt.

He wasn't sure what else to do, so he rocked her like she was a baby, and told her again and again that he loved her. It was the right thing, maybe the only thing.

"Forgive me?" she asked when her crying was down to hitches and hiccups.

"You know it," he replied. "Come to bed, Ruthie. It's all done now."

* * *

Theresa was still sitting in the waiting room at nine-thirty when visiting hours officially ended. Damon Blake had left at eight, telling her to call him if she needed a ride home. But she wasn't about to use one of the town's only policemen as her personal taxicab.

Doc Kensington, who had been an officious snothead twenty years ago and showed no signs of having improved his bedside manner since, informed her with the condescending attitude of an emperor toward a peasant that she should be able to see her father tomorrow.

Even so, she hadn't been able to bring herself to leave. Not without at least seeing her father, making sure he was alive.

A young woman, very overweight and with a sadly pretty face, approached timidly. "Miss Zane? I'm Megan McGuire, Kel's sister? I'm a nurse's assistant here?"

Theresa looked closer, trying to see a resemblance. Kel was tall and lean, his sister just the opposite. Her hair was a shade of orange so light it was almost tangerine, its frizzy texture making it look as if it was trying to escape explosively from beneath the clip she wore. Her eyes were much lighter than Kel's, a milky blue that seemed washed out against her fair, freckled skin.

"Nice to meet you," she said, setting aside the magazine. "Is my father okay?"

"He's resting, but I thought you might like to peek in? Just for a minute?"

"The doctor . . ." she broke off, and got up. "Yes, please."

She followed Megan through the quieting halls to Travis' room. Her father was sleeping deeply, the play of shadows turning his face alternately haggard as a corpse and then proud and noble as a warrior brave. She touched his hand, his brow.

"Hi, Dad."

"Maybe you shouldn't wake him?" Megan ventured.

"Okay." Theresa bent down and kissed his cheek, having assured herself that he was alive.

"I'll open the window a little?" Her round cheeks flushed, Megan crossed to the window with a mincing scurry that reminded Theresa of a quail. "It's warm in here, don't you think?"

Theresa shrugged; it was warmer than the waiting room but not uncomfortably so. She tucked the blanket around her father the way she remembered him doing the same for her when she was laid up with the usual variety of childhood illnesses.

"Thank you for letting me see him. I'll get out of your way now, and come back tomorrow."

Leaving the hospital, she walked through the mist that turned streetlights into haloed globes of gold. Her hands were deep in the pockets of her jacket, her hair gradually dampening and molding itself to her head. Soon she was eager to get home and dry, but despite that eagerness, she found her steps slowing as she got closer to Cliffwood Road. As she turned onto the woods path and began climbing the slope, she slowed even more.

Finally, realizing that if she walked any slower, she'd be going backwards, she mentally berated herself and picked up the pace.

The house looked bigger than she remembered. Huge. The size of Seacliff. And although she'd only been gone for a few hours, it had an aura of staleness and abandonment about it.

She let herself in, and right away Jack was twining between her feet, purring as if he'd never hissed at her. She scooped him up, propping his haunches in the crook of her elbow like she had once carried Lora, and Jack burrowed his nose into the ticklish spot beneath her ear. His clawless paws kneaded busily on her shoulder.

"So, you're finally glad to see me, hmm?" she asked. Her voice sounded too loud in the empty house.

Feeding the cat, making herself a snack because she'd missed dinner, and turning on an edited-for-television version of one of the Lethal Weapon movies helped her regain something of a sense of normality. But she was constantly aware of the quiet, constantly waiting to hear her dad come in.

This must have been what it was like for him when Mom took me away, she thought. When she herself had left the Phoenix house for her L.A. apartment, she never expected to hear Stephen or Lora, because neither of them had ever been there. That was a different sort of loneliness than this.

The movie ended at eleven and Theresa turned off the television. The news was depressing enough on a *good* day.

She was dry, warm, fed, and exhausted. But not in the least bit sleepy.

Something felt undone, unfinished. She'd been trying not to think about it ever since she left the hospital, but now it came to the forefront of her mind.

She went upstairs, to the room that had been hers as a child. Jack followed.

The door was standing halfway open and the light was on. She could see a slice of the bed, Kooky-Bear's black and white fur, part of Grandma Tashi's whimsical painting of Coyote the Trickster playing a prank on Brown Eagle.

Nothing to be afraid of. So why did the door have all the ominousness of a gloomy dungeon portcullis?

She pushed the door wider, revealing nothing but furniture, everything as it should be. Even the windowseat. Not a thing was out of place.

Theresa released the breath she hadn't even been aware that she was holding. Jack's warm fur oiled past her ankle as he went into the room. Straight for the windowseat, where he stood on his hind legs and began pawing at the overhanging edge of the cushion.

"There's nothing there," she told him. "I don't know why Dad said not to look . . ."

She trailed off, realizing that something *was* different. The seat itself no longer fit flush against the cabinet-front underneath.

All those times as a little girl that she'd tried to figure out how to open the fake cabinet doors, when it was the *top* that lifted? She'd never even tried that!

She tried it now. The top went up with a creak and a clatter worthy of shutters in a haunted house, and she leaned over to see what secrets and treasures were concealed inside.

"Oh," Theresa whispered strengthlessly.

In a bed of dust, blanketed by cobwebs, were the delicate birdlike bones of a child. The vacant sockets stared pleadingly up at Theresa.

Resting on the fragile cage of ribs was a necklace.

The necklace.

A central rose made of some glossy black stone, with a ruby at its heart, set in a heavy and ornate swirl of silver that made a pattern of leaves and thorns.

Among the bones were a few scraps of cloth, lace-trimmed linen so fine and old it looked ready to disintegrate if touched. The space was too small for the skeleton to have been laid out straight, so the legs appeared to have been drawn up and to the side, in a fetal position. A drift of colorless thready strands that might have once been hair pillowed the skull.

Long hair, that would have in life been sunny blond ringlets.

"Glory . . ." Theresa said, and then did something she had never done before – she fainted.

* * *

Jerry Forrester had been cruising on painkillers before; now he was floating. Floating serenely above everything. Not sure if he was awake or asleep, the images filling his mind seeming both dream and memory.

It was Angela, of course, Angela filling his mind. He'd loved her a little already, and suspected that the potential was there for her to be the first real love of his life. Always cast as the hero, how could he fail to fall for a girl who seemed a real live damsel in distress?

Not that she'd been chained to a rock for a dragon to devour . . . not really. Not literally. But that was kind of how it had been. She just didn't tell anyone. Didn't let on. Too afraid. Her stepfather had made her too afraid. If she told anyone how her mother's death hadn't been nearly so accidental as it seemed, her stepfather would make sure everyone knew it was her fault. Not his, but hers. Jerry had gleaned that much, but not much more.

His first look at her had been disappointing, dressed as she'd been in a shapeless sweatshirt and baggy jeans, her hair pulled back in a ponytail and her face too pale, too watchful. His mom had told him April Cliffwood's daughter was moving in, and shown him her high school yearbook in which April was an utter babe. Her daughter, on first look, hadn't measured up even halfway.

But, as he was a dude who prided himself on not being totally shallow and superficial, he didn't just write Angela off as a drab and be done with it. And he soon came to see that she *was* as pretty as her mother, maybe even beautiful. Just hiding it, or maybe not even knowing herself that it was there.

The scene that enveloped him now was of an afternoon in the woods, when he'd offered to walk her home – how '50's! – and she'd agreed. Usually, she'd turned him down because her stepfather either picked her up on his way home from the mill or called right after school to check up on her, and would hear it in her voice if she had disobeyed him.

But that day, her stepfather was in 'Frisco on a business trip, and Angela had agreed to walk home with Jerry. Walking through the woods, taking their time, talking and laughing. Not at all in a hurry to get to Seacliff, because he intuited that once she saw the house and was reminded of the rules, she would vanish inside and that would be that.

So he led her the long way, circling the hill and going down along the beach. He'd told her about the party his friends were planning to have that weekend, hoping she'd go, but she knew her stepfather wouldn't let her.

He remembered how they'd stopped and sat on the massive trunk of a redwood, and how when she had turned her head to follow the scampering path of a chipmunk, he'd reached out on impulse and undone her ponytail. Her hair, rich coppery auburn, fell loose around her shoulders and as she turned back, eyes wide in surprise, mouth open in a gasp, he had seen that he was right. She was beautiful.

Unable to resist, he'd kissed her. She tensed like she was going to smack the shit out of him, but then her hand stole to touch his face, wonderingly.

Again on impulse, he asked her to have dinner at his house, and then go to a movie. And she'd said yes, so they had, his folks and sister adored her, and even let him use the car though he only had a learner's permit so it was like a real date, and they'd driven down to Arcata for a movie. He hadn't even known what was playing; when they got there, they had a choice between a period piece, a tacky comedy, and the latest from Disney. They'd chosen Disney, been the oldest people there without a kid or two in tow, and they had a great time.

A great time . . . but the next day she was absent from school, and when he called, all she would tell him was that her stepfather had come home early, found her not there, and she was grounded. And her voice, oh, she had sounded so miserable, so dead!

Jerry tried to shake off that memory and the dismal events that had followed. He tried to focus on her hair, her lips, the way they'd held hands in the darkness of the movie theater and laughed at the antics of the animated characters.

No one ever said it was his fault. No one ever had to. If he'd left her alone like her stepfather wanted, maybe she would still be alive. But Jerry knew with all the certainty of his seventeen years that there was a big difference between being alive and living. That day was the only time he'd seen Angela really living.

What he felt guilty over wasn't what he'd done, but what he hadn't. He should have done more, should have made her tell him what was going on. They could have found some way to make it right, and put the light back in her eyes.

A damsel in distress, and instead of saving her, he'd let the dragon win.

His drifting mind seized on that. In the books he read, the movies he saw, the plays he acted in, good triumphed. But in the real world, too often evil walked away with the trophy.

Vote for the GREATER of two evils, he thought.

In a flash, it all came together in his head. He understood the connection, understood what kind of power was at work in Trinity Bay.

The greater evil.

* * *

Even at midnight on a Sunday, Nate's Bar was doing decent business. More than half the tables were occupied, as well as most of the stools along the bar.

The dart boards at the back of the room were the main center of activity, it being the final round of the weekly showdown between the Trinity Tigers and the Logjammers.

Theresa Zane paused just inside, looking around. Her jacket and hair were damp again, because the mist had turned to actual rain this time.

She hadn't been able to stay in the house. Her faint couldn't have lasted more than a few minutes, reviving on the floor of the bedroom next to the hidden compartment that concealed a child's bones.

All those years, she'd slept just a few feet away. Never knowing. And suppose she *had* been able to open it as she'd always tried? It gave her such a case of the creeps that she knew she had to get out. Get out and go someplace, anyplace.

Her choices were rather limited. This, the all-night grocery, or the donut shop.

Nate's hadn't changed a whole lot from when she used to stop by after gymnastics class two nights a week to see her father. Nobody had minded the bending of the rules, and she would sit drinking Shirley Temples with extra maraschino cherries, sometimes throwing darts, watching her dad mix drinks and draw draft beers and banter with the regulars.

The woman behind the bar, though, if that really was Danielle Kensington, had changed amazingly. Theresa remembered a pudgy girl with mouse-brown hair and braces that could set off an airport metal detector.

"Dani, is that really you?" she asked, taking in the French braid the color of ripe wheat, the dazzling smile, the sexy shape.

"Theresa! I heard you were back in town; it's about time you came to see me!"

"Phone works both ways," she said.

"Let me get you a drink. On the house."

"Something stronger than a Shirley Temple, I hope!" Theresa slid onto a barstool. "Hot rum truffle?"

"Alcohol *and* chocolate, what a mix!" Dani said agreeably, and went to work.

Warmth and welcome enfolded Theresa. Half the people here knew her dad and came over to ask how he was, offer condolences, promise to help out. She was reminded of what Damon Blake had told her. In a small, close-knit town like this, she didn't have to be alone with her problems. It didn't matter that she and her dad had Native American blood; fifty years ago, or even twenty, it might have made a difference, but not anymore. Not here.

Hard to believe that an hour ago she had been staring down at the remains of a murdered child.

"Here you go," Dani announced, putting the hot rum truffle in front of her. "Like the perfect man – rich and strong."

"I'll drink to that," Theresa said. Just as Dani promised, it was both.

Dani leaned on the bar. "Sorry to hear about your dad. He's a great guy."

"Yeah, he is. How'd he take it when you got his job?"

"Who do you think got me the job?" she laughed. Then, flicking her gaze toward the door as it opened, she groaned. "Oh, great, the High Poobah of all Creation has deigned to grace us with his presence."

Theresa looked, and her grip tightened on her drink when she saw Brad Thornton hanging his coat beside her jacket. Jerry's words rang in her ears – *I think he was after her, the son of a bitch.*

He surveyed the room, accepting greetings from some of the millworkers, coming off like he was just one of the guys. Then he spotted Theresa and Dani, and made a beeline for the empty stool beside Theresa.

"Well, hello ladies," he said. "Is this seat taken?"

The door opened again, this time admitting Damon Blake in faded jeans and a cream-colored sweater instead of his uniform.

"Sorry," Theresa said, manufacturing a smile. "I'm afraid it is." She waved to Blake, who grinned and raised a hand in return.

Thornton, only momentarily put off, shifted to the stool at the end of the bar.

"You've got good taste, Zane," Dani murmured, glancing approvingly at Blake. Louder, she added, "Howdy, Sheriff! Name yer poison, pardner!"

"Sippin' whiskey, ma'am," he replied, touching the brim of an imaginary hat. He sat down and winked at Theresa. "You're not the only one to tease me about it."

"And to think," Dani said, thumping a shot glass in front of Blake, "he comes from *New Yawk City!*" She shrilled the last, mocking a commercial that Theresa remembered from several years back.

"Past life experience?" Theresa suggested.

Blake chuckled. "Too many Westerns as a kid, that's my guess. My brother and I broke our arms once playing cowboys."

"You both broke your arms?" Theresa shook her head. "Your mother must've pitched a fit."

"Well . . . that's the funny thing . . . Derrek was trying to lasso the neighbor's dog, and it pulled him right into a tree. The rope tangled around my feet and knocked me down. I swear I didn't land on my arm, but sure enough, it was broken. In the same place as Derrek's. They told our folks they could have put the X-rays on top of each other and have them match exactly."

"Oh, bullshit," Dani said, genially enough.

"It's true," Blake said. "Read up on twin studies, and what you'll find won't make that seem weird at all."

Dani gave him a "yeah, right" look and hustled to the other end of the bar, where the Trinity Tigers wanted to celebrate their victory with a couple of pitchers.

Blake inquired after her dad, apologized for not being able to stick around. Theresa assured him that Travis was fine and she hadn't minded the walk. They sat for a while in a companionable silence, listening to the bar-chatter around them.

Dani went over to get Brad Thornton another beer, and he beckoned her close and said something that Theresa could barely make it out.

"I'm wearing them," he said.

Dani drew back, her brows knitting. "Wearing what?"

"Don't play that game."

Though Thornton was smiling, there was a cold hard gleam in his eye that Theresa didn't like one bit. Damon Blake's posture changed, becoming more alert, and she was sure he saw it too.

"Mr. Thornton, I'm not playing, I'm confused."

"The present you sent me, remember? I wore them, like your note said. I know you got Big Al to leave the package in my office."

"I don't know what you're talking about."

"Oh, I think you do. Why else would you be blushing?"

Theresa's gaze darted to Dani's reddened face.

"I'm not blushing. It's too hot in here."

"Well, someone's hot, that's a given." His voice dropped, and though Theresa couldn't make out the rest of his words, there was no mistaking that insinuating tone.

Damon Blake started to get up, but Dani hadn't made a career out of tending bar without learning how to handle herself.

"Yeah?" she said, unimpressed and unconcerned. "Well, far as I know, Hell hasn't frozen over yet. When it does, maybe I'll take you up on that."

"If you don't want it, why did you send me –"

"Hel-lo, Earth to Thornton, I didn't send you any package. Must be from a secret admirer, but it sure isn't from me."

Brad Thornton got up, looked like he was about to lose his temper, and then realized that not only were Theresa and Blake listening in, but by now most of the patrons were craning their necks in that direction, trying to see what was going on.

"I must have been mistaken," he said with a stiff dignity that made Theresa think of butlers. She bit her lip to keep from snickering. Thornton put several bills on the bar and walked out.

"Jerk," Dani muttered when she came back over to Theresa.

"What'd he say?" Damon asked.

"If I repeat it, you'll put me in the hoosegow for having a sewer mouth." She dipped a rag into a bin of crushed ice and water, and applied it to her face. "Whew."

"Hope you're not coming down with something," a man two stools over said. "I heard there's a bug going around. Mal Edwards' wife had it, and Celeste Haverley did too."

"Pop's a doctor," Dani said. "I'm not *allowed* to get sick!"

That earned a laugh, and Theresa would have put it out of her mind but it wouldn't go. Kept nagging at her like an itch she couldn't quite reach.

"Something on your mind?" Blake asked, not in the prying I'm-going-to-analyze-you way that Kel McGuire used . . . and which was probably totally unintentional, purely out of habit by now.

There was no way to put her nagging suspicion into words, but that wasn't all that was on her mind, was it?

She regarded him for a long, thoughtful moment. "Damon . . . if someone finds out about a crime that happened a long time ago, what should they do?"

It was his turn to give her a long, thoughtful look. "Not a hypothetical question, is it?"

Theresa shook her head. She sighed, making up her mind. "Can you come out to the house tomorrow? There's something I have to show you."

* * *

"Bitches," Brad Thornton growled in a voice light-years away from his normally slick and easygoing tones. "Bitches, all of them."

He was sitting at his desk, supposedly working but really just pushing papers aimlessly and looking over columns of numbers without really seeing them. His thoughts were on Dani Kensington and how she was messing with him. Coming on strong, then playing hard to get.

They were all alike. April had been like that, all flirty eyes and artful innuendo, driving him crazy. Wouldn't even sleep with him until after they were married. Just as if she didn't have a bastard daughter in tow and was probably getting it regularly from her hippie musician friends.

Angela had been just as bad. Oh, she'd seen how her mom played Brad like a fish. She knew how to work on a man. Prancing around the house in next-to-nothing, always making sure to announce it when she was going to take a shower. Making with the innocent act, as if she didn't know what kind of an effect her games were having on him.

Now along comes Dani Kensington with the same routine. Smiling at him, fawning over him. Sending him scanty briefs, for Chrissake. And then the I-don't-know-what-you're-talking-about spiel. She was getting off on it, that was clear. Getting off on teasing him.

He jabbed a pen at a stack of paper, thinking that if he could just get her alone, he'd put an end to all the bullshit. No more games.

That was probably what she really wanted. That was what they all wanted, down deep. For a man to just grab them. But they couldn't bring themselves to come right out and say it, so they did crap like this. Tease a man. Torment him. Make him crazy until he finally just snapped.

Then they could drag out the best weapon in the arsenal of women everywhere

– guilt. Oh, I didn't want to, oh, you made me, oh whine-whine-whine until a man would give them anything just to shut them the hell up.

Damned if he was going to let Dani Kensington do that to him. No more women trapping Brad Thornton, thank you very much. The minute a woman had that ring on her finger, she changed. Got high-and-mighty. Started making demands. Trying to control.

Like April. Telling him what to do, what not to do. Oh, she'd been a great one for ordering him around. Never a word against her daughter. Angela could do as she pleased, and let him just try to put his foot down, assert a little discipline, and April would be on his case like a pitbull.

He'd hoped it would get better after she died. With April gone, away from the bad influences of the Bay Area, in the quiet and sedate town of Trinity Bay, he'd hoped Angela would straighten up and fly right. But instead she'd only gotten worse. Sneaky. Disobedient.

Looking at him like it had been his fault her mother had died.

His fault, not hers.

All he'd done was try to protect her. Was that so bad? So he'd bent the truth a little! April wouldn't have wanted her only daughter to get the blame. Angela had gone along with the lie eagerly enough at first. She didn't want anyone to know what she'd done. But it had gotten all twisted around in that head of hers, until she had the gall to blame him!

Now along came Dani Kensington, thinking to start it all up again. Or maybe Big Al was right; maybe she was a lesbo and this was how she got her kicks, by taunting the straights. Either way, he wasn't going to put up with it. If she was going to mess with a man like Brad Thornton, she was going to get more than she bargained for.

He envisioned himself atop her, both of them writhing and sweat-slicked. And then, at the height of their raw, animalistic sex, putting both hands around her neck and squeezing. Squeezing until her face went purple, until her body went limp. Then bundling her into the trunk of his car and dumping her into the Agate River, right where the current swept strongly into the sea.

The vivid fantasy brought him to painfully hard erection. He knew he'd never do it, though . . . at least, not the way he'd imagined. They could do incredible things with forensic science these days. Better to make it look like an accident.

An accident, like April's tragic fall.

But people around him had a way of taking tragic falls, now, didn't they? April down the stairs of their San Francisco home, Angela from the bluff over the beach, even his lawyer . . . his oh-so-inquisitive lawyer. Falling, imprisoned in his car, from the high, narrow trestle bridge. Such a shame.

Now his thoughts gave way to a different fantasy. Dani Kensington in Seacliff, on the gallery, the sunlight filtering through the stained-glass dome on the roof casting her into blue and green hues like a mermaid. Pushing her, over the rail, headfirst onto the marble tile around the pool.

No, too suspicious. Even that small-town peace officer, Blake, would have some questions over that one.

But it still did make for a pleasant daydream. Teach her to mess with him.

A rap at the door interrupted his thoughts. He started to rise, but the stiffness in his pants made him sink behind the concealing desk. "Come in."

The door opened just enough to admit Celeste Haverley's skinny form, and she quickly closed it behind her. She was wearing a tan trenchcoat and sunglasses, her movements furtive, her cheeks filled with color.

"Afternoon, Mrs. Haverley," he said, politely as his strained emotions would permit. "I think your husband's down on the mill floor."

"I shouldn't be here. Oh, it's crazy. I know it is. If he finds out . . . but I couldn't stay away."

"That was a fine dinner you put on last night," Brad said when she showed no immediate signs of leaving.

"I wish you could have stayed for dessert."

He stared at her – there *had* been dessert, a chocolate cake from Wilson's Bakery. "Mrs. Haverley, is there something I can help you with?"

She undid the belt of her trenchcoat and pulled it wide open, like a flasher. Exactly like a flasher. Underneath, her small breasts were cupped in white lace, and her bony hips were sheathed in white panties with red ribbons.

Brad gaped. "It was you? Jesus! It was you?"

Celeste shrugged out of the coat and strutted toward him in nothing but her undies and high heels, running her tongue along her painted lips. "I can't stop thinking about you. Last night only made it worse. I know it's wrong. I know it's a mistake. But I have to have you again."

"Again?" The word burst out of him on a gust of laughter. "Please. Give me some credit!"

She faltered and looked at him. "But . . . Brad . . ." Then, shaking her head as if to shake off both his words and the incredulously unkind tone with which he'd spoken them, she hoisted one flat, scrawny buttock onto the edge of his desk and leaned closer. "I saw this in a movie once. Let's do it right on your desk."

"Are you kidding?" He shot to his feet, the previous troublesome erection having dwindled with amazing rapidity. "What the hell do you think you're doing?"

"Nothing we haven't done before," she insisted, her fingers reaching to skate down his tie toward his belt.

Brad backed up fast, the backs of his knees colliding with the seat of his executive chair and spilling him back into it. "Mrs. Haverley –"

"Oh, you may as well call her Celeste," Big Al Haverley snarled, pushing the door open. "Seen as how you two are such good friends."

"Al!" She whirled, gaining a sudden, striking, hunted form of beauty.

"Al, thank God!" Brad said. Then he saw the way the large foreman was looking at him, saw the way Al's fists were bunched. "Al, hey, hold on! It's not what you're thinking!"

"It is!" Celeste cried. "I'm glad you found out, Al, glad! Do you hear me? All the sneaking around . . . I'm glad it's over. I love him!"

"There's nothing going on!" Brad jumped up again, skirting the desk. "She came in here, started saying all sorts of crazy stuff –"

"You're nothing compared to him!" Celeste, still sexily posed on the desk, announced. "Nothing! He makes me feel like a real woman! I've had more orgasms with him in the past week than in the whole last *year* with you!"

Brad shook his head, numb and unbelieving. "I swear to God, Al, I've never touched your wife."

Al nodded soberly. "If I was in your shoes, Mr. Thornton, that's just what I'd say and how I'd say it. And seen as how you're my boss, it wouldn't be right of me to give you the thrashing you might deserve."

"Yes, that —" Brad began, shakily relieved.

"Not when I'm still on the clock," Al continued relentlessly. "Not on company time, you see. So we'll settle this later, you and me."

"It won't change anything, Al!" Celeste said. "I've had it with you. I'm leaving you. Brad and I belong together."

"Shut *up!*" Brad nearly shrieked at her. He turned back to her husband. "Al, hear me out —"

"Not on company time," Al said again. "Right now, if you don't mind me taking an early lunch, I've got some things to discuss with my *wife*."

She thrust her chin defiantly at him. "Forget it, Al! I've put up with your ignoring me long enough! It's time I found a man who really appreciates me!"

Al's fist whipped out. The blow knocked Celeste off the desk, where she crouched on the floor in a daze, one hand clapped to the side of her head.

"Get your coat on," Al said.

"Al —" Brad wasn't sure what he could say, and any possible words died in his throat as Al's flat gaze locked with his. Under that slow, lumbering anger, Brad saw a killing light that mirrored what must have been in his own eyes the day he'd pushed his wife down the stairs, then kicked her leather handbag after her to make it look like her feet had tangled in the strap.

Celeste saw it too, and whimpered as she struggled to get her arms into her coat. She threw a desperate, imploring look Brad's way, as if the crazywoman expected him to defend her, fight for her.

Al grabbed her by the arm and hauled her toward the door. "I'll see you later, Mr. Thornton."

"Al, listen . . ."

But they were gone, and Brad's legs didn't have the strength to go after them. He sank back into his chair, his mind aswim with what he'd heard in Al's voice, seen in Al's eyes.

What had he heard, seen?

Nothing less than his own death.

Unless he did something about it.

* * *

Theresa Zane hung up the phone, her hands cold and trembling at the implications of Jerry's call.

He'd been upset about more than he'd told her, and logy from the medication, but what he'd said about his conversation with Gary Haverley and greater evils was enough to chill Theresa to the marrow.

Celeste, too?

First Sandy, now Celeste?

What in God's name was going on in this town? What in God's name was going on with *her?* It all had something to do with her, that she couldn't deny. But it wasn't her that was in the most danger. Not right now.

She picked up the phone again, and flipped through the thin Trinity Bay phone book until she came to the H's. Dialed. Tried to imagine what she could say to Celeste Haverley, who hadn't liked her as a child and probably liked her even less now.

It rang and rang, with no answer and no answering machine. Gary would be at school, Al would be at the mill, and Celeste wasn't home.

That didn't mean anything. She could be out shopping, out in the garden, out gathering or spreading new gossip. But the sound of the phone, ringing endlessly into an empty house, chilled Theresa even more.

She'd never been in the Haverley house but could almost imagine the phone, a serviceable old-fashioned rotary, dull black. On one of those oddly-shaped tables some people called a "phone nook." In a hallway with fading wallpaper, and a shadow swinging slowly back and forth in the living room. The shadow of a woman's body, hanging by an electrical cord that had been tied first around a ceiling fan and then around her neck. Her sense of this was so strong and vivid that she could even see how one slipper had fallen from a dangling foot.

Theresa shuddered so hard her teeth clacked together. She dropped the phone into the cradle, then picked it up again. She'd call Damon Blake . . .

No. What was she thinking?

She couldn't call him over some silly idea that Celeste Haverley had hanged herself. She had death on the brain, that was all. Who wouldn't? She'd spent the night on the couch, foolishly afraid that Glory's bones would somehow animate during the night, that she'd awaken to their dry, hard touch on her hand, or on her face.

Ridiculous. The body wasn't going to move.

But then . . . the lower part of her mind, below the rational places where reason dwelt . . . that lower part insisted that the body had been disturbed now, the makeshift coffin had been opened.

Death on the brain. Sure. Her father was in the hospital, and she was alone in the house with the long-dead corpse of a child. Small wonder she'd be obsessed with the thought.

Yet she couldn't shake the certainty that Celeste was dead.

A car pulled up outside, and when she looked out and saw Damon Blake's patrol car, her mouth went dry. For a moment, she was sure he'd come to deliver some bad news. Her father had taken a turn for the worse, for instance, and they'd decided it would be kinder to tell her in person. Or he'd happened to go by the Haverley house and . . .

She bent to the sink, sure she was going to throw up, but the whirl of nausea passed. She splashed a handful of cool water on her face. Then, as she dried herself with a paper towel, she remembered that it was eleven-thirty, that Damon had promised to come by around noon so she could tell him what she hadn't been able to tell him last night, show him what was concealed in the upstairs windowseat.

He came to the back door and she met him there. She was fiercely tempted to put her arms around him, draw some of his casual strength into herself. That urge made her take a mental step back. She'd been drawn to men for a lot of reasons, mostly bad ones during her younger years, but never out of a sense of wanting strength and comfort and protectiveness.

"I hope I'm not taking you away from anything important," she said, inviting him into the kitchen.

"Sounds like it's important to you."

"It is, but damned if I know what it means, whether it's involved with anything else that's going on. I'm running in circles trying to make sense of it all."

"Well, you've already lost me." He smiled.

"I guess, since you're the police chief, I should start with the actual evidence." She took a deep breath, met his dark eyes squarely, and said, "There's a dead body upstairs, and I think it's been there for at least a hundred years."

"Show me."

She led him to the small bedroom, to the windowseat. Hesitated before opening it, insanely sure that there would be nothing but dust, that she and her dad were having a shared hallucination. But when she raised the lid, the fragile bones were there.

"Good God," Blake breathed. "Looks like a kid."

"A little girl," Theresa said. "Her name was Glory. Glory Cliffwood."

* * *

"I don't want to hear a word out of you," Big Al Haverley informed his wife.

Celeste huddled against the passenger door, rubbing fitfully at the swollen knot that had risen on the side of her head.

Even worse than the physical pain was the mortification that had come when Al practically dragged her out of the mill. She'd been careful going in, making sure she wasn't seen, and he just towed her along in full view of half the lumberyard crew. By now, most of them would be on the phone to their wives, sisters, sweethearts. And many of those would, having been victims of Celeste's own love of gossip and scandal, be wasting no time spreading the news. It would be all over Trinity Bay by the time Gary got home from school.

Sick embarrassment bubbled up inside of her, like heartburn, like nausea. She slouched in her seat, chewing on her manicured nails until they were ragged, staring out the window but not seeing the trees sliding past as they descended Mill Road.

She could feel Al's smoking-hot glare fall on her, and the first threads of fear wove through her anger and shame. This wasn't how it was supposed to go. This wasn't how it went in the exciting shows she watched in the afternoons. No. Not at all.

On the shows, the enraged husband would have attacked the other man, prompting the other man to pull a gun from his desk. But Al hadn't lost his temper. He lived in a state of constant grouchiness, sharp-tongued and quick-handed to her and the kids. Finding out about her and Brad should have sent him into a fit of fury. Then Brad would have been forced to defend himself, defend both of them.

Or an accident could have happened at the mill. Accidents happened at the mill all the time. Poor Lenny James last year, killed when a chain let loose and went through the air like a whip. Al was the foreman . . . Brad could have sent him to investigate an unsafe situation . . .

What was she thinking? She'd gone from an affair into fantasies about arranging her husband's murder?

Then again, why not? He could kill her easily enough. Probably would. She'd never seen him like this before. Mad, yes, but in a controlled, detached sort of way. Calculating.

She pressed against the door, which she usually hated to do on this section of road because there wasn't much shoulder before the land dropped steeply away to the tangle-growth gully of Leland Creek. Too easy to think about her car door popping suddenly open.

Too easy for Al to get rid of her that way! One good push . . .

Celeste whipped around, expecting to catch him about to do it, about to shove her from the moving car. He could tell everybody that she jumped.

He hadn't moved, his big hands still clamped on the steering wheel. He gave her a hateful, contempt-filled look, then returned his attention to the twisting road.

She sat back, and a flicker of dark movement caught her eye. There, in the side-view mirror. Something black. Not a rose, not the lovely black rose, but something even better. A sports car. Brad's car.

He'd come after them! Come for her! Just like in one of her shows. He would make Al stop, they'd have it out. Brad would have a gun. He'd reduce Al to a whining, pleading dog. Brad's own frantic pleas in the office would be revealed as nothing more than a ploy to gain time. Then, she and Brad would hop into his sports car and drive away into a life of passion and adventure beyond her wildest dreams.

Al tensed, looking in the rearview, and his glower deepened.

"I was almost ready to believe him," he said, as if to himself.

"What?" Celeste whirled on him. "Believe *him*? He denied everything!"

"Why the hell would he want to stick it to a dried-up old bat like you?" Al asked harshly. "That's what I was thinking. Now, he's coming after . . . maybe it was true, at that."

"Your wife confesses an affair, and you would rather believe the other man's lies?" she demanded. "Why? Because he's your boss? Your buddy? And for your information —"

"Shut up!" Al said, still fixed on the rearview. "What's he up to?"

She turned in her seat to look. Brad's car was closing in rapidly. She couldn't see him, just a hint of a man-shape behind the tinted glass.

"He must want to talk to us awful bad," Al said. "He's just going to have to wait until we get to the bottom of the hill. There's noplace here to pull off."

He was right on their bumper now.

"Showoff sonofabitch." Al braked, and the car jolted as Brad bumped them.

"There. Him and his fancy-ass car. Give him a scrape, that'll teach him to quit fucking around."

The black car slowed, and Celeste could see the man-shape waving his fist angrily. Or maybe flipping Al the bird.

Al only laughed, a humorless and angry laugh, and came down hard on the gas again. Their car surged ahead. An orange sign flashed by, too fast to read.

"Al, slow down, this isn't funny." Celeste held on to her seatbelt, trying not to look at the sun-dappled water of Leland Creek wending its way through the boulders below. "We don't want to crash."

"Oh, now you're telling me what to do? Ten minutes ago, you were set to leave me."

"Al, stop it!"

Brad's car had fallen back farther, but Celeste barely noticed. Orange sign?

Like a flare in her mind, she remembered the county work crew she'd passed on her way up. She remembered smiling pleasantly at the men in their bright orange jumpsuits, thinking that it was about time the potholes along Mill Road were patched, wondering what they'd say if they knew what the woman driving by was wearing under her coat.

Al had gone up at 6:30 A.M., riding with Henry Sorenson so she could have the car. The work crew wouldn't have been there that early.

"Al, you have to slow down! There's a –"

They came around a bend, doing almost sixty on a stretch posted to 35, and there were the cones, the tar truck, the roller. The flagger, a kid of about nineteen, was staring at them with his eyes and mouth three gaping circles beneath the brim of his hard-hat.

"Shit!" Al downshifted and braked.

The flagger dropped his "slow/stop" sign and ran for it in great bounding gazelle-like leaps as the Haverley car plowed through the first three cones. The rear end began to slide, tires shrieking.

Celeste screamed and braced her hands against the dashboard as they went into a loose, dizzying glide.

The back bumper slewed sideways and struck the steep hillside. The car rebounded away from the hill like a pinball, bumping over two more cones and the discarded sign. The stick snapped, the part with "slow/stop" on it bouncing up onto the hood like a last-ditch warning.

The front tires went off the road and onto the soft, gritty surface of the shoulder. Celeste's door slammed into a tree and dented inward, throwing her as far toward Al as the confines of her seatbelt would allow.

Then they were hurtling sideways down a slope that was nearly a cliff. They struck a boulder broadside and flipped. The roof crumpled and even through her own screams and the sounds of rending metal, Celeste heard Al's grunt, cut off by a horribly final crunch.

The world revolved again as the car tumbled the rest of the way down. It landed upside-down in Leland Creek, the cold water gushing through the shattered windows to douse Celeste.

She gasped, her throat so ragged from screaming that it felt like she'd been chewing shards of glass. Her gasp sucked in a lungful of water. Coughing, she tried to raise her head but in her disoriented state only dunked it back in the creek. She was still strapped in, belted securely in place, upside down.

Tucking her chin toward her chest brought her face out of the water. Her right arm hurt; she thought it might have broken when the car collided with the tree. She groped clumsily for the belt release with her left, then realized her legs were pinned. And by the warmth flowing up her body, she feared she'd peed herself.

She looked down, or up, or whichever way her legs were, trying to see what was holding them.

The entire front of the car had smashed in. What was left of the dashboard was pressed down on one leg, leaving it numb. The other had been gashed to the bone by a ragged scrap of metal. A dark scarlet tide was pulsing from her thigh.

Dimly, distantly, above the chuckling creek, she could hear voices. The work crew. Help. Help was on the way. All she had to do was stay calm.

She turned a little and saw her husband. Because the car had landed at an angle, Al's head wasn't underwater. If it had been, she might have been spared the sight of his skull cracked open like a walnut, of pinkish-grey brain tissue peeking through.

Any thoughts or chance of staying calm were dashed to pieces. She began to shriek and struggle, yanking at her seatbelt, hammering at the dashboard.

"Hang on, lady!" someone yelled.

So far away! What were they doing, stopping for a smoke?

Her head dipped into the creek again. Couldn't hold it up. Her neck was too tired. But when water flooded her mouth, she jerked and choked.

The next time it happened, it wasn't so bad at all. Her pains felt distant and insignificant.

Dark petals unfolded in front of her, drew her headfirst into their velvety midst, and closed around her with the warmth of an embrace.

* * *

She finished, not coming to any real conclusion but simply running out of words. She just folded her hands in her lap, the kitchen lights casting an indigo sheen on her black hair, and looked at him to see if he thought she was out of her mind.

Damon Blake gave it all very careful consideration before he spoke. He'd seen some unusual things in his life, twin-specific events too eerie to be coincidental. But none of that amounted to anything compared with the story Theresa Zane had just laid out for him.

The bones in the windowseat. The necklace, which both Theresa and Angela Cliffwood had depicted in sketches done many years apart. Ghosts and roses, cats freaking out, unfinished novels. Sandy Forrester. And maybe Celeste Haverley.

Theresa was still looking at him, her face set in an odd mix of determination and resignation. It occurred to him, not for the first time but perhaps for the clearest time, that she was one of the loveliest women he'd ever met. Even now, when she looked utterly exhausted, with her dark eyes ringed with bruised tension, she was beautiful.

"It's a hell of a story," he said finally.

"I know how it sounds."

"I know you do, which is why I won't say it. Who else have you talked to?"

"My dad, Kel McGuire, the Forrester kids. Partly, anyway. Dad found the bones yesterday. That had to be what triggered the heart attack. And he'd been reading my manuscript. That's what tipped him off. I didn't see it. I wrote it, and I didn't even see it. He read it and he knew."

"What about McGuire?"

"He's about ready to cart me off to Blue Lake. But *he* was the one who mentioned Sandy and the roses. Jerry and Charlie both confirmed it."

"Any ideas about what it means? Any ideas at all?"

"Sex and death," she said, without hesitation. "It all comes down to sex and death."

He mulled it over, not sure just what she meant by that. "The first thing I have to do is get someone from the county out here to examine those bones. Sheriff's Department. And a coroner, medical examiner, or forensic pathologist. They can determine how long they've been there, cause of death, all that. It's possible the child might've crawled in there, gotten trapped. I read something once about a bride, wanted to play hide and seek at her reception, and then she vanished. Fifty years later, a skeleton in a wedding dress was found locked in an attic trunk."

"That wasn't how it happened," Theresa said. "Someone killed her."

"Just between you and me, I think you're right. Not that it's going to do a whole lot of good. Whoever did it is long dead themselves."

She sighed and looked down at her hands. "Maybe the killer's dead . . . but the crime is still going on. Everything that's happened is a part of it."

"Theresa . . ."

"I know!" She raised her gaze to him, and the stark helplessness in it struck him like a slap. "You think I'm crazy. But it *is* all connected!"

He took her hand. "I don't think you're crazy."

"But you don't believe it."

"I'd be a lot more inclined to believe it if we had more to go on. I still don't see how the . . . similarities between you and Angela Cliffwood tie in with Sandy Forrester."

"I don't either." Her shoulders slumped. "Sandy had a fever and then got obsessed with sex and black roses. Then, the day we were all helping tidy up the Forrester house, Celeste Haverley begged off with a fever . . . and now, according to her son, she's obsessed with black roses too."

"I don't care to imagine Busy Bee Haverley obsessed with sex," Damon said dryly. "Besides, I've heard a bug's going around. Ruth Edwards had it, Nancy Ellsworth had it, and last night even Dani was coming down with something. And if you don't mind my saying, you look a mite peaked yourself."

She managed a faint grin at his overdone drawl. "I haven't been sleeping well. Not adjusted to the move yet, maybe. Or the change in climate. No fever for me."

"Insomnia?"

"No, that's Dad's department. I sleep like a dead thing and wake up like death warmed over." Her expression grew more troubled. "And there's the dreams . . . I used to dream quite often, but since I got here, I can only remember twice. Both nightmares. Both related to the rest of this."

Before he could answer, his beeper went off. "That means they're trying to raise me on the radio. I'd better go see what's up."

* * *

"And you said I wouldn't be done by noon," Nancy Ellsworth said triumphantly, sweeping into Kel McGuire's office with a stack of files and papers which she deposited with great ceremony on his cluttered desk. "Done, and it's precisely 11:57."

He applauded. "Great! Now you can start on today's correspondence!"

She rolled her eyes theatrically. "Do I get a lunch break?"

"You're the one who missed two days last week, not me."

"You know perfectly well that I was helping at the Forrester house on Tuesday. You even gave me permission, if you recall."

"Yes, but what about Wednesday?"

"I was sick! Some people get sick, you know. Some people don't ignore their body's cues until they drop dead in the harness. Wasn't I in first thing Thursday, bright eyed and bushy tailed?"

"So bright eyed and bushy tailed that I was wondering what you'd been up to," he agreed.

Nancy turned pink. "Wouldn't *you* like to know! Let's just say that I saw a side of Rand that I'd never seen before!"

"Let's leave it at that, shall we?"

"Of myself, too," she giggled. "I never thought I was the whips-and-chains type!"

"Need I remind you, Ms. Ellsworth, of the current outcry against sexual harassment in the workplace?" He said it mock-sternly, eyes twinkling.

"Oh, fine." She accepted the stack of unanswered letters he handed her and sashayed back to the outer office. In the doorway, she paused and looked back over her shoulder and pushed her lips into a seductive pout. "By the way, do you know anyplace where I could buy spike-heeled boots?"

"Get to work!" Kel laughed. "If Rand came in and heard that, he'd break me in half like a twig."

"Not without Mistress' permission!"

"Work!" He nudged the door shut with his toe, shaking his head to dispel the bizarre images that had lodged therein. Nancy gimme-a-he-man Ellsworth, playing dominatrix games? And Rand Kostas, who looked like the kind of guy who ate raw bear meat for breakfast, going along with it? Too much.

He checked calendar and clock, saw that he had a half hour before he was due for the afternoon therapy session at Silver Grove. Plenty of time to scarf down a sandwich while he finished going over the court orders on Sandy Forrester.

* * *

Damon Blake felt his gorge rise as the paramedics managed to pull Al Haverley's body from the mangled ruin of his car. But rather that turn away from the gruesome sight, he kept a look of professional detachment and concentrated on preventing the lookee-loos from getting in the way.

He'd seen worse sights . . . most of them in New York, the kind of things that had made him welcome the relative peace and quiet of Trinity Bay. The three-year-old whose mother had held him down on a lit burner because he wouldn't stop reaching for the pots on the stove, the teenage victims of the Screwdriver Killer, the old man who had lain unmissed in his apartment for two weeks after a heart attack and been found half-eaten by his own starving dog . . . those had been the worst.

But this was still pretty damn bad.

Most of the observers were from the mill, standing in a loose cluster behind

Brad Thornton, all of them wearing identical masks of strained shock as they watched Big Al bundled onto a stretcher and zipped into a thick plastic bag. Near the mill workers were several men in orange jumpsuits. One of them, a kid barely old enough to shave, was leaning against a tree looking like he was about to pass out.

They began lugging the stretcher up the steep path of devastation left by the tumbling car. Damon gave a stern warning look to all the locals and then descended to help.

Martin Arnes, one of the paramedics, looked up at him with a strained grimace. "Hell of a thing, Damon, hell of a thing! What's going *on* around here lately?"

Damon shrugged, knowing exactly where Marty was coming from. They usually got together to play poker more often than their professional paths crossed. Yet here they were, for the third time in less than two weeks. For the second time in as many days.

Once Al's body was loaded into the back of the ambulance, Damon followed Marty back down to where Celeste Haverley was still strapped upside-down in her seat. A piece of metal as sharp and serrated as the jaws of a bear trap had slashed her thigh to the bone, and she'd either bled to death or drowned when blood loss had left her too weak to hold her head out of the water.

Marty's partner undid the seatbelt and she crumpled onto the smashed roof. As they lifted her out, her coat fell open to either side like limp wings, revealing what she had on beneath. What little of it there was.

An incredulous, astonished murmur went through the observers. Damon gaped, his own words of only a short while ago clanging in his mind. *I don't care to imagine Busy Bee Haverley obsessed with sex.* But what other interpretation could he put on the fact that the lady had died in whorish lingerie?

They got her into the stretcher and covered her, then began hauling her up to the waiting ambulance.

Damon went over to the work crew. "You saw it happen?"

One of them nodded, the rest were still goggling after Celeste in a way that made Damon feel queasy.

"We heard them coming," the county worker said. "Coming fast, way too fast for the road. Then they roared around the corner, nearly ran Ted down." He jerked his thumb over at the kid. "Whammed into the hillside, bounced back, and over they went. Car rolled three times before it ended up in the creek. The woman was screaming, so I hollered for her to hang on. Then she stopped screaming, and made a godawful gurgling noise the likes of which I hope never to hear again. Then she was dead."

"How fast would you say they were going?"

"They must have come around that bend doing at least fifty, maybe more."

"What time was it?"

"About quarter to twelve. We were just getting ready to knock off for lunch."

Damon thanked him, got his name, promised to be in touch if he had any more questions. He approached Brad Thornton, who was staring at the car with an odd, unreadable expression. In other circumstances, Damon thought, it might have looked like satisfaction.

"Mr. Thornton?"

He jumped a little, and looked at Damon with sudden furtive wariness that instantly cleared into concern and attentiveness. "Chief Blake. My God, what a mess this is!"

"What can you tell me about it?" Damon asked.

"Mrs. Haverley came up to the mill, said she had a surprise for her husband," Thornton said woodenly. "They went into the conference room, it's just two doors down from my office. I heard them start in arguing –"

"About what?" Damon cut in.

"I was doing my best not to listen," Thornton replied, much too smoothly to be anything but a lie. "It might have had something to do with money. I know she'd been after him to ask me for a promotion, a raise. I'd even offered Al a managerial position, but he turned me down."

"So they started arguing. Raised voices?"

Thornton nodded. "Followed by something of a scene. He towed her out of the building by the arm, didn't even clock out for lunch. They got in their car and drove off."

"Big Al, he looked mad as hell," Stuart James volunteered. "I think if his wife had fallen down, he would have dragged her through the sawdust rather than helped her up."

"I can't believe they're dead," Thornton said. "I left just a couple of minutes after them. I heard the crash. When I got here, those men were trying to get them out, but they couldn't do it."

"Did you call it in?" Damon indicated the cellular phone that Thornton was clutching convulsively. The black casing was slick from the sweat of his palms.

"Yes. I said there'd been an accident. Then I called up to the mill and had some men sent down, in case the gas tank went." He gestured at the surrounding woods.

Damon fell silent. It all seemed pretty clear, pretty straightforward. Matched what everyone else said. Yet he couldn't shake the feeling that on the inside, Thornton was laughing at him. He'd had that feeling before about the man . . .

Come to think of it, the last time he'd had it had *also* been at the site of a car wreck, when Thornton's lawyer had gone off the Agate River trestle. Thornton had heard that crash too, since he and the lawyer had been on the phone at the time. Some bit of business they'd forgotten to discuss during their meeting.

"I guess everyone did all they could," Damon said, shaking his head and letting a hint of his pseudo-Western *durn shame* drawl creep into his voice. He kept a careful eye on Thornton, and was sure he didn't imagine the barely perceptible relaxing of his shoulders, the faint twitch of a relieved smile. "I'd best be going; I should break it to their kids before they hear about it through the gossip lines."

Thornton nodded and began dispersing his employees. As Damon got into his car and started the engine, he glanced in the mirror and caught Thornton watching him.

No, sir, Damon thought. *I don't care for that man at all.*

He put it out of his mind for the time being, and drove into town to tell Gary Haverley that he'd suddenly become an orphan.

* * *

The hospital had called a few minutes after Damon left, with the news that her father was awake, alert, and wanting to see her. Theresa scrawled a hasty note in case Damon came back, stuck it to the door, and locked up behind herself.

She found Travis sitting up in bed, the windowsill and bedside table already crowded with cards and flowers. His lunch tray was untouched, his face pensive as he stared out at the irregular sun breaks casting patterns of light and shadow on the bay.

"Hi, Dad. How are you feeling?"

"About how you'd expect." He squeezed her hand as she bent to kiss his cheek, and when she sat down in a chair just as uncomfortable as the one she'd sat in yesterday during her visit to Jerry Forrester – who was exactly one floor down, room 108 while Travis was in 208, a coincidence that she could have done without – he looked at her with a bleak and unsettling fear. "You did, didn't you?"

"Look in the windowseat? I did. How could I not? It's her, Dad. It's Glory."

"I know. Remember the other week when I said I didn't believe in haunts? I take it back."

"Strangest haunting I've ever heard of," Theresa said. "Haunting through my writing?"

"But it's true."

"Yeah." She sighed and picked up one of his cards to have something to do with her nervous hands. It was from Elsie, one of his friends at Silver Grove. "I told Damon Blake. Told him almost all of it, almost everything I know or suspect. He hasn't locked me up yet, so that's something. He wants to have someone examine the bones. Maybe they can do DNA testing, figure out who she was."

"A Cliffwood."

"Well, *I* think she is . . . the stuff I've been writing says she is . . . but that's hardly convincing evidence."

"She wouldn't be the first Cliffwood child to disappear," Travis said. "Not according to the old stories, anyway."

"What old stories? I did a paper on Seacliff once, and never heard anything like that."

"And you were, what, eight years old? Nobody's going to tell a kid about disappearing children."

"I'm not a kid anymore."

"And I heard all this a long time ago, and it might not even be true to start with. But according to what my father told me, after Jacob Cliffwood died, his wife Estelle remarried. Her new husband was a dozen or so years younger than her, but she was a good-looking woman and a wealthy widow to boot, so it can't have been that great a hardship for him."

"Oink, oink, Dad," she said automatically.

"Jacob and Estelle had three kids, a girl and two boys. The girl disappeared about a year after her mother remarried, and the youngest boy a few years later. They said the girl ran off, and the boy got lost in the woods, but there were those in town who thought something different. They thought Estelle's new husband might have done something to the kids."

"Done what?" Theresa asked, her hands growing cold on the scalloped edges of the get-well card.

"Your grandfather wouldn't tell me, but I later heard from Winnie Scribner –"

"Lan's mother?"

"That's right. Winnie said that the fellow . . . Reeveman, I think his name was . . . that Reeveman went insane. Thought devils were talking to him, everyone in town was against him because he was an outsider, that sort of thing. Winnie says he snapped, killed the kids, and that Estelle Cliffwood covered up for him. But then, you should also remember that Winnie and Myra Cliffwood hated each other like cats and dogs, and Winnie could have been spreading and embellishing stories to get under Myra's skin."

"What about Glory, then? How does she fit into it?"

"They say Estelle's other son Robert had a daughter who went missing right about the same time Estelle herself died."

"And who was the guy in the attic?" Theresa wrapped her arms around herself and shivered. Bad enough to think she'd made that up; far worse to think it had really happened.

Travis shrugged. "That, I don't –"

The door, which Theresa had closed when she came in, now swung open after a perfunctory rap. Doc Kensington sailed into the room like a galleon. He was a big man whose body showed evidence of all the bad habits he nagged his patients to give up – heavy jowls and belly, the chronically reddened nose of a long-term drinker, a smoker's rumbling cough. The hair he lacked on his head made up for it in his eyebrows, and his mouth was a tight little purse-string of disapproval.

"Ah, the pill-pusher," Travis said.

"Afternoon rounds," Kensington said with a nod at Theresa that was just as perfunctory as his rap on the door.

Travis glanced at the clock. "And it's only barely after noon."

"I can't dawdle. Arnes and Hamill are bringing in a pair of stiffs, and Welkes is on vacation." He snorted in disdain. "That means I'm in charge downstairs, too."

Downstairs. The morgue. Theresa shivered again.

"Who died?" Travis asked.

Theresa was glad he'd done it, because she'd been just about to ask it herself but it seemed that she was invisible. As a kid, she'd thought she simply lived below the sight-line of her friend Dani's father; he ignored both of the girls when they played at the Kensington house and even when Theresa had gone in for a check-up, the doctor had never actually spoken to her, always to her parents as if she wasn't even there. She would have expected that to change, but apparently it hadn't.

Turned out it didn't matter who asked, because Kensington didn't reply. He checked Travis' chart, grunted to himself, made a note, and took a look at Travis.

Still has his beside manner, Theresa thought, turning her head to hide a grin.

"Well, you're not going to die," Kensington said.

"Comforting," Travis said.

"But you're staying put for a few days. You're in no shape to cover for Dani tonight, no matter how she begs."

"Dani not feeling well?"

"Flu, that's my guess," Kensington said absently, scribbling a few more notes in the chart. "Fever, anyway. Home, fluids, bed rest, that's what I told her. Though whether she actually does it . . ." He cast his eyes heavenward in a manner that showed nothing but contempt for those who had the temerity to question the doctor's advice. "At any rate, she won't be working tonight."

"Have you seen anyone else with the fever?" Theresa cut in.

He favored her with a glance that told her it was none of her business.

But it was. She knew it. Somehow, it was.

* * *

Megan McGuire removed the thermometer from her mouth and studied it. "A hundred and two?"

It *felt* like a hundred and two, maybe more. Like her body had become a pottery kiln, surrounded by a hazy shimmer of heat. She opened her mouth at the mirror, and wouldn't have been surprised to see an orange glow coming from within.

No orange glow. Just her own hateful fat face, gawping like a toad. She closed her mouth and tried a wide smile, but it only pushed her chubby cheeks up so they nearly obscured her eyes.

Sighing, she slid open the mirror to find something to bring the fever down. Luckily, it was her evening off, so she could stay home without feeling guilty over calling in sick. Not that it was really like anyone would miss her. She was only a nurse's assistant, not a real nurse, as her parents and older sister never failed to remind her.

A few passes of a wet washcloth over her face made her feel a little better. She drank an extra glass of water and left the bathroom. Her apartment wasn't much, just a tiny studio with a kitchenette and a deck the size of a card table, but it was her own. And it wasn't as if she entertained much, anyway. Except for her brother Kel, and a couple of times that Brian Sorenson from down the hall had come over to watch her television when his own was on the fritz, no one had been over in the three years she'd lived here.

She got into bed and switched on her reading lamp. Her favorite book was on the bedside table. She'd read it six times already and liked it better each time. The main character's name was even Megan, Megan MacLean. She could almost imagine herself living that Megan's life, ever so much more romantic and exciting than her own.

* * *

If he was at school now, he'd be in biology class.

That was enough to bring a smile to Jerry Forrester's face. Being anyplace, even the hospital, was preferable to sitting in that dingy room that stank of formaldehyde from the pickled embryos displayed on the shelves. And watching a Scarlet Angel special on MTV was worlds better than listening to Mr. Mittleschut drone on about the difference between a mold and a fungus.

He shifted around, trying to get comfortable. His new stitches felt too tight, and he was morally certain that they'd done it on purpose to punish him for undoing their previous hard work.

On the television, the video for Scarlet Angel's first number one hit, "Heart of Stone," gave way to an interview with Nick Diamond's father, Tybalt Diamant Jr. Photos of Nick as a kid and Nick as a teenager appeared on the screen.

Jerry sat up fast and whammed his crazybone on the bed rail. He yelped, rubbing his elbow, but didn't remove his gaze from the TV.

Was it?

No, it couldn't . . .

It sure looked like . . .

Nah, no way.

But . . .

"Aw, come on!" Jerry moaned. "You're seeing things."

The picture changed, and now he was looking at Nick Diamond posed astride a motorbike. Looking, but not seeing, his mind still fixed on the previous image.

It had been a group shot, a bunch of high school kids at a pool party. Nick had been in baggy black shorts, and the arm with his trademark red-robed angel tattoo had been around a gorgeous brunette in a white bikini.

Theresa Zane.

It *was* her! He couldn't believe it, but it was!

* * *

Damon Blake showed up at seven, just as Theresa was poking through the fridge and realizing that she wasn't hungry for anything in it.

"I brought Chinese," he announced when she opened the door. "Wasn't sure what you liked so I got some of everything."

"I guess you did," she said as he began unloading white cardboard boxes from the two large brown paper bags. "It smells wonderful! But . . . what's the occasion?"

"Do we need an occasion?"

The frankness in his gaze hit her the same way the smell of the food had, awakening an appetite of a different sort. The husky timbre of his deep voice sent tingles through her.

"Do you sing?" she heard herself asking.

Damon laughed. "Not since church choir as a kid. You?"

"A little in high school, when I was dating a guy trying to start a band. I was never very good at it. He dumped me for a girl with a voice like an angel."

"His loss."

She grinned. "Thanks. I'll get some plates."

Jack came sniffing around, springing boldly onto the table and attempting to wedge his nose under the flap of a container of pork chow mein.

"Hey, fella." Damon scooped him up. Jack twisted in his grasp and looked searchingly at him, then batted him lightly on the cheek. "I think he likes me. Or he's hoping I'll share."

"There's enough here for six people," Theresa said as she opened the lemon chicken. "You weren't kidding about getting some of everything!"

She knew they weren't talking about what was on both of their minds. She had heard the news, which had flown from one end of Trinity Bay to the other at roughly the speed of sound. Everyone in town was ghoulishly debating what had caused the crash, especially given what Celeste Haverley had been wearing when she died. Just what had she and Big Al been doing in the final moments before the accident? In their morbid glee, it seemed to Theresa that she was the only one who understood that two people were dead.

A few slivers of pork satisfied Jack, who wandered off to doze by the fireplace. The rain had held off most of the day but now hissed down with a soothing sound.

"He's got the right idea," Damon said. "Perfect night for curling up in front of the fire."

"Shall I make cocoa?"

"No argument from me." He closed up the leftovers and whisked the dishes to the sink, and before she could stop him, was running hot water and squirting detergent.

"Oh, hey, Damon, I can do that."

"I always wash up right after dinner," he said. "Otherwise, I'd let everything pile up and my place would look like one of those bachelor pads."

"With dirty socks draped over old pizza boxes?"

"Eating off the butter dish because it's the only clean thing in the house," he agreed. "When my brother and I shared an apartment, you should have seen it. Disaster area. So when I moved out here, I said 'no more' and trained myself into a new set of habits."

"You could have worse habits," she said, handing him a towel as he stacked the plates in the drainer and pulled the plug. "Do you cook, too?"

"I can cook anything," he said confidently. "As long as it comes frozen and ready to microwave. Open my freezer and a stack of Stouffers' will fall out and bury you; open the fridge and there's barely a thing."

"Still, you're eating better than I did for the past year. I got by on vending machine fare and drive-through fast food."

"Oh, I'm not saying I don't do my share of that! The McD's out at North Valley has my order memorized."

She went into the pantry. "For your cocoa, you have three choices – double chocolate, chocolate raspberry, or chocolate toffee."

"Gimme a double," he drawled. "Ma'am."

"Anything you say, cowboy." She dumped the packets into two mugs. "Shall we see about that fire?"

Sitting at opposite ends of the couch, Jack sprawled between them and the warmth from the hearth baking at her legs, Theresa let the last of the day's tension slide away with a sigh. She felt at ease with Damon, more at ease than she'd felt with any man. Not bad, considering the first time they'd met he'd pointed a gun at her. Could that have been not even a week ago? Incredible!

"Nice," he said.

"Hmm?"

"The fire, the cocoa . . . the company."

"Yes. Very nice."

They sat in companionable silence a while longer, letting the crackle of the flames be the only conversation, and then she reluctantly brought up the one thing she didn't want to discuss but needed discussing.

"What happened with the Haverleys?"

He stirred the dregs of his cocoa, peering into the cup as if hoping to see some answers there. "The official story is that they were arguing, got going too fast, and when they saw the road crew, Al swerved to avoid them and lost control of the car."

"I heard that Celeste . . . that she was wearing . . ."

"Yeah. And the first thing I thought of was what you'd said earlier."

"Me, too. I didn't know her very well, but it sure doesn't seem like the kind of thing she'd do."

"I don't like it. The official story. It bugs me. If she did go up there to give Al a lunchtime thrill, why'd they start fighting about money?"

"Maybe it wasn't money. Maybe he was mad at her for pulling a stunt like that."

"Maybe it wasn't Al she went up there to thrill."

Theresa blinked at him. "Say again?"

"I talked to their son, Gary, and he was of the opinion that Celeste had had a case of the hots for Brad Thornton."

"Eew," Theresa said without meaning to.

"That makes more sense to me. A *little* bit more. It would explain why Al was so pissed. But Thornton and Celeste . . ."

"She's too old for him. Way too old." She hadn't told Damon any of her and Jerry's speculations about Thornton, but heard the dislike that had become utter loathing shine through clearly in her words.

He heard it too. "Something I should know?"

"I . . . I don't know. It might not be for me to say, it might not be true. But I can't see a guy like Thornton going for Celeste Haverley. Remember last night, how he was coming on to Dani? Celeste wouldn't have been his type."

"I got the impression he was covering, hiding something," Damon said. "Maybe I should talk to him again. But if you do know something, it might help."

"What, and make an enemy of the richest man in town? Who's also my next-door neighbor?"

"I'm not in Brad Thornton's pocket."

She flushed. "I'm sorry, I didn't mean to imply –"

"For what it's worth, I don't much care for the man. Never have. He puts up a good front, but a front's all it is, and it worries me that more people can't see through it. He always treats me like a small-town cop –"

"This *is* a small town."

"Like I am a know-nothing hick," he finished. "I don't think it's occurred to the man that I was a detective with the NYPD. He doesn't think he has to put on much of an act to fool me. He's up to something, hiding something, and it makes me right uneasy."

"Jerry Forrester thinks Thornton may have abused his stepdaughter," she said, staring down at her own folded hands. "He thinks that may have been why she committed suicide."

"Shit," Damon said softly.

"And if it's true," Theresa continued, still looking at her hands, looking at the pale curve of scar just visible beneath the cuff of her blouse, "then she and I had something in common, that might help explain this weird link between us."

He moved closer, bumping Jack to the floor. Taking Theresa's wrist, he turned it over and gently traced the scar. His grip tightened until it was just short of painful. "If I had my way, I'd string up any bastard who went after a kid that way."

She suddenly wanted to turn to Damon, wanted to kiss him, wanted to lose herself in the warmth and security of his arms. But not like this. Not when he was looking at her scar, thinking about how it got there. Not when she was feeling low and soiled, damaged goods. She'd gotten over the worst of that years ago, but bits of it kept creeping back.

"What's going to happen to Gary Haverley?" she asked, retrieving her hand and hiding the scar against the leg of her jeans. "He's not eighteen yet, is he?"

Damon let her change the subject. "I drove him down to Arcata this afternoon. His aunt lives there. She's a department secretary at the university."

"Claudia?"

"You know her?"

"She was one of April and Sandy's friends. April used to babysit me, so sometimes all three of them would come over. They'd do each other's nails, do mine too, make me feel like one of their group. Claudia was the bookish one."

"That's her, all right. She's going to take him in. I think it'll be good for him in the long run."

"How's he doing?"

"He comes across as a tough guy, handling it, puts on a 'good riddance' attitude about his dad. But he's shaken up, you bet. I asked if he wanted to see McGuire but he said no. Wouldn't fit his image."

"If he told Kel about the roses, the whole town would get quarantined for craziness," Theresa said glumly.

"I don't think he would. He's got other things on his mind. We're the ones fixated on the roses, remember? You, me, and Jerry Forrester."

"And my dad. I thought you didn't believe me."

"Didn't want to. Tried not to. But when they pulled Celeste Haverley out of that car . . . sex and death, just like you said. Right then, I believed everything you said, and felt ashamed I didn't accept it right from the start."

"Why? You hardly know me."

"But well enough to know you don't lie, and you're not nuts."

"That's a relief," she laughed shakily. "I must be sane, right, because they say a lunatic never worries about her sanity and I've done nothing but worry ever since I came here."

"There's one thing I want you to keep in mind," he said, capturing her hands again. "I told you yesterday and I'll tell you again now. You're not alone."

"Dear God, was that only yesterday?"

"We're in it together, and we'll get through it. Together."

She wanted again to kiss him, and this time didn't let anything stop her. She leaned over and pressed her lips to his, feeling his surprise and pleasure. He put one arm around her, his palm against the small of her back, and returned the kiss with a forthright intensity that left her gasping.

"Wow," she murmured when she drew away. "That was . . . sudden."

"But not unpleasant, I hope."

"Definitely not."

Jack shot to his feet and stood stiff-legged with his fur on end, then jumped onto Theresa's lap and landed badly, skidding on his hind claws and digging into her jeans. She cried out in surprise, her elbow striking the mug that had been resting on the arm of the couch. It smashed on the floor, spraying shards of ceramic and splashes of chocolate-toffee cocoa.

"Hey!" Damon exclaimed. He grabbed for Jack just as the cat sprang toward the back of the couch. "What's gotten into y—owch!" as Jack's head darted around and his teeth sank into the meaty part of Damon's thumb.

The flames leapt and flickered, fading briefly from warm orange to a faded, somehow cold yellow-blue. A draft chilled the back of Theresa's neck and brought goosebumps to her arms. Jack bolted up the stairs and vanished.

"Something's here," Theresa said. She rose, and Damon stood beside her. "Glory?"

At that, at the calling of the dead child's name, the house erupted in a scream of pure terror and agony. The windows shook. Damon's mug shattered too. Theresa's manuscript lifted from the table and took to the air in a whirlwind of pages. Upstairs, doors banged repeatedly open and shut. Jack blurred past them in an orange streak headed for the kitchen.

The fire gusted out, and ashes swirled up from the hearth. For a moment, they hung in the air and took on a shape, the sooty black image of a rose. Then the image burst apart into a fine grit of ash falling to the carpet.

Silence descended, silence except for Theresa's and Damon's rapid breathing. The sense of presences vanished. They realized they were holding onto each other as if caught in a storm, which in a way they'd been, though not a storm like anything they'd ever experienced before.

"Even if I didn't before, I sure would now," Damon said softly.

"There were two," Theresa said. "I felt it."

"So did I. Something . . . "

"Evil," she finished. "Something evil. And then Glory. She drove it off."

"I don't think you should stay here alone," Damon said.

"I can't leave. I can't run from this. I'm in it, and I have to stay."

"Let me run home and grab a few things, and —"

"Damon —"

"I'll sleep on the couch —"

"Damon, I'll be okay —"

"No way, Theresa. I'm in it too, now more than ever."

"Well . . . okay, if you insist."

"I insist. Want to come with me? I'll only be a few minutes."

"No, I'll start cleaning up." She looked in dismay at the scattered pages of her manuscript. "It'll take a while. But . . . do you go by Nate's on your way home?"

"The tavern? Sure."

"I'm worried about Dani. I know it doesn't make sense, but I don't want to see what happened to Sandy and Celeste happen to her. Doc Kensington says he told her to stay home from work tonight, but if Dani's anything like she used to be, she'll do just the opposite. Would you mind stopping by Nate's and seeing if she's there, if she's okay?"

"Will do. And then it might be a good idea, tomorrow maybe, to go around and talk to some of the others. The ones who've had this fever. Just on the off chance that there is something to it that connects to the rest of this." He kissed her quickly on the corner of the mouth. "Back soon. Be careful."

"I will. You, too."

He grinned at her and touched the brim of an imaginary hat, and the idea rose in her mind that they must sound just like the schoolmarm and the sheriff, her bidding him good-bye as he left to track down the rustlers and outlaws. It brought a smile to her face.

The smile faded, though, once he was gone and she was alone in the house.

* * *

No!

It could not be! It **would** *not be!*

His rage filled him until he thought he might simply fly apart, explode into a thousand furious pieces. He wanted to lash out, to crush and rend and rip and savage until there was nothing left of Damon Blake except for a sodden red heap that had once been a man.

But he couldn't.

Couldn't touch Blake. Not yet.

The only way he would be able to do it depended on a condition that he could not tolerate. He wanted to kill Blake before that came to pass.

She was his!

Didn't she know? Didn't she sense it?

Soon, she would find out about the gifts he was giving. But such a demanding woman! It wearied him, it wearied her. The energy required was considerable, and they both should have more time to recover in between. Time that he didn't want to waste. He had to prove himself soon, make himself known to her soon. He had never wanted a woman the way he wanted Theresa Zane.

Except once, and that woman had been forever beyond his reach. He shied away from even thinking about it, unwilling to bear the slinking guilt of his frustrated attempts, his failure.

Blake had to go.

He couldn't do it himself, but there were other means, weren't there? A nudge here and there . . .

The other women were nothing to him, idle trinkets that he collected in his pursuit of his true objective. But now he realized that their urges could come in handy.

It would be less satisfying than doing it himself, quicker than he would have preferred . . .

By this time tomorrow, Damon Blake would be dead.

And as for Theresa . . . he would have to do more. Even if it meant pushing both of them to the limit of their strength. He was determined to prove to her that he was the only one for her.

The only one.

* * *

"Aren't you going to take these cuffs off?" Dani Kensington said, shifting her shoulders and hearing the chain clink between her wrists.

"Maybe after I've searched you," Damon Blake replied, leaning close. "Thoroughly."

"Don't you touch me," she commanded, but even as she said it she moved her body in ways meant to tantalize.

"You have the right to remain silent," he replied, and ripped off her shirt.

She was braless beneath. With her hands behind her back, it caused her chest to jut forward dramatically. As she lunged against the cuffs, she was very aware of how her firm, full breasts bounced.

He filled his hands with them, his deep brown skin contrasting sharply with the pale globes and coral-pink nipples. "You don't seem to be concealing anything here!"

"Oh, you son of a bitch!" she moaned, writhing.

"Shut up." He went to work on the rest of her clothes, and in minutes she was stark naked, face against a wall with her legs braced wide apart.

She turned her head to the side, pressing her cheek to the wall. Out of the corner of her eye, she could see the rest of the squad room. Uniformed officers, young and sexy all, stood watching as Damon groped down her long legs. Watching with great appreciation. And waiting. Waiting their turn.

Chained, wickedly humiliated, helpless. Her pulse was racing, her body on fire.

Damon moved up again, squeezing her thighs, cupping her buttocks. Then his fingers probed between her thighs, over silky hair and satiny flesh. She gasped and pushed her hips back, rubbing against his hand.

Dani cried out in frustration as he released her and stood. She saw his face nearing her own. There was a devilish glint in his eyes, a cruel smile twisting his good looks. He grabbed her roughly and spun her around, throwing her face-down across a desk littered with citations and arrest reports. She started to get up but was driven back down as his weight came down atop her.

The other cops closed in, many already sporting huge erections, some handling batons in extremely suggestive ways.

Damon entered her from behind with one swift thrust. She cried out again, but in frenzied passion this time. He held her down and rocked and thrust until she was overcome by a savage orgasm. As she voiced her cries, another cop silenced her by filling her mouth with hot, throbbing flesh.

The rest of them surrounded her. Hands all over her body. Mouths on her, greedy and eager.

Dani Kensington descended into a frenzy of overwhelming lust.

* * *

Theresa had gotten everything cleaned up and was just putting the knocked-over phone back on the hook when it rang, startling her so that she promptly knocked it back off the desk.

She grabbed up the receiver, expecting it to be Damon with bad news. Instead, it was Jerry Forrester, sounding a little doped up but strangely excited.

"Mizzane! Hey! Why didn't you tell me?"

"About what?"

"About Nick Diamond!"

"Nick?"

"Did you used to go out with him?"

"Good Lord, that was ages ago! How did you find out?"

"I knew it was you! I saw your picture! Wow, Mizzane, you were a fox! Not that you aren't now . . . I mean . . . uh . . . listen, I was going to call you earlier, right after I saw it, but they gave me my pill and I cruised off into la-la land for a while, and then Dad and Jenny came over, they say hi, by the way –"

"Jerry, you're rambling."

"Am I? Sorry. It's the drugs. I feel all disconnected and shit. Sorry, Mizzane, but I do. Like my head's doing what my stomach does when you hit a bump in the road and it goes kinda *whoop* . . . how come there's no word for that? Everybody knows what it feels like, but there's no word for it."

Theresa chuckled. "Stay with it, Jerry. What's on your mind? And where in the world did you see a picture of me and Nick? It wasn't even Diamond back then, he was still Nick Diamant. He changed it around the same time he started his band. I guess you're familiar with Scarlet Angel."

"Oh. Oh, jeez."

"What?"

"You don't know. You haven't heard."

"Haven't heard what?"

"Mizzane, Nick Diamond is dead."

"Nick? Dead?" She searched herself for grief and found none, only a stunned but not particularly shocked acceptance. "Overdose?"

"Someone killed him last night in a hotel in San Diego. It was really bad. It's been all over the news. They don't know who did it. I was watching a special about him on MTV, and they showed a photo of him at a pool party."

"That one," Theresa said, nodding to herself.

"So, I'm like devastated and everything. I mean, here you knew him, and now he's dead. What a pisser!"

Headlights flashed across the front windows. Damon was back. In her ear, Jerry was waxing eloquent about how much he adored each and every Scarlet Angel album, how a couple years back he and Gary had lied to their folks and hopped a bus to Oakland to see them in concert and wound up sitting in the damn rafters but it was still the greatest show he'd ever seen . . .

She interrupted him kindly. "Jerry, I really have to get going."

"Oh, sure, okay, Mizzane. But can we talk about it sometime? I want to hear all about what it was like, you know, dating somebody famous."

"He wasn't famous then, and I'm sure it'd be a disappointing story. Still, if you really want to hear all that ancient history –"

"Yeah!"

"I'll come visit you tomorrow. We'll trade. I'll tell you about Nick when he was in high school, and you can fill me in on the latest."

She hung up and went to meet Damon at the door.

*   *   *

Megan turned slowly toward him, the wind that had been blowing her hair back from her face now tossing it around her shoulders like a torrent of liquid flame. "You came back," she said in dulcet wonder.

"I couldn't stay away." Alaric swept his gaze adoringly over her.

"What of Eleanor? You are to be married —"

He shook his ebon-maned head. "No. I will not marry her, not if the king himself orders it. You are the one I want, the one I love, the one I must have, else die!"

"Oh, Alaric!"

"Come with me and we'll quit this land, begin anew in another place." He sought the delectable sweetness of her lips in a kiss that seared her entire being and fanned alight the flames of the passion that had lain hidden within her since the moment she first set eyes upon his tall and magnificent form.

"Yes, my love, yes!" she cried, giving herself willingly into his embrace. His hands encircled her waist as he bent to kiss the hollow of her throat, the milk-satin smoothness of her shoulders above the emerald silk of her gown.

"Megan, my desire, my heart, my angel," he murmured against her flesh, his words caressing her soul just as his hands caressed her body. "Be mine for all time!"

She could not speak, only gasp in wonder and joy, carried away on the delicious tide as at long last his arms enfolded her.

*   *   *

He awoke with the sense of being in a strange place. Before he opened his eyes, he could tell that the blanket wasn't his own, that the soft surface beneath him was not his bed. The smell wasn't home, either.

The Zane house. He was in the Zane house.

Damon Blake opened his eyes to a pair of pale green ones that glowed with inner eerie radiance.

"Huh!"

Jack gave him the sort of contemptuous look that only cats can truly master.

His heart thumping, Damon sat up. "You gave me a fright, fella."

The living room was dark except for the thin shedding of light from the half-open door to the kitchen and the hallway upstairs. He picked up his watch from the coffee table and brought it close to his face. Three in the morning.

Jack pawed at the dangling watchband.

"Sorry, fella. It's not playtime." He stretched back out and fluffed the blanket over himself.

Jack hopped up, and Damon stroked him, expecting him to curl up and get comfy. Instead, the cat simply stood there, dead-center on his chest, and looked at him.

He shut his eyes and sought to recapture sleep, but the feeling of Jack's unwavering gaze wouldn't let him relax. He pushed Jack down, but the cat responded by jumping to the back of the couch and continuing to stare.

Fully awake now, Damon sat up again. In this place, it wasn't easy to ignore the weirdness of a cat's behavior. Not after what he'd witnessed earlier. He remembered hearing something about animals being sensitive to paranormal activity, and at the time he'd dismissed it as hogwash. Now, though, he was inclined to give it the benefit of the doubt.

When he got up, Jack trotted to the bottom of the stairs with his tail held high and meowed inquisitively.

His gun was locked in his car. Given the poltergeist display with the doors and Theresa's papers, he didn't want to see a loaded gun spinning through the air. Besides, he figured that whatever threats were in this house, a gun wasn't the answer.

Whatever Jack felt, Damon was now beginning to feel too. Like pressure, the flat and heavy weight of air before a thunderstorm. This wasn't the violent burst of a presence like before. This was more subtle. Insidious.

He followed the cat up the stairs. A linen cupboard and four doors, all closed. One was a bathroom. One was the bedroom Theresa said had been her brother's before he went to college and had then become her mother's sewing parlor. One was the room with the windowseat. And the last was the master suite. Theresa's room.

Jack went to Theresa's door and turned to regard Damon expectantly.

"I think he's trying to tell us something," he muttered to himself, mimicking countless movies with super-intelligent and heroic dogs. Then the darker realization came to him that Jack really was trying to warn him. That Theresa was in danger.

He tapped lightly, not wanting to startle her.

No reply.

A little louder. "Theresa?"

When there was still no answer, he tried the knob. It opened easily.

The curtains were open and the rain had ended, filling the room with pale moonlight. A handful of it was caught in Theresa's upturned and outflung palm, a sight that struck Damon with a powerful and erotic yearning. His gaze traveled from that hand to the rest of her.

She was on her back, the covers drawn to her waist, wearing quilted satin pajamas. Her hair was a black torrent over the pillow. Her lips were slightly parted, her lashes lay duskily against her cheeks . . . but her face had an unhealthy slackness to it, a pallor of grey. She didn't seem to be breathing.

He groaned under his breath, sure that when he touched her wrist he would find the cold flesh and stilled veins of a corpse.

The sense of pressure was stronger than ever, so strong that Damon had to force himself to draw air into his lungs. He took Theresa's hand, which was cool but not cold, and felt for her pulse. It was there, but slow, unnaturally slow.

"Theresa. Theresa, wake up."

She didn't move.

He shook her, and she lolled limply.

"Theresa!"

Her chest hitched, and she inhaled long and deep. Behind closed lids, her eyes rolled. Her fingers twitched.

He shook her harder, called her name again. Jack hunkered at the corner of the bed, watching him anxiously.

The pressure in the room grew until it was a palpable force, nearly pushing him down. His legs wanted to buckle, drop him to the floor. He felt Theresa shiver in her strange sleep and became aware of how cold the room was. Freezing. His breath puffed out in clouds, and the bare skin of his back and chest prickled into goosebumps.

"Let her go, damn you," he said through gritted teeth. "Let her go!"

Theresa winced, made a small sound that was part moan and part whimper.

Crushing. Cold. Dark. The feeling of being far down in an oceanic trench, isolated and alone, surrounded by sunless unmerciful water where pallid eyeless creatures swam.

"No," Damon said, just the effort of getting that one word out almost more than he could handle.

Then it broke. All at once. Gone.

The room warmed. The pressure dissipated. Theresa coughed and stirred, clutching at the blankets to tuck them around her shoulders. Her throat clicked as she swallowed.

"Theresa? Can you hear me?"

"Lemme 'lone, Mom, it's Saturday." Her voice was low and slurred. She rubbed her eyes, opened them. "Damon?"

Relief, huge and sudden, washed over him. "Are you all right?"

Confused, bleary, she peered at him. "What are you doing here? What time is it?"

"Are you all right?" he persisted.

"I'm tired," she complained, rolling away from him. "It's the middle of the night."

"Theresa, listen. Something was going on here. Something was in here with you. I almost couldn't wake you up."

"Damon, I just want to sleep." She burrowed into her pillow.

"I don't think you should be alone."

"Fine," she mumbled, scootching to one side. "There's room."

"Uh . . . that's not quite what I meant."

Theresa sighed and flopped onto her back. "Damon, what? It's late, I'm tired, I feel like crap. Can't we talk about it in the morning?"

She did look tired, he had to agree. Beyond tired. Not exactly sick, but drawn. Drained.

"I think you should see Doc Kensington."

"I don't like him."

"Some other doctor, then. I'll drive you."

"Don't need a doctor." Her words were turning thick again, her eyes only barely open. "Just need to rest."

Damon hesitated. What now? Bundle her up and take her to the hospital? And suppose they couldn't find anything physically wrong with her? Suppose they agreed with her, said she just needed some rest? They wouldn't believe him if he started talking about presences and pressure.

He decided to wait until morning, and watch over her until then.

After all, it wasn't as if any harm had been done.

He hoped . . .

* * *

Paul Kowalski hated working the night shift.

His boss knew it, though, the little whoreson. Trying to force him into retirement by making his job as unpleasant as possible.

Well, he was not about to retire! He was only sixty-three, still strong as an ox, more than able to keep up with men half his age. He was the best mechanic in town, hell, in all of Southern California, and they should be begging him to stay rather than trying to push him out.

The Joshua Flats Speedway was about the only thriving business in town, except for the burger place and arcade where the kids hung out. And that was the last place you'd find Paul Kowalski, let me tell you! Kids. No-good punks, all of them.

At three in the morning, the Speedway was all but deserted. The bleachers rose stark and empty against the vast star-pocked sky that domed the Mojave. The oval track was a black scar in the dusty earth, and beyond it were the sculpted hills and trenches where they ran motocross in the summer.

Only a few other sad sacks had the bad luck to be pulling the overnight detail. A couple of them claimed to prefer it, saying it was better to put in their hours out of the heat of the day. Paul thought they were idiots. Who wanted to sleep with the sun turning your cruddy trailer into an oven, so you woke up with the sweat running down your body and the sheets soaked?

There had been a demolition derby over the weekend, and the yard was full of mangled hulks. Paul was going over one searching for salvageable and reusable parts, just getting fed up enough with T.J.'s music to order the kid to turn it off – there was another one, a no-good punk, a longhair dropout delinquent – when his toolbox fell over with a discordant clang.

"You okay over there, Paul?" T.J. called from a couple cars over.

The kid was clever with his hands, Paul had to give him credit for that – not that he'd say as much out loud – and did decent work when he wasn't sneaking off to the shed for a smoke. Paul himself had quit eight years ago, regretted it every goddam day but wasn't about to cave in and go crawling back to Marlboro Country.

"Paul?"

Damn kid. Couldn't he tell when he was being ignored?

His back protested as he bent to pick up his toolbox. It was hurting worse than ever lately, the pills they gave him didn't do a thing as far as he was concerned, but he didn't dare make a peep about it because his boss would be happy for another reason to see him out the door and down the road.

Some life. Some goddam life. Wife left him and soaked him for every cent she possibly could. Good-bye to the nice air-conditioned house in Bakersfield, good-bye to his beloved and meticulously-cared-for '58 T-Bird. Hello Joshua Flats, hello trailer, hello piece-of-junk pickup. Some goddam life, yes sir.

He headed back to the car he'd been working on, and frowned when he saw a large shape looming nearby. "That you, Sas?"

What the hell was he wearing? A big black coat . . . no, a cape? And who'd let Sas out this late? Big as a truck, sure, but he had the brain of a six-year-old. His old aunties were always really careful with him.

But it had to be Sas. Who else could it be? No one in town even came close to that size. And, like a little boy, Sas always got excited about Halloween. Paul supposed it was possible Sas could have snuck out to show off his new mask.

"Little early for costumes, huh, Sas?"

Then the figure turned to face him. Paul stopped short and stared.

Not Sas. No way on earth.

The eyes . . . God and sonny Jesus, the *eyes –!*

He turned to run.

He was struck from behind, the impact driving him into the side of a car. Had his head struck the door panel, it would have knocked him out and spared him a good deal of pain, but his upper body went through the hole where the passenger side window had been.

Stuck clear to the elbows, arms pinned at his sides, he craned his neck to watch as the figure approached. He heard T.J.'s radio shut off in a hurried snap, heard the kid's alarmed cry and answering voices from elsewhere on the grounds.

No. What he'd though he'd seen couldn't be real. Some psycho, that was it. Escaped from an asylum. Strong, yeah, freakishly strong and crazy as the livelong day.

Paul kicked as hard as he could, aiming for the costumed freak coming up behind him and trying to thrust his body forward through the window in the same motion. His back went out with a feeling like a champagne cork popping out of the bottle.

Huge hands closed firmly around his ankles. Not hands. Gloves. Hot coarse leathery gloves.

He was too paralyzed to move, but not paralyzed enough to have lost sensation. His legs were lifted straight out into a Y-shape, giving Paul the mental impression of a wishbone about to be broken.

Instead of being ripped right up the middle, he was dragged backwards out of the car. Paul's face smashed into the dirt and gravel, his upper plate shooting out and three of his lower teeth cracking off at the gumline.

He was flipped over. The blood from his shattered nose ran down his throat. He tried to fight back, tried to do something, anything, but all his signals were scrambled.

"Somebody's beating up Paul Kowalski!" he heard T.J. yell, and then the kid burst into view between two rows of junkers. T.J. skidded to a halt, the wrench he'd had upraised like a weapon falling from nerveless fingers.

Fists that felt like iron mallets hammered at Paul's chest, his head. The maniac drew back for a moment as if surveying his handiwork, flexing his gloved fingers in an almost thoughtful manner.

Paul had plenty of time to study those gloves as he struggled for breath. They were tipped with claws. Short and thick claws. Dark, not ivory. Bearlike. More blunted than razored. Suited for gouging, not slicing.

The claws came down.

Tore my shirt, he thought. *Son of a bitch tore my new shirt.*

He laboriously raised his head and saw that it wasn't just his shirt, but that he'd been opened up. His insides were bulging out through the pale hairy skin of his belly.

The psycho leaned toward the exposed glisten of Paul's organs as if to eat him alive, then jerked up as if he'd heard something besides the clamor of approaching men.

An enraged, cheated sound issued from the snarling jaws of the mask. "Nooooooo!"

The gloves hands closed around Paul's throat. He felt the push of its claws on the sides of his neck and almost welcomed it, almost welcomed the end of the terrible pain.

Fading . . .

Paul was fading out, the shape over him losing definition, losing cohesion. He could even see the stars through it, the harsh white shopping-cart shape of the Big Dipper.

Fading . . . and gone . . . except for a fluttering black shadow that landed on his upturned cheek in a velvety butterfly kiss. Incredibly, insanely, he smelled perfume.

Gone . . .

But the pain was still there, and the shouts of the rest of the overnight shift rang loudly across the empty Speedway.

* * *

Theresa pulled herself reluctantly out of sleep to slap at the alarm clock.

Movement, someone else in her room, brought her awake in a hurry. She looked across at Damon Blake, who was sprawled in the chair by the window. He blinked owlishly at her as if he was as unsure where he was as she was about what he was doing there.

He straightened up gingerly, and she realized he'd spent half the night in that chair. That brought back foggy memories of him coming into her room, trying to talk to her. She hadn't wanted to listen, hadn't wanted to do anything but sleep.

"Morning," she said.

"Yes, ma'am." He was bare-chested, wearing pajama pants in a rich yellow color that set off his smooth brown skin gorgeously. He grinned a little guiltily. "Didn't mean to conk out on you."

"Watching over me?" She laughed at the idea, then stopped as she saw his expression. "What happened last night?"

He told her.

* * *

"We've got another one!" Mark Gladstone announced, waving a sheaf of papers.

"No, *we* don't," Derrek Blake said, reaching for the papers anyway. "Need I remind you, partner, it's not our case any more."

"Yeah, yeah, I know . . . the feds take over all the good ones. I knew I should have stuck with the Bureau."

"You'd never make it. Imperturbable isn't in your genetic makeup. So who's Number Five?"

"Paul Kowalski, and he breaks our pattern wide open. Diamond and the others were all about the same age, late twenties and early thirties. This guy's sixty-three."

"You're sure it's the same killer?"

"Same type of attack – beaten and torn all to hell, by weapons unknown. Black rose left on the scene. And this time, there's a witness!"

"So tell me, already."

"Witness is a sixteen-year-old greasemonkey, drug test negative –"

Derrek massaged his temples. "If they did a drug test, what he said must have been crazy enough to make them think they needed to."

"The kid – T.J. Lawton – said the killer was wearing a costume. Cape, mask, gloves, boots. Made up to look like a horror-movie monster. Said the guy tore Kowalski apart with nothing but his hands, then disappeared."

"Got away?"

"No." Mark paused dramatically for emphasis. "Disappeared. Like a ghost."

"Oh, come on."

"That's what he said."

"Did anybody else see the perp?"

"Just Kowalski, and his story backs up the kid's."

"*Kowalski's* report?"

"He survived, confirmed what the kid said. Mask. Gloves. Cape. They airlifted him to a hospital in Lancaster."

"Pennsylvania?"

"No, California. Happened in one of those tumbleweed towns in the Mojave. Apparently amazing he was still alive. Our killer unzipped his guts." Mark reached for the phone. "Lemme see if I can track down the hospital –"

Derrek pushed the disconnect button. "Lay off, Gladstone. The captain chewed your butt yesterday for calling long-distance to San Diego."

"You know I had to! When we heard about Nick Diamond, killed the same way as the others . . . how they were withholding certain details from the press to weed out cranks and fake confessions . . . I had to check and see if our black rose was one of those details."

"And you damn near made yourself a suspect," Derrek pointed out. "You know how twitchy they can get when a celebrity, even one like Nick Diamond, gets killed."

"But if Kowalski's still alive, he might be more willing to talk to us."

"Why? Why would he care about two cops from New York?"

"Well . . . because we believe him."

"Do we?"

"Don't we?"

"Just what do we believe? That some guy in a superhero suit and a monster mask is going around the country killing people?"

"Look, Derrek. *Something* is going on here. Something downright weird. Five attacks in under two weeks, all over the map. How's he getting there so fast? Why these particular victims? There's a link. There's got to be. Kowalski and the Lawton kid are the only ones who've seen anything. We have to talk to them."

"Mark, I'm going to talk real slow," he said. "It. Is. Not. Our. Case. Got it? The Spencer murder happened here, but the others were way outside our jurisdiction. The captain and the feds made it very clear that we were to let the big boys handle it. *Capishe?*"

Mark sighed grumpily. "There *is* a link."

"Let it go, Gladstone. We've got work of our own to do."

"What's the matter with you, Blake? Don't you want to be famous? Don't you want to be one of the men who caught the Black Rose Killer?"

Derrek groaned.

"Your name in the paper, your face on TV, think how proud your mother would be!"

"And the press ready to crucify you over the slightest mistake," Derrek said. "The public howling for *your* blood when the killer strikes again. Not to mention getting written up for failing to stay out of it like we were told."

"You have no sense of adventure."

"And you, my friend, have no sense of reality. This is our job, plenty of adventure without you trying to turn it into a cross between *The X-Files* and one of those buddy-cop movies."

"Why not? Denzel could play you –"

"And the kid who was Doogie Howser can be you. Leave it, Mark. We've got other work to do."

Mark blew out a breath in a disgusted snort, took the papers back from Derrek, and shoved them in a drawer. "Okay, okay."

"Good."

"Leo."

"What?"

"Not the Doogie Howser kid. Leonardo DiCaprio."

"Dream *on!*" Derrek Blake laughed.

* * *

He fought to regain control of himself.

For the first time, failure.

He'd been balked a few times, yes. Even blocked, held at bay. Denied. Infuriating as these things were, he had come to understand that there were defenses against him. Defenses to keep him from gaining the foothold that he needed.

When that happened, he simply accepted it and moved on. Such occurrences were rare, and he was usually able to convince himself that the women in question hadn't mattered all that much anyway. Most of the time, that was true.

But this . . . to be forced away when his work was unfinished . . . such a thing had never happened before. To have it happen now, when he was so close . . .

Theresa Zane wasn't like the other women. She was the one he wanted. The others were idle fancies. She was his chosen.

Alone, she couldn't stop him. He was sure of that. As rich and enticing as her spirit was, she was still just a woman. And women were trained by long millennia of society to bury and ignore their power.

He needed her. He would have her. No one was going to prevent that.

With Damon Blake dead, she would be weakened and distressed. She would be vulnerable. She would be his.

* * *

18

As they climbed out of his car in the Municipal Building parking lot, Theresa wanted to kiss Damon good-bye but knew it was inappropriate here in the very shadow of his workplace.

She settled for sharing a warm smile with him instead, and then they went their separate ways. He climbed the stairs and went inside, while she headed for Ruth Edwards' shop.

Part of her mind tried to tell her that it was wrong to be enjoying what she felt for Damon. In the midst of all this madness, how could she be sure that anything either of them felt was real? On the other hand, she needed him as an anchor against that very madness.

He was right. They were in it together. Maybe when everything was sorted out, when they'd figured out what was going on and made sense of the eerie events of the previous night, when all was well in Trinity Bay again, they would discover that they had nothing in common. For the time being, though, having someone to trust made her stronger.

For Me, Ruth's shop, was open. The string of tiny brass bells jingled as Theresa entered, but their festive sound did nothing to offset a sudden wave of apprehension. She wasn't sure which would be worse – finding out there *was* a link between the fever and the roses, or finding out there *wasn't*.

There was.

She stopped dead in her tracks, her gaze fixed on a rattan wastecan at the end of the counter. A tattered piece of cloth was flopped over the edge, a green scarf sewn with small black flowers.

Black roses.

"Be right there!" Ruth's voice, sounding cheery but a little strained, called from behind the curtain leading to the back room.

"Okay," Theresa called back. She bent and picked up the scarf, gingerly, as if it might suddenly coil around her arm like a snake.

It was cut in several places, attacked by scissors, but she could still see that there was a single dot of red in the center of each rose. No more than a dot of thread, not even visible until you looked at it closely, but there it was.

"Theresa, is that —" Ruth pushed through the curtain, saw Theresa with the scarf in her hands, and recoiled. She snatched it away, balled it up, and stuffed it back in the wastecan, pawing a layer of papers over it. "That's trash."

She'd wondered how she was going to bring up the subject, but there was no point fiddling around with small talk now.

"What did it make you do, Ruth? When you saw the rose. What did it make you do?"

Ruth's eyes bulged and her throat worked convulsively, but she said, "I don't know what you mean, Theresa."

"Please, Ruth." She touched the older woman's hand. "I won't think you're crazy. Something's going on, the rose is a part of it, and I have to figure it out. Please tell me. Something about sex, right?" She remembered her first visit to the shop, and drew in a breath. "You and Malachi —"

"No!" Her laugh was brittle and forced. "Nothing like that. This is silly."

"It's important, Ruth. I wouldn't ask, wouldn't pry, if it wasn't."

"I'm telling you, there's nothing."

"What's that? Nothing?" She pointed at the wastebasket.

"Oh, I didn't like how it turned out, so I threw it away."

"After you cut it to pieces?" Theresa persisted. "Ruth, I *heard* you last week. And I saw Mal on Sunday. Something happened between the two of you, and it's related to those damned roses!"

"It was only a dream!" Ruth snapped. "I should have known, but it seemed so real! I should have known that Mal would never do things like that. Why would he? Why would I even want him to? All just a dream, Theresa. I don't want anything more to do with it."

"A dream?"

"I don't want to talk about it any more."

"Why the scarf, Ruth? Tell me that, at least."

"I don't know why." Her laugh this time was high and wavering, almost lunatic. "But I do know I wouldn't leave it in the house, how's that for silly? I didn't want Toby to find it. Didn't want him anywhere near it! I should burn it, that's what I should do!"

"Why?"

"It's dirty," Ruth whispered. "Dirty, and evil." She shook herself as if waking from a doze, and smiled brightly. "So, tell me, what brings you by? Still got your eye on that blouse?"

"As a matter of fact, I do," Theresa said with a bright smile of her own. "I've decided I want it."

"Terrific!" Ruth folded the cinnamon, ivory, and violet top. "Let me find you a bag for this."

"How've you been?" Theresa asked. "Didn't you have that fever that's been going around?"

"Not going around very fast, and not much to worry about. I was only sick for a day, and have felt just great ever since." She accepted Theresa's money, made change, and gave her the bag.

"Except for the dreams," she prompted.

"Oh, well, that," she said in an of-no-consequence tone, leaving Theresa with the weird feeling that Ruth didn't even remember the conversation they'd just had.

She decided not to push it. "Hey, when they let Dad out of the hospital, we'd love to have the three of you over. I'll give you a call, okay?"

"We'd love to." Ruth winked. "And if you wanted to invite any other guests, like, oh, say, Police Chief Blake, it wouldn't bother us at all."

Theresa laughed self-consciously. "Uh-oh. Is it all over town?"

All at once, the levity went out of Ruth's mood. "Not without Celeste to pass it along. Isn't that the most terrible thing?"

"It is," she agreed.

"I swear, I don't know what this town is coming to," Ruth said. "First Sandy Forrester, now this. We must've been overdue for some bad luck. Ah, listen to me, I sound like Shauna Davis."

"How is Mrs. Davis?" Theresa asked slowly, a thought coming to her. "Seems like everyone else who was at our little cleaning party came down with the fever."

"Healthy as a horse, though if you ask her she'll give you a list of complaints as long as your arm."

"That doesn't fit . . . but then, I haven't had it either," she mused.

"What, Theresa?"

"Oh . . . nothing. Thanks, Ruth. Tell Malachi and Toby hi for me."

"I will. And if you or your dad need anything, we're here."

The two of them smiled at each other.

* * *

Damon Blake finished faxing the county office all of the reports on the Haverley accident and sifted through the more recent complaints. Not very many, thank God. Mrs. Reilly griping about the Peterson's dogs again, someone tried to jimmy open a pay phone out at North Valley, and a domestic disturbance.

"Hey, Scott!"

Scott James, a powerhouse of a second-in-command who more than made up for in dedication what he lacked in height, glanced up. "Yeah, boss?"

"What's this about Rand Kostas and Nancy Ellsworth?"

"Oh, one of the neighbors called in. Heard raised voices and thought there might be trouble. But Rand sure hadn't been beating on Nancy." Scott chuckled and shook his head. "If anything, the other way around."

"Yeah?"

"I guess you just don't expect to see a guy like Rand Kostas with rope burns on his wrists and ankles," Scott grinned. "Turned out they just got a little carried away with their game."

"Hunh," Damon said, mulling that one over.

The phone rang, and Scott was closest. "Trinity Bay P.D., Officer James speaking. Hey, Dani, how's it going? No, oh, damn, really? Okay, we'll check it out."

"Dani Kensington?" Damon asked as Scott hung up.

"Says someone broke into Nate's. Busted the fuse box, probably to try and get around the electric lock on the safe. I'll go take a look."

"That's okay, I'll do it. I was meaning to talk to Dani last night anyway, but she wasn't at work."

He crossed the plaza. The sky, heavily overcast to begin with, had now turned to a bruised purple-grey. The rain hadn't started yet, but he could tell by the smell of the mill that it soon would. Could even be that the winter drearies had begun in earnest, and they wouldn't see the sun again until the university offered its spring orientation for prospective freshmen. That, and graduation, guaranteed them several days of blameless blue.

Nate's was dark and silent as he pushed the front door open. The bar didn't open until later, but he knew Dani was in the habit of coming in early to get everything ready and use the computer in the back room. She already did most of the bookkeeping, and everyone knew that when the owner, Tom Harmon, nephew of the original Nate, retired, she would be taking the place over.

"Dani?" he called.

All of his senses snapped to full alertness. Something was wrong here, very wrong. Could be that whoever broke in had still been around, and Dani Kensington was facing more trouble than a possible burglary. He drew his gun and held it low at his side.

"Hello, Damon." Her voice, coming from behind the bar, sounded oddly flat and lifeless.

"Dani, are you okay?"

"Why wouldn't I be?" She stood from where she'd been crouched. The angle was wrong for him to see if anyone else was down there, hiding, maybe threatening and forcing her to talk. Her hair was in bunches and clumps, uncombed. Her eyes glittered in the dimness.

Damon swallowed, unease settling over him like a cloak. He heard nothing else, no furtive rustlings, no indication at all that there was anyone but the two of them in here, yet he was very sure they were both in real danger. "Scott says you had a little trouble here during the night?"

"You could say that. But then, you'd know all about it, wouldn't you?"

"What?" He took an involuntary step back, his hip bumping against a pinball machine that stood dark and silent as an Egyptian monument.

"I just want to know why, Damon," Dani said. "If you liked me, why not say something? Why do what you did?"

"Dani, listen, I —" *don't know what you're talking about,* he'd been going to say, but then he did. Her fever. The rose fever. It had given Sandy Forrester weird ideas about her son, and maybe had given Celeste Haverley weird ideas about her boss. Now it had done something to Dani, involving him.

"Don't lie to me, Damon." She brought up the shotgun, Old Nate's Blunderbuss as the regulars called it, and pointed it at him. "Don't lie to me."

He shifted his body slightly, his gun pressed against his thigh and out of her sight. The thought of having to shoot her made his stomach clench, but his nerves remained cool and his hands were steady. He didn't want to do it, but knew that he could if he had to.

"Okay, I won't." Jesus, that double-barreled Colt was older than dirt, having belonged to Nate's grandpa. Probably hadn't even been fired since then. An antique, carefully maintained but still an antique. If she did shoot, it might well blow up in her face.

"Even if it had just been the two of us, that would have been all right!" Dani said, now showing more animation, distraught though it was. "Why'd you do it there? Why with all the others?"

"Dani, put the gun down."

Had he thought they were alone in here? No. No. There was someone else. Someone watching this little by-play.

A presence. Oh, dear Lord, whatever had been in Theresa's house last night was here now. That same feeling of the air being too thick to breathe, of the room being too cold. As if, at any moment, the darkness might congeal into a solid form with deadly intent.

It was here. It was here and using Dani. Using her to get him out of the way so that Theresa would be on her own and unprotected.

Rather than argue with himself, he simply accepted it and moved on.

"Dani, whatever it was didn't really happen –"

"I know what happened, Damon. I ache all over from what happened. And I bet you thought you could get away with it, too. Who would I call? The cops? Ha! You *are* the cops! Who'd believe me? So I have to take care of this myself. Such a shame. I bet you didn't know that *you* were the one who tried to get into the safe, and when I found out, you tried to shoot me and make it look like a burglar did it. So I did what I could. Self defense."

He threw himself to the side even as she pulled the trigger. The shotgun roared like a wild animal. Glass exploded everywhere as the shot annihilated the pinball machine.

Dani, her face set in a grim mask, shifted her finger to the second trigger.

Training told him one thing – return fire before she could get off that next shot.

Instinct told him another. He jumped forward and grabbed the shotgun just as she fired. The hammer slammed down on the tender web of flesh between thumb and forefinger in a fierce bite.

Damon couldn't keep from yelling, but didn't let the pain stop him. He wrested the shotgun from Dani and shoved her with his free arm.

More glass jingled and crashed to the floor as Dani staggered back against the shelves of bottles. She stared at him, at what she'd done, hands clamped to her face and tugging the skin down into a hag's mask. Her eyes bulged. Her horrified scream trailed off as she fell down in a dead faint.

Once again, Damon felt the heavy and ominous presence vent its rage in a howl before it burst apart and vanished, leaving him alone and unharmed except for the white-hot spears lancing into his hand.

* * *

Travis Zane was sitting up in bed with a magazine when his daughter came in. "Theresa!"

"Hi, Dad."

"I hear you've been having company," he teased.

She grinned, but he noticed it seemed strained. "No wild parties. I told Jerry I'd come by this afternoon – he found out I used to date one of his musical idols and wants all the dirt. So I thought I'd stop in and say hi."

"Well, I've got some good news for you. Doc Kensington is planning to let me out of here day after tomorrow."

"How'd you talk him into that? Or is he sick of your griping already?"

"That could be it." His bantering tone faded. "He wants me to avoid any more shocks."

"So do I!"

"And speaking of shocks, what's been done?"

"The people from the county – Sheriff's department, coroner, I don't know what all – are coming out tomorrow to look at the . . . the bones. They would have been here sooner, but apparently autumn is drug-bust season." She cupped her elbows and looked worried. "They'll probably move her. I don't know if that's a good idea. She's been there so long –"

"Too long," he said gently. "She needs to be put to rest."

"Will they, though? Will she be buried, or will they bag her, tag her, and toss her in a landfill?"

"We'll see to it," he promised. "We'll see that she's taken care of."

"I . . . I took the necklace."

"You touched her? Theresa . . ."

"I had to. Whatever's going on, that necklace is a part of it. I might need it."

"Honey, what are you saying? What do you mean, need it?"

"Oh, Dad, I don't know." She ran her fingers through her hair in a gesture of distress. "But once they take Glory away, I might lose my connection with her. The necklace will let me keep it."

"I'd think you'd be ready to lose it."

"I can't." Speaking in a way that made it very clear she was trying not to alarm him, she told him about the events of the previous night. "Glory helped us, Dad. She's been helping us all along."

He sighed. "Your grandmother used to say there was evil in Trinity Bay. I always thought it was because of how the people treated her, especially Myra Cliffwood, that made her not like the town. But maybe she was right."

"She was right. Dad . . . how old was I when Mom's father, Grandpa Abbey, died?"

"You couldn't have been more than six."

"Did I go to his funeral?"

"Hell, no. Your mother flew back alone. We stayed home. Why?"

"I dreamed it," she said absently, rearranging his get-well cards from the gang at Silver Grove. "The night Jerry Forrester got hurt, I was dreaming that I was locked in a box as punishment for not being sad about my grandfather's death. But it was Glory. Reaching out. It must have been so awful for her."

"It's in the past. Let it go."

"I can't!" Her hands jerked, knocking cards over. "It won't let me go! I have to find out, Dad, and stop it. Somehow. Glory's trying to help, but I don't know what she wants me to do! How can I fight something like this? How can I fight it when I don't even know what it is?"

* * *

"Shit!" Derrek Blake dropped a cup into the stainless-steel sink in the police break room.

"You okay, partner?" Mark Gladstone asked.

"Must've spilled coffee on myself."

"Uh-oh, lawsuit a'comin'!"

Yet his hand was dry and unscalded. He couldn't have spilled. He tried to recall if he'd bumped against the machine while pouring himself a cup, and was sure that he hadn't.

And it didn't *feel* like a burn, either. Felt more like a pinch.

As he studied his flesh, it rose up into a blood blister so purple it was almost black. But after that initial sharp throbbing pain, it hardly hurt at all. Unless he pressed it, which sent sick waves rolling up his arm.

He hadn't done this to himself. He was sure of it.

"Damon?" he wondered aloud.

"Talking to yourself in there?" Mark called.

"Just thinking. I better give my kid brother a call."

"*Kid* brother? I thought you were twins."

"Hey, I'm older by all of six minutes, thanks."

"So why – oh, ah-ha!" Mark crowed. "It's like that, is it? 'In California, a man burns himself. In New York, his brother feels the pain. How? *Read the book!*'"

"Yeah, yeah, yeah," Derrek grumbled. "Laugh your ass off, partner, but I'm still calling him tonight."

"If you can put your mysticism on hold, I just got a fax from the hospital where they took Kowalski. He's dead. Bled out on the operating table."

"This mean you're going to forget about it?"

"No way. There's still the kid. And trust me on this, we haven't heard the last of our Black Rose Killer. You'll see."

Derrek sighed, and went looking for something to put on his hand.

* * *

The town turned out in droves at the news that another of Trinity Bay's women had snapped.

Sandy Forrester had done it in the middle of the night, Celeste Haverley had done it far out on Mill Road, but Dani Kensington had been considerate enough to do it in the center of town right before lunch on a workday. The plaza was crammed with people, the deli next door to Malachi Edwards' bookstore doing a booming business. Not even the steady rain deterred them.

Damon insisted it had been an accident, that Dani had been wound-up with worry about a prowler and fired at him by mistake. That didn't suit the town, though. They wanted to believe that Dani had lost it, which gave them much more interesting conversation.

Theresa had rushed over from the hospital as soon as she heard. Her promise to tell Jerry a very edited version of her brief stint as Nick Diamond's girlfriend would have to wait.

She stood with Damon, her arm around him as Marty Arnes treated his injured hand. She didn't believe his story, knew that he was hiding the truth for Dani's sake as well as to prevent panic. If the idea got out that there was some sort of contagious fever-madness, who knew what might happen?

Her intuition told her that it *all* had to do with her. Every one of the women who'd come down with the fever had been around her right before they started showing symptoms. She was . . . like a carrier of some sort. So she stayed at Damon's side and tried to keep well away from everyone else.

Dani Kensington had been taken to the hospital, having fainted or collapsed from shock, either way landing in a pile of broken bottles. She would need several stitches but wasn't seriously hurt.

Nate's was roped off with yellow police-barricade tape but the door was propped open, giving the crowd a good view of the wreckage of the pinball machine.

Theresa shuddered and looked away. If Damon had been a split second slower, that would have been him.

Whatever it was, it was using her as well as Dani. She realized that now. Her listlessness, her constant tiredness, were somehow tied in to all of this.

Or . . . was it *her*? Was she somehow doing it? Reaching out with her mind?

No, that was insane. She might not have liked Celeste Haverley, but Ruth and Dani and Sandy were all her friends. She had neither reason nor wish to hurt any of them. So it couldn't be that.

Something was using her. Drawing on her.

But what? And why?

* * *

Denied again! Outdone again!

The useless, skittish woman! He'd known the act of shooting might break his hold on her, but he hadn't counted on her to miss!

He was so weak that he could barely hold coherent thought together. He had overstretched himself, overtaxed himself.

Much as he hated to, he knew he needed a time of rest. A period of isolation and silence to replenish himself. Not even Theresa could help him in this case.

It would mean being away from her for several nights. Just the prospect made him want to shriek in rage.

He needed her. He had to have her.

All of his efforts could not have been for nothing. Soon she would find out what he had been doing for her. Soon she would be grateful, so grateful that she would accept his love willingly.

And then, oh, and then he would be renewed.

But to be away from her, unable to see her or feel her, was an agonizing prospect.

To be away from her and to know that Damon Blake would be with her . . . that was the most unimaginable of tortures.

If only that shot had found its mark! If only Blake had been blown backwards in a shower of blood, dying on the floor while scrabbling in a mess of his own insides! That would have made this weakness bearable, worthwhile.

He could no longer exert his influence on the others. It was costing him too much. They had been nothing to him anyway, mere diversions. And most were already almost lost to him, drugged or dead or having come to terms one way or another with the desires he'd awakened in them.

With a soft, painless tug, he broke with them and let them go. They gave him nothing but a pleasant distraction, and now he would be able to focus solely on Theresa Zane.

Once he was rested. Once she was rested, too. He realized he had been too demanding of her, taken too much too soon in his push to win her love.

There was only one left, one that he had to eliminate in order to show her how much he wanted her.

Unless Blake . . .

No. He would not let himself think of that. If she did, she did. And then he would be able to deal with Blake personally. Slowly.

And if not, if she didn't, then he would find another way.

Enjoy this life while you have it, Damon Blake, he thought as he felt himself begin to drift toward the somnolent rose-scented darkness of his sleep.

Enjoy it while you have it, for you won't have it long.

* * *

She wouldn't have expected to sleep well after the events of the previous twenty-four hours, but when Theresa climbed into bed Tuesday night, she slid down into a soft, restful dream.

Lora was in it, and Ruff, both girl and dog running joyfully along a pale beach of the sort Theresa had only ever seen in ads for travel agencies. She herself was half-reclined on a towel, the sun baking down with tropical warmth on her swimsuit-clad body, a rum drink in a tall fruit-choked glass scrunched into the sand beside her. The ocean breeze blew across her skin in gentle susurrations.

The buzz of the alarm wakened her and she reached lazily over to hit the snooze button. She sank back into the dream of the beach, and it felt wonderful in only the way that sort of thing could.

Nine minutes later, when the alarm went off again, she reluctantly let it go and surfaced into the waking world. She stretched without getting out of bed, aware that for the first time since leaving L.A. she'd finally gotten a good night's sleep.

Jack was curled on the other pillow, which at once pleased her and gave her a small flash of disappointment. Pleased because he was finally back to normal too, disappointed because a not-inconsiderable part of her wished that instead of Jack, she'd rolled over to see Damon.

But Damon wasn't here, wasn't even in the house. Yesterday's incident in the bar had convinced Theresa that he was more in danger than she was. She didn't know why she was so sure of that, but something told her that the presence in this house would sooner see Damon dead than let him get close to her. Although it clearly wanted something from her, too, she hadn't been physically threatened.

So she'd insisted he go back to his own place, where he would be safe. And declined, with a good deal of regret, his offer to accompany him. She couldn't run from this. Wouldn't abandon Glory, either. Not on what could be her last night in the house.

Besides, there was something she'd been wanting to try, something she didn't know if she could seriously sit down to do with anyone else around. And she knew she'd better try it before the people from the county coroner's office or whoever they were came to remove Glory's bones.

She dressed and headed downstairs. A stack of papers rested in the printer tray. She hadn't looked at them last night, too tired to do more than take her weary self upstairs, drowse through a warm shower, and then fall into bed.

Now, though, she would see what she'd written.

She remembered sitting down at the computer, calling up a word-processing program, and then poising her fingers over the keyboard. An initial feeling of foolishness had given way to a calm state, which had in turn deepened into something that could only be called a trance.

The last thing she clearly recalled was murmuring the invitation, "Tell me," and then beginning to type.

Time to find out just what she'd been told.

* * *

The girl held her breath as heavy footsteps stopped outside her door. It opened, and a thin slice of light fell across her.

She kept her eyes shut, feigning sleep. For a long time, he didn't speak, and she allowed herself to relax the tiniest bit.

"Wicked girl," he said quietly, the words slurred from his drinking. "I know you're awake."

She opened her eyes but didn't answer, fearful that anything she could say would only make him angrier.

"I'm just trying to do what's best for you. I've tried to raise you, and take care of you. All I asked was that you do as you're told. Was that so hard?"

She shook her head mutely. He came into the room.

"How many times do I have to explain things to you?" His voice rose suddenly into a shout. "How many goddam times?"

He moved with the speed of a striking snake, ripping the blankets off of her. She curled into a ball, covering her head.

Please, God, don't let him hurt me, she thought. Or, if that's too much to ask, just don't let him leave marks. Don't make me have to lie to anybody about where they came from.

He grabbed her shoulders and pulled her into a sitting position. One sleeve of her nightgown tore. Her hair tumbled across her face.

"Look at me, you little bitch," he snarled.

She looked up. His face was contorted with anger, a vein pulsing in his forehead. His breath stung her eyes. He shook her roughly. She bit back a cry of pain.

"I thought you were such a smart girl. Smart enough to follow a few simple damn instructions. But I was wrong. You're a lying, trashy whore like

your mother. You need to be punished." He held out the belt.

She stifled a moan as he doubled the belt between his hands and began slapping it against one palm. It made a sound like a riflecrack.

"Take off your nightgown," he commanded. The slur was gone. His eyes were feverishly bright.

She tugged the nightgown over her head, dropped it.

"Lay down. Don't make me tell you twice."

Shivering, she stretched out on the bed, facedown, holding onto the bedposts.

The belt hissed through the air and lashed across her buttocks. She shoved her face into the pillow, holding back her scream.

The second and third strikes landed on her back. The fourth striped her thighs. After that, she stopped counting.

After an eternity, the blows ceased.

She was a sheet of fire from her shoulders to the backs of her knees. She let out the breath she'd been holding. It came out in a shuddering sigh.

"It's for your own good," he said. "Somebody's got to teach you."

She suddenly knew what was coming next. He'd never dared before, though she'd often felt his eyes like hands upon her cringing skin. But now . . . oh, God, but now . . . her thoughts dissolved into incoherent prayers. No one to hear her scream, no mother here to help her, and if God was listening, He wasn't answering.

His fist closed around a handful of her hair and threw her onto her back. "Just a trashy little whore like your mother," he muttered. His breath was hot, vile. "I know you like it. You're just a slut like the rest of them. You're all the same. A bunch of sluts."

His weight pressed her down, forcing her thighs apart.

A yelp of horror burst from her and she twisted, trying to push him away. He slapped her, bringing blood to her lip.

"Shut up! You know you like it!"

Silent tears streamed down her face. She reached for the safe place, the place inside of herself where she hid when the beatings were bad. A place like a meadow, where nobody could go except herself. There were butterflies in the safe place, and warm sunlight. She would sit on the grass and watch the clouds float across the sky, and when she returned, it would all be over.

He rose up on his knees, grabbing her hips.

"Here it is, whore. Here's what you want."

The safe place shattered into a thousand spinning mosaic pieces and she was back in the real world, a real world now made up of red/black thunder, pounding pain, shame and filth and degradation. Her scream rang endlessly in her ears but never made it past her lips.

My punishment, she thought crazily. *Punishment for failing my mother.*

The man grunted and bucked like an inhuman thing, like a machine made in some medieval torture chamber and clothed in flesh.

Something cold touched her shoulder, an icicle chill that spread swiftly *down her arm and throughout her abused body and took away the pain. The abraded fire of her back, the horrible deep tearing ache in her loins, the stinging pinch-marks on her breasts, all faded away beneath that pervasive chill.*

Prickling with goosebumps, she turned her head slightly.

Something was there. A white form, blurry, indistinct. The girl felt no fear, only a strange wonder at this apparition. Wonder, and a startling awareness of empathy. She had the impression of a face, a child's face wracked with grief.

A small, pale hand reached out. She stretched out her own hand. Their fingers brushed.

The child's touch was cold, and as insubstantial as mist.

Then it was gone.

The man had collapsed heavily onto her, finished with his brutish act. He slowly got up, staring down at her in disgust.

"You made it happen," he said. "If only you'd obeyed me. It's all your fault. If anyone ever finds out, they'll know you for what you are. They'll hate you. Just like your mother." He gathered his clothes quickly, unable to look at her now, lip curled as if he'd touched something foul.

He left, closing the door behind him.

Alone in the darkness, the girl began to cry.

* * *

Theresa finished reading, aware that she was biting her lip against a chill and against memories of her own.

"Which of them was it?" she said. "Which of them, Glory? Was it Angela? Was it the other Cliffwood girl, the one Dad told me about? It wasn't me, that's not quite how it happened . . . but it's why you can reach me, isn't it?"

No one answered, but Theresa was sure she was on the right track.

It still didn't explain who, or what, was behind the rest of it. Was there some force in Seacliff that stirred up the darkest and most forbidden urges?

She'd been meaning to talk to Shauna Davis anyway. Maybe she could shed some more light on this mystery, even if it was something perhaps left unlit.

* * *

The painkillers had worn off and he wasn't supposed to take more for almost an hour.

"To hell with it," Damon Blake said, picking up the bottle. His hand was swollen like a rubber glove filled with warm Jell-O, and he fancied he could *see* it throbbing.

Of course, he couldn't get the child-proof top off . . . couldn't grip with his left hand hard enough to push down and turn with his right. He tried clenching it in his teeth but the bottle was too wide; tried bracing it between his knees but couldn't get purchase. He was about ready to draw his gun and blow the lid off when the phone rang.

"Morning, little bro," Derrek's deep and familiar voice said in his ear. "What have you done to yourself this time?"

"You always know," Damon said, grinning despite himself.

"It goes both ways. I'm just glad you didn't get shot."

"Almost did."

"What happened?"

He gave his brother the basics, leaving out everything about fevers and dreams and poltergeists and black roses. He could tell just by listening to his twin that Derrek was under stress enough of his own without him adding the unreal to it.

"Sounds like you lucked out, little bro."

"It's been quite a week, all right." As they'd often done during the times when they hadn't been assigned to each other as partners, he found himself relating his current cases to Derrek, leaving out all of the names and other confidential info in a habit that had long-since become ingrained. "How about you?"

Derrek sighed, and though that sigh crossed thousands of miles, it carried its full weight of exasperation. "Mark's driving me nuts, as usual. He's a good partner, but when he gets on one of these kicks it makes me want to clout him one."

"What's his beef this time?" Damon smiled. They had gone to the police academy with Mark Gladstone, and Damon knew that Mark's impulsiveness didn't mix with Derrek's practicality. Of course, that was partly why they made such good partners, tempering each other.

"The FBI stole *his* case." Derrek was rolling his eyes, Damon just knew it. "We got a body, done in a way that we knew it had to be a serial killer, and Mark was the first to track down the other victims. But then –"

"Told to back down, let the big boys handle it?" Damon asked.

"You got it. But this one's really put Mark's boxers in a bunch, because it's *inexplicable!*" He mimicked Gladstone on the final word, and both brothers chuckled.

Holding the cordless phone between his shoulder and ear, Damon went into the kitchen and wedged the prescription bottle into his silverware drawer. Pressing his knee against it, he was able to jimmy off the top. "What does he think it is this time? Secret society? Aliens?"

"Nothing that simple. We've got us some psycho who's been zipping all over the country, pounding men into hash, 'weapon or weapons unknown,' and leaves a black rose at each scene like some comic book bad guy. Only link we've been able to get on the victims is that they all lived in Bakersfield about the same time, ten, fifteen years ago."

"What do you mean, 'weapons unknown'?" Damon asked, then his jaw dropped and he spilled a roller derby of pills across the counter. "Hold on, back up, what was that about roses?"

"Unknown, that's what the forensics people told us. All they have is guesses. Could be claws, could be power tools –"

"Derrek, what about the roses?!?"

The pain in his hand was all but forgotten.

* * *

Shauna Davis opened Seacliff's back door, her greying hair covered by a kerchief in reds and yellows so bright it made the eyes water.

"Why, Theresa! What a surprise!"

"Hi, Mrs. Davis . . ." Now that she was here, she had no idea how to ask what was on her mind. "Can I come in?"

"Sure, if you don't mind the smell of wood polish. I'm doing the upstairs banisters today. Mr. Thornton's got some people coming out in a few weeks to look the place over. Hotel people!" She sounded so awed that Theresa had to hide a smile.

"Is Mr. Thornton here?" She didn't know if she could face him without spitting on him, now that she was sure in the hidden chambers of her own heart that Jerry was right about what he'd done to Angela.

"At the mill." Shauna clucked her tongue. "What with Mr. Haverley and all, he's got extra work piled up for him. He's arranging the funeral, too, you know. Paying for it out of his own pocket. I think he feels responsible, poor man."

Probably is, Theresa thought sourly.

Most places always looked smaller seen through the eyes of an adult. As a child, she'd visited April Cliffwood at the big house a few times, and thought it was huge and grand beyond belief. Seacliff's kitchen, though, had not undergone that shrinking of perception at all. It was huge.

Shauna kept up a steady patter of all the changes that Mr. Thornton was hoping to make as she led Theresa through the downstairs dining room and into the hall leading to what April's mother had always called 'the atrium.' Here, the ceiling soared the full three stories, topped with the blue and green stained glass dome. It was ringed with galleries at the second and third floors, looking down on the indoor swimming pool.

"It *would* make a good hotel," Theresa admitted, but she shivered as she said it. As if the weight of the building were pressing down on her. Or as if she were being watched. As if the presence that had been in her house the other night were here with her now, but dormant. Her gaze was drawn to one particular section of marble near the pool, where four of the large, square tiles didn't quite match the rest.

Around the pool, large ferns in brass pots and small white wicker tables and chairs gave the atrium a gardenish feel. On the south wall, sets of French doors opened onto the back terrace. To the north, a short, wide hall led to the foyer, where twin staircases swept grandly up to the second floor.

She tuned out Shauna Davis' ramblings and crossed the atrium. Through the French doors, she could see Seacliff's gardens and waterfalls, against the deep green of the trees. But not the rosebush. It was hidden from view.

On the way back, she paused at the place where the four tiles looked different. Up close, it was harder to notice. Only from a distance did the lighter hue give them away. It was a close match, though. She was sure that at some point in Seacliff's history, that section had been replaced. And she was also sure that it had something to do with what was happening.

"You feel it, don't you?" Shauna Davis broke off what she was saying to ask.

"Feel what?" Theresa's voice was unsteady.

"They say that's where she died," Shauna intoned ominously.

"Where who died?" Now she remembered what Shauna had said when they'd all gotten together to clean the Forrester's house. How Shauna was convinced there was a curse on Seacliff. At the time, she'd paid no attention, dismissed it. Now she wondered if she'd been too hasty.

"Bethany Cliffwood, Jacob and Estelle's daughter." Shauna pointed to the third-floor gallery. "She jumped from up there, they say."

"I heard she ran away," Theresa said, not mentioning the rest of what her father had told her. But now she knew those old suspicions were right. Bethany Cliffwood hadn't run away. Maybe she'd been about to try, when a fall had put all her plans of escape to an end. Just like Angela.

"That's what they let be said. But my family's worked here since 1900. We hear things. They told everyone she'd run off, so Estelle wouldn't have to bear the shame of having the whole town talking about how her pregnant daughter had killed herself."

"Pregnant," Theresa echoed dully.

"And this house has been a bad place ever since," Shauna said. "You didn't believe me the other day. I could tell. But you're having second thoughts now, aren't you?"

Without waiting for a reply, she went into the foyer and up the stairs. Theresa followed, though she'd already found out more than she wanted to know. But none of it was what she'd come to ask, so she couldn't leave yet.

"That's the portrait hall." She indicated a mahogany door. There was a little trolley, similar to what maids used, parked opposite it next to the gallery rail. A can of polish and a bundle of rags sat on top, and she went back to work. "Wellnow, I've bent your ear right off . . . surely you didn't come to just hear all that?"

"Mrs. Davis, have you been having strange dreams lately?" The question fell out of her mouth without any preamble. She couldn't help it. She was too unsettled, and being able to look down from the rail at the spot where Bethany Cliffwood's life and that of her unborn child had ended only added to it.

"Not a one," she said cheerily. "I've your grandmother to thank for that."

Theresa blinked, nonplussed. "My . . . my grandmother? Grandma Tashi?"

"Oh, yes, she and my mother used to be the best of friends. *Queen* Myra –" Shauna snorted disdainfully, "– hated it, but after all, Ma was only the housekeeper."

"So if she wanted to chum around with an Indian woman, what could Myra say, she was only a servant," Theresa said, nodding.

"Oh, and I had *such* a crush on your father when I was a girl," Shauna tittered. "Not that it ever came to anything, him being almost ten years older and all. I think I married Walt because he reminded me of Travis."

At this, Theresa had to suppress a snort of her own. Walt Davis, as far as her eyes could see, had not a single thing in common with her dad except for species and gender. She covered her bemused reaction by picking up a rag and helping to polish the rail.

"So your mom knew my grandma," she prompted.

"Yes, and whenever one of us kids took sick, I remember it was always Tashi's medicine that fixed us up better than anything the doctor could give us."

"Herb teas."

"I do wish your father knew her secrets. I could use some of the tea she used to mix up for my Pa's arthritis. Some days, after I've done all the floors, my back is singing like Jenny Lind. Oh, and Tashi used to make the most *cunning* little carvings and jewelry. Then, when I was about thirteen, I started having the most *awful* dreams." Her cheeks went scarlet and she began rubbing the rail with such fervor that it looked as if she was trying to erode it into nothingness.

"About what?" Theresa asked, though she had a pretty good guess.

"Things no woman should be thinking," Shauna said firmly. "Let alone a young girl. And nightmares, too. All mixed together. I'd hear the older maids talking, and the things they'd say! I don't know if they were real or dreams of their own, but it was shocking, let me tell you! I'd be working with them all day, and then when I went to bed my head would be so full of their stories that it was no wonder they'd follow me into my sleep."

Theresa made a noncommittal sympathetic noise and kept polishing.

"So, one day Ma sent me over to borrow something from your grandma – I don't recall what it was, might have been a spool of thread, or maybe it was molasses . . . no, I'm pretty sure she was sewing that day . . . wellnow, anyway . . . no, it *was* thread, because Tashi had me come up to her room with her so she could get it from her sewing kit. And that was when I saw it."

"Saw what?"

"She had something hanging over the bed, a circle of wood all crisscrossed with string and hanging with feathers and beads. She told me it was her dream-catcher, and I allowed as how I sure could use one. So she made me one. I've still got it."

"A dream-catcher! I had one too!" Theresa smacked herself in the forehead, leaving a splotch of wood polish that she wouldn't notice until later.

Her parents had argued about it, in fact. Lois had objected to Theresa having 'pagan trinkets' in her room, while Travis insisted it was part of her heritage and not pagan at all. But a few weeks later, Lois had 'accidentally' knocked it off the wall while dusting, and that was the end of that.

Bets on how long after her unremembered nightmares about Glory had begun?

"She knew," Theresa murmured. "Grandma Tashi knew."

* * *

Neither Kurt Masters nor Ellen Fielding looked as if they should be in the business of death.

Kurt, the coroner's assistant, was young and cheery and would have looked more at home doing something like water-skiing or snowboarding.

Ellen, a local anthropologist with ties to the university, was a petite older woman whose cloud of soft dark hair was shot with white, her movements quick and birdlike.

Theresa exchanged pleasantries with them that seemed absurd under the circumstances, offered them coffee which they declined, and watched as they went up the stairs to join the rest of the crowd.

She was willing to bet there hadn't been this many people in the house in decades. And all of them on their gruesome task.

The bedroom was full of deputies and other personnel. Damon hadn't shared any of their admittedly unorthodox conclusions on the identity of the body and the cause of death. Which meant they had to treat it as a homicide. They were photgraphing, measuring, collecting scraps of fabric and strands of hair, sifting the layers of dust. Even running a metal detector to look for bullets, coins, jewelry, or other clues.

Theresa listened to the murmur of voices for a while. What little she could make out was in a hushed jargon that could have been a foreign language.

She gave up and went back to her computer, trying unsuccessfully to lose herself in her writing. After a while, she became aware that she didn't have the room to herself anymore, and looked up to see Damon Blake.

"Are they done?" she asked.

"Not yet. But I'm the fifth wheel up there. They're wrapping the bones up now, going to take them to the coroner's office."

"Why?"

"To X-ray them, look for marks or scrapes that could tell them if any weapons were used, determine age and sex, study the dental work, things like that."

She was pensive, but let it go. Sensing he was about to ask her what had become of the necklace, which had been the first thing he'd noticed as this fun-filled carnival of forensics had begun, she changed the subject. "How's your hand?"

Damon let her change it, but also let her know with a look that he wouldn't be forgetting the other matter. "Not too bad. But something weird happened to me this morning."

"Me too."

"You want to go first, or should I?"

She indicated that he should, so he sketched out what Derrek had told him about the five murders, the roses left on the bodies, and the fruitless search to find a florist who knew of such a flower. "Black flowers are super-rare. The color on those petals only comes close to matching a Mexican species with a Latin name I won't even try to pronounce. Its local name is *la flor de muerte,* which translates as –"

"The flower of death," Theresa said. "Is that what they are?"

"Nope. They look like long skinny bells that hang down and flare out at the bottom. Nothing like a rose. And they only grow in that limited area, that climate."

"Which isn't much like here."

"We don't know for sure the roses at the murder scenes came from that bush."

She snorted. "Not for *sure,* yeah. But Jenny and I saw the cut stems. But you said these killings were all over the country. Who were these men?"

He took a piece of folded paper from his pocket. Derrek hadn't wanted to tell him, but after much persuading he had gotten his brother to give him the names. "Wayne Allen, Jim Navarro, Ben Spencer – Theresa, are you okay?"

"Go on," she said faintly. The blood had drained from her face, leaving it like a sculpture of milky amber.

"Nick Diamond, and Paul Kowalski," he finished. "What? What is it? Do you know them?"

Her head moved slightly. She thought she was nodding. One of her trembling hands floated up and took the paper.

"You know them?" He held her shoulders, as if worried that she might suddenly keel over. "How? Who are they?"

"Old boyfriends," she said from very far away. "Old boyfriends . . . and my stepfather."

* * *

"I'm telling you, she's fine. No one called you, *Counselor.* Your services aren't needed." Arthur Kensington crossed his arms implacably across his chest.

Kel McGuire put on his politest smile. "Physically, I know she's fine or else you wouldn't have discharged her from the hospital so soon. Just a few cuts from broken glass."

"Only a few stitches." Kensington backed into the house and made to shut the door in Kel's face.

"Still, I need to talk to her."

"As her doctor and her father, I'm telling you, for the third time now, Danielle is fine. Thank you for your concern."

"Dammit, Kensington, she took a shot at Damon Blake yesterday! And I heard you had to sedate her in the emergency room."

"Distraught. It was an accident."

"And part of my job is helping people who are distraught," Kel pointed out. "Dani's been through a traumatic experience. She needs to talk to someone."

"She has me."

Kel was getting that old familiar headache again. Normally, he loved his work and enjoyed being able to help people. But then, busy as he was, his job didn't usually consist of things like this. Talking to teens having trouble getting along with their parents, or spouses arguing too bitterly about the bills or the housework, or helping older folks come to terms with their declining health and abilities, those were all fine and well, a challenge he liked. He was left with the feeling that he had done some good for a change.

Getting past Arthut Kensington, though, was as formidable a task as Hercules facing the Nemean Lion.

"My Dani doesn't need psychiatric help," Kensington declared.

"I'm not a psychiatrist. I am, as you said, a counselor."

"She doesn't need counseling, either. She needs to be at home. Which she is, now. I told her it was a mistake to get her own place. Why would she need an apartment, when I'm living right here in town?"

Diplomacy prevented him from answering that one truthfully.

"Pop . . ." Dani said from behind him. "Pop, it's okay."

"You should be resting, young lady."

"I've been resting. He's right, I do need to talk to him."

Kensington harrumphed and scowled. "I don't think that's necessary."

Dani met Kel's eyes with a mute message of exasperation and fear. She had to be terrified about yesterday, and here he stood like a salesman unable to get a foot in the door.

"I *have* to talk to him," Dani said, squeezing past Kensington and onto the porch. "Everyone in town already thinks I've lost my marbles. If you keep me locked up in here, it'll only make things worse."

He expressed his displeasure by sweeping the door shut so hard the windows rattled all over the house.

Dani cringed, then offered a weak smile at Kel. "His bark's worse than his bite."

"I don't want to take my chances with either. Do you want to go over to my office?"

"Do we have to? Could we talk in the cafe instead? If people see us there, they'll know you didn't have to bundle me off in a straitjacket. Maybe it'll help."

* * *

Theresa didn't want to meet his eyes.

Damon didn't push it, just sat back and listened as she opened the doors of her most unpleasant memories. He could tell by the set of her body that she was expecting his reaction to be negative.

"After Mom divorced Dad, we moved around for a while. Up to Portland, where George was going to school –"

"George?"

"My older half-brother. By Mom's first husband. One of those hurry-up weddings right out of high school. I think ten years is about the longest my mother can sustain a marriage. George was fifteen when Mom and Dad got married. He didn't like it here. Hated this 'little nowhere town,' and couldn't wait to get out. He left for college when I was a baby, so I never really knew him when we were growing up. Mom lives with him now."

"When did she marry Kowalski?"

"When I was twelve. And I acted just like George. Didn't like Paul, didn't like our new house, my new school, any of it. I wanted to be back here with my real dad. Paul was . . . he was a control freak. Everything had to be just so, just his way. I was supposed to shut up, be good, and stay the hell out of his way. And Mom backed him up, to keep him happy, I guess."

A bleak, haunted look came into her eyes. "Wayne was my first boyfriend. I was fourteen. Paul and Mom couldn't stand him. And, being a typical teenage rebel, the more they nagged me about him, the more I went out with him. Then they did something I still can't believe. They made plans to go out of town for the weekend, told me that I was to have no one over. But it was a trick, all a trick. They went to a motel on the other side of town, then snuck back home to try and catch me doing something against the rules."

"I take it they did," he said.

"I'll say." She laughed, short and bitter. "We were having sex on their bed."

"Oh, man."

"Mom lost it. Screaming at me that I was no-good, grounding me for a year, threatening to make me go live with my father. So I yelled back in her face that I'd be on the next bus. Paul broke it up, told me I'd do no such thing, and gave me the 'while you live under *my* roof missy' speech. Then he gave me a spanking."

"You were fourteen, and he spanked you?"

"Turned me over his knee like a little kid. Then they sent me to my room without supper. I was infuriated, didn't know what to do, so pissed that before I realized what I was doing, I'd grabbed my stuff and ran away. I got picked up by the police trying to hitch a ride to Vegas."

Damon nodded. He'd seen it himself. "You're lucky they did pick you up. You could have wound up on the streets, strung out on drugs, dead in an alley somewhere."

"I know that now." She shuddered. "This is where you meet the *real* Theresa Zane, teen hellcat. I won't blame you if you're out that door any second."

He took her hands. "Not a chance. Whatever you may've been, it's behind you now."

Squeezing his good hand fondly, she went on. "I don't have to tell you how it went when the police brought me home. I bet you've been through all that yourself.

I wound up doing a stint in foster care while Mom spun a nice web of lies to keep them from giving custody to my dad. A bartender, wild women all the time, not a fitting lifestyle for an impressionable young girl. Eventually, they sent me back to her and Paul. But while I was in the home, I met Jim. And if they'd hated Wayne, they *loathed* Jim. Paul was, among other things, a firmly-entrenched racist. So here he was, tolerating his wife's 'little squaw,' but when I started hanging out with a Hispanic with a juvie record . . ."

"I can imagine."

"Through high school, I tried to get back at Mom and Paul by picking guys that they couldn't stand. Stoners, punkers, thugs, thieves . . . you name it. It's a good thing body piercing wasn't vogue back then, or I'd be wearing enough rings to set off metal detectors. I had to settle for doing crazy things with my hair and clothes. Somehow, with all of that, I held on to enough of my self-respect to keep from dropping out, to keep my grades decent."

"Didn't want to totally ruin your life to punish your mother."

"I guess. I did enough, though. I smoked, I drank, I took money from her purse, I fooled around. Got a real reputation, let everyone think I went all the way with every guy I dated even when I really didn't. I went with Ben for a while, and then met Nick. He was the jealous type, that particularly annoying brand of jealousy in which he thought he was allowed to chase every bippy that fawned over him when he played his guitar, but if another guy so much as looked at me, he'd get mad." She groaned. "Now I find out the jerk went and got famous; he was one of Jerry Forrester's favorite musicians. I even saw him on a poster in Jerry's room, though didn't recognize him. Jerry wants to hear all about it. I think I'll lie."

Damon look down at their linked hands and his attention was drawn to the scar on her wrist. "When'd you do this?" he asked, tracing it with a fingertip.

"After my stepfather raped me," she said flatly. "I'd been at a graduation party at Nick's. Mom was out, but Paul was home. He'd never done anything before to make me worry about him trying to touch me. 'Little squaw,' after all. But that night he started yelling at me, calling me a slut and a whore, saying that if screwing was all I was good for, he was going to have his share. I remember laughing at him, taunting that even if I let him, he wouldn't be able to get it up. I was wasted, almost ready to pass out, so it's mostly a blur. But when I woke up and realized what had happened, I did this."

He'd told her before that anyone who would do something like that to a kid deserved to be strung up, so he couldn't deny a certain slinking gladness that Paul Kowalski was dead, that his last few hours had been an agony of fear and suffering.

She pulled her sleeve up a little. "Broke the bathroom mirror and cut myself. Bled all over the place. It was like getting hit with a bucket of ice water, making me see what I was doing to myself. So I bandaged it – though I left the bathroom like it was, and when Mom saw the mess she nearly killed me –"

"Didn't you tell her?"

"I did. She called me a liar and slapped my face. I let her have it right back, and told her that I was leaving. Dad had given me a car as a graduation present, so I threw my stuff in, pulled out all my savings, swiped Paul's ATM card and booped myself an extra three hundred bucks – if he thought I was a whore, damned if he was going to get away without paying – and off I went." An exceedingly hard edge had crept into her voice, the sort of edge that could cut sheet steel.

"And Travis didn't know any of this."

"Oh, no. Mom went above and beyond to keep it from him, and I didn't want to admit any of it. I should have. Should have told him right from the start. Maybe things would have been different then."

"He still doesn't know?"

She shook her head. "And that's how I'd like to keep it. No point in bringing it all back up now. Mom's in Portland living with George; she divorced Paul two years after I moved out. George is welcome to her. Let her be a grandmother to his rotten kids, not my Lora."

The thump of footsteps from overhead reminded them that they weren't alone in the house. They both jumped a little.

"Must be done up there." He started to rise, but she held his hand a moment longer.

"So, tell me, sheriff, now that you know the whole sordid story, what next? I'm not the innocent schoolmarm you thought I was." She masked with levity a deep concern, and he understood that she was afraid of him walking out, of him not wanting her.

"Ma'am," he said with a smile, "you're not watching enough of my kind of movies. It isn't always the schoolmarm. The soiled doves and dance hall girls with hearts of gold are much more interesting."

* * *

The Trinity Square Bar and Grill was kitty-corner across the plaza from Nate's. From their booth by the front windows, Dani Kensington could look through a smeary grey world of rain to the place where her mind had fallen apart.

She was all too aware of everyone else in the 'Grill watching her. Keeping a careful eye on her just in case she should pull an Uzi from a hidden holster and go on a mad shooting spree. Or that she'd suddenly rip off her sweater to reveal banks of dynamite lashed to her torso, enough to take out herself and everyone around, as well as a big chunk of central-town real estate.

"But you won't," Kel McGuire said from opposite her.

"I didn't know you could read minds," she said as lightly as she was able.

"Job requirement. You're not going to hurt anyone, Dani. It was an accident. An isolated incident."

"Like Sandy Forrester? A few more 'isolated incidents' like that and half the town will be in the hospital." She poked at her fries, which, like her burger, looked so naked without her customary dousing of catsup. Today, though, she couldn't face the thought of anything red, because it reminded her of blood and what could have happened.

"Want to tell me about it?"

She looked over at him. Her father had bitched about McGuire ever since he came to Trinity Bay, feeling somehow threatened that McGuire would cut into his place in the community. She supposed Dear Old Pop's fears hadn't been unfounded. Used to be that people here went to him with all their concerns, but now they took many to Kel. The older folks in particular. And she didn't blame them; her father more often than not would brusquely tell them they were getting old and would just have to live with it, that it beat the alternative. But Kel had started Silver Grove, encouraged activities and outings and exercise, and as sweet white-haired Elsie Donbury had gigglingly confided to her one afternoon, also told them that sex was one of the best things they could do to keep healthy.

Now here was McGuire again, trying to cut in on what Dear Old Pop believed should be his business. Taking his only daughter away. Butting in. And she was glad. Pop was not the most sympathetic of ears, and she'd been unable to tell him the lunatic thoughts that had been running around in her head the past few days.

Pitching her voice low, not wanting to air all this to the general public, she told him how she'd gotten feeling feverish Sunday night at work. With her late-night schedule, she usually didn't get up until well past noon, and when she woke on Monday, she was drenched with sweat. Her father told her to stay home, drink fluids, all that good stuff, and she had obeyed like a dutiful daughter.

"As opposed to today, when I am defying and betraying him," she added.

"Overprotective."

"To say the least. You should have heard him when I got my job at Nate's. And when I wanted to move out on my own –!" She clutched her chest dramatically.

They laughed, and for Dani it was a tremendous relief. She'd felt like she was tottering on the edge of some chaotic abyss ever since waking up yesterday morning, and to laugh felt so right, so normal, that for the first time she could almost believe that she wasn't going crazy.

"Go on," Kel invited.

"All the rest of Monday, it was like my brain was out of focus. I'd start to do something, forget halfway through. I kept thinking that someone was looking in my windows, or listening in on my phone. Next would be the tin foil hat to keep the Martian mind-control rays away, you know? Paranoid ideations."

"I forgot your degree was in psych."

"Bartending is only part mixology," she said.

"What happened next?"

"That was when things really got freaky. I stayed home Monday night, I know I did. But when I woke up Tuesday, I was sure I had gone out . . . and that I'd gotten arrested. By Damon Blake. And . . . and . . . he was searching me, stripping me, I was in cuffs . . . there were all these other cops around . . . " She shook like a dog casting water from its coat. "When I woke up, I ached all over but I felt so *good*, oversexed and tender but just fantastic."

Kel cleared his throat, and she saw that he was struggling hard to hold onto his professional decorum. "An erotic dream?"

"But it seemed so *real!* I was sure it had happened, didn't know what to do next. That was when I started hearing it."

"Hearing voices?"

"Well, *a* voice. Telling me that I couldn't let Damon get away with that. Telling me I had to do something about it. Ordering me. Constant. Nagging. Persistent. Always there. Command hallucinations. Just wouldn't let up, wouldn't let up, so finally I went down to Nate's. Pulled the fuses. Called the police station. The voice told me that Damon would come over, even though it was Scott James I talked to. Loaded the shotgun. Waited. Sure enough, it was Damon. And then it was like I wasn't in control of myself. Like I was just watching from inside myself. Then, once he got the gun away from me, I knew I'd imagined all of it. My God, and I'd nearly killed him!"

"Command hallucinations can be very persuasive, even undeniable."

"No, Kel, it was more than that. This was like being controlled. Like the voice in my head was taking over my body. Like a puppet."

"It may have been delirium from the fever . . ." he sounded uncertain and stirred his iced tea viciously, the spoon clacking and clanking against the glass. His voice dropped to a mutter. "At least there weren't any roses . . ."

"Roses?" Her voice quavered, and Kel looked up sharply.

"What is it, Dani?"

"The . . . the wallpaper in my bathroom has roses on it. It was there when I moved in. Kind of ugly stuff. Climbing vines, pink roses, little gnomes wearing caps and curly shoes. But on Monday, every time I went in there, I kept thinking they should be black. So I took a marker and started coloring them all in. Once they were all black, I was finally able to get to sleep."

"Black roses," Kel said.

"And Tuesday, whenever I'd hear the voice, I'd have olfactory hallucinations too. Smelling roses, but not like any I'd ever smelled before. What does it mean? You said Theresa; does she know what's going on?" Her eyes widened. "Is it . . . paranormal? Was I possessed?"

Kel exhaled. "Dammit, I don't like this, Dani, I really don't. I'm no parapsychologist. I don't believe in ghosts, demonic possession, or psychic powers. Don't start thinking that way. You know as well as I do that there's weirdness enough in the human mind without resorting to that."

"So I'm losing my marbles."

"I didn't say that –"

"Well, what *are* you saying? What did cause it, then? Is it going to happen again? I don't know if I can stand hearing his voice anymore. I don't know if I can stand seeing him again, and he comes into the bar all the time, trying to pick up on me!"

"Damon Blake?"

"No! I wasn't hearing *his* voice in my head."

"You mean you recognized the voice? Whose was it?"

"Brad Thornton's," she said.

* * *

Kurt Masters and Ellen Fielding were the last to finish their work and get ready to leave. They came downstairs carefully, bearing the small bundle between them.

It was of dark green heavy plastic, zippered in a semicircle like a sleeping bag, and looked more like a wrapped pile of sticks than anything resembling a human body.

Damon and Theresa watched them descend. He could tell by her face that she was torn by several conflicting emotions. Relief that the horrifying find was being removed from her home, concern for the lost spirit of the poor dead child, and even sadness because she was, in a way, losing a friend.

"Any ideas on cause of death?" Damon asked. He'd almost said *how she died*, but that could lead to them wanting to know why he was so sure of the gender, and he'd just as soon not get into that with these two. Let them handle the scientific end of things. He and Theresa would deal with the increasing weirdness of the rest of it.

"Hard to say on just a preliminary look," Masters said. "We'll be able to do a more in-depth analysis when we get them to the lab. But I did spot what looks like a skull fracture, that could have been consistent with either a blow to the head or a fall onto a hard surface."

"Marks along the pelvis suggest that one of the hips was dislocated, too," Ellen Fielding added, and beside Damon, Theresa blanched.

They carried the bundle out to their truck, and although there wasn't anyone else in sight, Damon was suddenly glad it wasn't obviously a body. The town gossip mill had enough to grind for the moment. Especially as the parade of county vehicles hadn't gone unnoticed. Lan Scribner would be sniffing around soon enough.

"How old is the house?" Fielding asked.

"About a hundred years old," Theresa said.

"And no one's looked in that cabinet all this time?"

"It was stuck shut."

"The moisture of decomposition might've swelled the wood," Masters said cheerily. "Place must have been unoccupied for a while, or the smell would have tipped them off."

"Yeah," Theresa said faintly, looking unsteady. "It was a guest house until my grandparents moved in, back in the early 1930's."

Damon felt none too steady himself. The images the words conjured were distinctly unpleasant. A lot easier to deal with dry, brittle bones. You could almost trick yourself into thinking those bones had always been clean, never sheathed in flesh.

Apparently oblivious to their reactions, he went on blithely. "I'm guessing it's a kid, maybe nine or ten –"

"Most likely female," Fielding cut in as they slid the bag into the back of their truck.

"And from some of the other things we noticed, scratches in the wood and such, she might have still been alive."

Theresa held on to Damon's arm. "Buried alive."

"Entombed alive," Masters corrected. "We'll never know if she was put in there or if she crawled in on her own."

"According to local folklore," Theresa said cautiously, "Three of the Cliffwood children – the family who lived in the main house – disappeared back around the turn of the century. A teenage girl and a little boy, then another girl several years later."

"Cliffwood, eh?" Masters jotted it down in his notebook. "Any first names?"

"Bethany for the teenager, Glory for the other, and I don't know about the boy," Theresa said.

Damon glanced at her sharply. Bethany? Her visit to talk to Shauna Davis must have turned up that bit of info. But it sounded familiar, damned if he could remember why.

"I don't think this body was a teenager," Ellen Fielding said.

"Glory Cliffwood." Masters wrote it down and circled it.

Theresa relaxed a little.

Still trying to recall why the name Bethany rang a bell, Damon let his gaze wander away from the truck. A flicker of movement in the corner of his eye, like a curtain sheer stirring in the breeze from one of the upper windows.

But the windows were closed, and the pale shape behind the glass was no curtain. It was a wraithlike form, staring down from the bedroom, from the very windowseat that had until recently held the bones.

Theresa was asking what sort of tests they were planning to run and what they'd do with the remains when they were finished. Damon murmured, "Back in a sec," and did a slow fade toward the house.

Jack was on the stairs as if waiting for him. Damon crossed the living room soundlessly and crept up, using the sides of the treads to avoid any creaks.

The bedroom door was half-open. He pushed it silently the rest of the way, sure that by now the phantom would be gone . . .

. . . and there was the child, her fair skin and white dress and platinum-blond hair as translucent as the mist that came off the bay. Damon could see the pattern and texture of the wallpaper through her.

The brightest thing about her was the necklace, silver and black with the red gem in the center, a ghostly image of the solid reality that Theresa had described.

It was like a gear shifting in his mind. He'd experienced the poltergeist events of the other night, heard the scream, sensed the threatening presence first in Theresa's room and then again at the bar. He hadn't thought he still harbored any doubts. But this, actually seeing a ghost with his own two eyes, set him firmly and irrevocably on the path of believing.

"Glory," he whispered, not meaning to speak and inwardly cursing himself as he did for now she would vanish.

Instead, she turned slowly toward him and he saw her eyes, blue and shimmering with tears. The room was very cool, almost chilly. He moved forward as she stretched her small fingers searchingly toward him.

Contact was like attempting to grasp cold smoke that curled around his warm skin. A communication passed wordlessly between them, and he understood that even the decent interment of her bones wouldn't let her be at rest, not until the force behind the black roses was somehow nullified. Until then, she was bound to this world, to the estate, trying to warn those who were in danger.

Like Theresa.

It wanted her. Wanted to possess her, body and soul.

"I'll protect her," Damon promised, though he had no idea how he could defend Theresa against an unseen, unholy menace.

Satisfied, she looked back out the window at the open rear of the truck, where the pitifully small bag rested.

"They won't hurt your bones –"

She shook her head as if that didn't matter to her, and a longing came to him, her only wish, to have them buried near her parents.

"Okay," he said.

A slight smile turned up the corners of her mouth, and then she disappeared as he'd known she would, growing paler and less distinct, the room warming as she was lost to view.

* * *

"Brad Thornton's voice," Kel mused.

"I know how it sounds," Dani said, flapping her hands in frustration. "But that's who it sounded like. He was in the bar on Sunday night, too, coming on to me. Jerk. Like I'm supposed to be impressed by a rich older guy with a sports car and nice hair."

"According to all the commercials, you *are* supposed to be impressed," Kel said dryly.

Dani methodically mooshed a fry into potato paste with her spoon. "This is going to come out like more of the same paranoid delusional crap, but maybe it's him doing it. Maybe he's, I dunno, psychic or something."

"Dani," he said warningly.

"Okay, okay. Then what? Shared psychosis? Some sort of contagious mental illness? At least you won't ever be out of a job."

"Contrary to popular belief, not everyone in this line of work is hoping their clients never get better."

"That more describes Pop," she said sourly. "But come on, Kel, help me out here! I don't want to move away; I love my job, I love this town."

"There's no reason you'd have to move away."

She swept her hand at the plaza. "What about them? Now that I'm officially a crazywoman? I stay, everyone avoids me like a leper, and I end up a weird old woman living alone out on Agate Way with fifty cats, talking to myself and having the local kids chant mean poems at me when I go to the grocery store."

"That's a little extreme, isn't it?"

"Is it?" She challenged him with her eyes, and he broke away first.

"People are still going to talk, no matter what Damon Blake or you or I say. He's willing to leave it at that, an accident, a case of mistaken identity. You were keyed up, expecting to see Scott, and when he came in instead –"

"What, because he's a black male? Oh, great, I'm not loony-tunes, I'm just a racist," she said sarcastically.

"Or should I make something up? Tell them that it was all a state of delirium brought on by the high fever, caused by a temporary swelling of the brain tissue?"

"Could that have been it?" she asked hopefully.

He grimaced. "People don't usually root for a swelling of the brain tissues. Besides, your father says you're perfectly healthy –"

"It would be a blotch on his profession if I wasn't," she said. "When I was fifteen, I got mono, and he denied it until I passed out in school one day. Then he tried to blame it on something I ate. Shoemaker's kids shouldn't go barefoot, doc's kids shouldn't get sick. Makes him look bad. Or maybe, half-assed analysis time, it has to do with Mom dying so young, that if he never admits there's anything wrong with me, there *won't* be and he won't lose me too."

"Sounds like the two of you could benefit from family counseling."

Dani threw back her head and laughed. "I don't want to be anywhere nearby when you suggest *that* to Pop!"

Kel's beeper went off. "It's Nancy. Excuse me a minute."

"Sure thing." She smiled brightly, but as he went over to ask Gertrude Mittleschut if he could use the phone, her smile faded into a thoughtful expression.

Maybe they had studied the same things, taken the same classes . . . but for Dani, the main thing she had learned was that *anything* was possible. The brain was a powerful and mysterious thing. Who was to say that in all those uncharted folds and lobes there *wasn't* an area given over to the talents usually dismissed as supernatural?

Let Kel think what he wanted. She had some ideas of her own.

And just maybe a few questions for Mr. Brad Thornton . . .

* * *

They shook hands, after Masters and Fielding had stripped off their rubber gloves, and exchanged good-byes all around, and then the small truck drove off and left Theresa and Damon alone.

He'd come back out with a peculiar stunned expression, the look of someone who'd just gotten a shocking revelation, but she hadn't been able to ask. Now she did.

"Where were you? What happened?"

"I saw her," he said, heading back into the house. "Glory."

"You did? She's still here?" Theresa looked around as they came in, half-thinking Glory would be waiting for them at the top of the stairs. But the only one there was Jack, sitting with his tail curled primly around his forepaws and his ears up alertly.

"I even . . . talked to her," Damon said. "Except she didn't really talk . . . she touched me, and it was like I knew what she wanted me to know." He grasped her by the upper arms, pinned her gaze with his. "I know why those men were killed. I don't know how, but I know why. It wants you, Theresa. It wants you for its very own, and it'll kill to get you."

"What wants me? The presence? What is it?"

"I wish I knew. Ghost, demon, *something*."

"And why would it kill Wayne, Nick, the others? I haven't even seen any of them in a dozen years! That doesn't make sense! None of them mean anything to me. It's sure as hell not like I loved them! Especially Paul! I won't go so far as to say I'm glad he's dead —"

"I would," Damon practically snarled. "We can't expect this thing to think like us. Maybe it's trying to kill off your past lovers so it'll have you all to itself, maybe it's trying to win you over by getting rid of the people who've ever hurt you. I don't know." He paused and drew a deep breath. "But I think you should leave Trinity Bay. Right away."

"Leave? Damon, if you're right, if this . . . whatever it is . . . is after me, what makes you think I'd be any safer someplace else? It reached all the way to New York, didn't it?"

He closed his eyes briefly. "Damn."

"I've done enough running. This thing may want me, but that doesn't mean it's going to get me. Sure as hell not without a fight. My grandmother knew about it —" she quickly told him about the dream catchers.

"So it can be stopped."

"I don't want to just stop it. I want to get rid of it. Forever. For me . . . Sandy, Dani, Angela . . . everyone whose lives have been messed with."

"And Glory. As long as it's still around, she can't go wherever she's supposed to go."

"You didn't tell me that. Now I really can't run from it. That poor child has spent almost a hundred years in pain, Damon. I have to help her."

"I'm with you, but how? How can we fight something like this?" He patted his holster. "Guns aren't going to do us much good against a ghost."

"There has to be a way. We've just got to find out everything we can, and hope it has a weakness."

* * *

"Hi, Nancy, you paged me?"

"Kel, oh God, thank goodness it's you!"

"What's happened?" He had never heard Nancy so shaken. "Are you all right?"

"I'm fine . . . it's not me . . . Kel, it's your sister."

"Megan?"

"Brian Sorenson just called. He lives next door to her, you know, Henry's son . . ."

"Sure, sure," he said. He knew Brian and Henry; had talked to them both five years ago when Brian's interest in role-playing games convinced his father that he must be a suicidal devil-worshipper. "What about Megan, Nancy?"

"She . . . she . . ."

He knew what she couldn't say and could barely bring himself to say it either. "Dead? She's not dead, not Megan?"

"Brian thinks she is. He was passing her apartment, and saw her through the window . . . on the bed . . . a pill bottle . . ."

"Did he call the EMS?"

"Yes, the paramedics are on their way and so are the police, he called them first."

"I'm going over there."

"Kel, I don't think –"

He hung up, and it was only then that he became aware that his voice had risen during the conversation. Gertrude Mittleschut was staring at him with her mouth in an 'O', and a hush had fallen over the others.

"It's happened again," Vince Garrick said. "Another one."

Dani rose to deliver an angry retort, but Kel didn't stay to hear it. He tossed a few bills at Mrs. Mittleschut and hurried out the door.

* * *

Theresa handed Damon the stack of papers. "This is what I wrote this morning. I tried to tap into Bethany, the other Cliffwood girl."

He snapped his fingers. "Bethany Rose!"

"What?"

"There's a portrait of Jacob Cliffwood in the town hall, of him on the dock next to his boat. It was named the Bethany Rose. I knew I'd heard that before!"

"He named it for his daughter . . . Rose must have been her middle name . . . that fits."

"And she supposedly disappeared."

Theresa nodded and tapped the papers. "If what's in here is true, she was murdered."

"You realize this isn't exactly the usual way of gathering evidence."

"This isn't the way I usually write, either. But these girls, these poor dead girls, are a key to figuring this out. It's not like you could charge Bethany's stepfather, or the man from the attic, with the crimes anyway. They're long dead."

He riffled the pages. "So you sat down and . . . what? Summoned up her spirit?"

"I'm not sure what I did. It was like being hypnotized. I didn't know what I was writing until I finished and read over it. But I'm not imagining things, Damon. I'm not making things up."

"I know."

Damon sat down on the couch and began to read. Theresa curled up beside him, already having committed the words to memory but looking at them again.

* * *

"What have you done? What have you done, you wicked, sinful girl?"

"Mama, please! It wasn't my fault!" she sobbed, trying to cover her face as her mother's blows rained down on her head and shoulders.

"I'm supposed to believe that Adam is to blame? Why on earth would he want a slat-thin thing like you, unless you tricked him into it, seduced him!"

"Mama, I never did! He came into my room! I didn't want to! Please!"

"It wasn't enough for you to come between your father and me. Now you think you'll take Adam away? You think you can force him to leave me and marry you, all because you went and got yourself with child?"

"I came to you for help!" Bethany wailed.

"Oh, I'll see to it that you're helped, all right. Helped right out of this plan of yours. You stay right there. I'll see about that baby in your belly."

As her mother stormed down the hall, leaving her alone in the parlor, Bethany straightened up and regarded her tear-streaked face in the glass over the mantle.

Why wouldn't Mama believe her? Surely Mama couldn't think that Bethany wanted Adam Reeveman's attention! She hated him, hated the way he followed her with his eyes, hated him even more since the night he had come into her room and pinned her to her bed, forcing part of himself into her and making her bleed.

She saw another reflection behind her, that of Adam himself, leaning in the doorway with a snide smile.

"I told you she wouldn't believe you," he said. "Now you've gotten yourself in trouble, little girl. If you'd kept silent and done as I said, we'd have come through this with no trouble."

"Why did you do this to me?" she wept.

"How could I resist?" Even now, here in her mother's very parlor, he dared to saunter over to her and run his finger down the side of her neck, over the silver necklace her father had given her, down over the modest swell of her chest. "A tempting creature like you, playing at being the innocent but luring me with your glances, your smiles, your wiles?"

She twisted angrily away. "I never did any of that!"

"It's not like I was the first. I know about you frontier girls. You're fourteen, ripe for wedding and bedding. Probably been going behind the barn with young boys since you were twelve. No wonder you were ready for a real man."

Bethany slapped his face and burst into renewed tears. She tried to shove past him, but he grabbed her and flung her against the wall. The corner of the mantelpiece dug sharply into her shoulder.

"Don't make it any worse for yourself," he snarled.

"How could it be worse?"

He raised his hand to strike her, but the sound of her mother approaching made him swiftly retreat to the opposite end of the room.

"Even now, Estelle," he said as Mama came in, shaking his head as if in utter disbelief. "Even now, she was begging me to leave you and marry her. From that one night, that one drunken night when I fell prey to her seductive charms, she's imagining that I would —"

"Mama, he's lying, can't you see that he's lying?" Bethany shrieked.

Estelle came toward her, a cup in her hands. It was brimming with a black, noxious, oily-looking liquid. "Drink this."

"What is it?" Bethany backed away.

"Oil of roses, ergot, other herbs. Drink it, and we'll be rid of the proof of your shame. This will flush that baby from you. And then I can decide what must be done with you. I won't have you living under my roof and trying to steal my husband. And give me that necklace. You're not worthy of it. Your father should have given it to me, not to you."

She clapped her hands over it, feeling the cool stone petals press into her palm. "No! It's mine!"

"Give it to me; it's much too valuable for an irresponsible girl of your age." Mama thrust the cup at her.

"I won't drink it!"

"Hold her, Adam," Mama ordered. "You bear some small part in this, so you had better do as I say!"

Bethany ran for the door, bumping Mama and nearly making her drop the cup of witch's brew. She slipped past in the midst of their startled exclamations. She dashed up the stairs, meaning to lock herself in her room.

As she was hurrying down the hall, Adam appeared at the end. He'd taken the back stairwell, knowing her plan, and now he was between her and the safety of her room. As if her room could ever be safe again, after what had happened to her in there.

She turned and ran back to the main stairs, up and up to the third floor, where the domed skylight painted the wood in shades of the sea.

Adam caught up with her at the rail and seized her. She struggled with him, kicked at him, but to no avail. He held her as she heard the steady, unrelenting tread of her mother drawing near.

"Now," Mama said. "Now you'll drink, you wicked child."

Between the two of them, they made her open her mouth and swallow the thick, gagging-foul liquid. It burned a molten path down her throat and her stomach clenched into a cruel knot.

"There," Mama said, satisfied. "That will put an end to one problem. Now for the necklace. Give it to me, Bethany, this very minute."

Horrible wracking cramps lanced outward from her middle, but she still held protectively to the necklace. She shook her head, unable to speak.

"Give it to me, I say!" Mama strode forward and snatched at the silver

chain.

Bethany lashed out, hitting her mother in the face, but Mama was too strong. She shoved Bethany back.

Her waist struck the rail, sending an even fiercer cramp exploding through her. Bending double, clinging to the rail, she heard Mama screaming curses at her, tearing at her hair and her dress.

Then the railing cracked, and Bethany tottered outward. Terror overwhelmed everything else and she reached desperately for Mama to save her.

Mama reached, but only to grab the necklace. It pulled tight around Bethany's neck, strangling-choking as her feet swung out over the drop.

She beat at Mama's grasping hands until they lost their purchase, and her last thought as she plunged with the taste of rose oil rich and dark in her mouth was that she had kept her necklace, and her baby, after all.

* * *

22

Most of Trinity Bay attended the Haverley funeral on October first. Everyone in town had known, if perhaps not particularly liked, either Big Al or his wife.

Kel McGuire stood among the crowd, observing the rest of the family with empty detachment. Al's sister Claudia, the oldest boy Billy, the daughter Annette with her husband and kids, and Gary. On each of their faces, he saw a sense of unadmitted freedom mixed with their shock and grief. Had he been wearing his counselor hat, it would have confirmed much of what he'd always suspected about the inner workings of that particular clan.

But he wasn't wearing his counselor hat today. He couldn't offer words of comfort to the Haverleys. Couldn't do much more than stand in the little cemetery behind the schoolyard and listen to the service without hearing it, the weight of a paperback heavy as a stone in the pocket of his suit jacket.

He was aware of the skittering glances of his neighbors, who knew that this wouldn't be his only trip to the cemetery this week. Who didn't meet his eyes because they also knew that few of them would join him on that next visit.

After all, it wasn't as if any of them had known Megan. His sister had lived in an unhappy invisibility for most of her twenty-four years, only drawing unkind attention despite being one of the sweetest and dearest people Kel had ever known.

He steeped in guilt, simmered in guilt. Here he was, a man who had devoted his life to the helping of others, and he hadn't seen how much his own sister was suffering. Too busy with his work to notice that Meg's shyness had taken a turn to quiet desperation.

The scene was going to stay with him the rest of his life. Scott James had tried to keep him from entering her apartment, but he wouldn't be dissuaded. All the way over, he'd been unable to remember the name of the complex, only that the kids called it Nerdwood Lane because nearly all of the units were rented out to an assortment of Trekkers, computer geeks, gamers, and introverts like Meg.

Weirdwood? Wyrmwood?

Only when he'd pulled into the little parking lot and read the sign – Birdwood Lane – did the truth of it smack him between the eyes. Suicide. His younger sister had overdosed, ended her own life. So he'd been as prepared as it was possible to be when he went to her apartment, through the cluster of onlookers gathered around the ambulance.

The neatness of the room had been the first thing he'd noticed. Considerate Megan had done up all the dishes and tidied the place. She'd left her home as ordered as if she was going on a vacation and didn't want to come back to a mess.

Except, of course, for the scatter of small blue tablets that had rolled off the edge of her nightstand, and one that had partly dissolved in the ring of condensation around the base of the glass she'd used to take the rest.

Her hair had been loose, a frizzy cloud on her pillow. He couldn't recall the last time he'd seen it unconfined by a clip or a hairband. And she'd been wearing a brand-new silky nightgown of a brilliant emerald green, when Meg usually favored plain tones that let her fade into the background.

She looked more like a woman who'd fallen asleep awaiting a lover than someone who meant to die.

A book had been clasped in her hands, resting on the large soft hills of her breasts. The book he now had in his pocket.

He took it out and read for what had to be the hundredth time the sticky-note pasted to the front cover. Meg's round script, no mistaking it.

If sleeping is the only way I can be with him, then I'll sleep forever, it said.

Kel peeled the note off and studied the cover though he'd already committed the images to memory. It was a romance novel, *Blissful Conquest* by Serenity Townshend – there was a pen name if ever he'd heard one. The artwork was typical of the genre – ruggedly handsome man in an open shirt leaning over a woman whose green gown seemed about to fall from her lush bosom, a windswept sea and brooding castle in the background.

He turned it over and read the back-cover blurb. Fire-haired Megan MacLean and grey-eyed Alaric Hawke, the only man who could tame her willful spirit and awaken the passion in her soul.

This was why his sister had killed herself? This piece of trash? She'd yearned so strongly to identify with a bodice-ripper heroine that her own life had seemed worthless?

Angrily, Kel stuffed the book back in his pocket. He knew it wasn't really to blame, that making Ms. Townshend and her unrealistic characters responsible for Megan's death was as senseless as blaming movies and video games for the increase in teen violence. The underlying problem had to be there in the first place.

He realized that the service had ended, that people were filing past Claudia Haverley and her brother's orphaned children on the way to their cars. He knew he should join them, but couldn't bring himself to do it. It wasn't their grief he was thinking of, it was his own.

Someone was waiting for him by his car. Mary Christiansen, the head nurse at the Medical Center, Meg's supervisor.

Kel sighed heavily and approached. "Hello, Mrs. Christiansen."

"Mr. McGuire, I know it's hardly the time or place, but I wanted to let you know how sorry we all are about your sister. If there's anything we can do . . ."

"The pills. They were from the hospital?"

She nodded. "We've never had anything like this happen before. We are always so careful about the med room."

"Did Meg have keys?"

"The Schedule Fours . . . that included the Halcion tablets and other sleeping pills . . . weren't locked in the cupboards."

He sensed her concern went beyond that of his loss, and would have assured her that his family had no intention of suing. But it probably would have been a lie. He himself might harbor no such ill will, but his parents were another matter. They would be all too willing to point fingers at anyone they could for Meg's death, anyone but themselves for having raised her under constant scrutiny and scorn.

"Was she at work Tuesday?"

"Yes, for the evening shift. I even thought that she seemed much happier than usual. Brighter. I remember wondering if she met someone. But all she said was that she'd been feeling sick the day before, and was much better now. It was such a shock to hear what happened."

"Sick?" Kel asked.

"Just a mild fever, she said."

He stared at her. "A fever?"

"I heard there's one going around. But like I said, she was fine on Tuesday, bright and more cheerful than I'd ever known her to be. I don't understand it, Mr. McGuire. We're all so sorry."

"Thank you," he said absently, and accepted the motherly hug she gave him.

He slid into the driver's seat and sat lost in thought, his mind busily totting up the similarities between Megan and Dani. Fever . . . Dani's delusional obsession with Damon Blake and Megan's with the fictional Alaric Hawke . . . one instance of violent acting out and one suicide, both spurred on by those same obsessions . . . but Dani reported being hounded by voices and command hallucinations, and if Meg had, she'd concealed it well.

Now add Sandy Forrester into it . . .

And Celeste Haverley? Gary said she'd been sick one day last week.

But so had Ruth Edwards, and Nancy. Neither of them had suffered any bizarre delusions or strange behaviors . . . not that he knew of, anyway. And while he might not have known about Ruth, he worked with Nancy. She'd been her usual saucy self.

Was he making conspiracies out of coincidences? Looking for some outside culprit to blame for Meg's death? Unwilling to look at the cold truth and his own part in it? He hadn't done nearly as much for his sister as he could, always too busy and her too timid to ask.

Ridiculous to blame phantom fevers. He was scared and upset, like everyone else in town, grasping for explanations, trying to see patterns where there were none. In a place as quiet and peaceful as Trinity Bay, they'd gone off the charts in terms of deaths and assaults in the past two weeks. No wonder everyone was on edge.

He couldn't let that get in the way of his judgement. Had to keep a cool head, or he'd wind up sounding just like Dani Kensington and Theresa Zane. Raving about ghosts, demonic possession, psychic powers.

To coin a phrase, bullshit.

* * *

"Theresa, hon, quit fussing over me, I'm fine," Travis Zane said with a chuckle. "I'm not going to drop dead on you. Don't worry."

"How can I not worry?" She thumped his overnight bag down on his bed. "This isn't a good place for you right now, Dad."

"Oh, now she's trying to shuffle me off to the old folks' home," he said to Jack. "So's she can be alone with her new boyfriend."

"It's not like that!" she protested. "Your last heart attack was brought on my a bad scare, remember? I don't want it to happen again!"

"I doubt there's any more bodies hidden around the house, unless you've had a busier few days than I thought."

"Dad, I'm serious!" She turned to face him with her hands on her hips. "Let go of the Zane stubbornness for a minute and listen to me! What Damon and I saw the other night would have scared the hell out of anyone, and it's not over. There is something here, something in this house. Not just Glory. And it's not friendly. It's fixed on me, Dad. Anyone around me is in danger. I don't want you to get hurt because of me."

"Who's the stubborn Zane now? You can't expect me to leave my only girl alone to fight a ghost, or whatever it is."

"I don't know what it is, but I've seen what it can do. People are dead. I'm like a carrier or something, infecting people with this thing. Then it gets into their minds somehow, makes them do crazy things."

"Honey, it's not your fault –"

"There's not a whole lot of difference between it being my fault and it being because of me," she argued. "Either way, I have to do something about it. Quick, before more people suffer. Look at what happened to Kel McGuire's sister! I only talked to her for a few minutes Sunday night, and now she's dead."

"That hardly had anything to do with you."

"How do you know? My God, Dad, I don't even dare leave the house! Practically every woman I've talked to since I got here has been affected by this. All but Mrs. Davis, and I almost know why. I almost understand. It's at the back of my brain. It has to do with something Grandma Tashi gave her. A dream catcher. Like the one I used to have, remember?"

"Sure, your mom broke it. But Theresa, your grandmother made those as a hobby. She had one in her room, and so did your Aunt Dorry. Besides, it's to ward off bad dreams, not evil spirits."

"What if it's an evil spirit *causing* the bad dreams?" she countered. "What if Grandma Tashi knew about it and was trying to protect herself, her family, her friends?"

"I've never had any troubles like that."

"It only affects women." She swallowed, and looked at her father with dread in her eyes. "And some men . . . men that have . . . uh . . . been involved with me. Romantically."

"What are you talking about?"

"There's a lot about my life that you never knew, Dad. That Mom didn't want you to know because she thought you'd take me away from her, and that I didn't want you to know because I was ashamed. But when I was a teenager, I . . . slept around a lot. And I just found out that . . . that a bunch of my ex-lovers are all dead. All killed. Murdered. Since I came here. Since all of this started. By someone or something that no one can identify." She gave him a quick rundown, glossing over the gory parts and not mentioning any names, no names, certainly not that of her stepfather. "The roses, Dad, see? The roses are a link. Sandy was fixated on them, so was Ruth, and Celeste. And I bet Dani and Megan McGuire were, too."

Travis had grown pale. She was terrified for his health, but she had to impress upon him how grave the situation was in hopes that he would agree to stay out of it. If he moved in to Silver Grove, just for a while, she would know that he'd be safe. She could confront whatever force had focused on her without worrying that its manifestation might trigger another heart attack.

"Do you believe me, Dad?"

"I believe you, honey."

"Do . . . do you still . . ."

"I still like you fine, still love you. I should never have given in to Lois when she wanted to take you away, but back then, no judge was going to take a child away from her mother. I've never been anything but proud of you, Theresa."

She hugged him, tremendously relieved.

"But I'm not going to Silver Grove," he finished. "I'm staying right here. If it's the death of me, at least I'll go out trying to help my daughter." The firm set of his jaw told her that he was going to win this one, that she couldn't out-stubborn him this time.

"Okay, Dad. Okay."

"So, just what are we up against?"

"I wish I knew." She told him what she and Damon had observed, and what little Damon's brother had been able to piece together from the various police reports on the murders. "Somehow it knew who they were, where they were. *I* didn't even know where they were. It can . . . appear, I guess . . . anywhere, and it's strong, inhumanly strong. The only witness said it looked like a guy in a monster-movie costume. The Phantom of the Opera or something."

Travis fell silent, mulling it over, and Theresa unpacked his bag. "Honey, I don't mean to pry and I don't mean to be indelicate . . ."

She looked at him with arched eyebrows. "What?"

"These men who've been killed . . . they were all your lovers?"

"One way or another, you could say that," she said bitterly.

"But . . . what about . . . other targets?"

A folded shirt dropped from her hands. "Oh, my God! Steven!"

* * *

He dozed, floating easily in the midst of stolen dreams.

Images surrounded him, warmed and soothed him for all that they were images partly composed of rape, violence, incest, brutality. The darkest secret fantasies, the hidden lusts and longings of the souls. Some were pitiful in their innocence, others of sufficient depravity to bemuse even one such as himself.

Among the dreams were memories of his own, of the screams and pain and blood of the men he'd killed. Savage triumph. A sense of power. Oh, yes. No one developed more of a taste for power than those who had been utterly helpless.

Soon he would be rested enough to rouse again. Rouse and continue his work. This time, he was determined not to fail.

* * *

"Help you, Chief Blake?" Lan Scribner rose from his desk in a hurry, smoothing his comb-over and trying to make it look as if he hadn't been napping with his feet up. He was still wearing the somber dark suit he'd worn to the Haverley's funeral.

Damon grinned. "I'm not here on official business, Lan, relax. I was wanting to poke around the archives."

"Brave man. Ever seen it down there?" Lan shook his head. "This is one of the oldest buildings in town, and I think they stored everything down cellar. Probably find the original land charter."

"I hear your family knows a lot about local history," Damon nudged casually as he followed the older man down a claustrophobic flight of wooden stairs lit by a single cobwebbed bulb.

"Oh, yeah," Lan said. "Mind your head here, the doorjamb's low. "There's been Scribners in Trinity Bay ever since it was founded. My great-grandfather Elias, and Jacob Cliffwood, they were with the Gregg Expedition in 1849, the group that discovered Humboldt Bay. You know, they named that bay Trinity at first, then changed it. So when old Jacob came a little further north, he used the same name, as he liked it better."

The basement of the Leland Building was a long, narrow L-shape stacked to the beams with old crates, cardboard boxes, and filing cabinets. On quick look, it seemed to Damon that it was organized in sideways geologic layers, the newer stuff at the front, the older getting pushed progressively backward to become more cluttered and crammed.

"How do you find anything down here?" he wondered glumly, knowing how he was going to be spending the rest of his day.

"Luck, mostly," Lan replied. "What in particular are you looking for?"

"The real olden days. I'm trying to find out something about Jacob Cliffwood's kids." He pointed into the dusty, shadowy recesses of the basement. "Back there, right?"

"The missing kids?"

"You know about that?"

"Oh, sure. My aunt Kate, my dad's sister, she married Abraham Cliffwood. Oh, and was my mother dead-set against it? You bet! Kept telling Kate that she was a fool to stay, that her children would be snatched away by the boogeyman or somesuch."

"Why'd she think that?"

"Ah, I'm sure it was mostly to get under old lady Myra's skin. They hated each other like a pair of queen cats, I tell you. My mom just couldn't stand it that her own sister-in-law went and married Myra's nephew."

"No boogeyman, though."

"Nope. Though both of my cousins did come to a bad end. Barbara, she did the same thing as the McGuire girl. Sleeping pills. And Edward wound up in a sanitarium."

"Bad luck house?" Damon said it lightly, but meant it underneath. He couldn't stop thinking about what Theresa had given him to read yesterday. It had all the elements of one of those books his mother enjoyed . . . a brooding house full of family secrets, a domineering matriarch, a lecherous stepfather, an innocent girl caught in the middle. But this was even stranger, because the past was literally coming back to haunt them.

"Oh, absolutely," Lan said in all seriousness. "Bad luck house. Old Jacob started that mill with John Leland as a partner, then squeezed him out. Added insult to injury by marrying his daughter to get his hands on her inheritance, and used that to spruce up Seacliff. He built that house on the sweat and tears of his betrayed partner, so if anyone deserved bad luck, it was him."

"He died in the mill, didn't he?"

"Out on the skid road behind the mill. Redwood log was sliding down, hit a stump, flipped up and over, and son of a bitch, crushed him like a beer can."

Who needs the archives? Damon thought. "Then his wife remarried, right?"

"Right. Reeveman, his name was. From Back East. He only lasted about five years though."

"What happened to him?"

"Drowned. Took old Jacob's boat out and drowned. Guess that was the last straw for his wife's sanity. Two of her kids had gone missing in the past few years and the other one had been sent away to school, so she had no kids around, lost her husband. Had a hard time keeping servants, too."

"Lan, do you know anything about a necklace?"

"What necklace?"

"Silver, with a black rose on it?"

"It sounds familiar, but darned if I can remember why. I seem to think I saw something like that in a portrait once. You could check at Seacliff; the last I heard Thornton still had all the ancestors on display in the second-floor gallery."

"Thanks, I might do that." He had no idea how he was going to approach the subject with Brad Thornton, though. "When Jacob's kids disappeared, was there much about it in the paper, do you think?"

"The paper wasn't much back then. Came out once a week. But yeah, there might be something. Mind me asking why you're interested in all this old stuff?"

"Just curious. If they're going to turn Seacliff into a hotel, it might be nice for us all to know a little more about the place's history."

Lan gave him a look that said he wasn't fooled for a minute. "Oh, that right? You know, Officer, some folks who've been here a while might tell you that sometimes it's best to let the past alone."

"What about you, Lan? What might you say?"

He stared into the depths of the basement moodily. "I'd say that sometimes it's best to go a step further, and tear out the past, roots and all, burn it, and scatter the ashes."

* * *

"Damn, damn, damn," Theresa chanted as she hung up the phone.

Travis looked at her sympathetically. "Didn't sound like it went very well."

"I blew it. I really blew it. Steven thinks I'm ready for the men in the white coats. Thinks the stress of the divorce, the move, and living in L.A. made me snap. He wouldn't listen to me." She dropped into a chair and ran her hands through her hair, groaning. "He's halfway ready to file a restraining order, and as for seeing Lora over Christmas, he doesn't know if it's such a good idea. The man is in danger, damn it, and I can't get through to him."

"Want me to try?"

She grimaced. "I don't think it would do any good. But there has to be something I can do! I can't just sit back and let this . . . this . . . whatever the hell it is tear Steven to pieces. What would that do to Lora?"

"We could see about contacting the police down there in Phoenix."

"First off, how would we convince them? Damon's brother, or this partner of his, might believe us, but they're in New York. And even if we did, what could they do? Put him under police protection? Against what? What good would guns be against something like that?"

"A priest, then?" he suggested, only half-joking.

"If I thought it would do any good, I'd convert to about any religion that didn't require me to make human sacrifices, but there isn't time! It could wake up any minute and decide to finish its work!"

"What do you mean, wake up?"

She paused, surprised at what she'd said. "I don't know. But the past couple of nights, ever since it tried to make Dani kill Damon, I haven't felt its presence. I've been sleeping fine, getting enough rest, dreaming like I normally dreamed. And on some instinctive level, I guess I knew that was a part of it."

"So you're aware of this thing."

"Somehow . . ." she trailed off. "I was thinking about getting myself a dream catcher, but now I'm not so sure. Blocking this thing isn't the answer. I've got to find a way to stop it, to destroy it. Otherwise, it could just keep coming back."

"If it does . . . kill –" he dragged the word out of his mouth reluctantly, "– Steven, then what?"

Theresa sat down, wrapping her arms around herself to ward off a chill. "Dad, I don't even want to know."

* * *

23

Jerry Forrester sighed in delight as the cool evening mist hit him. "It's so good to be out of there!"

The orderly chuckled as he wheeled him toward the rattletrap Chevy that was the Forrester family car. "No matter how nice we try to make the place, everybody's always happiest to be going."

His dad ambled on his right, and although Charlie had visited every day, Jerry couldn't get over how bad Dad looked. Like a scarecrow, but not the cheery Ray Bolger variety. A week plus of life without Mom was wearing on the old guy, wearing on him big-time.

Jenny did her best to make up for it, babbling with enforced effervescence about how glad she was to have Jerry finally coming home, how she'd gotten his room ready for him, how she was even cooking meatloaf for dinner, his favorite. Her little arms were burdened with a cardboard box crammed with Jerry's new menagerie of plushies, most of which would probably wind up joining Jen's already large collection. He especially noted her eyeing the two Beanie Babies that she didn't already own.

Jerry closed his eyes and turned his face toward the soft grey sky, for a moment putting everything out of his mind – the fact that his mom was still sitting in a soft-walled room somewhere, that his best friend was at a funeral party for his dead folks, and anything and everything having to do with black roses –and just relishing his freedom and the sea-scent of the air.

He was out of the hospital, he was going home, and for the first time since his mom had come at him with a knife, he could really believe that he wasn't going to die.

The worst was over.

* * *

Damon listened to Theresa's recounting of her conversation with her ex-husband, and his heart went out to her. Even though the marriage was over, she wasn't like some embittered divorced spouses who would happily see their one-time partners slowly put to death.

"There has to be something we can do!" she finished. "Should I go there myself, talk to him in person? He already thinks I've lost it. Might even think this is some weird scheme of mine to get Lora away from him."

"Or that you're doing it yourself," Travis threw in.

"That *I'm* the killer? Dad, that's crazy!"

"No crazier than the rest of this, from his point of view anyway," Damon said. "We know you aren't, but I can tell you right now what my brother's partner would say."

"What's that, that the only way to get rid of this thing before it kills anyone else is to shoot *me?*"

"Pretty much."

"Because I'm the key, I'm the . . . the what? Source of its power? Somehow, it knows things that even I've forgotten, or don't care about anymore. It's digging into my memories to slaughter men from my past, men I haven't even thought about in years." She flopped on the couch like a dropped rag doll. "What the hell kind of ghost *is* this, anyway?"

The three of them lapsed into a grim silence, interrupted only by Jack's eager/wistful cry from the window – it sounded like *eh-eh-eh-eh-eh*, his tail whipping back and forth as he hunkered down as if to launch himself through the glass at the birds beyond.

Damon didn't want to ask, least of all in front of her dad, but cleared his throat so self-consciously that both of them were suddenly looking at him.

"Don't take this the wrong way," he said, trying to soften it with his best cowboy grin, "but is your ex-husband the . . . only other possible victim?"

Travis sagged in his chair in a posture of relief, letting Damon know that he'd been wanting to ask the very same thing but wasn't sure how to do it without coming out sounding judgmental and controlling – like a father, in other words.

"Yes, just Ste –" Theresa closed her mouth with a snap. "Oh. Wait." Color flooded her cheeks. "Uh . . . there was one other."

"Before or after?" Damon asked.

"Before. The first semester of college." She avoided looking at either of them. "A party, my roommate Ramona's older brother was on leave from the Army and had a party. Ramona took a bunch of her friends. I'd been meaning to change my ways, now that I was away from home, fresh start in a new place. But old habits and all of that. It was one of the brother's friends. Just a one-night thing. After that –" here she cast an appealing glance at her father, "I did change. No more parties, no more drinking, no more guys. Just me and my books, good little student girl, until I married Steven."

He reached over and patted her hand. "It's all behind you, honey."

"It's like it happened to someone else. More like something I saw in a movie or read in a book than something I actually lived. That girl . . . that wild girl . . . it's like that wasn't even me."

"What was his name?" Damon asked.

"Tony."

"Tony . . . what?"

She dropped her eyes again, and painfully admitted, "I don't know. He was Italian, he was in the Army like Ramona's brother, older than me by about five or six years . . . that's all I knew."

"These killings," Damon said. "They've been in . . . in order?"

Theresa nodded.

"So this Tony person would be next on the list."

"Yeah, but what do we do? He's not any more likely to believe us than Steven! What would we say, even if we could find him? Hey, Tony, you probably don't remember, but this one-night-stand from ten years ago is your death warrant?"

"We've got to try anyway." Damon grabbed paper and pen. "Is there anything else you remember? What about the roommate? Still in touch with her?"

"Ramona? No, she moved out of the dorm halfway through the school year to live with her boyfriend. My next roommate, Tammy, was as studious and unsociable as I was trying to be. Ramona's last name was Ruiz, though. Her brother was Manuel. They were local, from Phoenix, I remember that."

"That's a starting point, at least. We can worry about the rest if we find him."

* * *

Another funeral over, another inappropriately-named funeral party out of the way. The business of death taken care of. Loose ends neatly tied up.

A long, hard day. But now it was over.

Brad Thornton eased off his shoes and rubbed his feet. Hundred and forty bucks, and still pinched his toes. But then, he hadn't worn them since Angela's funeral, almost a year ago.

Big Al and his bitch of a wife were closed books. He'd miss Al, both as a friend – conveniently forgetting that in their last not-so-friendly exchange Al would have twisted his head off like an apple off its stem if he hadn't still been on company time – and even more as a worker.

Al had known the sawmill inside and out, known all of the workers and all of the details. Brad was a good ad-man, a good slap-the-back fellow, but when it came down to the actual hands-on of running the place, he was without a clue.

Still, that was the whole point of being management. He didn't have to know how things actually *worked.* Just needed to know how to push the papers, sign the forms, make the deals, and keep the grunt labor motivated.

And if all else failed, he would just sell the damn thing. Bring in an outside company to run it, maybe see about that long-delayed oil rig project. There would be layoffs, though, a blow to his popularity in the community. Even turning Seacliff into a hotel, with the jobs that would create and the tourism it would bring, couldn't offset in the eyes of the town layoffs at the mill.

As if the mill had been open and running ceaselessly and profitably for a hundred years. Far from it! Brad knew all about how the mill had been 'temporarily' shut down during the eco-freak years. What were a few hundred men out of work, a few hundred families going hungry, stacked up against a few mangy owls?

He'd brought the mill back, made it operational and profitable again. Because he knew a truth that seemed to have escaped some others. Shouting about the environment was fine for the hippies, college kids, potheads, and 'shroom munchers, but in little towns like Trinity Bay, built on reliance on the forests and redwoods, the working man was more interested in keeping cash in the pocket and food on the table.

April hadn't understood that. Had turned her back on what, while not a fortune, was a sizable chunk of change. She'd let the mill sit and molder, costing money in taxes and even more for repairs when he eventually got it going again.

He shuddered to think what Seacliff would have looked like if it hadn't been provided for in the conditions laid out in old Myra Cliffwood's will. It would have been as bad as the mill, peeling paint, broken windows, water damage, infested with rats and bats and other assorted wildlife. Maybe even a few of those damnable owls.

The house was quiet around him. Not silent, not the way its large halls and cavernous atrium caught and held the distant rushing of the waves. But it was a soothing sound, drowning out the babble of the television in the servants' wing where the Davises had their apartment. Walt was half-deaf, wouldn't admit it or suffer the indignity of a hearing aid, and made up for it by cranking *The Tonight Show* to a point where even the thick walls couldn't muffle it completely.

Brad went into the atrium, mindful of how sock-feet could be treacherous on slick marble, a tumbler of Scotch in one hand.

The room was dark but for the row of lights that were set into the walls of the pool. It turned the rectangle of water into a mystical, rippling jewel and cast flickering light-wraiths up along the gallery rails and dome of blue and green stained glass.

He wasn't much of a swimmer, but he enjoyed sitting by the pool. Would enjoy it even more when the hotel plans were complete and Seacliff was full of guests. Guests who would bring their daughters, who would dive and frolic like bikini-clad naiads before dolling themselves up in elegant gowns to dine in the sumptuous dining room.

Now that was a prospect that suited him far more than running a sawmill.

He sat back on one of the lounge chairs – tubular white metal with cushions of waterproof swirled blue and green – and sipped his drink.

The place wouldn't be nearly so quiet then, but it was a price he was willing to pay. The murmur of voices and music from behind closed doors would be more than offset by the benefits.

Who knew . . . maybe some of those lush bikini-nymphs would even dare each other into girlish games of skinny-dipping, sneaking down to the pool when the rest of the guests and staff were asleep. Never knowing how well the upper galleries might cloak an observer in deep shadows.

Angela certainly had never noticed. Not that she'd gone skinny-dipping, not that timid slut. No, nor even a bikini. Plain white one-piece. But even so, it had shown off her legs and ass and tits to good advantage. Watching her slide through the water with her torrent of hair streaming back . . .

He chuckled ruefully as he realized he was getting hard. All dressed up and noplace to go. Not much use thinking of Angela, who had been dead and gone for a year. And it wasn't as if she'd been much of a lay anyhow. Crying and carrying on, just like she *hadn't* been spreading them for that Forrester kid, and who knew how many other besides. Just like her mother.

And then to think that his own damned lawyer had accused him of chasing the girl! Some loyalty, that! Okay, sure, he'd been April's lawyer first, but it wasn't as if he'd ever really gotten to know the woman.

Or was it? For all Brad knew, April could have been carrying on behind his back with her lawyer. After all, it had come as enough of a shock to him just to find out she'd even had a lawyer in the first place! And then to find out about Seacliff, the money, and everything else she'd been keeping from him . . . and to think, a marriage was supposed to be based on trust.

Well, she hadn't trusted him, that was plain enough. If she had, she never would have come sneaking home that night when she'd told him that her dance show was going to go until midnight. Never would have come home and found him in Angela's room, checking out her sleeping daughter.

It wasn't like he'd even touched the little bitch! But April had taken it all wrong, and to shut her up, he'd finally had to just push her down the stairs. He hadn't even really intended to kill her, just get a moment's peace, but down she went. And then Angela had seen the whole thing, been ready to call the police. It had taken all of his craft and cunning to convince her that it was as much her own fault as it was his.

And then it had just been the two of them. The two of them, and Trinity Bay. His wife's secret inheritance. For Angela's own good, he was sure it would be better to move north, away from the corrupting influences of the Bay Area and April's meddling hippie friends.

Coming to Seacliff had been like coming home. From the moment he'd walked through the door, he'd felt as if he was in the presence of an old friend. An old friend who had just woken up, but was very glad to see him.

Everything would have been fine if not for the damn lawyer. Sniffing around, saying things to suggest that he didn't believe April's death was as accidental as it sounded.

Brad grinned to himself. Fixing the brakes had been easy – long before there had been Brad Thornton, advertising genius, and Brad Thornton, college football hero, there had been Brad Thornton, gifted mechanic. At least as far as fixing brakes. He'd learned that little trick from his own father, who had gotten rid of Brad's hellish shrew of a mother that way.

Yes, after that, all it had taken was a phone call. Ringing up the esteemed Mr. Smythe's car phone after he'd left Seacliff hadn't really been necessary. The brakes would have failed sooner or later. But calling him up, laughing at him, mocking his suspicions about April's death, making him mad, knowing that anger caused the foot to come down even harder on the gas pedal . . . that had been the fun part.

Then, just when he'd known Smythe's car was speeding down the hill toward the bridge, he'd taken the big risk, told Smythe that his brakes were out, and listened with something akin to glee as the car lost control and smashed through the picturesque rail. Smythe's terrified shrieks on the way down nearly split Brad's phone in two, only ending in the final splashing crunch of the car plowing snout-first into the swiftest part of the Agate River.

Oddly, or perhaps not, thinking about that didn't make his erection go away. On the contrary, in fact.

Something moved in the shadows above him.

Brad caught himself just as he was reaching into his lap, recalling his earlier thoughts about how the gallery was a good hiding and observing place. He picked up his glass instead, as if that was what he'd been about to do all along. Would not do for the dumpy Mrs. Davis to catch the lord and master with his hand down his pants, now, would it?

Yes, there was someone up there. He didn't tilt his head for a deliberate look, but resentment bubbled in his veins. Sneaking about, was she? Spying on him?

He sipped more of his drink, then saw the movement again. But it hadn't come from above, as he'd first thought. From outside. On the terrace. Outside in the darkness of the terrace garden, moving from the concealment of one shadow to another.

Brad leaned back and let his eyes drift mostly shut, appearing to be resting, while really watching intently from under lowered lids.

Too big to be a cat or a dog, and the wrong shape. A person. Not a grown man. A woman, or maybe a kid.

He didn't know any women who might come creeping around the back door after dark, but he did know a certain kid. A certain bratty neighbor kid who at first look seemed like a budding young fag, but was still able to corrupt stepdaughters. A certain bratty-neighbor-fagboy who had just been let out of the hospital tonight, according to local scuttlebutt.

Some people couldn't leave well enough alone.

He'd escaped with his life from his murderous knife-wielding psycho mother. One would think that would leave a kid with a healthy respect for authority. But instead of staying home like a good boy, here he was, probably still with the antiseptic stink of the hospital on his skin, snooping around Seacliff.

And just what did young Mr. Forrester hope to find, anyway? There was no Angela here, not anymore, no Angela to let him in the house although Brad had expressly forbidden it. The time for amateur heroics was long past. Couldn't rescue a fair maiden who was rotting in the ground.

His lip wanted to curl but he forced it to relax. Probably, his own brush with the Reaper had given the little whoreson time to think, time to dream up lies. What did he hope to find? Some proof that Brad had caused Angela's death, maybe? That would be a good trick, since he'd been as stunned by her suicide as anyone else. Certainly hadn't pushed the bitch off the bluff.

Or . . . maybe Angela had said something to him. Yes. Brad had had that thought before. Made the Forrester kid think that what was going on was against her will. Now here came the bold knight, better late than never, looking for some proof?

"Let him come, then," Brad muttered, but without meaning to.

Like someone else had spoken. Someone right beside him. The devil on his shoulder. Just like in the cartoons he remembered watching as a child. Devil on one shoulder, angel on the other. Except in his case, there was no angel steering him toward the straight and narrow. No angel? Hell, not even Jiminy Cricket.

It was the stress, of course. The stress of losing his wife, moving to Trinity Bay. He'd certainly never had any such silly ideas before that. Devil on his shoulder. Voice in his ear. Yeah, right. But it was impossible to deny that low, seductive whisper. He'd heard it the strongest on the night he'd finally given Angela what she deserved.

Wicked girls. Oh, yes. Wicked girls liked nothing better than to ruin a man. Even from beyond the grave. They worked their wiles on men, promised them life and then let it be torn away in blood and pain. Made them so distraught that they chose the cold embrace of the sea. Left them to die in lonely misery, hungry and afraid.

And now, even a year dead, here was Angela trying to ruin him again. Sending her would-be boyfriend around to try and get the goods on him. Just what did the bratty fagboy hope to see, anyway? Did he think he'd catch Brad attacking some jailbait runaway hitchhiker? Or find him gloating and chortling over a diary in which he recorded all of his acts, a diary which could then be spirited away to that idiot cowboy cop Damon Blake?

"If you come in here, my fine young friend," Brad said softly into the depths of his glass, an ice cube bumping against his lips as he spoke, "you'll regret it. There are laws against trespassing, you know. But come on. Come on and try."

Then the figure moved again, furtive through a patch of turquoise glow from the pool, and Brad saw that it wasn't Jerry Forrester at all.

* * *

But Jerry Forrester *was* outside of Seacliff. He wasn't entirely sure *why* he was, just that he'd been unable to sleep, felt the need to go for a walk.

Not smart, he told himself as he got dressed in the red glow of his clock-radio. He'd only been out of the hospital for a few hours, and no matter how bright a front he was putting on for Dad and Jenny, he was far from feeling up to snuff.

What he should be doing was pulling up his covers and drifting off in the safe cocoon of his room, his rock posters on the walls, his programs from drama club productions stuck in the corner of his mirror under a shelf of books ranging from Shakespeare to stage make-up. He was home, after all.

Home, where his own mother had carved him up like a Thanksgiving turkey . . . and now she was gone. According to Dad, she was in her ward at Blue Lake State, raving, and in restraints because she kept trying to hurt herself. Claw at herself.

He did his best to put it out of his mind, but it wouldn't go easy. He missed her, the house felt wrong without her, but at the same time he was scared half to death.

So he'd gotten up, moving with the sly stealth of any seventeen-year-old boy sneaking out past curfew. Jenny's door was propped open, his little sister curled in a tangle of blankets with one foot sticking out – and she had wasted no time commandeering those two Beanies, he saw. Dad's door was shut tight, and Bingo was stretched out in front of it like a draft-stopper.

His restless feet had carried him past the Zane house and along the woods-cloaked path he used to take to see if Angela was there and her stepfather wasn't. The path that had led him to his encounter with the weird apparition near the black rose bush.

He had to see it again. Not the ghost; he didn't particularly want to see anything that creepy on this dark and misty night, but the rosebush. Maybe seeing it would help him understand how much of this was real, and how much was his own drug- and stress-induced lunacy.

By day, the rosebush had been a deeply colorful jewel against the lighter green of the undergrowth. By night, it was a hulking snarl of black and blacker, marred only in a few places by lighter sheared-off ends of stems.

Jerry stood beside it, breathing its rich scent that was more like dark chocolate and heavy spices than anything floral. He didn't know a whole lot about plants, but wasn't it true that they closed up at night, then opened to the sun? Or were roses open all the time once they'd bloomed? And did they even bloom this late in the year? He wasn't sure, but could see for himself that all the flowers were unfurled, glistening faintly in the mist. If the moon came out, he thought, the whole thing would shimmer like satin.

His chest ached along his various fresh scars, and his head was swimmy from the exertion of the walk after so many days doing nothing more strenuous than hobbling back and forth to the bathroom. He lowered himself into the damp grass, knowing he was courting pneumonia but unable to face the trek back without a little rest.

The moon did come out then, peeking briefly through a gauzy rent in the clouds. And he was right, the rosebush, adorned in mist, did shimmer. It was at once beautiful and scary, the way certain sports cars or guns were.

He was just getting up, having decided he'd rather wipe himself out than stay here bathed in that spooky light, when three figures appeared. Three female figures, melting through the mist.

"Oh, jeez, I'm having a MacBeth moment," Jerry moaned, recalling a scene from the play he'd held a minor role in last summer at the university. "Enter three witches."

Except they weren't witches, no trio of hunched hags. They were girls. A blonde no older than Jenny, a brunette of about fourteen whose dusky black hair was the exact same shade as the rose petals, and an auburn-haired girl of his own age.

He recognized the last one, and the strength ran out of his limbs. His arms, which he'd been using to push himself up, went limp and Jerry thumped back down on his keister.

"Angela," he breathed.

She heard him, turned toward him. If he hadn't already been on the ground, he would have collapsed. Her face was sad, so unbearably sad.

Of the three, she was the only one not appearing to wear a necklace. She looked so out of place, the other two in their old-fashioned clothes and hairstyles, Angela in what looked like the same nightgown she'd been wearing that awful night on the bluff.

"I'm so sorry," Jerry said, not caring that tears were running down his cheeks. "I should have done something. I should have helped. If only you'd told me."

Her pale, pale hands reached out. Jerry got clumsily to his knees, Romeo in blue jeans with nary a balcony in sight. But rather than clasp his outstretched hands, Angela pointed.

He followed with his eyes, and frowned in puzzlement at what he saw.

Someone was creeping through the manicured garden toward the back of Seacliff. From his spot out here at the edge of order, at the beginning of the wild woods, he could see the intruder but couldn't be seen himself.

Now Angela's cool, insubstantial fingers curled around his, and though she didn't speak, he somehow understood that the terror was going to begin again. The force that had been born of the roses would be wakened by the violence that was about to happen.

Unless he could do something to stop it . . .

* * *

Dani Kensington wasn't sure what she expected to find at Seacliff. Probably nothing. Very unlikely that she would poke her little nosie up to a window and see Brad Thornton in the middle of some hellish rite – pentacles of goat's blood, black candles, daggers with bone handles and cruelly jagged blades.

Yeah, pretty darn unlikely. Though in a way, it'd be kind of nice. At least then she'd have something to go on other than her own inner conviction that Thornton was responsible for what had happened to her.

So here she was, Dani Kensington, Girl Adventurer. Some joke for a babe that was pushing thirty, skulking around in the dark like Nancy Drew all grown up.

Or, really, it was closer to the way the dippy characters in horror movies behaved. Here she was all by her lonesome, going up to take a look at the haunted house. In the dead of night, no less.

Though, really, if she'd been in a horror movie the way they were making them nowadays, she would have to be a.) ten years younger, b.) wearing a babydoll nightie, and c.) fresh from a steamy clinch with her boyfriend . . .who would by now be nailed to a tree with a post-hole digger rammed through his chest.

But what else was she supposed to do? Sit in her apartment and stare at the colored-in roses on the bathroom wallpaper, waiting for the voice to start up again? And just what would it make her do this time?

Even if she couldn't catch Thornton in the act, at the very least maybe she could find some proof. Either that he was, or wasn't, involved. Then she could decide where to go from there.

It had been years since she'd been inside Seacliff. The events of late 1978 and early 1979 had been the talk of the schoolyard, and though Dani had been too young at the time, good stories, like jump-rope rhymes, were passed down from one year to the next. By the time she was eleven, Barbara Cliffwood's Christmastime suicide and her brother Edward's subsequent breakdown had been re-told and embellished in the gore-crow way that only pre-teens could love.

The house had been five years vacant the summer that Dani was twelve. She hadn't found a best friend to replace Theresa Zane, and her status as the heftiest and clumsiest kid in her class didn't help her in the popularity department. Trying to make herself included, she'd gone along with a slumber-party dare to go into the abandoned manor.

And now here she was again. Considerably older, and hardly bearing any resemblance to the girl she'd been. The gap in the fence that had once threatened to wedge her like a cork in a bottle now only gave her a problem topside.

The garden offered plenty of hiding places. She'd waited until she saw Thornton's car come back, until a light had gone on, and then off, in the master suite. The windows of the housekeeper's apartment in the east wing were flickering with the glow of a television, and the French doors leading from the atrium to the terrace were touched with soft blue.

The gap in the fence was on the east end. She caught a glimpse of Walt Davis, zonked out in a recliner while Jay Leno bantered with Tom Hanks. She passed by as quietly as a breath of wind, though as loud as he had the volume, she probably could have tap-danced her way across the terrace.

The moon came partway out, leaving her horribly exposed for the split second it took her to react. She hunkered down in the shelter of a large planter, realizing that her getup – black leggings, black sweatshirt, even a black bandanna to cover her hair – was fine for the shadows but against the pale surface of the moonlit terrace made her stand out vividly.

Even more carefully now, she all but oozed her way from one planter to the next. The garden was set up in a series of steps, rockeries, and waterfalls, which gave her a convoluted but mostly secure path to the patio and the French doors.

She came to the wall, slid to the edge of the doors, and pressed her face to the glass.

Right away, she spotted Thornton. Sitting in a lounge chair, the dancing rippling radiance from the pool moving over him. Head tilted to the side, eyes shut. A tumbler loosely grasped in one hand, resting against his thigh. Maybe a quarter-inch of liquid remained in it, and Dani wasn't guessing apple juice.

Well. There he was.

Not summoning any demons, mixing up any mind-control potions in a mad scientist lab. Not even watching a Friendly Psychics infomercial. Just a forty-something wanna-be studmuffin sound asleep after a hard day and a few drinkie-poos.

Feeling absurdly let down, Dani eased back along the wall and wondered what to do next. It wasn't like she would find crumbling ancient tomes full of magic spells, open on his desk with the good bits carefully underlined.

What now?

Talk to him?

There was a bright idea. Oh, pardon me, Mr. Thornton, would you mind confessing that you took over my mind and made me try to kill a cop?

Still, dammit, she was here and she had to do something. If she didn't, it might happen again. Could happen again, at any time. She'd always been proud of being an independent thinker, and hadn't learned how to resist her own Pop's strong will just to be turned into a puppet by Brad Thornton.

She looked again, and he was gone.

Gone?

Then he moved, a sudden dark blur against the glass, throwing his weight against the door just as he twisted the handle. It swung out hard and fast, smacking Dani in the forehead and making stars dance in her eyes.

She stumbled backward, caught her heel on the raised lip of a flowerbed, and wheeled her arms for balance. The door flew the rest of the way open and Thornton was there, his good looks contorted in a mask of hate. He grabbed Dani and yanked her upright.

"Let me go, you bastard, I'll scream," she said, dizzy but tugging for freedom anyway.

"Trespassing little bitch," he snarled – actually *snarled!* – and punched her in the stomach.

Dani's breath, which she had drawn in hugely to scream so loud they'd hear her in Crescent City, gusted out. Bile splashed the back of her throat and she was sure she was going to throw up, fought it because she hated throwing up more than anything else.

While she was occupied trying to regain control of herself, Thornton swung her around, bent both arms painfully behind her back, and propelled her ahead of him into the atrium of Seacliff.

Her feet tangled and down she went. One leg shot backward, colliding with Thornton's, and he slipped. They crashed together at poolside. With her arms pinned behind her, she could do nothing to break her fall except twist so that she landed on chest and shoulder instead of squarely on her face.

Even if she could have gotten her breath, she knew there was no reasoning with him, so she wrenched loose, rolled, and raised one knee in a vicious angled bend just as he tried to throw himself on her. Missed his groin, got his hipbone so solidly she felt it reverberate up her leg.

She didn't slap or claw, but drove the base of her hand at his nose, meaning to shatter it and send splinters into his brain, all the books and movies said it worked, right? Probably go to jail but who cared?

He turned his head, not enough to avoid her blow entirely. She bashed him in the cheekbone, making the eye on that side squint shut and begin to water.

His hands closed around her throat.

Dani left off pummeling at his face and tried to pry his fingers from her neck. He was spitting curses at her, hitching his body so they both slid across the marble tile to the edge of the pool. Then he was half-straddling her, pushing her head backward and down.

Cold water soaked her hair, then her scalp. Then shifting blue light surrounded her as he forced her head underwater.

* * *

When Brad Thornton popped out of the doors like a well-dressed jack-in-the-box and grabbed the secret agent woman, Jerry left off trying to sneak and broke into as fast a run as he could manage.

Like most of Trinity Bay's younger citizens, he knew about the gap in the fence and had done his rite of passage back when Seacliff was abandoned. He passed the Davises' window and flash-thought about knocking, hollering for help. But everyone knew Mrs. Davis slept like a stone, and her husband, who had been the school janitor up until last year, couldn't hear a bomb blast.

He skidded across the patio and nearly went face-first into the edge of the open door, catching it by the handle and avoiding a collision by more luck than anything else.

Two struggling figures were at the side of the pool. The woman in black was submerged to the shoulders, huge bubbles rising and exploding, and in a cartoon, her screams would have pealed to the skylight with each bursting bubble. Her legs kicked and flailed, her hands grasped desperately.

Thornton knelt over her, stockinged feet and shirtsleeves, tie pulled askew, just a businessman relaxing after a long day. He was holding her under with one hand, and the other was ripping at her clothes.

Intent on rape or drowning or both simultaneous, he didn't notice Jerry until Jerry slammed both doubled fists down on the back of Thornton's neck in a half-assed maneuver that worked a hell of a lot better than he had any right to expect.

"Huhg!" Thornton grunted, falling sideways.

The woman toppled the rest of the way into the pool, then came up with a splash and a gasp. The bandanna had come off her hair. It was Doc Kensington's bartender daughter, Dani, the one who had shot up Nate's the other day.

Jerry didn't care if she'd shot up the entire town. He caught her wrist and tried to haul her out.

He saw her eyes widen, saw the warning begin to form on her lips, and then a glass tumbler with a thick bottom cracked against his skull. Wetness that reeked of alcohol sluiced over him, and he plunged into darkness.

* * *

Unable to sleep, Kel McGuire sat in front of the television. He was staring without seeing at a program on the culture of teen violence, something that normally would have interested him keenly, but none of it was sinking in.

He thought briefly about having a drink, but rejected the notion for four reasons – he wasn't much of a drinker, didn't have anything in the house but cooking sherry and an old bottle of Bailey's, he knew that it wouldn't help, and lastly, understood that facing his parents would be hard enough without also dealing with a hangover.

They were arriving tomorrow from Connecticut. He glanced at the notepad beside his phone. Three o'clock, at the somewhat inaptly-named Arcata-Eureka Airport – it was in McKinleyville, after all. Mental reminder to clean out the car before going to pick them up. It wasn't that he was a slob, far from it, but his car did tend to collect the clutter reflective of his typical busy day.

Kel sighed and slumped lower in his chair. He should be thinking about Megan, grieving for his sister, but it was hard to do while simultaneously trying to steel himself for the morrow. He could already hear the accusations, worsened because they were right, damn it, they were *right!* Why *hadn't* he known something was wrong? *Was* he too caught up in his work to notice his own family?

The guest bedroom was ready. He knew they would insist on staying at a motel, but also knew that if he didn't make the token offer, he'd hurt his mother's feelings.

He slumped even lower, mulling on and marveling at the terrible hold parents had on their children. Even grown up, thousands of miles from the place he'd lived his first twenty years on Earth, with a job and house and life of his own, his parents still had that hold.

No matter what you did for a living, how much money you made, who you married, where you lived, your parents decided for themselves if you were a success or not. If you didn't meet *their* expectations, even if you turned out phenomenally wealthy or famous, you were a failure in their eyes forever after.

Kel thought ruefully about a guy he'd known in college. Went on to become a multimillionaire industrialist, married to a gorgeous actress. Practically had the world at his feet. But because he hadn't followed in his father's footsteps and become a fisherman, he would always be a disappointment.

And so would he. Dad was a psychiatrist, Mom a pediatrician, and to make matters worse, his older sister Gwynne had *exceeded* parental hopes and was this very moment attending a conference on neurology in Vienna. Not just attending, but *presenting,* her paper on chemical mapping of brain function or whatever it was – Dad would know it word for word, Kel hadn't a doubt – had been exceptionally well-received.

Which was something of a relief, really. It meant Gwynne wouldn't be here until Sunday, and would have to leave again Monday. Less than twenty-four hours, all told, of family togetherness. And some of that time would be spent sleeping, as well as at the actual funeral and reception after.

He was sure that would still leave plenty of time for getting in digs at his career. Never mind that his counseling practice was thriving, that he'd single-handedly built Silver Grove from a shoddy adult-family home into one of the finest elder-care facilities in the county. Never mind that he was liked and respected here in town. By all but Arthur Kensington, but when you came right down to it, Art and Kelwyn McGuire Sr. had a fair amount in common when it came to parenting . . .

No, he wasn't a doctor, had settled for a Master's degree. At least it was in psychology; he could still hear his mother trying to mollify Dad by pointing out that Kel was *almost* a "real" scientist; he could have been a liberal-arts major or something . . .

Almost a real scientist. Like Megan had *almost* been a nurse, which wasn't as good as being a doctor but was still in the medical field . . . but she could have at least been a nurse, maybe a surgical nurse or a trauma nurse . . . oh, Megan had been a catalog of failed hopes as far as Peg McGuire had been concerned.

Poor Meg, his poor dear sister. Who had gone into the health-care field simply because it had been ingrained into her since birth, but who never would have been happy as a surgical or trauma nurse, because Meg had actually discovered that she liked *helping* people, taking care of people. The same sort of thing that Kel had discovered in himself. For the two of them, it had never been "How do I treat this case?" but "How do I help this person?"

Now she was gone, and not only had he been unable to help her, he hadn't even realized she needed help. He'd thought all Megan needed was time. Time out from under the parental thumb, out from under Gwynne's shadow. To live without Mom constantly at her about her weight, Dad constantly at her about her grades.

Kel couldn't slump any lower in his chair, so he gave up and slid onto the carpet, his long legs stretched out in front of him, toward the clunky little woodstove that stood self-importantly on its brick hearth.

He'd been so proud of Megan! Although he was much closer in age to Gwynne – Meg had been a late surprise for his parents – he'd always had more in common with her.

Or so he'd thought. But now, now that she had done something so drastic and incomprehensible – he was always going to think of suicide that way, no matter how many times he encountered it – he wondered what else about Megan he hadn't known.

The romance novels, of course, he knew about that. Knew that they represented something of an escape for Megan. The excitement, adventure, and passion that she felt she would never know in real life.

But what had brought her to this point? She'd been showing none of the signs that Kel associated with suicidal behavior. None. She'd been slowly but surely coming out of her shell, accepting herself for who she was rather than who she'd failed to become.

Was that it? The "what I've missed" syndrome? He had run into it before when he'd worked with chronic mentally ill patients. They spent long years in a decompensated state, got on a new med that started clearing them up, and then suddenly seemed to realize how much of their life had been such misery and chaos of thought. Unable to deal with that, they sometimes became overwhelmed and stepped out.

Not Megan. He couldn't see anything like that happening to Megan.

What had it been?

What could make Meg, who was so painfully honest that she would drive all the way back to the market if they gave her too much change, steal that bottle of sleeping pills from the hospital?

He realized his hands were clenched tight, his mind back in turmoil. Seeking answers. Demanding answers. When there were none to be given. Nothing but her note, which only created more questions.

If sleeping is the only way I can be with him, then I'll sleep forever.

He picked up the paperback, trying to understand how his sister had come to be so obsessed with a fictional hero that she took her own life in the apparent belief that she would wake up in his world. That was, at least, what her note implied.

An unwelcome thought popped into his head: *she dreamed it, she dreamed about him, just like Dani Kensington dreamed about Damon Blake.*

He restated his former opinion on the matter. "Bullshit."

The book had clearly been read several times. A favorite. Her small apartment had been full of books, many of them this same turbulent *affaire-de-cour* sort, with the Serenity Townshend books occupying a place of honor on the top shelf, above even Bertrice Small.

He riffled the pages absently, then started as something caught his eye. He dropped the book and it slid partway under the couch. Fishing it out, he tried to find that page again.

"You didn't see what you thought you saw," he told himself sternly.

There it was. A doodle in the margin. Meg was no artist, had never been. But he could still tell what it was supposed to be.

"Megan, my desire, my heart, my angel," he murmured against her flesh, his words caressing her soul just as his hands caressed her body. "Be mine for all time!"

Next to Alaric Hawke's declaration of love, Meg had drawn a thorned black rose.

"No," Kel said, shaking his head. "No, no, no, this is not what it looks like."

Angela . . . Sandy . . . Theresa . . . Dani . . .

Megan?

"No. Impossible."

There were no such thing as ghosts. No such thing as psychic powers.

"The dead do not reach out from beyond the grave to make people kill themselves over romance novels!" Kel said angrily, slapping the book against his knee.

There had to be a perfectly good, perfectly reasonable explanation . . .

All he had to do was think of it.

* * *

His eye was puffing shut, he had a red blotch on the side of his neck that was sure to bruise, and his hand was cut and gouged by broken glass.

"Drunk," Brad Thornton muttered. "Drunk, the funeral, so much stress. Wasn't wearing shoes. Slipped on the floor. Hit my head."

"Should I call the doctor?" Shauna Davis worriedly asked her husband.

"No doctor," Brad said thickly. The smell of Scotch hung around him in a cloud.

"He'll be all right," Walt Davis said. "Help me get him to his room, then bring the first-aid kit."

"Should get him out of those wet clothes before he takes a chill." Their eyes met, and the unspoken thought flew between them – that instead of finding their employer only half-soaked, they could have found his drowned body floating in the pool.

"I'll do it." Walt worked one shoulder under Brad's arm. "Mind that glass."

"I see it, I see it," she said. "Soon as we get him patched up, I'll get the broom."

"Good thing you heard him holler," Walt said. It was the closest he'd come to admitting he was half-deaf, and they both knew it.

"Woke me up," Shauna said, troubled. "Why, at first, I thought it was a woman's scream."

"Gee, thanks," Brad groaned, staggering heavily against Walt.

"Don't you worry, Mr. Thornton," Walt said. "Come with me. This-a-way. We'll use the elevator, okay, stairs might be a bit much tonight."

The elevator had been added in 1960, following old Myra Cliffwood's first stroke, which had come so close on the heels of her cousin Edward's marriage that the unkind tongues of town had much to say on the matter. It was an ornate brass cage climbing the side of the front hall, and it clanked and rattled like a jalopy on a cold morning. But it got them to the second floor, and Walt began shepherding his boss down the wide hallway.

"Ammoss fell inna pool," Brad said with much difficulty.

"Yessir, that would have woke you up," Walt replied jovially, mentally adding, *woke you up at the Pearly Gates, most likely*. "Might have tipped one too many, maybe."

The master suite was at the end of the west wing, overlooking the bay and coastline. Right time of the year, the barking of sea lions added their chorus to the music of the waves.

Brad reeled across the room and plowed face-first onto the bed. "Nummore. Overdiddit."

"Lemme help you out of those wet things." Walt began the matter-of-fact business, remembering the advice of his uncle, who had worked for one of those snobby East Coast families. Rich as they were, that didn't stop them from getting piss-drunk and carrying on like any low-class caveman who mashed beer cans on his forehead. The thing to do was just take care of them, and never mention it again or you'd find yourself out of a job.

Brad complied, shucking his shirt and pants and then putting his bathrobe on over undershirt and shorts. Shauna knocked discreetly and came in with the first aid kit, clucking her tongue as she swabbed the blood from his hands and applied Band-Aids.

The stinging of the antiseptic roused him somewhat, and he gave them both a shamefaced look. "Sorry to wake you, but thanks."

"You're welcome, Mr. Thornton, not a problem at all," Walt assured him. "We'll get it all cleared up, you can count on that."

"We're just glad you're all right." Finished, Shauna picked up his blood-spotted shirt. "I'll get this in the laundry right away."

"I owe you," Brad said, with the best smile he could muster in his condition. "Have to think of a nice way to pay you back."

"That's not necessary," Walt said. "We'll go now and let you get some sleep."

"No, I mean it. You've both been a tremendous help to me ever since I came here, and I want to show you how much I appreciate it. What would you say to a nice vacation? I know you've been talking about visiting your son in Idaho."

"Wally and Irma?" Shauna turned to Walt excitedly. "Oh, we've been wanting to see their new house!"

"My treat," Brad insisted. "My way of saying thank you."

"We'll talk about it in the morning," Walt said, nodding. *When you're sober*, he added to himself. "Very kind of you to offer."

"I won't take 'no' for an answer." Brad grinned, and there was something in it that gave Walt a little chill. "I can manage without you for a few days, at least."

"Well, like I said, we'll talk about it in the morning. 'Night, Mr. Thornton."

"Good night, and thanks again."

They left, closing his door behind them, and returned to their own little rooms above the kitchen. Shauna was on Cloud Nine, already planning what to pack and what they could do while they were in Idaho, but Walt only bobbed his head and grunted in the right places.

Weird, Thornton wanting them to go on vacation right now. Maybe he was embarrassed they'd seen him like that, wanted time to recover his dignity.

But he couldn't shake the feeling that there was more to it than just that.

* * *

"Finally," Damon Blake said as he hung up the phone.

"Something?" Theresa Zane asked hopefully as she came from the small kitchenette with two cups of coffee. She sat down at Scott James' desk, pushing a stack of DARE fliers out of the way.

"We're getting closer. That was the right Manuel Ruiz. He hasn't heard from his old buddy Tony in about four years, but he gave me the last name. Monatella. And another stroke of luck, if it pans out – he's from New York. Right in Derrek's territory."

"But will your brother help? Won't he think we're nuts, or joking, or something?"

"He might think that if it was anybody but me. He knows I wouldn't joke about anything this serious. Before I call him, though, I want to see if I can find out a little more about our man Tony."

"Even if we can find him, though . . . what then?"

Damon shrugged. "Hopefully, we can convince him he's a potential target of a serial killer and he'll agree to let Derrek and Mark put him under guard."

"What about Steven?"

"Trouble is . . ." He was wearing his hat today, and tipped it back on his head in the unconscious gesture of a cowpoke regarding a difficult trail ahead, "in New York, we've got an edge. We've got a pair of detectives willing to believe us and go along with this crazy plan. It'll all have to be done off the record, so to speak. Derrek and Mark wouldn't be on official duty. Getting the police in Phoenix to do the same thing . . . I just don't know, Theresa."

"Should *we* go, then? To Phoenix?" As soon as she said it, she shook her head. "No . . . Steven already thinks I've lost it. He wouldn't let us in. But, dammit, there has to be *something!*"

"We don't even know if we can stop this thing," he reminded her. "Guns aren't going to do any good. All we might be doing is putting ourselves in danger."

"We already are," she said, looking pointedly at the fading bruise on his hand. "What about a priest?"

"You mean an exorcism?"

"Maybe . . . do they still even do that? You were the one who said you were in the church choir as a kid. Me, I've only ever been in churches to go to weddings."

"That was a lot of years ago. I wouldn't know where to start looking. I just can't see taking this story to Reverend Carmody."

"Well, keep trying to find Tony, then; I guess it's all we can do right now." Theresa picked up the manila folder containing the faxes Damon had received from his brother.

"I wouldn't," he warned. "It's not pretty."

"I have to know."

The first page made her gasp, the second made her moan sickly, and the third made her slap the file shut before she had to race for the tiny restroom.

"My God, what could do that kind of damage?" she whispered.

Damon removed the folder from her shaking hands. Derrek's overzealous partner Mark Gladstone had, although he'd been told to stay out of it, managed to collect reports on all of the murders. Even the Nick Diamond case, which was being handled very close to the vest as the deceased was a drug-using teenager-boffing celebrity.

"They're really all dead. Dead!"

"Don't freak out on me, now, ma'am," he said gently.

She shuddered and took a deep breath, then got a grip on herself. "Okay. I'm okay. But this can't happen again. We have to find some way to stop it."

"Working on it." He turned back to the computer. The wonders of the Information Age, when a few clicks and keystrokes could call up details on nearly everyone. Even starting from a tiny town like Trinity Bay. Soon he'd narrowed his search to the Anthony Monatellas of the right age group, four of which lived in New York, two of which had military backgrounds.

A few more clicks and a flurry of typing later, all that info was zipping electronically on its way to Derrek. His private e-mail; the last thing they needed was some right-of-disclosure snoop getting his hands on it.

"Why hasn't it been in the papers, on the news?" Theresa wondered.

"It will. Only a matter of time. Right now, everybody's keeping it quiet. Could you see the headlines? The coroners can't even figure out what killed these men, the only witness swears it was someone in a monster get-up or superhero suit. Crazed Werewolf Vigilante Stalks America, Film at Eleven. People might panic, there would be a glut of fake confessions and maybe even copycat attacks. Diamond being a rock star only makes it worse. Front page stuff, all the way."

"What's going to happen when someone finds the link?" she asked, meeting his gaze. "When they trace it all back to me? People might think *I* did it. That I'm a witch, a psychic, who knows?"

"Thought all the psychics worked for 1-900 hotlines," he said with a grin.

"I'm serious, Damon."

The grin vanished. "I know. But listen. You haven't done anything. You've been right here in town; there's no way anyone could prove otherwise. Don't worry about that."

"Am I going to be visited by any of the 'special' branches of the FBI?" It was her turn to grin, but there was more apprehension than humor in it.

Damon knew just how she felt. He'd read a statistical study once that showed more people believed the Air Force was covering up the existence of UFOs than actually believed in UFOs in the first place. Paranoia was more a part of modern life than ever, and nobody trusted the system, the politicians, the government. Life in the new millennium, and wasn't it a blast?

He thought about Mark Gladstone, who eagerly embraced all of it. Every conspiracy theory that came down the walk was worth a look. And who knew? Maybe Mark was better prepared to deal with the world as it was than the rest of them were.

"Where does it end?" he murmured. "After what we've seen, does it mean we have to open the door to the rest of it?"

"Abductees, Bigfoot, the Loch Ness monster?" Theresa chimed in.

"The *real* reasons behind the deaths of J.F.K. and Elvis."

"Top secret enclaves where hideous experiments are carried out on death row prisoners."

"Covert societies controlling things at the highest level."

"Want to move to the mountains and build a survivalist shelter?" she asked.

"Is that a proposal?" he countered with a wink.

They laughed, easing some of the tension, then realized they were no longer alone in the office.

* * *

"I can't believe I'm doing this," Derrek Blake grumbled.

"What, helping your brother? Tracking down a vicious psychotic killer? Protecting the innocent?"

"Encouraging you."

"Oh." Mark Gladstone chuckled, braked hard to avoid a cyclist with a death wish, and made a left turn. "Well, then, you shouldn't have told me."

"You're my partner."

"That's right. And in this screwy world, a good partner's about the only one you can trust."

Damon's message had come in just as he was getting ready to leave for the day. He didn't mind the night shift, which was always something of a coin-toss. During the day, it was busy, and you never could tell whether you'd get something interesting or more of the same old, same old. At night, though, it was either quiet, or the really wild stuff went down.

But by the end of it, especially when he had to stay late for a meeting with the captain followed by an hour-long mandatory training on riot gear, he was ready to go home, grab a hot shower and something to eat, and fall into bed. Instead, here he was, doing what Mark had cheekily termed a 'pre-emptive homicide investigation.'

The first Tony Monatella was the ultimate blue-collar man, putting in overtime every week at a plumbing and pipe-works factory. He was none too happy about talking to them, especially with his supervisor hanging over them and giving him the evil eye.

"No, I never knew anyone named Ruiz. Know a Manuel, but his last name's Chavez."

"You're sure about that?" Mark asked, making a note.

"Sure."

"What about Arizona? Ever been there?"

Monatella looked at Mark as if Mark had just asked him if he had ever had carnal relations with an octopus. "Arizona?"

"I think that's all we need," Derrek said. "Thank you for your cooperation, Mr. Monatella."

* * *

"Mr. Forrester," Damon said. "What can I do for you?"

Charlie Forrester was always uncomfortable around Damon, and by the look of it, he was more so now. Though they hadn't found any wacky tobaccy or other questionable botanical products at his house, though he had never been busted, he went through life knowing that everyone in town figured he was a pothead anyway.

And here he was in the police station. A first, to Damon's knowledge.

"Hi, Charlie," Theresa said warmly.

He smiled tentatively her way, and turned back to Damon. His Adam's apple bobbed beneath his scraggly grey goatee and he first pushed his hands into his pockets, then pulled them out with a guilty twitch as if he thought they might suspect him of hiding something, then let his long fingers wander in distress up to fiddle with the hand-carved wooden totem hanging from the zipper tab of his jacket.

"It's my boy," he said. "My boy Jerry."

"What's the matter?" Out of the corner of his eye, Damon saw Theresa straighten up in concern.

"Uh . . . have you seen him?"

"Didn't he get released from the hospital yesterday?" Theresa asked.

Damon wondered briefly if Charlie was so absent-minded that he'd gone to visit and found his son no longer in his room over at the Medical Center.

"He did. But he's not home. He was gone when I got up this morning."

"Gone?" From what Damon knew of Jerry Forrester's condition, the kid was in no shape to have taken himself to school or anyplace else.

"And I'm getting a little worried," Forrester concluded. "The doctors said he should take it easy for at least a week."

Glancing at the clock – 10:13 AM – Damon asked, "What time did you notice he was gone?"

"Around nine." He noticed the glance, and hurriedly explained, "I first thought he might have just gone to Gary's, you know, to see his friend. Then I remembered there's nobody at that house. So I called the school thinking he may have gone, but they hadn't seen him. Just Jen. She says his door was shut and she didn't look in when she got up."

"Gary Haverley has a car," Theresa said. "Maybe they went out."

"That could be it," Damon said. "A little irresponsible of them, maybe, but I bet Jerry was tired of being cooped up."

"I just want to know he's okay. Things . . . things have been bad lately." He still looked like Ichabod Crane, but now it was more like how Ichabod might have looked after his encounter with the Headless Horseman. Starkly haggard, older than his years, eyes staring glazed from hollow purpled sockets.

"I'll get in touch with Claudia Haverley in Arcata, and start asking around," Damon said.

"Thanks." Relief sagged his thin shoulders. "Bye, and thanks. See you, Theresa."

"Take care, Charlie. Let me know when he turns up. And if you need anything, Dad and I are right next door."

They watched him go, and then Damon said, "I don't like it. Jerry's lucky to be alive. What's he thinking, pulling a stunt like this? Probably went over to the school to bask in the attention."

"He's a good kid."

"I know that, but he's also a ham."

"I don't think he would upset his father just for attention. He could be with Gary. They've both had a hard time. Lives turned upside down. They could be down at the mall in Eureka, hanging out, trying to get feeling normal again."

"I hope that's it. Still won't save them from getting a lecture from me." He dug out the card with Claudia Haverley's home phone number on it, making that his first call even though he figured he'd get the machine and would have to try her at work.

To his surprise, Gary Haverley answered.

And to his growing concern, Gary swore that he hadn't seen Jerry since the last time he'd paid a visit to the hospital. Damon had been lied to by enough people to know that he was telling the truth.

Several fruitless calls later, he looked over at Theresa. "Nothing. Nobody's seen him. I think I better ride on over to the Forrester house and look around."

"You don't think . . ." She closed her mouth, but he could read it on her face. She was thinking about Angela Cliffwood.

"I don't," he assured her. "I'll find him. He'll be fine. You'll see."

* * *

Monatella's Grocery and Deli was a bright, clean, well-lit, appealing place in a decaying neighborhood where windows were barred, walls were tattooed with intricate and overlapping graffiti, and the gang of young thugs sitting on the stoop of a boarded-over apartment building looked at Blake and Gladstone with the flat, evaluating eyes of reptiles.

They didn't bother telling the kids they were cops. The kids knew from the moment they stepped out of the car, probably even before.

Something was wrong with the scene, and Derrek couldn't initially place it. Mark got it before he did.

"Laptops instead of boom boxes? There's a switch."

"Lot quieter," Derrek said.

"No complaints here."

They went into the deli, which was thick with delicious aromas. The man behind the counter, slapping together a thick, greasy, utterly wonderful-looking pastrami sandwich, was tall and well-built with close-cropped dark hair and a tattoo of a rose on his bicep.

That gave Derrek and Mark both a nasty jolt. It was a red rose, and a banner with the name 'Gina' scrolled across the thorny stem, but a rose was a rose was a rose. Shakespeare. No, Dickinson? Bronte? Derrek couldn't remember, and it had gotten stuck in his head the way a sliver of popcorn kernel could sometimes get stuck in the teeth. Maddening. Frost? No, that was the one about the tree.

Derrek shook his head to rid himself of the inane ramblings and cleared his throat to make himself heard over the late-lunch crowd. There were four tiny tables wedged into the front section of the store, all of them full, and several more people and clerks in attendance.

"Mr. Monatella?"

"Be right with you!" the big guy shouted over his shoulder. He plunked a pickle down on the plate beside the sandwich, added a bag of chips, and slid the whole works down the counter to a diminutive old man who looked like a shaved chimpanzee. Wiping his hands on a rag, he came over to them. "Yeah?"

"I'm Detective Blake. This is Detective Gladstone." He flashed his badge.

"Yeah?" Monatella said again, the set of his bristly eyebrows informing them that he wasn't surprised. "Help you?"

"We need to ask you a couple of questions, Mr. Monatella."

"Right now?" He gestured at the line of customers.

"They're real quick ones," Mark said. "Mr. Monatella, do you know a man named Manuel Ruiz?"

Wariness flickered in Monatella's inky eyes, and for a moment Derrek was sure he was going to stonewall them. But then he nodded. "Yeah, I was in the service with Manny Ruiz. Haven't seen him in oh, four-five years. Why?"

Derrek and Mark glanced at each other. Pay dirt.

"You ever visit him in Phoenix?"

"Long time ago. What's this all about?"

That was the tricky part. Derrek could only imagine this burly ex-soldier's reaction if they told him he might be marked for death by some *thing* that killed by weapons unknown. He'd want to know why, and Derrek didn't even know. His twin hadn't seen fit to brief him on that part.

"It's related to an ongoing case, Mr. Monatella, which we're not currently at liberty to discuss," Mark said smoothly. "You know, the usual bureaucratic bullshit."

"Gotcha," Monatella said, and, amazingly, that was all. "Anything else for you today?"

* * *

Some hero.

That was the first thought that percolated through the cloudy swamp of his mind.

Some hero.

On the heels of it came a voice, a familiar wiseass voice.

For some reason, they always cast me as the bad guy and Romeo here as the hero . . .

He knew that voice. Gary. Gary Haverley.

But Gary wasn't the bad guy this time. Gary wasn't even in this play.

And he wasn't much of a hero.

He'd failed. He'd blown it big time.

Again.

Which went against everything he'd wanted and hoped and yearned for and loved since he was in elementary school.

Since he and Gary used to duel it out like Spiderman and the Joker in the Haverley's treehouse – those two didn't go together, but Jerry liked Spidey's easygoing wisecracking good-guy nature a lot more than the gloomy and brooding Dark Knight. Not to mention getting to spray Silly String all over the place as makeshift web-shooters. And Gary was a natural to be the Joker, with a maniacal laugh that could make dogs bleed from the ears.

Since the fourth-grade production of Little Red Riding Hood, in which he'd stolen the show as the huntsman who rescued Red and Gramma from the evil wolf.

Always wanted to be the hero.

But when Angela needed a hero, he'd let her down. Let her down and watched her die. Watched from below as she jumped, her hair and clothes whipping around her as if the wind itself was trying to push her back up the bluff. Watched the spray of blood that looked black against the deep grey of the sky as she struck the first rock, her body cartwheeling, her scream cut off. Watched her turn limp as a bundle of rags, sliding into the sea-churned shallows where the rocks poked up like a monster's teeth.

Some hero. All he'd been able to do was be the first one to reach her, to pull her out of the water even though Traci Neeman yelled at him not to move her, either thinking she might still be alive or not wanting him to mess with any evidence, he didn't know, didn't care. Pulled her to a flatter rock that stuck its wet black back above the waves.

Angela. Poor broken Angela. He hadn't saved her. Hadn't helped her. Might have even contributed to her death, because he had the feeling that her stepfather's abuse had picked up after she started going out with him.

Yep.

Some great goddam hero.

Now here he was again, having blown it a second time.

He couldn't even remember why.

He ached all over – Jesus, did he ache! Felt like everything had torn loose inside of him and was floating around in a dank soupy mess.

His head pounded. He opened his eyes, saw nothing.

Blind. I'm blind.

Gary's voice again: *maybe it's just dark, quiche-for-brains.*

Oh. Yeah. Maybe it was just dark.

He moved his arm and it did what he wanted it to, rising slowly to let his fingers do the walking through his hair. Yuck. Tacky-crusty with dried something, and he didn't have to be on Final Jeopardy to come up with "What is Blood?"

There was also a swollen lump the size and shape of half a grapefruit, more crusted blood, and a few chunks of glass embedded in his skin.

Stuff like this never happened to Arnie/Mel/Sly/Jean-Claude/Pierce. Blown it. Big time. The bad guy had gotten him.

It all came back in a rush. The ghosts by the rosebush, Dani Kensington dressed all in ninja-black, Thornton trying to drown her in the pool. His rescue effort. And then getting hit with something. A glass, must've been. Full of booze. He could smell it, dried onto his clothes and skin and mingling with the stink of his own blood.

Jerry realized that it wasn't as dark as he'd initially thought. Or his eyes were getting used to the dimness. Either way, he could see a little. Shapes bulking in the gloom. Furniture, some of it draped in tarps or sheets. Good thing he hadn't mistaken them for more ghosts. One more shot of adrenaline right now might just kill him.

He was on a floor, a bare, wooden, very dusty floor. Cold, too, but not freezing. Hungry and thirsty, though compared to the rest of his complaints, the last two were pretty minor.

A low, miserable groan escaped him as he levered himself into a sitting position. His stomach slid side to side and he was sure he was going to barf. Barf until he ruptured something, and then he would die. At the moment, dying didn't seem like such a bad prospect.

But he neither barfed nor died, and his head only gave one apocalyptic throb before settling back down to its regularly-scheduled programming . . . in this case, a marathon of headaches.

His hearing was messed up. Aside from his own sickly-thumping pulse beating in his ears, he could hear his own rasping breath in stereo.

No, not in stereo. He wasn't alone.

He tried to turn around but it was too much, so he scooched on his butt in a dusty circle. There, behind him, was an old-fashioned bed, one of the kinds that short people needed a little staircase to get into. The staircase was there too, pushed to the end of the bed and holding some old crockery.

Dani Kensington was sprawled facedown on the bed. Still in her outfit of ninja-black, which he now realized was just a pair of plain leggings and a big baggy sweatshirt that came halfway to her knees, though the bandanna had come off of her hair and lay in an indifferent crumpled wad on the floor.

He poked it and found it still damp. However long they'd been here, it hadn't been long enough for the cloth to dry.

She was alive, hurt but alive. Her clothes were okay, so maybe Thornton hadn't done anything to her that way.

Maybe there was still a chance to get out of this. This time, he would do it right. This time, he wouldn't fail.

In what he now figured was Seacliff's attic, Jerry Forrester took a deep breath and silently repeated that vow to himself.

* * *

26

Scott James hadn't become a police officer for the usual reasons. Not at first.

He hadn't joined the force to protect and serve. To uphold the rights of the innocents. Even to have the legally-sanctioned opportunity to beat the shit out of the scum of society.

Nope. None of that.

He'd become a police officer first and foremost to prove, to himself and everybody else, that he was as capable a man as any. To earn, through badge and uniform and gun, the respect that had been denied him the previous years of his life.

Oh, it had been okay when he was a kid. He was the youngest of the Trinity Bay Jameses, a big and close-knit family. He had cousins in every town from Crescent City to Garberville, it sometimes seemed. Every couple of years, the whole sprawling clan would get together for a week-long campout at one of the region's seaside or mountain paradises. Much charred animal flesh would be devoured, much beer would be consumed, whole herds of marshmallows would be toasted and slurped scalding-hot from sticks and long cook-forks.

The Jameses were all markedly similar in appearance. Fairskinned blondes who sunburned easily, so gallons of sunblock were also used at these family gatherings. The men were broad-shouldered and husky, the women proudly full-figured.

But they were also tall. The biggest of the Jameses, Paul, was six-foot-eight and his name had proved to be either prophetic or convenient, as during the tourist season, he dressed in red flannel shirts, jeans, and work boots, and despite the fact that his lush beard was as yellow as a daffodil, turned up in vacationers' photo albums from all over the country posing with their kids as legendary lumberjack Paul Bunyan. He'd even been known to dye a white bull blue every now and then, when the animal rights people weren't looking.

Even the women were tall. Giants. Rubenesque Valkyries. Cousin Freida stood just shy of six feet and modeled plus-size lingerie with a smoldering challenge in her cornflower eyes.

Scott had reached five-foot-four at age thirteen, and there he'd stayed. Runt of the litter. Never sickly, never scrawny. Just short.

But short was enough. The rest of the family towered over him, and ranged from teasing with bluff good humor to downright vicious taunting on the parts of some of the more thick-browed knuckle-dragging cousins.

Unable to find his manliness on the football field – he'd been a gifted baseball player in junior high but quit in high school after always being called 'Shortstop' even when he was pitching became too much to bear – not wanting to work the woods like his brothers, Scott had turned to other ways of proving himself.

The armed forces were out, because he knew he'd only be letting himself in for more of the same. Boot camp would be just another form of the hell he'd already endured. Besides, it would take him away from home, and much as they infuriated him, he loved his family and his neighbors and wanted to stay close.

So he'd signed on with the Trinity Bay P.D. And life was good.

Then he'd found that he had a real knack for it. Damon Blake, who had trained in perhaps the toughest city in America, had told Scott on many occasions that his skills were being wasted in a tiny town like Trinity Bay. He could do well, Damon said, and be a credit to, any detective division in the state.

Flattering, but he was happy here. He didn't fancy himself Sherlock Holmes or one of those brilliant TV sleuths, though he did get a kick out of old *MacGyver* reruns. Every now and then, even in Trinity Bay, he had occasion to use his skills and that was enough.

Damon had asked him to go over the Haverley deaths. Not really expecting him to find anything. It looked like a clear-cut accident. But they had to go through the motions in case there was ever a need, ever a demand for a deeper investigation.

Scott hadn't minded at all. Gave him something to do. He even felt that he owed it to Al and Celeste. Though he hadn't particularly liked either of them, their house was just down the street from the James place. He'd gone to school with Billy, even dated Annette during those awkward adolescent years when all the girls were taller than all the boys anyway so it didn't matter.

So, on what could well be the last sunny Friday of the year – every sunny day in October was like that – Scott found himself on his way out to North Valley, to Otto Otter's Auto Works.

There *otter* be a law, he thought as he pulled up under the sign which featured a cartoon otter in a topcoat and English driving cap standing beside an old-fashioned runabout.

Gus Sorenson was expecting him and came out to meet him, wiping his oil-stained hands on a rag before sticking one out. Gus could have passed for a James in terms of size, but was dark-complected and surly of aspect. He was perhaps one of the least-popular men in town, but no one would ever dare treat him so. Not only did he look like he could crack a skull in the crook of his elbow, he owned the only two tow trucks in town and would be just as happy to leave you sitting by the side of the road as long as he pleased if he thought you deserved it.

Scott shook Gus' hand and smiled, though inwardly a part of him still grimaced in disgust at the fact that when he looked straight ahead, he was looking not at eyes but at coverall. Coverall with a patch, God help us, of that same chipper chap of an otter grinning from the pocket.

"So you wanna see the mess that Big Al left, hunh?"

"You know how it is," Scott said. "The family'll want to know if there were any mechanical problems."

"So they can sue me?" Gus glowered, his eyebrows drawing together fiercely. "Don't count on it. I didn't work on this baby. Al did all that himself, or took it to that dipwad in Eureka. If something did fail, it wasn't because of me."

Scott made a non-committal noise. He knew that Big Al and Gus had had a major falling-out a couple years back at Superbowl time, regarding a bet. Ever since, Al swore up and down that he wouldn't let Gus touch his car even if he was the last mechanic on God's green earth.

"Could have even been that no-good kid of theirs, tinkering around," Gus added.

Scott made that noise again. The last thing Gary Haverley would have done was tinker with the family wheels. He didn't even tinker with that puke-green Mustang of his.

Gus led Scott around the shop to the auto graveyard. It was his first up-close peep at the wreck, and he sucked in a breath that was partly admiring. The car was totaled. Some of it could be attributed to the efforts of the paramedics, who had torn what was left of the front doors off to get at the occupants, but the rest was caused by the tumble from Mill Road into Leland Creek.

Scott walked around slowly, taking it all in, shaking his head to himself.

Most of the damage was to the front, which was crunched in so that it was nearly unrecognizable as a car. More like some weird modern-art sculpture that everyone pretended to understand while the artist secretly smirked at what suckers they were. The sides were bashed to crap too. The rear was mostly okay, one corner dented from a rough meeting with the hillside and a scrape scrawled above the license plate.

Scott paused, backed up. He hunkered down next to the scrape, noticing but not commenting on Gus's snort of contempt that he should fix first on the least of all the injuries to the vehicle. Kind of like seeing a savaged corpse and noticing that the poor guy also had one mean bastard of a hangnail.

He ran his fingers around it thoughtfully. Al's car was the copper-brown color of an old penny. But there was paint embedded in the scrape. Black paint.

Easy to dismiss as the result of a parking-lot fender bender, but something clicked over in Scott's head. Just the first little twinge of speculation. Like a tiny magnet, it drew other random bits of information to itself. Things he'd heard, or even overheard.

Who'd been the last person to talk to Al and Celeste Haverley?

Who did Gary Haverley think his mom had had the hots for?

Who had been first on the scene, who had struck Damon as being a little off in his reactions?

Who drove a black car?

Why, what do you know, each of those questions had the same answer.

Which made Scott wonder . . . who had Celeste *really* put on those scanty panties for? Did that have the same answer too?

And who would Al have been pissed at if he'd found out?

Who should he maybe have a little talk with, just to set his mind at ease?

Scott straightened up. "Well, Gus, if you do find anything, be sure and let us know."

"I will," Gus said with a slightly predatory gleam, and Scott knew that he'd search extra hard, happy to have something to blame either on Al or on one of his competitors.

In the meantime, Scott had a little searching of his own to take care of. He tipped a farewell wave to Gus and headed back to his patrol car.

* * *

Kel McGuire was waiting by the windows, waiting for the plane, knowing that he would see his parents the moment they appeared at the top of the staircase-on-wheels.

He might as well have been hungover, since he felt like crap without having taken a single drink. Hadn't been able to sleep. Up all night thinking about Megan. Trying to understand what had been going through her mind. Trying *not* to think about the similarities between what had happened to her and what had happened to Dani Kensington, Sandy Forrester.

"Get your head out of the sand, damn you," he muttered to himself now, only realizing he'd spoken aloud when he saw Shauna Davis glance over curiously at him. People who talked to themselves in public, especially *counselors* who talked to themselves in public, might find themselves out of business before much time went by.

Just to show how far into this ridiculous scenario he was sinking, he actually caught himself wondering if he should ask Mrs. Davis her opinion. As if he didn't know what her answer would be. Hers was not exactly a cool and rational head on matters of the inexplicable.

It *wasn't* a matter of the inexplicable! He was giving in to the comfort of looking for external sources, trying to play Pin the Blame on something, anything.

With conscious effort, he forced it all out of his mind and nodded to Mrs. Davis. She smiled back, hesitated, and then ventured closer.

"I'm so sorry about your sister," she offered.

"Thank you," he said, the words coming automatically and numbly to his lips after all the times he'd had the same brief exchange during the past few days. To stop her before she could start adding the usual empty sayings about Megan being in a better place, he looked at the suitcase that sat obediently behind her. "Going on vacation?"

"Yes," she said, more brightly. "Walt and I are going to spend a few days with our son Wally in Idaho. Here comes Walt now. He was just getting a newspaper and some airsickness medicine for me. Not that I'll need it, at least I hope I won't. But better safe than sorry."

"Words to live by. I hope you have a nice time."

"Oh, wellnow, I'm sure we will. I'm just glad Wally could put us up at such short notice. Irma's probably having a fit, poor dear. She never feels like she does good enough, you know the sort, especially when her mother-in-law comes to visit."

"Spur of the moment thing, then."

"A present from Mr. Thornton. Isn't that nice of him? He even paid for our tickets. Like a Christmas bonus, a few months early."

"I'm sure he appreciates how hard you both work," Kel said, beginning to feel like he had been drawn into the conversational equivalent of quicksand. Walt Davis was no help, standing there with a paper in one hand and his gaze fixed on the sunlit twinkle of a descending plane.

"We try," she agreed. "Lord knows how we'll manage when Seacliff becomes a hotel. All those people! Mr. Thornton said he'll be hiring more staff to help out. Maids and cooks and the like. But he still wants us to stay on. I don't mind telling you, I was worried for a time that he would let us go, and hire on some younger blood to take care of the place. Not like we've been there forever, mind you. But my family's always worked at Seacliff, and I was just so glad to get my job back when he and Angela moved in!" She caught herself and turned apologetically red as she remembered that Angela Cliffwood was also a suicide.

The loudspeaker announced the arrival of the flight, and Kel excused himself. "My parents," he explained. "Have a good trip, Mrs. Davis."

Still bushing, fearful she'd offended him, she scuttled away to rejoin her husband.

And there they came, his father tall and stooped and the sun shining on the smooth skin of his bald pate, his mother diminutive and ethereal as her older daughter, with her hair still showing a few strands of apricot. Mom was lugging a cat-carrier in each hand, and Kel sighed, pressing his fingertips to his forehead.

Pinkie and Percy, how could he have forgotten Pinkie and Percy?

Please, he thought, *let the motel allow pets. It's a tourist area, a lot of tourists are retirees who travel with their surrogate children of the fur-person variety, please.* Because if the motel didn't, he knew that he'd be having a couple of houseguests. Houseguests who were not only cats but Persians, who would shed clumps of sneeze-making hair just from someone walking by.

If he'd been a cynical man by nature, he might have even suspected that Mom had brought the cats solely to punish him. After all, the housekeeper could have looked after Pinkie and Percy just as well.

Didn't matter now.

Kel moved forward to greet his parents.

* * *

"Miz Kensington? You okay?"

Dani opened her eyes to Jerry Forrester's pale, unwell face against the darkness of a room that was at once large and claustrophobic. There was a small circle of light, too, coming from one of those keychain squeezy-flashlights.

She tried to speak, and her throat clenched into a knot of pain. That was when she remembered Thornton choking her.

Choking her and drowning her. The after-taste of chlorine was thick in her sinuses. Her eyes felt raw, her head felt waterlogged.

She was laying on her stomach, the side of her face pressed against a mildew-smelling expanse of scratchy linen. There was a sensitive swelling bump over her ear from where Thornton had clubbed her unconscious.

Dani sat up woozily, and immediately began to shiver. Jerry, though he looked in far worse shape than she felt, assessed the situation and tottered over to drag a curtain off of the highboy it had been draped over. He hauled the heavy fabric over to Dani and she wrapped herself in it, hoping it was free of spiders but also aware that at this point, spiders might be the least of her worries.

"What time is it?" she rasped, each word pushing through her throat like the last glob of toothpaste coming out of the tube.

Jerry clearly hadn't expected the question, and floundered for a moment. Then he pushed up the cuff of his jacket and brought his watch close to his eyes. "Uh . . . almost two. Friday."

"Been out for *hours*!" Dani leaned forward over her knees and cradled her head in her hands. "How about you? Are you all right? I thought he'd killed you." Talking was easier now, but she would have given anything for a drink of water to soothe her abused throat.

"I feel like shit, and if I live, the doctors are gonna kill me. They made me promise I'd take it easy."

"And taking it easy doesn't include breaking and entering, assault, and then getting beat up and locked in the attic," she concluded.

"I thought that's where we were. How'd we get up here? Did . . . are you . . . did he . . . ?"

She shook her head. "No. He didn't. He might've, he might still try, but he didn't. And if he *does* try, I'm going to rip his balls off."

"He's crazy," Jerry stated flatly.

"No argument from me."

"He can't keep us here. Sooner or later, he's going to have to come back. And when he does . . ." Jerry, one of the most peaceable kids Dani had ever seen, smacked a fist into his palm with murder in his heart.

"Slow down, okay? You've got guts, but you just got out of the hospital! You jump on Thornton again, he's liable to take you apart."

"I don't care."

"Well, I do. I want to see him suffer as much as you do, but we've got to think about getting out of here first."

"What happened after he knocked me out?" Jerry prodded gingerly at his head, where grew a lump that put the one Dani had to absolute shame.

"I yelled, or tried to." She cupped her neck in one hand and swallowed, wincing. "Knew I didn't have much of a chance of waking up Walt Davis, but I had to do something. Screamed and ran for it, but in all the water, I slipped and he caught me. Choked me some more, then dragged us both to the elevator. I was only barely hanging on, and you were out cold."

"Why didn't he just finish us off?"

"And spoil his fun?"

"Yeah, gotcha. So before anybody could come along and catch him, he brought us up here. Then what?"

"Called me a bitch and a whore and some other names, promised he'd be back to 'deal with me,' then knocked me out."

"He killed Angela. Not like he pushed her or anything, but he drove her to it. And I think maybe he *did* kill his wife. We're next. Unless we can get him first."

"He could come back with a gun," she pointed out. "What then? I don't suppose you're armed."

"Well, no . . . are you?"

"Just this." She unhooked her fanny-pack and dumped it out. Packet of tissue, lip balm, fifty cents, keys, ah, there it was. Pocket knife. The little folding kind that really wasn't good for much more than opening envelopes and cardboard cartons.

Jerry took it, opened it, and pressed his thumb against the dull blade. He raised his eyebrows at her.

"I know, I know, but the end is reasonably pointy. If I shoved it into his eye, maybe his neck . . ."

"Still not much good if he has a gun."

"How about you? The good Boy Scout, packing a Swiss Army knife?"

"I wasn't a Boy Scout." He emptied his pockets, both the ones in his jeans and his coat, adding his array of junk to hers. Video game tokens, half a roll of butterscotch Life Savers, movie ticket stubs, wallet, change, comb.

"Okay . . . we're screwed," Dani announced. "Can I have a Life Saver?"

"Go for it. Hey, maybe we can find something up here to use."

He swept his little flashlight around the attic. Now that her vision had adjusted, Dani could tell by thin seams of brightness here and there that it was indeed daytime, and sunny too. But the attic was well-shuttered, the roof in good repair.

She huddled into her dusty musty curtain, letting sweet butterscotch-flavored saliva trickle down her wounded throat.

"How about these?" Jerry came back with a couple of . . . what were they? Swords? Yes, strange but true, swords. Maybe bayonets.

"Where did those come from?"

"The Civil War, I think," he replied dubiously, holding one up.

"I think we'd have better luck with the pocketknife. Do you even know how to use a sword?"

"Sort of . . . I took a class this summer in stage combat. But really, that was just teaching us how to miss and make it look good."

"So we dazzle Thornton with your acting ability, and while he's applauding, we make a break for it?"

He grinned at her. "Sure, that sounds like a plan. Unless you see anything here we can build a tank out of, like on those old shows with that big black guy."

"I got news for you, Jer, the *A-Team* we're not. Hell, we're not even the *Golden Girls*."

Blank look from her co-prisoner, and Dani only laughed.

"How'd you get into this mess, anyway?" she asked when her mirth had subsided.

He told her about his late-night walk, and then, his voice growing ever softer and his expression saying that he didn't expect her to believe him, told him about his encounter at the rosebush.

"I saw Angela. She wanted me to stop him. She pointed to you. If she hadn't, I never would have seen you, never would have followed."

"Lucky for me that you did!" It was her turn then, and she told him in very abridged terms about her dream, her obsession, her urge to shoot Damon Blake. No sense going into all the gory details, not to a seventeen-year-old kid who, despite his condition, was still a bundle of raging hormones.

He didn't once look at her with disbelief, but simply accepted it. Except . . .

"It wasn't Thornton. Wasn't him doing it. Something else. Something that's been here for a long time. That's what Angela was trying to tell me. It's using him, maybe, like it was using you."

"But what *is* it, then?"

He had no answer for that, and for a while they sat each lost in their own thoughts.

"What about starting a fire?" Jerry abruptly asked.

She waved at their collection of belongings. "You smoke? Me either."

"Wait, wait. I don't smoke, but . . ." He reached into the inside pocket of his jacket and came up with a matchbook from Jordano's restaurant, and a couple of mints from same. "Forgot these."

"A fire," Dani mused. "Lord knows there's enough junk up here to burn merry hell. But what happens to us? The fire department comes, but they're not going to know anyone's in the attic. They'll think it was the wiring, lightning, spontaneous combustion, I don't know. They might even suspect arson, but a lot of good that'll do us if they find our bodies in the ashes."

"Yeah, the son of a bitch would probably leave us up here to burn. But couldn't we break out a window, yell for help?"

"Maybe . . . it's worth thinking about. But I'd rather just get out."

He nodded and sat back down on the floor, shoving the swords under the bed. They struck something with a muffled clicking-clunking sound.

Jerry bent down and pointed the flashlight underneath. "There's a blanket down here."

"Pull it out," she said. "Might be better than this curtain."

He did, and there was a rattling noise as things rolled around.

"Oh, jeez!" Jerry went even whiter, and Dani was sure he was going to keel over in a heap. Instead, he picked up something and held it aloft. "Jeez, first MacBeth and now Hamlet, jeez, jeez, jeez!"

Dani stared at it. A skull. A human skull, yellowed with age, teeth snaggled and black and rolling loosely in the jaw.

"Alas poor Yorick," she said faintly. "I knew him well."

"Actually, it's 'I knew him, Horatio,'" Jerry corrected as if from a great distance, and then he did keel over.

The skull rumbled across the floor like a bowling ball, struck the base of a circular table, and split apart in a dry shower of dust.

* * *

"'Kay," Mark Gladstone said. "That's the guy. Now what?"

The remains of lunch were littering the front seat. Derrek Blake scooped the last of the macaroni salad out of a cardboard tub with a plastic spoon. "Good question."

"Be a shame to see him killed off . . . he runs a damn good deli. Excellent pastrami. Mind telling me how you know he's the next victim?"

"Uh . . ."

"Or, rather, how your brother knows?"

"He didn't say."

"But he's sure."

"Reasonably. Damon wouldn't joke about this. It rocked him when I told him about our case."

"Aha!"

"What?"

"*Our* case."

"Shaddap."

"The others were all in Bakersfield around the same time. This guy, you tell me Phoenix. What gives? What's the link? What's the key? How does your brother know Monatella's next?"

"I told you, he didn't say." Derrek was as frustrated as Mark.

"We could be wasting our time here."

"I know. But if there's a chance, any chance at all, that Damon's right, we might have an opportunity to nail this killer."

"And I want that as much as you do, partner . . . but I'd like to know what I'm getting into beforehand."

"So would I." Derrek rummaged in the glove compartment for antacid. Excellent pastrami, yes, but he was going to have heartburn the rest of the day. "Also, what do we do about it? We're both on duty all weekend. Can't stake out the deli, not without giving the captain a reason why, not when we've got a pile of other stuff to take care of."

"If it *is* the Black Rose Killer, only nighttime's the problem."

"You want to spend the next few nights parked here?" Derrek bobbed his head toward the group of kids, still sitting on the stoop, pretending not to keep an eye on the cops. "Whole neighborhood will know something's up. What do we tell Monatella when he wants to know why we're staking out his place?"

"Too bad we can't arrest him."

"On what charge?"

"My point exactly. But it would make sure he'd be inside, safe."

"Trapped like a caged rat if the killer did come looking."

Mark rolled his eyes. "No killer, no matter how *weird*, is going to come looking for his victim in a police holding cell."

"Hey, partner, you're the one who was trying to convince me that we were dealing with a *what*, not a *who* here. Suppose you're right and it is a *what* . . . you think bars and locks and our fellow brothers in blue are going to stop it?"

"Yeah, like in *Terminator*, 'there are thirty cops in this building;' twenty-nine, twenty-eight . . .'"

Derrek crunched up a third antacid tablet, this time not blaming it on the pastrami.

* * *

The section of Mill Road where the accident had taken place had been closed off for three days following the Haverleys' deaths. Wednesday and Tuesday, everyone headed their to work had to take the old access road, an axle-buster of a rutted dirt track that looped around the back side of the hill.

The mill had been closed yesterday, so that all the workers could attend the funeral. But then, this morning, everything was back to business as usual. The mill open, the road open.

Scott James pulled off the road and got out of his car. He knew it was a waste of time; by now, any tracks or other possible clues to suggest that another vehicle had been involved would have been eradicated by the morning shift's traffic.

Signs of the wreck hadn't completely vanished. The hillside headed down to the creek would bear the scars for quite some time. Torn-up bushes, split rocks, trees that had been scored down to the naked white wood. Strewn glittering sprinkles of glass, and the red and amber shards of brake lights, hazard lights. Some twisted shards of metal. Copper-brown paint on the rocks. And, winking back the sun in bright flashes, a side-view mirror that had been ripped completely off and lain unnoticed until the clouds cleared.

He prowled back and forth along the steep path of destruction. The county work crew had long since finished up and departed. He'd read over their statements. Not one mention of another car. They'd heard the Haverleys' car approaching, going fast.

But then, just a couple minutes after the crash, Brad Thornton had shown up. In his sleek black sports car. Used his cel phone to call for help. Said he'd left for an early lunch just after Al and Celeste.

Convenient . . .

Okay, he thought. *Let's try this on for size.* Thornton and Celeste are carrying on an affair behind her husband's back. Sure, she doesn't seem like his type; he seems more like the sort who'd be looking for a trophy-babe half his age. But what the hell. Got to take it where you can get it, and besides, at night all cats are grey.

So she goes up to the mill for a little afternoon delight. Careless, risky, but the risk might be part of the turn-on. Knowing Al might find out. But this time, Al *does* find out. Loses his temper. Doesn't take it out on Thornton then and there . . . why not? Maybe promises to come back later and rearrange his dental work, but first he's got to deal with his straying, cheating wife.

Then what? Then Thornton, to save his own ass, chases after and tries to run them off the road?

Scott hooked his thumbs through his belt loops, staring at the wavery white fan of reflected light the broken mirror threw onto a boulder, not really seeing it. Eyes open, mind open, thinking it over.

Could work. Maybe he was just trying to scare Al, warn him off. Maybe he's hoping Al will lose control, knowing that his sports car will handle better than the Ford. Either way, they get going fast. Come around that bend, and bang, there's the work crew. With Al barreling down on them, damn near running over their flagger, they wouldn't have noticed Thornton's car, or maybe he fell back and stopped before he would have come into view.

Then down the hill and into the creek. Neither of them left alive to tell what really happened. And here comes Thornton, was just going to lunch, heard the crash, oh-my-God-are-they-all-right.

It made an eerily persuasive sense, but Scott knew he would have to come up with something a lot more convincing before he voiced so much as a single word of his speculations to anyone. Even Damon. Even his own family. No, strike that, *especially* his own family. Badmouthing Thornton, the man who had re-opened the mill and given Lenny and Stuart good jobs, that was just not done.

But it was kind of creepy how accidents and death surrounded the man. First his wife, then his lawyer, then his stepdaughter. Talk about a run of bad luck.

Plus Lenny, and now Al and Celeste. Thornton sure went to a lot of funerals.

Or was he looking to pin something on Thornton, unconsciously blaming him for Lenny's death? It had been an accident, everyone agreed on that. The subsequent safety investigation hadn't turned up anything that would have pointed a finger for laxness or corner-cutting. But if Thornton hadn't re-opened the mill, Lenny wouldn't have been there when that chain let go and snake-whipped through the air.

And the stepdaughter, that had been suicide. The lawyer, another car crash, and there were plenty of people able to swear that Thornton had been in his office when it happened, halfway across town from the Agate River Bridge.

Scott would be the first to admit that sometimes his inquisitive mind led him down the wrong paths. That was why he was always so careful to check and double-check, especially now that he was an officer of the law and his deductions could have real impact on the well-being of the people he was supposed to serve.

Measure twice, cut once, that was the law of the saw that had been a favorite in the James clan since time immemorial, but it wasn't too shabby applied to police work, too.

What to do, what to do?

Go on up to the mill and take a look at Thornton's front bumper?

That would be fun to explain, if Thornton came out and asked what the hell he thought he was doing poking around the executive parking space. If his suspicions were totally on the wrong track, all he'd do by voicing a whisper of them would be to get on Thornton's shit-list. And Thornton did seem like just the sort who'd find some reason to fire Stu because of it. Then Scott would be on his family's shit-list as well.

But suppose Thornton did have something to hide? Maybe he deserved to sweat a little.

And maybe Scott would find just what he was looking for. A fresh scrape of copper-brown. What then, boys and girls?

He wasn't exactly sure what then, but he knew what his next step had to be.

To the mill, then.

* * *

She was *not* going to cover him with that blanket. Not one that had been wrapped around a bunch of old bones for God knows how long, absorbing God knows what kind of rot and disease.

But the damn curtain was too heavy, so Dani dumped it on the floor and picked up Jerry's flashlight to do a little exploring. An attic treasure hunt.

And just maybe find a way out of here while she was at it.

She'd been able to get Jerry onto the bed, though moving his dead weight onto that high mattress had nearly made her black out from the effort. The shock, the shock of pulling a human skull out from hiding, had been too much for the poor guy on top of everything else he'd already suffered.

If she got the chance, she'd clobber Brad Thornton an extra time for Jerry, too. Maybe the blow-dried whoreson had something against her, maybe he was pissed that she had rejected him and in his mind that gave him the right to do something about it, but who did he think he was beating up and imprisoning a kid who wasn't even eighteen?

She found a large trunk with a flat top, the sort of thing she and Theresa might have called a hope chest back in the days when they were pre-teens each hoping for a chest. Right on top was a handmade quilt, neatly folded, faded and musty but looking like it had never been used.

Wary of quilt-dwelling bugs, she shook it out and thwacked it a couple of times just to make sure. When nothing scuttled or flew out, she took it back over to the bed and tucked it around Jerry.

He needed a doctor. He needed to be out of here. Her first-aid training only extended to doing the Heimlich if one of Nate's patrons sucked a beer nut down the wrong pipe.

The mental image of Nate's, bottles glinting in the red and blue neon of the Budweiser sign, a foamy misty smell hanging around the taps, the juke playing a steady stream of good old rock and roll, only served to make Dani more thirsty and determined to get out of here. Jerry needed a doctor, and maybe she could do with a check-up herself, but right now, more than anything else, she wanted to plunk her butt down on a padded leatherette stool and lift a chilled bottle to her lips.

Well, no . . . more than *anything* else she wanted to punch Brad Thornton's teeth so far down his throat that he could re-chew his last meal. But after that, the beer came a close second.

She looked around for anything else they might be able to use. The Cliffwoods had stored quite an array of old furniture and stuff over the years, and as a kid she would have loved to spend hours up here poking around, playing dress-up with the old-fashioned clothes, having tea parties with the ugly but doubtless expensive china. Right now, though, she wished they'd been collectors of more weaponry than a couple of beat-to-hell cavalry sabers.

The more she looked, the stranger something seemed. The corner by the door – which was locked, of course, she had figured as much but wouldn't it have just been *too* funny not to check and then have it turn out to be open? – was where the bed was. Not cloth-shrouded like the rest of the pieces. A bed, a little table, a stool, an open box of wooden toys. A mirror hung on the wall, cloudy glass like a blind eye.

Set up like a room, almost.

She peered into the mirror and regretted it at once. If she looked this bad in the meager light of the keychain flash, she didn't want to think about what daylight would reveal. Puffy, red eyes. Puffy black-and-blue neck. Her hair, though, was not in the least bit puffy. Lank. Stringy. Swimming always did give her bad hair.

"Who gives a damn?" she croaked. "When you get out of here, you can go straight to Red's Salon and have Red make it all better. With a stop by Nate's on the way."

Set up like a room. And a bundle of bones under the bed.

Too easy to imagine some Cliffwood child, retarded or deformed, locked up here away from the prying eyes of the town. Growing up in the dark attic. Growing insane.

Dani shuddered. If she went on in that vein, soon she'd be imagining the bones drawing together, knitting themselves into a semblance of a human form, rising . . .

Too late; she already *was* imagining it.

"It was probably just a medical skeleton," she told herself in the gloom. "Like Pop has in his office. Fell off the stand. That's all."

To get her mind off of it, she resumed her explorations. The few small windows at first gave her a burst of hope, especially when she saw that some of the boards nailed over them from the inside had fallen aslant. But then she remembered the storm shutters that had been placed all over the outside of the building.

Even the attic.

Damn.

Decorative, made to match Seacliff's trim . . . but they prevented her, even if she was able to yank off all the boards, from getting out.

The only window not covered was a tiny round one at the end of the attic. To get to it, Dani had to duck-walk crouched under the sloped ceilings. She brushed past an old box of papers, and mice erupted from it like blackbirds baked in a pie.

She squealed and was instantly ashamed of herself. They were only mice, tiny brown ones, not giant repulsive rats.

The window was the size of a ship's porthole, divided by two wooden pieces that made it resemble a cross-hairs on a rifle scope. It was caked with grime from the within and sea-salt from without. She could do something about the grime, scrubbing it off with the sleeve of her sweatshirt.

She was at the extreme west end of Seacliff now, looking through the blurred and filmy glass at the ocean and its tumble of rocks.

Even if she could break it, even if she was as limber as a circus acrobat, she would still be looking at a three-story drop straight down.

Muttering a few choice curses, she duck-walked back to Jerry. Still out, but now he seemed to be sleeping. Good; he needed it.

If there was an attic section to the east wing too, it wasn't reachable from here. No way to check the windows there, not that they'd be likely to be any more helpful.

Ding-Bong!

A high chime and then a low tolling one, muffled but audible even here.

Doorbell? Had to be.

She shouted, but her throat felt like it first cracked, then split, and all that she voiced was a feeble yap. She flung herself at the attic door, hammering on it, kicking it.

Ding-Bong! Ding-Bong!

Jerry mumbled and turned over. Dani ran to him and shook him awake. He emerged reluctantly, thickly, and looked up at her as if he hadn't a clue where he was, who she was, what was happening.

"Come on, Jer, look alive!" she pleaded. "Someone's at the door!"

"Mr. Thornton?"

"No, the front door!"

Ding-Bong!

"Yell!" Dani said. "Make noise! Knock stuff over!"

He scrambled from the bed and joined her at the attic door, throwing his shoulder against it, hollering for all he was worth. "Up here! Help! Hey! Up in the attic! Help us!"

* * *

"Normally, we're not even supposed to take a missing persons report until someone's been missing for twenty-four hours," Damon said. "But given Jerry's medical condition, I think we better not wait."

Charlie Forrester scrubbed his hand fitfully up and down the side of his face. "You tried Gary?"

"I tried Gary. Also swung by the school, the plaza, and Galaxy West."

"Christ, Jenny's going to be home from school soon. What do I tell her? First her mom, now this!"

"It's going to be okay, Charlie," Theresa said. "Can you think of anyplace else he might have gone?"

"A walk, maybe, but . . ." his eyes widened with bleak horror. "You don't think he passed out in the woods, fell down, hit his head, something like that?"

"Next thing I'm going to do is take a roam through the woods," Damon promised.

They'd already been down to the bluff under the beach at Theresa's insistence. Unlike the smooth sandy expanse strewn with picturesque driftwood and tuft-grass over by the campground, the other beach was narrow and rocky and hard to get to. A favored party-spot for Trinity Bay's teens, because few others cared to take the trouble to get there.

But they'd found no sign of Jerry there, not on the beach and not amid the tumble of boulders at the extreme west end of the point. If he had jumped, which Damon doubted, then any evidence had been carried out to sea.

"Are you going to get dogs?" Charlie asked.

Damon looked at him blankly for a moment. "Dogs? Oh, for tracking?"

"I sent Bingo out to see if he could find him, but Bingo's no hunting dog."

Bingo, currently sprawled on his back with his forelegs held up to his chest and his hindlegs sprawled and his tongue hanging out the side of his mouth, thumped his tail on the linoleum agreeably at hearing his name.

"I'll give Chester Underwood a call if it comes to that," Damon said. "He's got some of the best sniffers in the county. Mind if I take a look through Jerry's room?"

"Go ahead." Charlie stared glumly down at his hands. "I was gonna go visit Sandy this weekend. They said I could come visit, as long as I didn't mind an attendant staying in the room." He rambled on, not seeming to expect any replies.

Damon glanced at Theresa and motioned with his head toward the hallway. She followed him to Jerry's room. No notes. A pair of sweats and a T-shirt crumpled on the floor. Closet door, one drawer, standing partly open.

"He got dressed before he went out," Theresa said.

"Maybe Charlie's right. If he went for a walk, state he was in, would have been easy to overdo it. Let's go exploring, shall we?"

A patrol car passed the house as they emerged, Scott James behind the wheel. Damon raised a hand, and Scott waved back. Seeing Theresa's sudden worried look, he slid an arm around her and gave her a brief, comforting squeeze.

"It's not your dad."

"I didn't think he would have just cruised on by without stopping if it were, but still . . ."

"If you'd rather head on home . . ."

"Trying to get rid of me, sheriff?"

"No, ma'am! But you've been helping out down at the station all morning —"

"It's not like I'm doing volunteer work! It's my fault that man is in danger. And Jerry's a friend. I'd hate to see anything happen to him."

"We'll swing by your place too. Maybe Travis has seen him."

* * *

Thornton hadn't been at the mill, hadn't been in all day according to Stu. Something about business meetings. Scott hadn't figured on finding him at home then, but it had been worth a look.

No luck. Nobody answered the door, and a quick look through the garage windows showed that not only was Thornton's car gone, but the Davis' was too. Place was empty.

Even if it hadn't had that empty *feel* about it. Cop instinct could sometimes go astray.

Cop instinct could well be going astray in more than that, leading him on these nutty suppositions that Brad Thornton had been involved in the smash-up that had killed the Haverleys.

He waved to his boss as he passed the Forrester house, deciding that he probably wouldn't be telling Damon how he'd spent his day. Damon did his best to keep his opinions under wraps, but the entire force, all six of them, knew that it annoyed him no end that Thornton's impression was that every one of them were small-town doofuses who couldn't find their own butts with both hands and a guide dog.

Wouldn't do to bother Damon with his own ponderings. Besides, it looked like the boss was having a busy day of his own. Another anonymous tip that Charlie Forrester was growing the old weed out back of his workshop? They'd never turned up anything, but every so often, someone would point the finger of accusation and it would look bad if they didn't at least make a show of checking it out.

Scott shook his head. They were lucky Charlie didn't sue them for harassment. At least Damon was spending the day in much more palatable company than he was. He'd take Theresa Zane over Gus Sorenson anytime. Not that she'd look twice at him . . . she wasn't a tall woman like five-foot-nine Dani Kensington, but she still had a couple inches on a certain officer of the law. Plus, rumor was that she and Damon had, as the boss might say, hit it off right well.

He was distracted from these thoughts by the sight of a sleek black sports car shining in the parking lot of Jordano's.

MYDLITE.

"Found you, Mr. Thornton," Scott said smugly to himself. He pulled into the parking lot and did a slow cruise down the row. It was late afternoon, not yet the cocktail hour, so Thornton's car lacked much in the way of company. But it was parked nose-in, in the front rank. Couldn't see the front from here.

He chose a spot at the far end where he'd have to walk past it on his way to the doors. Tried to look casual, like he was giving the car an appreciative once-over rather than scanning it for clues.

"Something I can help you with, Officer?"

And here, right on cue, was the man himself. Scott turned and affected a warm grin. "Just admiring your car, Mr. Thornton. Beauty, isn't she, the way the sun sparkles on her?"

Brad Thornton did not look well. For one thing, he had a bruise on his cheekbone that wasn't quite a shiner. For another, one of his hands was partly gloved in Band-Aids. And last but certainly not least, there was a skittery quality to his gaze that set off Scott's interior bells and whistles.

But he grinned back, a big showy salesman's grin. "I didn't know you were into sports cars."

"I like to look," Scott said. "Couldn't afford anything this sweet on my salary."

Oops, that might sound like he was mooching for a bribe . . . there were those in town who thought Thornton already owned the department – more fuel to the fire that annoyed Damon Blake – the way he supposedly had the Town Managers squarely in his pocket.

But Thornton merely ran an adoring hand along the hood and started reciting the car's statistics. While he was doing that, Scott dipped his eyes and there it was.

For a second, he thought he'd so utterly convinced himself that he *would* see a scrape that his mind had obligingly manufactured it. But that was a real scrape. A small one, the paint only minorly scored. He'd need a good close look to be sure, but it seemed to him that there were some flecks of coppery brown along the edges of it.

He opened his mouth to bring it to Thornton's attention, then changed his mind. The man was acting off, edgy.

Instead, he said, "Hurt yourself, Mr. Thornton?"

"Slipped in the shower," Thornton lied. As if he didn't even have to lie all that well to fool a hick cop like Scott.

He pretended to buy it all the same, and stood back as Thornton got behind the wheel and started up the engine in a throaty, contented growl.

* * *

By suppertime that Friday, a low-key panic was gripping Trinity Bay.

Not only was Jerry Forrester missing, but now Dani Kensington was also nowhere to be found. Her father's strident demands mixed with the rumors that flew from one end of town to another at the speed of gossip, roughly twice that of sound.

Damon Blake spent the evening organizing a search party to start combing the woods the following day. Forecast for early morning clouds, rain by noon.

Theresa Zane and her dad stayed up half the night with Charlie and Jenny Forrester, waiting by the phone for some word.

Brad Thornton sat in his darkened study, drinking Scotch and listening to the voice of the rose whisper to him about wicked girls . . . wicked girls and the wicked things they did.

* * *

Dani Kensington was cold. Damn cold. Not to the point that she could see her breath, but suffering a damp chill that sank into her limbs.

She wanted to burrow deeper into the makeshift nest of old curtains and quilts, and would have had the first two orders of business not involved liquid.

They'd set up an old spittoon behind a dressing screen for privacy. Dani made that her first stop.

One order of business taken care of, she went to the trundle cart that was near the door. It chilled her even more to think of how she and Jerry, following their frantic attempts to attract the notice of whoever was ringing the bell, had collapsed into exhaustion. And at some point while they were sleeping unaware, someone had rolled that cart in.

Someone? Why be coy? Thornton. Their captor. Proof that he didn't mean to kill them right away, but was holding them prisoner while deciding what to do. He'd come in here, maybe stood over them as they slept.

The cart was the sort of thing that room service might use. Or a maid bringing afternoon tea to the lady of the manor and her elegant friends.

She'd do about anything for a cup of hot tea. Hot tea with honey would feel good on her sore throat. Maybe help the racking chest-deep cough that she was developing. Probably pneumonia. Dunked in the pool, thirty hours or so locked in the attic. Pneumonia. Wonderful.

The cart held no tea, but there were a few plastic sports bottles of water, a wooden bowl of oranges and bananas, a stack of wrapped sandwiches from Tom's Market, a bag of chips, a packet of oatmeal cookies. Hungry after their long ordeal, they'd devoured half of it last night.

Dani opened another water bottle and peeled an orange, the acidic juice stinging all the way down. Her stomach clamored until she had also finished off a banana and half a sandwich. Then she made herself stop. No telling how long this was supposed to last them.

According to Jerry's watch, it was almost dawn. By now, they would have been missed. She had been scheduled to work from four until two last night, and her absence sure wouldn't have gone unnoticed. Not on a Friday night, a payday Friday night, especially. And Jerry . . . as foggy as Charlie Forrester may be, even he would have realized it wasn't right for his convalescing son to be away from home so long.

Trouble was, who'd think to look here?

He couldn't really expect to keep them like this. It wasn't as if he had the whole vast house to himself. Maybe Walt Davis wouldn't hear them pounding and yelling, but his wife would eventually start to wonder at all the noise.

Finished with her meal, she went back over to the bed. How long were these little flashlights good for, she wondered?

If anyone had told her that she would be climbing into bed with a cute seventeen-year-old, she would have responded with a toss of her hair and a laughing comment about the cruel joke God had played on humanity when He made women peak in their thirties and men in their teens.

Now here she was actually doing it, and all she could think of was that perverted schoolteacher from Washington that had been in all the papers. But this was hardly a case of older woman initiating young boy into the pleasures of sex. This was two battered survivors trying to conserve warmth.

She could just hear it now:

They said they had to stay warm . . . wink-wink.

I bet she kept him warm, all right!

Haw-haw, snort, guffaw.

Like he'd be capable even if she was so inclined. Assuming they got out of here, it would be back to the hospital for him, and probably a room across the hall for her.

She crawled back in and pulled the quilts over her head, using a trick she'd employed as a child and letting her exhalations help heat the air trapped beneath the covers. Full, almost comfortable, and the pain in her throat momentarily eased, she was on the verge of falling back asleep when she heard the rattle of a key.

Hide and he'll go away! she thought.

No. Dumb.

She sat up instead, meaning to grab one of those antique swords from beneath the bed and cleave it through his stinking pus-filled brain.

The door opened just as she swung her legs out of bed and she froze, caught in the beam of a flashlight much brighter than Jerry's. A dark shape loomed behind the fierce yellow-white circle.

"Why am I not surprised?" Thornton's voice, gravely and slurred. "Wicked slut like you. That's your game, huh? Lead men on, tease them, but it's little fagboys that you really want."

Dani stood up, her fists clenched at her sides. No time to dig for a weapon, but that was okay. She'd use her bare hands if she had to. "Let us out of here."

"Oh, no. Oh, no. I think not. Not until you've paid."

"Dream on!"

"This is how you want to play it, huh? Bet you're all hot inside, just aching for it, but you like it rough, don't you?"

He set the flashlight on a stool, its beam pointed upward at the cobwebbed beams. Dust motes swirled in that harsh shaft of light. It was one of the big jobbies, heavy plastic. Good head-cracking weapon if she could just get ahold of it.

As he advanced, the sour reek of his breath preceded him and the bartender in Dani figured that had they been at Nate's, she would have confiscated his keys about five drinks ago.

"Back off," Jerry Forrester said, sitting up with his eyes still sleep-bleary but his face contorted with hatred. "Back off, you shit, or I'll kill you."

Thornton laughed. "Like to see you try, fagboy. You just sit tight and behave, and maybe I'll let you live." His shirt was unbuttoned, hanging over a plain white undershirt, and he pushed the sides apart to reveal the butt of a pistol stuck in the waistband of his slacks. "You move, and I'll blow your scummy little balls off."

The sight of the gun froze Dani and Jerry. Thornton drew it, beckoned with it. "Wicked girl. Come here."

* * *

Saturday dawned through a thick mist, the sun invisible, only the gradual lightening of the day proving that the earth had turned on its axis at all.

Kel McGuire left his own home as quietly as a thief laden with valuables, though he was laden with nothing more complicated than a pair of running shoes and a forest-green jogging suit.

How long since he'd risen before the sun to go for a brisk run? Too long. Always too many other things to do. But this morning, waking early to the sound of his father's snoring from the guest room and the knowledge that Pinkie and Percy would have laid claim to the living room, he knew he needed to get out of the house.

Contrary to his expectations and/or hopes, his parents had insisted on staying with him. At this time of family tragedy, they needed to be together. All of them. Even Gwynne, when she arrived tomorrow.

They'd spend the previous evening in Arcata, talking to the funeral director and a minister. Peg McGuire had made some token noises about having the body flown home to be interred, but Kel's arguments that Megan had chosen Trinity Bay had been accepted with only minimal fuss.

With all of that, followed by a trip into Eureka for a late dinner, it had been nearly midnight by the time they'd returned to Kel's modest house. He hadn't even checked his messages. Plenty of time to do that when he got back.

He ran along silent grey streets, the thumping of his footfalls the only sounds in the stillness. By the time he reached the plaza, a few other people were moving about. The paperboy, a delivery man. Wraiths in the fog.

The only place that seemed alive was the donut shop. Remembering his father's fondness for maple bars, Kel detoured across the street and into the warm, sweetly-scented place.

Lila Renshaw was at one table, her walker resting beside her chair. Her grandson

Grant was with her. Kel knew them both and admired them. Too many families these days were all too eager to shuffle their aging relatives off to places like Silver Grove once frail health or mental deterioration had begun.

A homeless man known only as Dobie gave Kel a terrified look, gathered up his newspapers and coffee, and fled out the door. Although Kel had never given him reason to think so, Dobie was convinced that Kel was just waiting for the moment to slap him in detox, dump him in a shelter, or use bus therapy to ship him down to San Francisco or up to Portland.

Scott James, sitting at the counter, watched Dobie's rushed exit, and shared a rueful grin with Kel. "I get that same response from him, but only when I'm in uniform."

"Off-duty today?" Kel sat two stools away and asked for orange juice. Noreen Sorenson, Brian's younger sister, plunked a container down in front of him and mumbled something incoherent through a wad of gum.

"Supposed to be, but Damon tapped me for the search party."

"Search party? It's a little late in the season for lost hikers, isn't it?"

Scott looked at him blankly. "What?"

"What?"

"What lost hikers?"

Kel opened his orange juice and took a drink, then grimaced and did his best to hold it shut while he shook it. "Let's start over. What search party? Who's lost?"

"Jerry Forrester, and maybe Dani Kensington too."

He accidentally eased his hold on the sides of the container while still shaking, and juice squirted out over his hand. "Jerry? Dani? What happened?"

Scott explained – Jerry missing since sometime Thursday night, Dani never showing up for work last night. It was mostly Jerry that everyone was worried about, of course, but Art Kensington had been on the phone all evening demanding of anybody and everybody that they find his daughter.

Kel thought of the unheard messages waiting for him on his machine and winced. "They had a row the other day. Maybe she just needed to get away for a while. Though leaving Tom in the lurch like that . . . not even calling him . . . that's not like Dani."

"Well, she hasn't exactly been herself lately," Scott pointed out carefully.

"Not feeling well," Kel corrected. "And upset by the incident on Tuesday."

"Yeah, I bet."

"Dani . . . I hope she's all right! When and where is the search party gathering?"

"Nine, out at the Forrester place. Damon's getting Chet Underwood to bring his dogs, going to see if they can track Jerry. Luckily, it hasn't rained yet."

Kel drank the orange juice though he didn't really want it anymore. His thoughts were more occupied with Dani Kensington than with Jerry Forrester. Jerry probably *was* with Gary Haverley; the two of them had been best of buddies since kindergarten and were old pros at covering up for each other. Damon Blake may have been sure that Gary was telling the truth, but Gary was nearly as good an actor as Jerry himself. No, it was Dani's absence that bothered him.

He recalled their last conversation, over at the Grill, the day Megan had died. Her symptoms. Paranoia. Delusions. Command hallucinations. Her obsessive idea that Brad Thornton was putting thoughts in her head.

"Oh, God. I hope she didn't do anything stupid."

Scott had been outlining the day's planned search procedure when Kel interrupted. "Something going on that I should know about?"

"No . . . no. Just thinking out loud." He bought a dozen donuts, three maple bars and the rest at random. "Nice talking with you, Scott."

Scott followed him out. "Hold up a minute, Kel. There's something I have to ask."

Kel stopped in front of a used bookstore that had so many posters and fliers papering its windows that it was nearly impossible to see inside. "I'd be glad to help with the search party, sure."

"Great, but that wasn't it. I need to know . . . is there any chance that Dani Kensington might have done something to Jerry?"

"Kidnapped him, boiled him up in a cannibal stew? That's preposterous, Scott. You've known Dani even longer than I have."

"All my life," Scott said. "She was a senior when I was a freshman."

"Then you know she would never do anything like that."

"Yeah . . . but I also would have said she'd never take a shot at Damon Blake. I know you and he have made it sound like an accident, but I also know you're covering something."

"Well . . ."

"If there's a chance she's a danger to herself or others," Scott said, "aren't you obligated to tell the police?"

"Duty to warn," Kel agreed reluctantly. "Okay . . . I am worried that she might try to hurt someone. But it's not Jerry Forrester I'd be concerned about. She's . . . fixed on someone else."

"Damon?"

"No. Not anymore. She thinks someone *made* her shoot at Damon."

"You mean, as in, took over her mind?"

He nodded. "I'm worried that she might have tried to act on it. I should have talked to her more the other day, but Megan . . ."

Awkward remorse twisted Scott's face; he'd clearly forgotten all about Kel's personal grief. But he persisted nonetheless. "Do you have any idea where she might be? Who she might be fixed on?"

"She could have gone up to Seacliff," Kel said heavily. "Seacliff."

* * *

He woke from his dark slumber, roused by what he sensed.

The man's twisted lust, the woman's fear. He knew her; she was one of those whose dreams he had touched.

Like a farmer, he had helped to grow what seeds lay dormant in the fertile soil of her mind. Cultivated them. Fed on them. Mere sustenance. Mere diversion.

She was the one who had nearly been his tool. In her vulnerable state, still caught in the cold fever of his passage, it had been an easy matter to make suggestions. If only she had been successful!

And now here she was again. In his domain this time. His castle, his prison. Here, he was the lord, the king, the god . . . but also the trapped, the confined, the imprisoned. Only through dreams could he taste freedom. Through dreams, and through his missions of love's dire vengeance.

The man. Twisted lust. The same twisted lust that had awakened him from a longer sleep. Years spent in timeless solitude, the emptiness of the house touched only by the faint ghosts and residues of past emotions. But then the man had come, and in him had been already-sprouting seeds.

So easy. So easy to nudge here, encourage there, until the man acted on those impulses. Oh, and then the rapture of it! Riding unseen, hearing the girl's cries, feeling the softness of her cringing flesh, wallowing in the man's bestial pleasure.

If not for the man's presence, awakening him after so many years, he would never have come to his current level of power. Never noticed the woman he desired above all others, the one he would have as his own. Forever.

His past failures now seemed far distant. Of no consequence. The merest flick of his awareness told him that the one called Kowalski had died after all, died following many hours of suffering and terror. As he had been the worst of them, it was easy to convince himself that he'd let Kowalski's life linger on deliberately.

The other failure . . . Damon Blake was still alive, still untouchable. Good and bad, that. Good that he had not sullied Theresa Zane's body with his. Bad, for now there was even less chance of killing him.

But the business at hand did not involve Blake. It involved the man, Thornton. Driven over the edge, into the madness that had always lain just below the surface. Building. Rising. Volcanic. Explosive.

Thornton was no longer useful, no longer needed.

He was awake now.

Awake, and would soon finish his work. Once Theresa Zane was his, he would never need to sleep again. They would be one. He would get offspring upon her, and grow stronger than ever.

Awake and hungry.

He reached out to Thornton. Men were more difficult. Nearly impossible. Only the ones like Thornton, like the ones who had been called Adam and Joshua and Edward, the ones who were not only living within his limited sphere of influence but who also harbored those seeds of lust and destruction in their souls, only those could he use. Draw from. Feed on.

Ah, but the women . . . so rich, their dreams! So alive, their spirits!

He reached out to Thornton, and insinuated sly seductive whispers to spur him on in his tormented sexual violence.

Quivered with excitement as Thornton seized the woman. Yes, yes!

The youth sprang up – foolish boy! Didn't he see the gun? But no, he fancied himself a hero, and Thornton had his hands full with the woman. The two of them might overpower him, stop him. Stop the flow of emotion.

Would not be allowed.

He knew the youth, had seen images in the dreams collected from the first of the women he had touched during his adoring pursuit of Theresa Zane.

Gathering his strength, pulling what he needed from Thornton, he flung those images at the youth. Let him see what his mother saw, know what his mother knew. Let him lose sight of his surroundings!

Yes!

See how the youth's head snaps back! See how his eyes go wide and blank! He thinks himself home again, in his own room, one hand curled around the stiff spear of flesh rising from his loins. He sees his mother standing over him, lush body nude and exposed. He feels the hotness of her breath, the slickness of her tongue. He is lost.

The woman, Dani, fought Thornton, struggled. Screamed the youth's name through her injured throat. To no avail. The youth stood spellbound. Horrified, but at the same time darkly aroused, his blood pulsing.

More energy. More power. Their lusts gave him his strength. Especially those that were overripe with shame. Forbidden. Taboo.

Thornton dragged the woman from the attic. At the small landing on the top of the stairs, he tried to hold her with one hand while he groped for the latch, the lock, the key. He left his light. They could not see well in the dark, poor weak creatures.

He *could see in the dark. He lived in it, loved it. It was a part of him.*

* * *

"This is crazy," Kel McGuire said.

"Seems like the whole town has gone a little crazy these past couple of weeks," Scott replied.

"Maybe something got into our water supply."

"Doesn't it strike you as a little odd?"

"That was a stop sign."

"You want me to put on the siren?"

"The whole thing strikes me as odd. But that doesn't mean I have to buy into all of this nonsense about conspiracies and psychic powers."

"Better explanation?"

"Mass hysteria?"

"I don't buy it. Look, Kel, I know people here are a little quirky. But just because the whole town is speculating that some *thing* caused all that's happened, doesn't mean it didn't."

"Just because you're paranoid doesn't mean they *aren't* out to get you," Kel said sourly.

"I thought having an open mind was a necessity in a job like yours."

"Having an open mind and readily accepting the idea that the women of Trinity Bay are being mind-controlled into weird sexual fantasies are *not* the same thing. What about you? Aren't police officers trained to look for *rational* explanations?"

"Yeah, unless there aren't any. Remember your Holmes?"

"Whatever's left after eliminating the impossible?"

"That's right."

"No, that's not *right!*" Kel said angrily, whumping his fist against the dashboard. "Not when what we're talking about *is* impossible!"

"Why'd you come, then?"

"Because whether I believe it or not doesn't matter, if Dani does."

"And if she does . . . the Dani I know is no shrinking violet. She would have gone up there to confront Brad Thornton."

"But even if she did, that's where it stops making sense," Kel protested. "If she showed up at Seacliff last night, raving about mind control, Thornton would have called the cops."

"Maybe."

"What do you mean, maybe?" His eyes narrowed.

"Well," Scott said, "would he, if he did have something to hide?"

"My God, the whole town *has* gone crazy! You included! Next thing you'll be saying is that Thornton really *does* have psychic powers, and when Dani found him out, he murdered her and buried her body in his backyard!"

"All I'm saying is it's worth a look. And that's what I'm going to do. Have a look. No harm in that, is there?"

* * *

Someone slapped him across the face.

Jerry Forrester's head rocked to the side.

Jolted from his daze, jolted from the horrible, unimaginable vision, he cried out in loathing and surprise.

"It wasn't real, Jerry."

He whirled, and there she was. Angela. Standing with her hands folded demurely in front of her nightgown, hair loose over her shoulders. As big as life, but not as solid. He could see the rest of the attic through her.

"What you saw wasn't real. Just a dream," she said.

"Are . . . you?"

"We're trapped, Jerry. Bethany, Glory, and me. All of us trapped. Until it ends. Until it's over. But first you have to stop him."

"Thornton?"

"Don't let him do to her what he did to me," she pleaded.

Then she vanished like fogged breath fading from a windowpane, and other sounds intruded. Cursing, struggling. The rattle of the door in its frame. Scraping, scratching.

In a flash, he knew that Thornton was trying to lock it again. Lock him in. So that he could have the leisure to do what he pleased with Dani Kensington.

He ran to the door, and just before he got there, he heard a fleshy thunk, a garbled bleat of pain, and then the crashes and thumps that could only be a body falling down a flight of stairs.

Jerry was about to cheer, when Thornton's voice snarled from the other side of the door.

"Bitch!"

Then a shot, loud as cannonfire in the enclosed space.

* * *

Theresa was dreaming. Even in the dream, she was aware that she was, but remained powerless to change anything, or wake herself.

Dreaming. A vivid, bizarre dream of taking Lora to Disneyland. Her mother had been there, having arranged to meet Theresa with a box of her old belongings.

But for some reason they met in a parklike meadow that sloped toward a bandstand/stage, when Theresa was fairly sure the Happiest Place on Earth boasted no such feature. Then, after her mother departed, Theresa and Lora were left to go through the large cardboard box at night, after the theme park had closed.

And it began to storm. Lightning striking.

Among the belongings, which had turned out not to be Theresa's at all but a bunch of old junk her mother had wanted to get rid of – even in the dream, she was self-aware enough to suspect it was some sort of subconscious commentary on how she was still burdened with her mother's emotional baggage – was one of those metal and wire clothes-drying whirligigs.

Theresa kicked it over quickly, before it turned into a lightning rod, and grabbed up Lora to flee to the shelter of a rocky ridge.

There, they huddled, Lora scared and crying, while thunder shattered the sky. When the rain came, it hadn't been rain at all but sheeting pellets of white-hot lightning-fire that stung Theresa's back and shoulders as she hunched herself over Lora to protect her.

Then the fiery hail ended, and a weird glow spread across the field. There were shapes in it. Wraiths and ghouls. The cast of the demonic finale to Fantasia, racing and cavorting across the smoldering grass. Theresa tried to shield Lora from the frightening sight, but the noise – howling-gibbering-screeching-roaring – had been enough to shake the rocks against which they crouched.

A shadow rose behind the ghastly turbulent parade, a shadow of inky blackness.

It unfurled wings that blotted out the sky, outstretched arms that cast long-fingered darkness over the land. With it came a bone-deep chill.

Cold and dark. Blackness and chill. Blotting out everything.

The other dream images faded, and Theresa felt herself slipping into a heavy cocoon.

Had to wake herself!

With the last effort of will she could muster, she tore through the thickening weblike membrane that separated her from the waking world.

She lurched upright with a start, the cold wrapping her like a blanket and the word "No!" on her lips.

Jack, who had been curled in a tidy orange and white ball on the other pillow when she went to bed, was now in a tense, stiff-legged pose. When Theresa sat up and switched on the bedside lamp, he turned his wide green eyes on her.

"Started again," she said to the cat, dismal but unsurprised. She'd hoped it was over, and in the past few days had even allowed herself the luxury of thinking it had all been a series of gruesome coincidences compounded by severe stress.

But now she knew better, and was ashamed at herself for grasping at those flimsy hopes.

It had started again.

It was back. *It* was awake. She didn't know how she'd sensed that fact, but she believed it completely.

But there was more that she'd sensed. Not *it*, but *he*. Whatever presence stalked her, she was now more sure than ever that it was male.

* * *

Jerry started toward them, meaning to help, and all of a sudden Dani saw his body go rigid. His eyes became huge unseeing circles that swallowed his face. The color drained from him until he was milk-white, corpse-white.

Even as she struggled with Brad Thornton, Dani's main concern was for Jerry. He was having a heart attack, seizure, stroke, something.

But Thornton propelled her to the door. Terribly strong. Unnaturally strong. His mouth was a leering bestial snarl. Although she was a tall, fit woman, she could not break free.

Beyond the door was a landing, a cramped flight of stairs, and another door at the bottom. With one hand, Thornton pinned her against the wall. He used the other to swing the attic door closed, cutting them off from the flashlight, leaving them enclosed in the dark.

She heard the scrapes and rattles of him fumbling with the latch and lock. Distracted. She couldn't see him any more but that only seemed to make her hearing more acute. His ragged, eager panting. A wet sound as he smacked his lips in anticipation.

Disgust shivered through her. He sounded like an old hound dog slurping up Gravy Train. The idea of him making that noise over her body repelled her even more than the thought of his touch.

Dani pulled away, and he yanked her back just as she expected. She raised her elbow and drove the bony point of it dead-center in his chest. Then, cat-quick, swung that same arm down so that her clenched fist struck the hard bulge at his crotch.

Thornton choked out a pained cry. Dani tried to pull away again, but at the same moment he shoved at her in a reflexive motion.

Stairs beneath her sneakers. Then Thornton's fingers closed on the collar of her sweatshirt, yanked it taut against her throat. It hurt terribly, so Dani pushed against him with all her might.

The cloth, old and worn from many washings and wearings, gave way before his grip did. It ripped straight down the back as she tumbled down the stairs.

Revolving, battering against sharp angles of wood. Like the time she'd put her Barbie doll in the dryer and given it a good spin.

She slammed against the lower door and her jaw clacked shut so hard she could have bitten off her tongue. For a moment she could only lay there in her contorted pose, amazed that she hadn't broken her neck.

From above, Thornton said, "Bitch!" in a voice that could have belonged to a bear or a wolf, had such creatures been given the power of speech.

Then he fired, the muzzleflash flaring.

The slug punched into the door, four feet above Dani's head, showering her with chips and splinters. Now she was deaf as well as blind, but she groped up the panel for the handle, offered a brief but very fervent prayer, and turned.

It opened, spilling her into the third-floor hall of Seacliff.

* * *

Jerry grabbed the heavy-duty flashlight, having the same thought that Dani had not long ago. Good blunt instrument as well as light source. He reached for the doorknob, his face still tingling from the slap that had shocked him out of scenes best left uncontemplated.

He heard running steps, knew that Thornton was plunging down the stairs in pursuit of Dani.

Locked!

No!

Dammit!

Then he turned the knob the other way and the door swung toward him, almost knocking him on his butt. He speared the bright beam down the stairs and caught a glimpse of Thornton just making it out the lower doorway.

He made it to the hall in a series of graceless bounds that left him lucky to avoid taking a fall of his own. The hall stretched the length of the west wing. Forest green carpet. Wood paneling. A bunch of those little tippy tables that seemed made for tripping over.

At the end of the hall, Dani Kensington was running hell-for-leather with Thornton hot on her tail. They'd left a pretty respectable path of destruction – three of those tippy tables were upended, broken vases, scattered knickknacks, and a spindly bench that looked too fragile to support any weight were strewn behind them. Either caught by racing feet or frantically flung behind Dani to deter her pursuer.

Jerry went after them. Heard another gunshot, this one echoing and rebounding, and a crystalline explosion.

At the end of the hall, it opened onto the gallery that ringed Seacliff's atrium. Dani and Thornton were at the rail, him grappling her. The gun was nowhere to be seen. High above, one of the blue panes of stained glass in the dome had been smashed by a bullet.

Dani's sweatshirt was in tatters. Thornton had her pinned against the rail, spitting filthy words at her. He no longer bore any resemblance to the suave-if-slightly-sleazy man he'd been. Now he was frenzied, deranged.

Jerry saw the gun. Way the hell over there. Thornton must have tossed it aside when he caught Dani.

He went for it even though he'd never fired a gun in his life. Couldn't be that hard. Couldn't be that much different from the arcade games, right? Even though he had never been very keen on electronic mayhem, he'd played a few. Training his generation to be psychotic life-disrespecting killing machines, wasn't that how it went?

Dani was dishing it out, not slapping and scratching at Thornton in the way they often showed women's' feeble defense efforts in the movies, but really whaling on him in the best Sigourney Weaver and Demi Moore tradition. Had Thornton been just a regular guy, he would have been curled in a ball begging for mercy.

But he wasn't. Not anymore. Something, whatever it was that came out of the rosebush and made people crazy, had gotten into him. Made him strong, made him impervious to pain.

Well, Jerry thought as he closed his fingers on the gun, *let's hope it can't make the asshole bulletproof.*

CRACK! Both Dani and Thornton jerked as the railing they were leaning against took a sudden outward jolt.

"Let her go!" Jerry demanded, getting into a half-kneeling crouch and leveling the gun at them.

Thornton didn't even look around. Jerry didn't dare shoot for fear of hitting Dani, and plus Thornton's back was to him. He wouldn't have expected it, not after all Thornton had done, but the prospect of shooting him in the back just smacked of chickenshit-edness.

He pointed it at the ceiling and squeezed the trigger. It went off like the end of the world right beside his ear, the recoil slamming down his arm. The bullet plowed into the plaster and sent chunks hailing down on Jerry.

But it got Thornton's attention. He turned, lips pulled back from his teeth as if he might just fall upon Jerry and rend him to bits.

"Goddam little fagboy!" he growled. "Thought you could fuck these wicked girls behind my back, didja, fagboy?"

An eerie calm settled onto Jerry and he only shook his head as if bemused. "That's a contradiction in terms, dickweed. If I was a fagboy, why would I be wanting girls?"

Behind Thornton, Dani clung to the rail trying to catch her breath. As well as she'd been fighting, he had still messed her up pretty badly.

Jerry focused on Thornton, who was puffing and snarling so ferociously that Jerry wouldn't have been surprised to see him undergo some lycanthropic transformation. Instead, Thornton just charged.

"Oh, shit," Jerry moaned, having really hoped they could get through this by bluffing. He fired.

* * *

Kel was surprised when Scott didn't pound on the door, shout, "Police!" or anything. The burly young officer just crossed his arms in front of his face, lowered his head, and went straight through one of the foyer windows like a bull charging a matador.

But then, given that they'd heard three gunshots in the last few minutes, Scott probably had the right idea.

They'd pulled up, and Kel had seen just what he'd expected to see. The big house dozing peacefully in the cool grey dawn. Just as they'd gotten out of Scott's car, though, the first shot had split the air.

He clambered in through the broken window, knowing it was okay for Scott to have barged on in without a warrant, given that there was an assault in progress, but completely unsure how the law applied to counselors in way over their heads. All he knew was that he couldn't wait on the porch, that he had made a life out of helping people and wasn't going to back down now.

Scott screeched to a halt and looked frantically around. He had drawn his own piece but no targets readily presented themselves.

Then a voice, barely recognizable as Brad Thornton's, came from the atrium. Something about a goddam fagboy. Answered by another voice, the words unclear. Jerry Forrester.

Rocked to the core – what the hell was Jerry doing here? – Scott and Kel raced to the atrium. High over them, on the third floor, they saw Dani Kensington holding onto a sagging piece of rail, beaten and bleeding.

A fourth shot. A man staggered backward, driven by the impact. He struck the rail right next to Dani, and with a grinding squeal of tortured wood, the rail gave way under his weight.

Dani uttered a rusty croak perhaps meant to be a scream. She and Brad and the section of splintered railing catapulted out.

"No!" Kel and Scott and Jerry cried in unison.

Dani plunged into the pool, missing the edge by half a foot. Brad wasn't so lucky, landing half on the concrete lip that surrounded it. His arms shot upward, clawing at the dome far above. Pieces of wood clattered on the marble, splashed into the water.

On the upper gallery, Jerry appeared, the gun dangling from his hands. He looked down, then dropped the weapon and swayed.

Kel was sure that he was about to follow the others over, but instead Jerry crumpled to his knees, then onto his side.

Thornton slid bonelessly into the pool, a scarlet cloud forming around him. His shirt was dark with blood from where he'd been shot. Dani surfaced, gasped, and went under again with her hair a trailing mass of dark blond.

Scott kicked off his shoes, dropped his gun on a lounge chair, and dove in.

* * *

Theresa had bundled herself up in a quilt and taken her tea out front, relishing the pearly quality of the morning and the silence. She'd heard an engine go by while waiting for the water to boil, but now the day was all her own, as if she was the only person on earth.

It helped her to shake off the last vestiges of her bizarre dream. Not that it changed her belief any. She still knew that it had begun again.

If she got herself a dream-catcher like Shauna Davis had, would that help? Or would it only protect *her*, while still letting the events continue on their evil course? *She* might sleep well, but would the killings continue? Would she still be a carrier, a nightmare Typhoid Mary, infecting everyone around her? Would the force that had already come close to killing Damon keep trying?

And even if all of those things could be forestalled, what if just any old dream-catcher wouldn't do? She no longer had the one her grandmother had made for her as a child. Grandma Tashi had known about this thing; what if she also knew the secret of keeping it away, a secret that some other craftsperson might not know?

She thought of her Aunt Dorry, Travis' older sister. But Aunt Dorry had died a few years back, and while she had enjoyed and embraced her heritage, her knack went more toward the making of jewelry.

Gunfire.

Theresa spilled hot tea on herself but barely noticed. The shots had come from Seacliff.

She hurried back inside and called Damon Blake.

* * *

At the end of the day, that long, long day, a group of five (six including Jack, seven or more including Glory or any other ghosts that might be hanging around) gathered at the Zane house.

Damon couldn't have been more worn out if he actually had spent the day tromping through the woods, though the search party had been canceled before it even got underway.

He'd endured a grueling conversation with his brother, Derrek wanting to know how and why and what Damon knew. Derrek wouldn't have had him committed if he told the whole story, but there just wasn't time. Plus, despite all that they *did* know, they couldn't *prove* diddly-squat, and trying to explain would have taken more time than he'd had.

Kel McGuire sat on the couch, resigned to having a thorough inspection by Jack – the smells of Pinkie and Percy, his parents' cats, were just irresistible. Kel himself kept shaking his head in slow, steady arcs. He didn't want to believe the strangeness that the rest of them had accepted so readily – well, *more* readily – but he was running out of arguments against it.

Scott James, on the other hand, had treated it simply as a matter of course. His suspicions and hunches had led him to conclusions of his own, and the important thing was that they'd also led to Seacliff in time to save lives.

Travis Zane was holding up darn well, though clearly worried about his daughter. Theresa herself was also worried, not for her own safety so much as her concern about what might come next. The presence that had fixated on her had been absent for a while, but she was sure that it was back now. Which meant the danger to Tony Monatella and Steven Taylor could be imminent. Not to mention the danger to Theresa herself.

Though it went against procedure, Damon had laid out everything for this group. He'd already broken the rules by letting Theresa see the faxes from Derrek . . . who had broken the rules by sending them, and Mark had broken the rules in obtaining them . . . the cycle of guilt just spiraled on and on until it was pointless to worry about. After all, dealing with a spirit that could apparently possess people did fall outside normal procedure.

There would be no stopping the town talk now. But it was odd how quickly the finger of blame had shifted from pointing at Dani Kensington to pointing at Brad Thornton. Once the story had come out of how he'd held Dani and Jerry prisoner in the attic, beat the living tar out of them both, and then tried to kill them, people who had only a few days ago raved about what a great guy Thornton was were now claiming they'd known all along that there was something not right about him.

And there was no way of Thornton telling his side of the story. When he'd fallen from the gallery, he had fractured his spine and skull. He was paralyzed from the waist down, and brain damage was likely even if he regained consciousness after the surgery to remove the bullet from his chest.

Dani Kensington had fared considerably better. Choked, nearly drowned (twice), pushed down the stairs, and beaten up, she also had pneumonia and a collapsed lung. But she had come through it without any broken bones, a small miracle in itself. Two cracked ribs, a sprained shoulder. She was nearly one big bruise from head to toe. But she was alive, and had been able to talk to Damon.

Jerry Forrester was right back in his old familiar hospital room. When he'd passed out on the gallery, his knee had come down squarely on an upthrust stake that had once been part of the railing. He'd needed surgery to replace his ruined kneecap. Plus removal of a chunk of glass embedded in the puffed knot on his head. His collection of bruises was half as extensive as Dani's, and he had a mild concussion.

Following their renditions of what had happened, Damon and Scott had been all over Seacliff. More bones – another undiscovered skeleton. Which meant another visit from the county, another old mystery that would be treated as a homicide.

Theresa and Damon suspected, from what she'd written while in her weird trances, that the bones belonged to the 'attic man' who had killed Glory. Not that they could share those suppositions with the medical examiners.

"So it *was* Thornton?" Kel mused, as if trying to convince himself.

"No," Theresa said, exasperated. "Not just him. He didn't have anything to do with what happened to Sandy. Or to your sister."

"But after what Scott turned up about Al and Celeste," Damon said, "we'll be going back and taking a closer look at the crash that killed that lawyer. Smythe. Bet my hat he was involved in that."

"And Angela, and possibly even April," Theresa added. "But what's the point? He's dead."

"There will still be an investigation."

"Is Jerry going to get in trouble?" Travis asked. "That family's been hurt so much lately. I'd hate to see it happen."

"Not a chance," Scott said. "Self defense. Kel and I were both witnesses to that."

"What if the rest of it was just coincidence?" Kel suggested. "Sandy, Megan . . ."

"Come on!" Scott leaned forward, his eyes blazing. "Get over it and open your eyes! The roses, you can't explain those away. Dani's wallpaper, Angela's sketchbook . . . hell, man, your own secretary's a part of this!"

"Nancy? That's ridiculous . . ." he trailed off. "Though she did . . . no. No. Never mind. That has nothing to do with –"

"What?" Scott pressed. "Her sudden interest in bondage?"

Theresa's and Travis' eyebrows went up in nearly identical gestures.

"And what about her tattoo?" Scott continued. "I didn't know about these roses at the time, so I didn't think anything of it. But when I went over there responding to that call, she was in a robe, and it showed a lot. Including the tattoo."

"A black rose," Theresa said. "It was a black rose, wasn't it? Ruth Edwards was sewing them on a scarf."

"So why didn't they experience the rest of the symptoms?" Kel said. "Why didn't they act out?"

"It's their fantasies," Theresa said slowly, as if feeling her way through the explanation even as it came to her. "Sexual fantasies, dreams. They actually believe their most hidden desires, even the ones they never admitted to themselves, were becoming real. Maybe Ruth and Nancy . . . maybe theirs were just fantasies they could live with. And not suffer any guilt or compulsions that seriously got in the way of their lives."

"We know Nancy's acting on hers. The part I can't believe is that Rand Kostas would be into it too." Scott shrugged. "Goes to show, you never can tell about people."

"And Ruth and Malachi were having some troubles themselves," Travis said. "They've worked through it now, though."

"I think I know what it might be," Theresa said, still speaking slowly, uncertainly. She got up and went over to her desk, grabbing her battered old dictionary and turning to the I's. "Inchworm . . . incorporate . . . aha! Incubus."

"Incubus? What's that?" Travis asked, frowning.

"Some kind of demon, I think," Damon said.

"The male version of a succubus," she said. "A demon, a spirit . . . a sexual vampire."

* * *

30

The necklace was in the bottom drawer of her dresser, wrapped in a dishtowel. Theresa unfolded the cloth and looked at the heavy silver leaves, the smooth black petals.

It hadn't tarnished. Theresa remembered a silver pitcher that her mother and Paul Kowalski had gotten as a wedding gift, and how only a few years of disuse and confinement in a high cupboard later, it had been dark with corruption.

This necklace, which had spent a hundred years without benefit of polishing, was as bright and shining as if it had only come from the jewelry store that day.

She turned it over in her hands, looking for inscriptions and finding nothing. Where had it come from? Jacob Cliffwood had apparently given it to his daughter Bethany Rose, but where had Jacob gotten it? What power did it hold?

Not content with being a logger baron, Jacob had also dipped his fingers in many other pies. The fur trade, railroads, even smuggling. One of Trinity Bay's most enduring and endearing legends was of a sea cave in the bluff beneath the manor, accessible only from the inlet on the other side. Jacob's boat, named for his daughter, had been more than a fishing craft or pleasure cruiser. He hadn't been anything so exotic as a pirate, but according to old tales, he had done more than a little traffic in bootleg booze and foreign goods.

Which meant that the necklace could theoretically have come from anywhere. Maybe it originally had been only what it appeared to be. An expensive, ornate adornment. Maybe it hadn't acquired any unusual aspects until later. Until after it had graced the necks of not one but two murdered girls.

She had no idea if it was something that could help her or not. It was somehow linked to the living rosebush too, had to be.

A glance at the clock showed her it was midnight. The witching hour. Thanks to half a dozen cups of coffee, she had reached that state of gritty-eyed wakefulness familiar to her from her college finals.

The house was still, their company having long since departed.

Jack looked at her as if to ask, *Well?*

"Okay," she breathed. Her fingers trembled as she undid the clasp and lifted the necklace in front of her. She put it on.

The metal was cool even through her sweater. When she tucked it inside, it felt like ice against her skin before quickly warming to body temperature. The black rose rested just at the top of her breasts, the touch of the unfamiliar stone silken and sensual.

She closed her eyes and waited for something to happen. Some revelation, understanding, something. But the only thing she was aware of was her own heartbeat.

When she touched the red jewel at the center of the rose, she could swear she felt her pulse echoed in it.

Jack regarded her steadily, unnervingly. She reached to pet him, and instead of arching to meet her hand as he usually did, he remained as still as an Egyptian statue but for the slightest of twitches at the end of his tail.

She eased open her bedroom door and listened. The normal night-quiet of an occupied house – the faint whistle of the heater vents, the gurgle of the pipes, the dripping of condensed moisture from the eaves, her father's low snores.

Theresa crept downstairs, took her jacket, and went outside.

The mist that had lain over Trinity Bay all day had thickened into a fog that put her in mind of Victorian London. Not hard at all to imagine Jack the Ripper with his doctor's bag, or Dr. Jekyll out twirling his cane.

Don't scare yourself, she cautioned. *Don't get yourself all worked up over imaginary monsters when there's already a real one to deal with.*

She could just see herself panicking and running off the edge of the bluff. That wouldn't do at all. So she made herself walk calmly, hugging the woods until she reached Seacliff's manicured lawn.

A shadow detached itself from the night then, and Theresa very nearly *did* panic and bolt. Would have, if her feet hadn't been rooted to the spot. But when the shape came closer, she saw it wasn't the demonic creature she'd been half-expecting to see. It was Damon Blake.

"Taking a stroll, ma'am?"

"You shouldn't sneak up on people like that!" she laughed nervously.

He'd changed out of his uniform, and now she had the weirdest feeling that she was seeing the *real* Damon Blake. Well-worn tan-brown jeans. Faded denim shirt the color of the dusty desert sky. Long brown trenchcoat, the leather buttery-soft with age. Even cowboy boots with fancy stitching. He lacked only the hat and the sexy low-slung double-crossed gunbelts to make the picture complete. Well, that and the horse.

"I thought I might find you out here. Theresa, mind telling me what the hell you're doing?"

"You know what I'm doing. I'm going up there."

"We still don't know how to deal with this thing. Wasn't the plan that we'd do some research in the morning? Read up on folklore?"

"And in the meantime, people could die. It's using me, Damon. Feeding off of me. That's what made me so lethargic. It takes from me, and uses what it takes to kill. I can't sleep – *can't* as in I don't dare to sleep. That's when it's strongest. But I also know I can't stay awake forever. So that means I have to confront this thing now. Tonight."

"And do what?"

"I don't know. But I won't sit around and wait for it to kill someone else. I'm tired of only being able to react. Maybe by going up there, I can find out what it is, what it wants, what its weaknesses are."

"I figured you'd decide that."

"Are you going to stop me?"

"No, ma'am. I may not like it, but you're right. So I'm tagging along."

"Damon, no!"

He came closer, took her by the shoulders, looked squarely into her eyes. "I'm afraid it's not open for discussion. Either I'm coming with you or I'm following after, but either way, I'm not letting you go up to that house alone."

"You're a brave, crazy man," she said.

"That's right." He bent down, and she tipped her head up, and they sealed their bargain with a warm, sweet kiss.

* * *

She was coming.

He sensed her presence drawing nearer.

Not alone.

Blake was with her, Blake had even dared to kiss her. But that was all right. It realized now that Blake was no danger. No threat. For once Theresa Zane learned the true depths of his emotion, his promise, his power, she would see that he was a thousand times more than Damon Blake could ever be.

And once she'd seen that . . . why, perhaps she would return the favor that he'd been showing her. Hadn't he done murder to prove his love? Hadn't he rid her of old sorrows, old pains, old . . . shall we say, thorns in the side? It was only reasonable that she might do a similar deed for him.

Yes. Kill Blake herself.

Then, once she had spilled blood and taken life, she would really be his. They would be joined by bonds even stronger than those of passion or love.

The time he'd been waiting so long for was almost here.

She *was coming to* **him!**

She was coming to him, and once she knew all that he was, all that he could give to her, she would be his willingly. Even eagerly.

He shivered at the prospect, anticipating the feel of her skin, the scent of her breath, the heat of her body.

Honored. Yes, she would be honored that she had been chosen above all others. She would gladly accept his embrace, bear his seed.

Be one with him, in the rose-darkness, forever . . .

* * *

Her house had been night-quiet.

Seacliff was tomb-silent.

The Davises were staying with their son and daughter-in-law in Idaho, and it seemed that Brad Thornton had purposefully gotten them out of the house to give himself the time and privacy to finish his business with Dani and Jerry. Damon had contacted them to inform them of their boss' death, and they weren't due back until late Monday.

During the day, despite the best efforts of the authorities, nearly everyone in town had found some reason to drop by Seacliff and gawk. Not that there was much to see. Just a broken pane in the stained-glass dome, a sheet of plywood nailed over Scott's unconventional entryway, and yellow police tape strung across the doors.

Now, though, as Theresa and Damon approached, it would have been easy to believe that it hadn't been a matter of hours but of *years* since anyone had set foot on the property. Looming in the fog, Seacliff held a menacing air equal to that of any centuries-old castle fully populated by chain-dragging woe-crying specters.

Damon lifted the tape and they ducked under to the porch.

"Will we need to bust in another window?" Theresa asked in a whisper.

"As it happens, I've got the keys." He unlocked the front door. It swung open on well-oiled hinges, with nary a haunted house creak to be heard, but Theresa's mouth went dry with dread anyway.

She didn't let that stop her from being first inside, over Damon's hissed warning.

"Jesus," she said. "Do you feel it?"

Damon nodded. "Like what I felt that night in your house. Pressure. Not as much, though . . . more . . . diffuse. But it's here, all right."

Theresa moved deeper into the foyer, her eyes sweeping across the grand staircases and chandelier. She and Damon had both brought flashlights, not wanting to risk undue attention from anyone in town who might be awake and looking up at Seacliff and wonder at lights in the windows.

"Where do we look?" Damon wondered. "The attic?"

"I don't think so. Those weren't his bones."

"What makes you think that?"

"I just do. Whoever that was, he was a victim too, in a way. While you were busy with the people from the county, I went through some of the back issues of the *Gazette* –"

"Down in the archives? You probably could have just asked old Lan; he knows everything."

"Yes, but he was up here hanging on your every word. I think the bones in the attic belonged to Joshua Cliffwood. Bethany's brother, the one who disappeared."

"I thought he was just a kid when he went missing."

"That's just it, Damon. He never went missing at all. He was locked in the attic for all that time. Even if he wasn't insane going in, he must have quickly gotten that way." She hunched herself deeper into her jacket, cold. "But that wasn't what I was looking for. This . . . incubus . . . has been here for a long time. And all that time, his influence has been affecting people. The Cliffwoods have always tried to keep it hushed up, but there've been a lot of problems with their family. Everyone knows about how April's aunt killed herself and her dad had a breakdown, but even a lot of people who *worked* at Seacliff ended up committing suicide or going nuts. Shauna Davis was right all along. It gets into people. More of a foothold in those who were already having some problems, maybe, less in others."

"What do we do, then? Burn the place?"

Thereeeeesa . . .

"Did you hear that?"

"Hear what?"

Thereeeeesa . . .

"That!" She turned in a circle, trying to pinpoint the source of the ghostly keen, but saw nothing.

"I don't hear anything."

"It's him. Calling me."

Damon was staring at her as if he didn't at all like the way she looked. "You shouldn't be here."

"Where else can I go? We've been over this. His reach is too long. No matter where I went, eventually I'd have to sleep. And then he'd be there. Seeking me out."

"What do you say? Fire? We burn the place to ashes, that'll get rid of him."

"I doubt it. It's not the *house* itself." She let herself relax into a state similar to the trance she'd been in when she wrote about Bethany Cliffwood's fatal fight with her mother. "The house is just . . . closest."

"Closest? To what?"

"To . . . to where he . . . is. Where he lives. Where he was . . . born."

"Theresa, I'm not getting you."

"She was still alive when they buried her," Theresa said. "Dear God, still alive."

Like a sleepwalker, she went into the atrium, directly to the patch of marble that didn't quite match the rest. It didn't surprise her at all to see that the broken section of railing on the third floor was in the exact same spot. Brad Thornton and Dani Kensington had fallen from the same place that Bethany had, though they'd landed closer to the pool.

Damon followed her, increasingly concerned, but Theresa could say nothing to comfort him. She touched the black rose through her sweater, pulled it out. She felt the jewel pulsing, pulsing.

"Here," she said, stopping. "She fell, bones shattered, full of that poison her mother had given her, dying, dying, unconscious but still clinging to life, that poison working through her system, trying to abort the baby. Then . . . then . . ."

She exhaled in a sigh and would have fallen if Damon hadn't supported her. "Then what?"

"Dragged her outside. Reeveman and her mother. Dragged her outside, and buried her. Even though they knew she was still alive. Buried her, but first her mother took her necklace." She held it, tight, the rounded edges of the petals pressing into her palm.

"Where he was born, you said," Damon said. "Where he was born. You mean this thing, this incubus, is Bethany's unborn child?"

Theresa nodded. "Conceived in shame, born in death, and the rosebush, the black rosebush, grew from the grave he and his mother shared."

* * *

He called to her, called.

So vital and alive! So beautiful!

Even more so than her grandmother had been.

Tashi Swiftwater . . . copper skin, proud features, ink-black hair in a braid to her hips . . . first seen when she'd come seeking work at Seacliff, only to be turned haughtily away by the one called Myra. Envious, sour Myra, whose dreams hadn't even been worth his notice.

Ah, but Tashi . . .

Glimpsed, yearned for, and then gone.

And then returned, not to Seacliff, but married to Thaddeus Zane and living so close, so close that he was ever aware of her. Wanting her. Reaching out for her, for one single night sinking into the softness of her dreams.

But she had recognized his touch, known him for what he was. Rather than accept him, she had in her stubbornness refused him, pushed him away, woven spells to hold him apart from her. Armored herself and her children.

Now her granddaughter. Even more lovely in a different way, her mind strong but not so forceful, not so determined. Not so versed in the ways of the world beyond that which the eyes beheld. A child of an age that didn't see the need to shield the soul against unseen powers.

Accessible.

Inviting.

He called, called.

Felt her response, felt her let go her hold on the waking world just a bit, just enough to bring her partly into his realm.

She was curious. Wanting to know more about him, about how he'd come to be. Fine, let her know, let her understand.

Awareness and pain had come hand-in-hand, his first sensation that of blackly burning agony, of unbearable crushing. Then, bursting into his still-forming mind, the desperate betrayed anguish that had been his mother. Helpless. Bound together, her death and his. And the intense searing hatred that filled him at the realization that he would be denied his life.

Somehow, that fierce flame of emotion had sustained him. Sustained him in spirit even as flesh dissolved into the damp earth, even as the poison that had failed to destroy him continued seething beneath the ground.

Then, roses.

The woman who would have been his grandmother, the jealous Estelle who had let her daughter die rather than lose her young husband, found enough grief in her heart to mark her daughter's secret grave with a rosebush.

* * *

"The rosebush," Theresa said again. She shuddered and her vision cleared. Damon released her as the strength flooded back into her limbs. "That's the key."

"You mean, if we destroy the rosebush . . . ?"

"Maybe. It's worth a try." Her expression was bleak but firm. "I understand now.

But no matter how sad, how tragic, how pitiable the origins, we have to stop it."

She took a step toward the French doors leading to the garden, and the temperature in the atrium plummeted.

Damon's startled exclamation puffed out in a cloud. Thin ice crackled as it formed across the pool. Along with the cold came a terrible pressure, heavier than it had been that night in her room, heavier than they could resist. Unable to move, the air having the consistency of deep-packed snow, Theresa seized the back of a lounge chair for balance.

A whirling anger assaulted her mind. Then all light was snuffed out, and she didn't so much *fall* asleep as she was *yanked* headfirst into it.

Sad, am I? Tragic? Pitiable? When all I've done for you, I've done for love?

Let me go!

Why won't you see? I love you, Theresa Zane! I want you! You are mine, you will be mine! Forever!

No!

Quit fighting me! Look, look what I have done for you!

Oh, God! Wayne!

See? I did what you wanted! See his terror? See his pain? Watch, how he suffers! There! Repayment for how he hurt you!

He didn't hurt me!

He used you, discarded you, deserved to die!

No!

And this one! Look, Theresa. Don't avert your eyes. Don't let the blood bother you. It's no less than what he had coming to him. That's what I gave them. What they deserved. And that's what I gave you! I have set you free, Theresa, almost free!

This isn't what I wanted! Never what I wanted!

You don't know your own heart, Theresa. Not like I do. I have seen into your heart, into your soul. I know the hurt they caused you, and to prove my love I have punished them for it!

That's not love! That's insanity! Murder!

Revenge! Revenge for you, my Theresa!

I'm not your Theresa!

No, not yet . . . not yet. But soon. Soon. I promise. When you are free, you'll know that I was right to do what I did. When the last of them are dead, their holds over you will be gone as well. Then you'll be able to stop tricking yourself, and see clearly. You'll be mine then. Mine, my lover, my mate.

No!

It will be so! I am more than any of them could ever be . . . than all of them together could ever be! I am what you need!

I don't need you! Don't want you! You will never have me!

Stop doing this to me . . . to yourself . . . to us! Why do you fight so? Haven't you seen what I've done for you? Don't you know what that means?

You're a killer!

Because of you! For you! My strength comes from you, Theresa, haven't you realized that? It's your soul's secrets that let me appear to those men, your darkest hidden emotions that lead me to them. You wanted them dead. You carried the bitterness against them, locked far down in your heart.

Locked so tightly that even you may not have acknowledged it, but you can hide nothing from me.

You are wrong! What you see in me, you see through your own warped mind! It's your bitterness, your anger. Not mine!

Is this the thanks I get? I rid you of those who have hurt you, but all you can do is answer me with hostility? I love you!

You know nothing of love! All you know is death, lust, and obsession! You tell me to look at what you've done to my past lovers; what about what you've done to my friends? What about Sandy Forrester? Dani? Ruth? Was that your idea of love?

They were nothing to me! Mere . . . diversions. Appetizers. Distractions. I swear to you, I'll get rid of what I took from them. I'll get rid of all the other dreams that women have dreamed to me. There will be only you, Theresa, only you.

You will have nothing from me! Nothing! Now let me go!

Why won't you listen to me?

If your strength comes from me, then I can take it back! Get out of my mind! Out of my dreams! Leave me alone!

It's not that easy, Theresa. You cannot deny me. Whenever you sleep, I am with you! We are a part of each other now. Once you see, once you fully understand, what I am and what I can do, then you will change your mind.

I do see what you are! You're a monster, a demon, a vampire!

I am love! Look what I will do for you! Come with me, see for yourself!

I'm not going anywhere!

Oh, yes, my Theresa. Oh, yes you are. You sleep already, so you are in my world now. You will come with me, and I will show you my power. And then, then maybe you'll repent this ingratitude and welcome the honor that you've earned! Come with me, and watch!

* * *

Damon crawled to Theresa, who had collapsed onto a lounge chair. The thin fall of frost that covered the room had powdered her hair, her eyelashes.

He couldn't stand. The pressure was too great. Had he thought it was bad before? The sort of steel-crumpling pressure that destroyed submarines? That had been nothing compared to this. This was like being on another world, a frozen moon of Jupiter where the gravity was far greater than that of Earth.

Still, he pulled himself to Theresa, his lungs and heart laboring valiantly in his chest.

She was asleep. So far under that he knew he wouldn't be able to wake her this time. Yet even in sleep, her face was a mask of distress. Her eyes rolled sluggishly behind their lids. Her lips moved, but he couldn't make out what she was trying to say.

It had begun, and there wasn't a damn thing he could do to help.

* * *

Derrek Blake always knew he had been on stakeout too long when Mark Gladstone's theories began to make sense to him.

Last night, the topic had been 'aliens among us,' one that he was able to discount and refute no matter how many instances Mark dredged up.

Tonight's topic was a little more persuasive, the idea that the ancient Egyptians and Mayans had both been inspired by the same lost culture. The list of similarities in their styles of building, pyramids, sun gods, advanced building techniques known no where else in the world at that time.

Derrek found himself nodding, and Mark took this indication of agreement as a springboard to jump to a few conclusions about Atlantis and the *true* origin of secret societies.

Whose influence was still with us today, undeniable, just look at the back of a dollar bill and you'll see for yourself, the eye and the pyramid, symbol of the Illuminati, and the pyramid and the eye, which supposedly represented the sun god by some chain of logic that had left Derrek in the dust.

They were parked across the street and a half a block down from Monatella's Family Grocery and Delicatessen, and except for the spectacle of three hookers chasing a transvestite down the sidewalk, had the night to themselves. At 3:20 AM, even the muggers were abed.

Mark had managed, with his usual flair for the creative, to convince their captain that they'd gotten an anonymous tip that Tony Monatella was the next potential victim, probably a copycat killer or empty threat but the caller had known some details about the Spencer murder that hadn't been generally released, so it was worth checking out. Derrek didn't like it, although it was interpretively true. But it had gotten the captain to give them permission to keep watch on the place for a few nights.

Or maybe she just wanted Gladstone out of her hair as well. He was a good cop, but his intuitive leaps were hard to follow and harder to document or explain in court.

So here they were, two detectives on a Saturday night, and for the past few minutes Derrek had been developing a strange feeling of foreboding. And with it, the certainty that his brother was in trouble. Damon knew a lot more about this than he was telling, and Derrek knew he was holding back because what he had to say was so crazy that he worried even his own big brother wouldn't believe him.

What had his twin gotten himself into? Had he, out there in his serene coastal podunk town, met someone who claimed to have a psychic connection with the killer? Or something even more preposterous? It bothered Derrek that his brother might be wading in Mark Gladstone's waters, bothered him more that it had created this weird barrier of holding back and uncertain distrust between them.

He had tuned Mark out completely, but his head had kept up its unconscious habit of nodding in the right pauses and places. Now he tuned back in and found with some dismay that they'd come back to Mark's all-time favorite, the business about the government's highest elechons being secretly controlled by this Illuminati bunch, who, because of their links with Atlantis, had access to life-extending technology . . .

"Wait," Derrek pleaded. "Enough, Mark, okay? For a little while, enough."

"Too much all at once? Sorry. Yeah, when I first started realizing just how it all fit together."

"I need to stretch my legs. Maybe take another walk in front of Monatella's. You coming?"

"Sure." Mark opened his door and got out.

Tony Monatella lived with his elderly father, the wizened gent they'd noticed on their first visit to the deli, in an apartment above his store. Tony himself was widowed, his wife Gina lost to a brain aneurysm four years ago, boom, no warning, right in the middle of the lunch rush one Tuesday.

The Monatellas had no criminal connections, and the one time a two-bit hood trying to build a name for himself had gone to hit Tony up for protection money, Tony had sent the hood on his way with two busted wrists and a nose that would never be the same. Kids didn't even mar his storefront with graffiti.

Tony was known throughout the neighborhood as a decent hardworking man but also one tough son of a bitch, and nobody screwed around with him.

Mark's line of thought had evidently been pacing Derrek's, for now he said, "Some of the other Black Rose victims were in pretty good shape. Navarro taught phys. ed. But none of them were as big as Monatella, or as well-trained. Our killer might have his hands full with this one."

"Yeah, if we're dealing with a normal man here."

Derrek stopped, and so did Mark, and they looked at each other.

"Wait a minute," Mark said, a huge grin spreading across his face. "Isn't that *my* line? When did you start thinking like me?"

"I don't know, but I wish it would quit." Derrek turned up the collar of his coat against the wind and crossed the street. His sense of foreboding had grown worse. Now he was sure that not only was Damon in danger, but he and Mark were, too.

"Just between you and me, partner, all of a sudden I have the *worst* case of the creeps," Mark murmured, scanning the empty night around them.

"So do I. Come on."

They were right in front of the deli, peering up at the dark windows of the upstairs apartment, when someone screamed. A man. A big man.

"Go!" Derrek had noticed before that, his reputation as a tough son of a bitch notwithstanding, Tony Monatella also believed in security measures. The bars and locks on his store would have deterred all but the most bullheaded of thieves, which meant it also deterred the police.

He ran past Mark to the alley, to the fire escape. From above, the first scream was followed by a second that was brimming with more terror than anyone should ever know.

"Holy shit!" Mark said. "What could make a shaved ape like Monatella scream like that?"

Derrek didn't answer. Didn't want an answer. Didn't want to know. But it went with the badge. No backing out now. He scrambled up the fire escape, seemingly taking forever, Mark at his heels.

A second voice joined Monatella's. The father, caterwauling his son's name.

With no time to waste, Derrek shot the lock off the kitchen window and shoved the pane upward. Someone had set a row of potted plants on the sill, and they detonated in bomb-blasts of ceramic and potting soil as Derrek climbed through. He raced through the kitchen, barking his shin on a chair, and threw himself to one side of the swinging half-door that led into the living room. He knew Mark was with him though he couldn't hear a thing above the combined shrieks of the elder and younger Monatella.

Mark put his back to the wall. Derrek jerked his chin down and Mark nodded. When they moved, it was as one smoothly-functioning unit. Derrek thrust the door open and Mark went through, dropping to his knees as Derrek came up behind him. One high, one low, both with guns at the ready. By the book.

The fabled book had no suggestions how to handle the situation they faced as they burst into the small but tidy living room.

Monatella's father was on the floor, a lamp in pieces beside him. Derrek knew right away that the old gent had tried to smash it over the head of the intruder that had ahold of his son, and paid a heavy price. He was semi-conscious, and from the way one leg was oddly shortened and twisted, they were looking at a hip fracture.

Tony himself had been backed all the way across the room, his wide shoulders pressed to the wall between a crucifix and a picture of the family back when Tony must have been no more than ten years old. His short-cropped hair stood on end in his fear. His screams had stopped because his jaw now sagged like a cloth sack of crushed eggshells. One arm hung limp at his side, and the other, dripping from a series of short defense wounds, grasped drowningly at the arm of the intruder.

The intruder had Tony pinned to the wall, with the heel of one hand planted firmly against his forehead and the other in a fist against his chest.

No. Wrong.

The other in a fist *through* his chest.

Wide claws, not razor-sharp but blunter, made for gouging, had punched through the skin and flesh, the first two fingers to the right of the sternum, the second two to the left, passing between the ribs and then curled down and under so the claws re-emerged. The intruder had Monatella by the ribcage, blood gushing down.

Monatella's boxers were already soaked crimson, and in lieu of his screams, he now made a sucking-whistling noise that came not only from his gaping mouth but also from the deep, brutal rents in his chest.

But that wasn't the worst.

The smell . . . the smell of the intruder filled the room, overpowering the stink of blood and loosed bowels. It might have been a pleasant scent – cinnamon, musk, dark chocolate – had it not been mixed with other odors.

Part of the reek triggered a bizarre association in Derrek's mind, reminding him of the first time he and Virginia had gone away together. Three years of dating, he'd finally talked her into it, yes, come on, Virginia, don't make me wait, just like Billy Joel sang so energetically. A cabin upstate. They'd done it like rabbits, glutted themselves on sex, until they couldn't even *think* about it anymore. And the bedroom, the cabin's bedroom, had been filled with the odor of their frenzied passion.

The other part of the reek also reminded him of Virginia, but a few years later, visiting her in the hospital. She'd been diagnosed with the ovarian cancer six months after their wedding, and died shortly before their second anniversary. On his last visit, sitting beside her as she slept in the heavy grip of drugs, her body withered, that smell had clung to her like a stale perfume.

Cinnamon, musk, dark chocolate . . . and sex and death.

But even the smell wasn't the worst.

The worst was their first look at the Black Rose Killer.

Derrek Blake felt his rationality go with a painless tug. They had charged through the kitchen door and right into Hell.

* * *

Theresa was gone.

That chilled Damon worse than the freezing temperatures in the atrium. One moment, she'd been in that unnaturally deep sleep, but now she was gone.

Her body hadn't moved, but her face had gone as dead and slack as a corpse. Her eyes no longer rolled, her lips no longer tried to speak. The only way he could tell she was still alive was from the faint clouds that formed as she exhaled.

But she, the inner, the *essential,* Theresa, was not there.

It's taken her along, Damon thought. *Oh, God, it took her along.*

* * *

With a soulless laugh as ominous as an eclipse, the intruder bunched its arm and braced its other hand more solidly against Tony Monatella's head. An oval of plaster had cracked behind his skull.

Mark Gladstone, who had spent his life training his mind to deal with just-about-fucking-anything, only hesitated for a split second. Beside him, Derrek was frozen like a waxwork.

"Stop!" Mark bellowed. "Police!"

Then, not bothering to wait and see if the creature surrendered, he started shooting. Because things like that were outside. Outside the law, outside the realm of human experience. Outside of everything. The Black Rose Killer would never stand trial. No, when it came to *things* like that, the old ways were best. Old ways like stakes and hammers, silver, fire, cold iron.

Cold iron.

He realized that even though he'd emptied the clip and hit every time, the bloodless holes didn't harm the intruder in the slightest.

The edges, the image of it, seemed blurred and unreal somehow, leaving Mark with only vague impressions. A towering body-shape that dwarfed even Monatella, muscular but oddly *underdeveloped* somehow, even childlike. It was partly wrapped in a shadow that looked like great batlike wings one second and a flaring cape, the color a deep velvet-black, rustling with a sound like wind through leaves, and giving off the rich dark scent of roses. The rest of it was thorns . . . thorns for claws and teeth . . . and eyes that were orbs of midnight with ruby-red pupils.

Derrek snapped out of his horrified daze and echoed Mark's shout, "Police!"

"Blake!" The fury in that inhuman voice was indescribable, and the creature's shock was only surpassed by Derrek's at hearing his name on the lips of this monster.

As the two of them stared at each other, Mark took advantage of the distraction to reload, slamming in a new clip. Monatella was still against the wall, but had given up his struggles and now just slumped. If he hadn't been pinned there, he would have slid to the floor.

Derrek and Mark opened fire together.

As before, the bullets didn't harm the thing, only made it stagger a little from the impact.

Then it struck back in the most gruesome way imaginable – it clenched its fist that was still buried in Tony Monatella, and in a hideous crackling and snapping sound that took Mark years back to the time the family dog had gotten ahold of the Thanksgiving turkey carcass, pulled Monatella's breastbone and half his ribcage out through the ripped skin of his chest.

It flung its trophy, the stiff spiderlike cluster of bone trailing shredded organs and spraying blood. Something warm and wet smacked against Mark's cheek, the rest hit Derrek. He stumbled back, pawing at himself, gagging.

Monatella dropped, thankfully landing face-down. As the creature stepped away from him, Mark noticed a flutter of movement and saw a black rose land on Monatella's back. His sunken, swaybacked back, Mark's mind insisted on noting with clinical revulsion.

"Blake," it said again, packing more hatred into that one syllable than it could have fit into a roaring rant.

But as it crossed the room, it faltered. Looked at Monatella's outstretched hands, the lake soaking into the carpet beneath the body. From there, it looked again at Derrek – Mark had lost whatever marginal interest he might have held for the creature

— and then at Monatella, in an agony of deprived wrath.

It couldn't attack Derrek, Mark realized. It had come for Monatella, and now that its job was done, it had to go back to wherever it had come from.

An icy wind buffeted him and the creature began to fade like dissipating smoke. For a moment, Mark thought he saw another figure near it, an unfamiliar woman with black hair and dark eyes filled with grief and horror.

Then it was gone, and if there had been a second apparition, she was gone too.

Mark patted his arms and torso, amazed to be alive. He hurried over to Derrek, who was fighting to keep from vomiting. But every time his sight fell on the mangled bones on the floor, he came nearer to losing that battle.

"Come on, partner," Mark said, feeling more than a little like throwing up himself. He steered Derrek toward the kitchen, away from the mess. Through the open window, they could hear sirens. The neighbors had heard all Hell break loose — literally — and now the cavalry had arrived.

Mark pushed Derrek into a chair. His partner gazed up at him, disconnected.

"Damon. It mistook me for Damon!"

"Later," Mark promised. "Stay put. The old guy needs help." He put his gun on the table, cautiously stuck his head out the window and hollered to the units out front so they didn't come rushing in and blow him away before they realized he was one of the good guys, and went back out into the living room.

Mr. Monatella was out, and Mark could only hope that he'd lost consciousness before witnessing his son's death. Mark knelt beside him and gave him a quick once-over. Broken hip, probably a few sprung ribs. He figured the creature had simply backhanded the old man away, and his old brittle bones had done the rest.

When he was sure there was nothing more he could do for Mr. Monatella, Mark rocked back on his heels and distanced himself from the sound of the boys in blue rushing up the stairs that led from the apartment to the deli below. He closed his eyes to the sight of Tony Monatella's body, wiped at the trickle of wetness on his cheek but didn't bother looking at his hand, just rubbing it against his pants.

Deep, steady breaths. Through the mouth so as to minimize the stench of blood and the cloying-floral-rank odor of the creature.

He had no trouble accepting what he'd seen. All he wanted to know now was whether it was of this world or another . . . and most importantly, how to get rid of it.

Oh, yeah . . . and whether or not his inventive mind could come up with a convincing story to explain how he and Derrek had fired a total of three clips at the murderer, hitting damn near every time, and yet Monatella was still the only source of blood in the room.

* * *

See? Did you see my strength? My power? Bullets, human weapons, are nothing to me. They cannot harm me. Cannot kill me. What a man you have in me, Theresa! You should be honored that I have chosen you!

. . .

Don't turn away from me!

. . .

I'm speaking to you, woman! Don't reject me. Don't you dare reject me. I have chosen you, and I will have you. You're mine, Theresa. Why can't you accept that?

If that's what you want, why not just hold me down and rape me?

So cold! You sound so cold, and so full of rage! Why do you fear me? That's not what I want! Rape? I want your love! I want you to come to me willingly, give of yourself to me.

What you've already done to me is worse than rape. You've gone into my mind, into my soul, stolen from me, violated me in the most terrible way possible.

No, it's not like that!

You've drained away my . . . my life force . . . like a vampire sucking blood. Your strength comes at my expense, and you expect me to be impressed by that? Grateful? Honored? Don't flatter yourself! I despise you!

No! I will not listen to that! You haven't understood, haven't learned anything! What I've done, I have done for you! Why is that so hard for you to believe? These are your dreams I'm making real, your wishes come true at my hand!

These are not my wishes, not my dreams.

They are! Though you won't admit them to yourself, I know you better! Look at this one, Kowalski, your mother's husband!

Don't show me that!

You wanted him dead. You wanted him to die in pain and fear.

I left that part of me behind.

You can't leave anything of yourself behind, Theresa. You can't cut the past from you like a lock of hair and forget about it. It's in the texture of your soul. I can feel it there. You wanted him to die.

Him . . . maybe. But not the others!

Better! See? You can accept it! Soon you'll know what a great and glorious gift it is that I am offering you! With the sufferings of your past repaid a hundredfold on those who created them, you will be free!

I don't want any kind of freedom, any gifts, offered by you. The price is too high!

Price? What price? All I want is you! Your love, given to me willingly. Your love, and the warm cradle of your body to bear my seed.

. . .

Why do you shudder so? Look on me, Theresa!

No.

I know the form I wore to do my work was unappealing, but I can be anything you wish. Anyone you wish. Let me show you.

God! Get out of my mind! I feel it – burrowing, like worms! Get out!

*I'm just looking. See, what about **these** men? Men that are considered handsome, desirable, famous by your world's standards. What would you prefer, Theresa? This one, older and sophisticated, that white-silver beard and those piercing eyes, the accent? Or this one, with near-perfect symmetrical features, such beautiful dark skin, such a bright and brilliant smile? Or this one –*

Quit it! It doesn't matter what movie star you make yourself look like! I've seen the real you. That's no form you choose for convenience and physical strength. That's you. Ugly, vile, monstrous.

What difference does it make? I can appear to you in any form you wish! Isn't that what matters?

No, because underneath, I'll always know the truth.

Then love me as I am! Love me in this form! The things I can give you . . . you would be the envy of all the world's women! I can make you immortal, my Theresa, if only you will consent! Think of it! You and I and our children, all of us gods upon the earth!

I'd rather die.

I won't allow it. You may try to anger me, but I will not strike out at you. What would I be to kill you out of love? No, I see now. I see why you still refuse, resist. I've not yet proved myself to you. Of course. These others, lovers, yes, but brief affairs that never fully claimed your heart.

Don't.

But your once-husband . . . he's another matter, isn't he? He came after those others, and you went to him with trust and caring. And he betrayed you. Turned his back on your hopes and dreams. Put his own comfort above your desires.

Leave him alone!

Such a hold he still has on you! He denied you your own daughter, sent you off to live alone in a foreign place. Had he loved you, he would have done anything to see you happy. But his selfishness was like a knife, cutting the bonds between you. Yes, I see it now. The others may have meant little to you, but the hurt he caused was the worst of them all. You won't truly be free until he, too, is dead.

No! Damn you, leave Steven alone!

You still think that you care for him! After he treated you so cruelly! What will it take to open your eyes? What will it take to reveal to you the small but well-nurtured bloom of hatred in your heart?

I don't hate Steven!

Oh, but you do, my Theresa. You do. Let me show you.

* * *

Damon hovered over her, not sure what he should do. Go for help? Couldn't leave her alone. But with the way the weight of the room was pressing down on him, he knew he couldn't carry her.

She stirred and moaned softly. He leaned close, but rather than awaken, she rose briefly into that state he'd seen before. Eyes rolling. Lips moving in indecipherable silent speech. Her forehead knit in tension.

Though he knew it wouldn't help, he shook her, called her name. She only lolled in his grasp.

He stared at the necklace she wore. Was it causing this? Helping the incubus dominate her?

Tear it off? But what if that stranded her, left her body as an empty shell?

What if it was the only way to bring her back?

He took hold of it, the stone that formed the rose normally cool but now warmer than the room, warm as a loving caress, the jewel in the center throbbing slowly against his palm with a rhythm that matched Theresa's slowed pulse.

As he touched it, she lapsed back into gone-ness.

But even before he heard the ghostly whispers from behind him, Damon Blake knew he was no longer alone.

* * *

She expected to see the Phoenix house, but instead, the swirling blind nothingness parted to reveal a night-swept landscape. Theresa knew by the scent of the salt-sea air that they were still in Trinity Bay, even before she recognized Seacliff.

Not Seacliff as she knew it, but as she remembered it from old sepia-toned photographs dating back to the turn of the century. The east wing hadn't been built, the long low stable was a barn and carriage house, the stained-glass dome atop the central section was missing and in its place was a cupola with a narrow walkway around the outside.

"Theresa."

His voice was even deeper than Damon's, a hollow throbbing voice devoid of any humanity. She didn't want to turn, didn't want to see him. But an awful compulsion took hold of her, turning her to face the incubus.

He stood between her and the rosebush. In this strange between that was neither a true vision of the past nor a dream, the rosebush had grown to monstrous size. Its branches moved endlessly, restlessly, scraping over one another like a nestful of snakes, the hearts of the black blooms glowing with scarlet light that threw blood-shadows over the grass.

The incubus wore a new face. Not one taken from her memories of movies and People magazine's "Sexiest Men" issues, not the half-seen visage he'd worn when slaughtering Tony Monatella.

Instead, he stood before her as a tall young man, with black hair that tousled rakishly over his forehead and was pulled into a Mozart-style ponytail in the back. His skin was very fair, his eyes as dark as her own. He wore garb better suited to the last years of the 19th century, fitted well and stylishly to his well-built frame.

What all the best-dressed vampires are wearing these days, she thought, and laughed.

"Why do you laugh?" His tone was wounded.

"It's just another mask," she said.

"No," he protested. "This is how I truly am. How I would have been, had I been allowed to live. Bethany's son. The last of the Cliffwoods. Heir to Seacliff."

"It's a mask, a lie, like all the rest. How stupid do you think I am? This is your world, your dream-world. I've seen how you really look."

"But I've told you! It doesn't matter! I can be whatever you want me to be, Theresa. I can make you a queen, a goddess."

"You're a parasite. A leech. I don't want anything to do with you." She began walking away, through knee-deep grass toward the bluff.

He circled around in front of her and seized her by the wrist. There were ruby flickers in his eyes, and she sensed him struggling to maintain control.

"I've warned you not to resist me!"

"And I've told you no!" She tried to pull away, but his grip was fearfully strong. All too easy to imagine him twisting and tearing, one easy gesture on his part but her arm would be gone at the shoulder.

"I'm surprised at you. I would have expected you to bargain for your ex-husband's life."

"It wouldn't do any good." Clamped around her wrist, his hand had begun to subtly change. A greenish tint was creeping into his skin, his nails hardening, curving into thorn shapes. "I'd never trust you to keep a bargain."

"It hurts me when you speak to me so."

That was enough. Theresa lost her temper. "Oh, poor baby, tough shit! You kill people, drive others crazy, destroy lives, violate me, and then come across whining and petulant when I don't fall madly in love with you. Grow up! Take a hint! You can't have me!"

She had taken, at her agent Suze's insistence, a women's self-defense course when she moved to L.A. Hadn't been needed until now. But she pivoted, skidded the heel of her shoe down his shin and crunched it onto the top of his foot.

It was only then that she realized her own costume had changed as well. Half Victorian, half fetishist, complete with high-buttoned, outrageous high-heeled shoes. His trousers shredded, and the pointy heel impaled his foot.

At the same time, she grabbed his index finger and tugged it sharply backward. He yelped and leaped back, letting go of her.

Theresa ran, meaning to head for the guest house. Home. Safety.

But the rosebush, the writhing and animate rosebush, blocked her way. It sent out thick thorny tendrils, expanding and growing, like the wall of brambles that had barred the prince from the Sleeping Beauty. Roses, bigger than her head, swiveled to follow her progress and watched her with their cyclopean crimson eyes.

She veered left, toward the bluff. If this was partly a dream, then leaping might end like one of those falling dreams, with her jolting awake, in a cold sweat but unharmed. Then again, if this was partly real, she might well jolt herself right into oblivion.

It didn't matter. More thorny branches thrust up from the earth. She was hemmed in, surrounded, her only open path leading toward Seacliff.

"Theresa, stop this!" her would-be suitor called.

She ignored him and ran toward the house in that slow-motion syrupy movement characteristic of nightmares. Her high shoes were awkward on the uneven ground, her skirt snagging on twigs. It was a long black skirt with a ruffled lace trim around the hem, but the front of it was open so that her stocking-clad legs were visible all the way to the garters.

Above, the tight corset cinched her waist, making it nearly impossible to get a deep breath, while her breasts bounced and wobbled and threatened to explode out of their confinement. No blouse. Her hair combed up in a bun with a few wispy curls hanging down. A black velvet ribbon around her throat, with a cameo that felt, to her questing fingers, like a rose.

Good God, what I must look like! she thought as she neared the house.

"Come back!" he bellowed, his breath hot on her bare shoulders.

She risked a glance back. He had given up the pretense of masquerading as a Cliffwood and had taken on a horrific demon's guise. He charged after her on taloned claws, tail lashing behind him like a whip, leathery wings half-flared. Then he sprang high, took to the air.

Theresa saw his shadow tracking across the field, thrown there by the moonlight. She heard the flap of his wings, and then silence as he began his dive.

Trusting to instinct, she threw herself aside and rolled at the last minute. The cold backwind of his passage stirred the grass. His claws caught nothing but air. She scrambled to her feet and dashed the rest of the way to the house.

No terrace, no multi-layered garden. Not at this Seacliff, this image from the past. And the atrium, as she yanked the doors open, had no pool. It was a marble-floored ballroom, currently dark and empty except for six polished ebony caskets lined up in two rows of three. All were closed, and each had a single black rose resting atop the lid.

She intended to go straight through the atrium and out the front door, but the layout had changed. Instead of the foyer, she was in a long hallway with many doors opening off of it. All of the doors were different, none matching the decor of the house.

Here was a door with a poster of Buffy the Vampire Slayer on it. Now, *that* was apt. It looked familiar but she didn't have time to think about it, just went through.

Skidded to an appalled halt at the sight.

It was Jerry Forrester's room, and Jerry was on the bed with Sandy bent over him . . .

Theresa reversed out of there so fast she nearly broke her ankles in those damned high shoes. All the way across the hall to another door, this one an anonymous interior door that popped open when she ran into it. She stumbled on the edge of a rug and fell to her knees at the foot of a bed, where Ruth Edwards was getting a paddling from her husband.

"Theresa, no!" the incubus shouted from the end of the hall. "I've told you, they mean nothing to me! There's nothing to see!"

She didn't believe him, didn't want to see more, but there had to be a way out of here. She tried door after door – Nancy Ellsworth standing over her caveman boyfriend, wearing a pair of boots that put Theresa's own kinky shoes to absolute shame . . . a heavy iron-bound door more suited to a castle, behind which Megan McGuire was clasped in the embrace of a handsome rogue . . . she passed by the frosted-glass door that read "Trinity Bay Police Department," dreading what she might see on the other side.

Though the hall never turned, it somehow circled around and dumped her right back into the atrium where the six coffins stood in their somber rows.

He was waiting for her.

Panting, a stitch in her side, feeling dirty all over and *dirty* all over from the nasty yet weirdly thrilling scenes she'd beheld, Theresa stopped.

"I've decided," he said. "If my final demonstration doesn't sway you, doesn't convince you of the worth and strength of my love, then I shall have to reconsider."

"And let me go?" she gasped.

"No. And do what you suggested." His tongue darted out and slicked his lips. "Throw you down and rape you. *Then* there will be no more of this foolishness. Once you've felt me within you, once your own body has surrendered, once my seed ignites the fire of new life in your womb, then you'll come around."

Theresa shuddered. "I won't —"

"No more of your talk. I have work to do. You've left me no choice. It must all be done tonight, no matter how it tires me. No matter how much of your energy I must draw upon to sustain myself. You'll be a little older come daybreak, my Theresa, but it won't matter to me."

He snapped his wings to their full extension, thrust his clenched fists into the air. The room rippled, and when it cleared, there were *seven* coffins. Six closed, one open.

"The last task," the incubus said. "Tonight it ends."

* * *

Damon Blake looked up as the girls approached.

It said a lot about his state of mind that he was actually *relieved* to see three ghosts closing in on him.

He'd seen two of them before. One was Glory, just as she'd been when he'd met her in the Zane house, long blonde pincurls around a sweetly angelic face. The tallest of the trio was someone he knew, Angela Cliffwood, in the same simple nightgown she'd been wearing the night she'd jumped. The third was a petite young brunette, busty beyond her years, with a peculiar white fire burning in her eyes.

"He must be stopped," the brunette, Bethany Cliffwood, said firmly. "My son must be stopped."

"Ma'am," Damon said, "I'm more than willing. Tell me what I need to do."

Angela shook her head. "*You* can't, Chief Blake. But you can help *us* do it."

"It's his fault," Glory breathed. "He's the one who made them do bad things to us."

"But it was their fault too," Angela argued. "Their . . . their lusts woke him up."

"Whose fault it is doesn't matter!" Bethany hissed, her eyes blazing brighter than ever. When she looked at Damon, he swore he could feel the heat of her gaze leaving a searing path across his skin. "His for encouraging them, theirs for waking him, mine for bearing him, my mother's for what *she* did, Adam Reeveman for what *he* did . . . it doesn't matter. He *is*, and for the first time in a century, I have the chance to put an end to it. Once and for all."

This little miss, Damon thought, *is purely loco*. But he didn't have any better options. He glanced at Theresa, still insensate and barely breathing. "What do you need from me?"

"The same that *he* takes from this woman," Bethany said. "Give us of your strength."

Apprehensive, but lacking any other choice, he let them encircle him.

* * *

This time, it was worse.

This time, rather than being a passive observer, Theresa was actually *within* the incubus. Seeing through his eyes. Hearing, smelling, feeling all that he sensed.

She knew what it was to manifest, to bring a physical form from the nothingness. She knew the tremendous physical power in this chosen body, the potential for destruction.

The darkness cleared, and she saw what she had expected and dreaded to see. They were in the backyard of the Phoenix house. At this time of year, the desert night was cold, the sky overhead like an upended bowl of black crystal studded with knife-sharp stars.

With inhuman ears, she heard the sudden speeding up of a canine heartbeat, followed by a low growl of fear. The incubus had appeared just a few feet from Ruff's doghouse, and, like Jack, like Jim Navarro's dog, Ruff was reacting to the invasion.

Ruff, stay! Theresa tried to yell, remembering what Damon had said about Jim's dog, neck snapped, body thrown carelessly aside. And that had been a trained German Shepherd; Ruff was a smaller and more amiable retriever mix.

Let him come, the incubus thought with a chortle.

Ruff emerged, cowering low to the ground, whining and baring his teeth. Theresa willed him to keep back, keep silent. Incredibly, he obeyed and slunk away, quivering.

You are more worried about the dog than the man, the incubus noted, amused. *Perhaps because the dog never hurt you, never betrayed you.*

Steven never hurt me or betrayed me either, she thought.

Poor Theresa . . . even now, you won't admit the truth? Look inside yourself. When you left him, it wasn't just because of your disagreements over your career. Look . . . look . . .

Things began flashing past her then, like images from a scrapbook, clips from films. Theresa Zane, this is your life! Or, at least, here are all the things about your husband that really got under your skin!

"My wife doesn't work. She's a writer."

The same furious, frustrated annoyance bubbled up inside of her as she heard those words, a pale echo of Steven's voice. Even after the *Lora and Ruff* books had become popular, even once talk of a television show had begun, he'd kept on with that condescending attitude toward her writing. Not *real* work.

And then there'd been the way he'd treated Lora. "You're too easy on her, Theresa!

You're going to spoil her!"

Not that he was ever cruel, abusive. No, not that. But always holding too-high expectations, demanding too much, pushing too hard. Had to talk early, walk early, potty-train well before the average age, learn French, learn to read, keep her things neat. In Steven's world, there was nothing worse than wasteful, unstructured time when it came to Lora. She knew that currently, their daughter went to school five days a week, had piano lessons Monday and Wednesday afternoons, gymnastics lessons Tuesdays and Thursdays, and Pee-Wee Soccer every weekend. When was Lora supposed to have time to *play*, to just be a kid?

Those were the biggies, compounded by a host of tiny nagging nits that the incubus insisted on showing to her in detail. Every habit of his that irritated her – the way he showered with the curtain outside the tub so that water ran all over the floor, the way he had selective blindness about where he left his clothes, the way he sneered "Tell me *another* one" at the nightly newscasters when he felt they were full of shit ,which was most of the time – all of those minor but unendearing quirks were blown up, distorted, magnified.

He's a decent man! Theresa insisted. *All couples have a few things they can't stand about each other. You're making too big a deal of it.*

She struggled to get her anger under control, sensing that it was the key. The incubus dug up her negative feelings, amplified them into rage, and then destroyed the ones responsible. She couldn't allow herself to dwell on anything negative about Steven. Who *was* a decent man, a good man, a good husband and father.

What about the way he cheated on you? she thought.

What are you talking about?

Don't play the fool, my Theresa. Well before you decided to divorce, he was bedding that woman. An affair with his secretary, how trite! Because **she** *was always there for him.* **She** *wasn't distracted, paying more attention to silly books and a spoiled child than to her own man. She doted on him, cared about his every need.*

You're lying, Theresa thought desperately, trying to force from her mind all of the things that she had noticed and wondered about during that time. Late nights at the office, blond hair in the laundry, whiffs of unfamiliar perfume . . . the speed with which Steven had gotten together with Cheryl once Theresa had moved out . . .

The more she tried *not* to think of those things, the more they jumbled and clamored in her mind. All that time, the signs had been right under her nose, and she had pretended not to see.

Oh, Steven, you bastard, she thought without meaning to. That opened the door on her anger, and as if he'd been waiting for just that moment, the incubus pounced. He plunged into the river of her emotion and drank of it as if it were blood to a vampire's fangs, or water to a parched plant, drawing it eagerly and hungrily into himself.

Then, overbrimming with stolen energy, he ignored Ruff's terrified howl and wrenched the patio's sliding glass door out of its tracks to enter Steven's house.

* * *

It wasn't an unpleasant sensation. Reminded Damon Blake of the way a cool bath slowly leached the warmth from a body.

They didn't bite him or do any of the other things he'd been worried they might need to do, just stood around him with their hands linked. With his every exhale, he felt a little more tired, and they looked a little more substantial.

"When they return, we will be ready," Bethany announced.

"Wait, what do you mean, return?" Damon asked. "I thought you were going after him."

"We cannot," Glory said. "We're bound to this place. All of us died on these grounds, and cannot leave."

"But he died here too!"

"He's not like us," Bethany said. "When he comes back, he will be weary from the killing. At his weakest. That is when we will have our only chance at finishing him."

"You mean a man's got to die in order for this to work?"

"What is the life of one man, more or less?" Bethany's eyes flashed anew. "Men cannot be trusted! They lure you with promises and lies, and then when they've had what they want, they turn their backs on you! They are selfish, vain, arrogant beasts!"

Damon reeled back from the intensity of her white-fire eyes, but didn't give up. "Can't you stop him now?"

"We can't *reach* him now," Angela said. "Not until he comes back."

"Not all men are like that! Jerry's not like that, neither am I."

"Jerry . . ." Angela said sadly. "I know, Chief Blake."

"My papa wasn't like that," Glory chimed in.

"Neither was yours," Damon told Bethany. "He loved you. Gave you that necklace. Named his boat after you."

"My father promised me that he would always be there for me, always look after me. And then he died, and left us with our mother, who brought Adam Reeveman into our lives. So he lied too! He broke his promise too!"

Damon abandoned that argument, seeing it would do no good. "I can't sit around and wait while an innocent man gets torn to pieces."

Bethany laughed. "Innocent? There is no such thing! If it were only men, why shouldn't my son be loosed like a plague among them? Why shouldn't they be made to suffer for all the pain they cause? But it's not only the men. Others suffer for this too. His very presence killed Glory, killed Angela. He's the worst of them all. He has to be destroyed, you know that as well as we do. And this is the only way."

"But we can't do it without your help," Angela said. "He's too strong for us alone."

Glory touched Damon's hand, and this time he actually felt it. Not like smoke but not quite as solid as flesh, either. "Please help us. We just want to be done here. We just want to rest."

"Where will you go?" he asked. "What'll happen to the three of you?"

"We'll finally go where we belong," Angela said. "We won't be trapped here anymore."

"But *where?*"

Bethany smiled, for the first time showing something other than bitterness.

"Heaven? Hell? Reborn into new bodies? The beyond is what you make of it. And we have been here too long."

* * *

The familiar house seen through demon's eyes. Everything in it turned into a mockery of its former self. A place where Theresa had once been content, happy, loved, was now a place of nightmares.

She couldn't let this happen! Even if Steven had done all of those things, he didn't deserve to die for them. And Lora certainly didn't deserve the horror of having her father brutally murdered.

Why do you keep fighting me? Give in, Theresa! Share this moment with me! When you feel the flesh part under our claws, when you feel the hot bulge of his organs pushing through the skin, when you smell the blood and taste the mortal fear, you will know what it is to step above mortality!

She blotted his invasive persuasions from her mind and conjured the image of the necklace. Smooth sculpted silver. Satiny black. Its solid weight resting on her chest. She focused on it, concentrated on it. Willed herself back to it, and her body.

No, you don't! You will take part in this! Don't you dare leave me! Don't you dare deny me! Not after all I've done for you!

Ignoring him. Thinking of the necklace. Picturing it against her sweater.

She was dimly aware of the incubus moving faster now, on a whirlwind path of devastation through the house. Paintings and prints ripped from the walls. Furniture upended with crashes and splinters. The television imploding in a whiff of ozone. From the second floor, cries of alarm. From the back yard, Ruff's frantic barking, the sound of him pulling at his chain.

Then, just as she felt herself begin to lift away, she heard Lora's voice wailing in fright.

Don't you leave me! the incubus shouted, but she separated from him with a soul-jarring weightless drop.

But rather than return to her sleeping, empty shell, she went to her daughter.

She knew she couldn't stop or sway the incubus. All she could hope to do now was spare Lora the trauma of having to witness it.

Or, worse . . .

She thought of the German Shepherd, of Tony Monatella's father. The incubus could only hurt those who got in the way of his wrath. If little Lora gave him the chance, Theresa knew he wouldn't hesitate at lashing out at the child. After all, if Theresa was to whelp his unholy spawn, what use would she have for her living, human daughter?

Intangible as a wraith, she passed through Lora's door and saw the child sitting up in bed, holding her stuffed doggy tight-tight-tight, her green eyes wide and shimmery with tears in the glow of the *Blue's Clues* nightlight.

Lora looked right at Theresa, and gasped, "Mommy?"

* * *

33

Of all the ungrateful, willful, stubborn, foolish women!

Now his rage knew no bounds. That she could keep refusing to see what was right before her eyes, refusing to accept the wonderful gifts he gave her!

She was no longer with him, but they were still connected. Oh, yes. Still connected.

He reached out and found her, drew on her to gorge himself more than ever before. Yes, glutted, stuffed, until there was more than he could contain and the excess crackled off of him like sparks. The sheer force of it hurled objects from his path as he rampaged up the stairs and along the hallway.

The master bedroom's door opened and there he was. Steven Taylor, the man who had shared Theresa Zane's bed for years, who had been the recipient of her willing caresses, her eager touches. There he was.

In the boiling-over of jealousy, the incubus barely noticed that the man was holding a gun. Once he did spy it, he laughed, a great and booming disdainful laugh that blew wallpaper into tatters. Ridiculous little gun! If the others hadn't been able to stop him, what hope did this one man have?

Thinking of that brought back the thought of Blake, the amazed shock of seeing Blake in that apartment. But the scent had quickly told him that it wasn't Damon Blake but one very like him. Identical, their scents very similar but not quite exact.

Yet, somehow, that Blake had known about him. Tried to stop him.

Well, it had failed, and this Steven with his tiny gun would fare no better.

He knew how he must appear, a huge hulking shadow charging through the gloom. Then, as Steven raised the gun, the incubus reached the fringe of light from the open bedroom door. At that moment, he spread his wings as wide as the hallway would allow, slashed the air with his claws, and gaped his jaws wide to reveal his thorny teeth.

Steven froze where he stood, amid the sudden acrid reek of urine. Behind him, visible through the open door, was a woman by the side of the bed.

***This** was the woman he'd forsaken Theresa for? Slim, pretty, with small but high breasts well-exposed by the peach-colored teddi in which she slept . . . but compared to Theresa's dark beauty, this*

Cheryl was inexcusably bland. And spiritless, too; as she glimpsed him, she uttered one high-pitched scream and then fainted across the bed.

He sensed Theresa nearby, knew from the tender outpouring of love that she was with her daughter. Knew also that she had finally realized that she couldn't stop him from doing what must be done. That was the first step toward acceptance, and following acceptance would come desire, devotion, adoration. There was still hope for them!

Of course! What had he been thinking?

It wasn't the husband at all! Theresa only wanted to let him live so the child didn't have to see the gory aftermath of his work. She didn't care whether Steven died or not, probably preferred that he did, as long as it wasn't in the presence of the child.

He should have seen it before. It wasn't as if he had no compassion, after all! He held no grudges against the girl. Lora was no threat to him. Indeed, Lora might grow up to be just as appealing as her mother, a fitting earthly mate for one of the sons that Theresa would bear.

No wonder she was so upset with him! He must have come across as an insensitive boor!

As a favor to her and Lora, then, he decided to be done with it quickly. Much as he would have liked to draw it out, inflict a new and agonizing injury for each year that Steven had been with Theresa, he was willing to sacrifice his own wishes for hers.

The man still had not moved. He stood there in a puddle of his own piss, the gun forgotten. His throat worked, as if he thought he were shrieking for help, but nothing emerged.

The incubus advanced. He was tiring rapidly, so even if he'd been so inclined, he might not have had the stamina to fully torture Steven as he'd planned. His rest of a few days hadn't fully refreshed him, and there was a limit to what he could do without overtaxing himself and Theresa. He was quickly approaching that limit. After tonight, they would both need a good long rest. Preferably in each others' arms.

As he got within arm's reach, Steven snapped out of his stun and made one last attempt at self-defense. He pointed the gun at the incubus and tried to fire, but nothing happened. Gibbering now, Steven scuttled backward, groping for the safety switch.

That time, the gun went off. The bullet sank into the tissue that made up his chest and stuck there harmlessly. No pain, of course, just a dull thud that informed him the shot had struck.

He swatted the gun away. Now, too late, Steven tried to run. But he hadn't even gotten two steps when the incubus' hands closed on the sides of his head.

He turned the man so that he could watch his face.

Squeezed.

Dug his claws into the scalp where Steven's sandy-brown hair was just beginning to thin.

Steven was trying to pry loose, but his efforts were of no more consequence or bother than those of a fly.

Squeezed harder . . .

crackle

And harder . . . now the man's eyes, an arresting dark green, were protruding frog-eyes and his mouth was stretched into a cavern. Dank sleep-breath with a faint toothpaste undertone wafted into the incubus' nostrils.

There came the first signs of blood, from the nose and the ears.

Steven was making some sound now, not a groan and not a whimper but full of pain and pleading.

crackle

Steady, relentless inward pressure against the sides of his head, feeling the shift and give as the bony helmet of the skull began to split apart into plates.

He was aware of fists battering feebly at him, then coming up to grasp his wrists and pull. All to no avail.

Peering directly into Steven's eyes, seeing full comprehension there of what was about to happen, the incubus drove the heels of his hands inward with all the force he could, at the same time gouging through the scalp to peel flaps of hair and skin away from the naked bone.

crunch!

The eyes burst from the head as if seeking escape.

It was done. He let go.

* * *

Theresa rushed to her daughter's bedside. "Oh, Lora, oh, honey!"

"Mommy!" Her tremulous fear turned into delighted excitement. "Mommy, what are you doing here?"

"You're dreaming, honey."

Lora's face screwed into a frown. "Dreaming?"

"Yes, see?" Theresa extended an arm, pushed it through the mattress. It was spongy but not resistant, prickling slightly along her skin. "Only a dream."

Unspeakable sounds of violence came from the hall, and Lora's gaze flicked nervously that way. "What's happening, Mommy? Is it the bedbugs?"

Theresa winced. Bedbugs. Cheryl had made the mistake of saying goodnight to Lora with the old adage about not letting the bedbugs bite. To an imaginative, vulnerable five-year-old, that had resulted in many nightmares.

"Shh, shh," she said, trying to stroke Lora's tangled ebony hair, barely able to feel it beneath her insubstantial hand. "You're going to be just fine, Lora. I promise."

To soothe the girl, to drown out the noises, Theresa began to sing "Colors of the Wind" from Disney's *Pocahontas*, which had been Lora's favorite lullaby as a toddler. She only faltered once, at a gunshot from the hall.

Amazingly, the song worked its old magic, and Lora yawned, lay back down, and cuddled up with her stuffed doggy. "Will you sit with me for a while, Mommy?"

Theresa nodded and smiled, with effort. Lora wasn't the only tired one. Exhaustion was creeping through her limbs, making her eyelids heavy.

"Now, go to sleep, honey," Theresa said.

Lora murmured something, sighed, and slept.

Theresa looked at her with sorrow. Steven was dead. She could already feel the beginning of the dissolution that meant the incubus was finished. He would be pulled back to his strange realm, taking Theresa with him.

Tears slid from her eyes, over her cheeks, dropped onto the backs of her hands. She wept for Steven, but mostly she wept for Lora. In the morning, she would find out that her father had been killed, and what would that do to her?

In the mirror over the white dresser, Theresa saw herself fade into nothingness.

* * *

She faded back into herself, again wearing her spanking-governess fetish outfit, in the Seacliff that wasn't.

He stood before her in his Cliffwood guise, smiling proudly. "You're free, my Theresa! Free of every man that ever hurt you! Now we can become one!"

Theresa attacked him. She had no intention of doing it, but found herself in a fit of anger flying at him. He staggered back at the viciousness of her assault, but easily overpowered her and held her by the wrists.

"I have tried over and over to be reasonable," he growled, his eyes changing to red-slit black orbs. "But you continue to resist me, defy me. I give you one last chance to accept me, Theresa. Let me be anything you want. Let me make your dreams come true. Don't make me force myself upon you. Show me, let me be the mirror of your desires."

His mind burrowed into hers again, slimy serpents working through the hidden caverns of her thoughts. As he did so, his features began to change, taking on aspects of various men she'd seen and entertained idle fantasies about.

A vindictive grin twisted her lips. She brought one image to the forefront of her mind and *pushed* it at him as hard as she could.

The incubus, seeing himself wearing the face and form of Damon Blake, roared in outrage and struck out at her. She didn't have a chance of keeping her balance in those high shoes, and slid partway across the floor on her back.

"You wicked bitch!" he bellowed. "You've had your chances. Now you've left me with no other choice. I'll have you physically, Theresa. I'll have you *now!*"

Swirling nothingness engulfed them.

* * *

"Now!" Bethany joined hands with Angela and Glory.

Damon gritted his teeth. They were drawing on him, draining him. A deep and awful lethargy pressed him down to the cold marble floor. Breathing became a chore, movement an impossibility. It was all he could do stay conscious.

A smoky form manifested on the other side of Theresa, looming over her. It was so hideous, so abhorrent, that if Damon had been in full possession of his body he would have fled like a pack of hounds were on his heels. As it was, all he could do was lay in a fetal position and stare as it became fully solid and spread its dusky rosepetal wings.

Theresa opened her eyes, but the same lethargy that held Damon also held her. "No," she whispered. "I refuse."

"I *will* have you!" the demonic creature declared.

"You'll not," Bethany said. "We will put an end to you."

The incubus sucked in a gasp, and slowly turned his head to look at the trio of young girls, their expressions grim, their hands linked. "You would all be nothing if not for me! Dead and gone, burning in Hell like the wicked girls that you are! Because of me, you're spared that! Strike out at me, and you'll only destroy yourselves as well!"

"It's worth it," Angela Cliffwood said. "Die!"

"Begone!" Bethany shrieked.

"Go away!" Glory added her cry to theirs.

Theresa, with a titanic effort of will, rolled from under the incubus' descending thorn-tipped hand. She thudded to the floor beside Damon, and he found the will himself to draw her protectively into his arms. They clung to each other, shaking, as the opposing sides in this conflict of the dead and damned siphoned off their strength.

No bolts of spectral energy shot back and forth between them, no swirling ectoplasm marked the battle. It was all invisible, or taking place on some level where it was beyond the perception of normal human sight. But Damon could sense the tremendous tides, surging as Bethany attempted to drive her son into the death from which he'd arisen, as he fought to avoid that banishment.

"The necklace!" Glory called to Theresa. "Smash it! Now!"

"Can't . . . move," Theresa groaned.

Damon inched his hand to the rose pendant, which had swung down to rest on the swell of her breast as she lay on her side. "Take from me."

"Damon, no, it'll kill you!" she protested weakly.

"Do it!"

With a strangled sob, she closed her hand over his, and the draining intensified. Before the incubus could steal it from her, she sat up, Damon's hand falling away.

She didn't bother with the clasp, just yanked and it broke. Holding it by the chain, she whirled it once and brought it down on the marble.

The black rose shattered.

The incubus shrieked. A shockwave burst from him that caused the French doors to explode outward onto the terrace. The stained-glass dome high overhead split into shards and caved in, raining onto the ice sheet that covered the pool.

"Well done, ma'am," Damon said, and everything went dark.

* * *

Noooo!

He screamed his denial, too late, too late!

Already, his power was running from him like blood from a wound.

Diminishing! Dying!

Undone by his own mother! By she who had ignited the spark of his life, nurtured him on the flames of her undying bitter rage! That she should do this to him! That the others should go along with it! That even his Theresa could be so blind, so stubborn to help them!

He would not allow it!

Whirling from the three dead girls, he ran. Before the glass had even finished pattering from the ceiling, he was at the doors, out. Into the night. Running for the one last place that would give him safety and shelter. Not even they could harm him there.

Oh, and then he would have his revenge! He would rest, recover, and then return!

He heard the ecstatic cries of the dead girls as they were released. With the necklace broken, the power that bound them to this living world was gone forever. As were they. No more would he share Seacliff and the garden with them. They were gone, but he remained.

He had won.

* * *

Bethany and Glory cried out, their uplifted arms and faces suddenly bathed in the most glorious light Theresa had ever seen. It surrounded them, absorbed them. Then it winked out, leaving a dazzling afterimage floating in Theresa's vision.

"Oh, my God," she breathed.

"He got away."

Theresa jumped at the voice, stared in surprise at Angela. "You . . . you're still here?"

"I never wore it," she said, gesturing at the broken necklace. "That wasn't what kept me here. I still have something to do. And so do you. He got away, but he'll be back. Unless you can get rid of him once and for all."

"What do I have to do?"

Angela told her.

"Okay." She went to Damon, found him alive but unconscious. She briefly touched his cheek, but didn't try to rouse him. There wasn't time.

Although tired and achy, she couldn't let herself rest. The moment she tried to do that, she knew she wouldn't be able to hold off sleep. And once asleep, she'd be back at the mercy of the incubus.

The stable was divided into a garage and a storage facility for all of Walt Davis' landscaping equipment. The garage half was locked, but the other wasn't. She found what she needed on a shelf above the workbench, and carried it around to the place where the wilds encroached on the garden.

The rosebush rustled with eager expectancy as she approached. In the whisper of the wind through the leaves, she could hear her name.

Thereeeeesa.

The branches strained toward her, as if yearning to draw her into their thorny embrace, press petals against her cheeks and lips in night-fragrant velvet kisses.

She paused.

A tremor of erotic longing made goosebumps rise on her skin.

What the incubus in person hadn't been able to do, the rosebush itself did, making her weak-kneed with desire. What unknown pleasures did it offer? What secrets did it know?

Shouldn't she be, after all, honored to be chosen?

Didn't she deserve to explore those dark passions?

Her breath quickened, her insides felt fluttery and melting. She wanted to shed her clothes and feel the brush of petals all over her body, the lovebites of thorns on her breasts and thighs.

Anything she wanted.

It promised anything she wanted.

Any man . . . even any woman, child, animal. All that she wanted, whatever she wanted.

She closed her eyes and the tempting images swirled through that inner darkness.

But then, suddenly, absurdly, a fragment of song occurred to her and brought with it memories of going to midnight movies with Nick, all of them laughing and throwing rice-toast-toilet paper, shouting at the screen. The total ludicrousness of it was like a slap.

"No more!" Theresa yelled. She upended the gascan, the fluid gurgling out to drench the rosebush and soak into the earth beneath.

It lashed out, thorns raking across her forearm and leaving ragged scratches. A branch snarled in her hair, but she pulled the box of wooden matches from her pocket anyway and skidded one down the sandpaper strip. It bloomed into flame.

The rosebush lurched as if trying to pull itself up by the roots, dragging her to her knees by the hair. A swipe of a rose-laden branch tried to knock the match away, igniting a few leaves. The bush beat itself against the ground, snuffing out.

Theresa got another match, then a fierce yank to her hair made her spill all the others. She struck it, lit it, and at the cost of more thorn-slashes, thrust the burning match down toward the roots. The flame tasted a puddle of gasoline, and blue fire fanned out in rippling circles.

whoosh!

Flame raced up through the rosebush. Theresa smelled singeing hair and tore herself loose, leaving clumps and strands hanging from the thorns. She scrambled away on hands and knees, then got unsteadily to her feet.

Someone touched her shoulder.

Theresa spun, sure it would be him, the incubus, that this insane nightmare would never end. But it was Damon Blake, looking haggard and unwell but there, whole, alive. The leaping flames were reflected in his dark eyes.

It couldn't escape. The rosebush began falling apart. In the center of the inferno, a manlike form was writhing in torment, screaming in pain and fury and denial.

Then gone, crumbling to a heap of ash.

Theresa leaned against Damon, and he leaned against her. With their arms around each other, they watched as the rosebush was reduced to embers.

That final lingering sight, of black roses wreathed in fire, would stay with her for the rest of her life.

* * *

One last thing to do.

One last thing, and then she, too, could be finished.

She heard the considerately hushed laughter of the night-shift nurses, the muted beeping of medical monitors, a radio softly playing a rock-and-roll tune.

Heard the labored breathing of the patient in the bed.

Angela Cliffwood looked down at her stepfather and thought about forgiveness, absolution, mercy.

As if realizing he was no longer alone, Brad Thornton opened his eyes. They instantly widened with shock as he saw her standing over him.

If she did nothing, she knew, he would live many more years. Many more years unable to move his legs, feed himself, speak coherently, control his bowels. Some would think that death might be preferable to a life in that condition.

But then . . . they didn't know what would be waiting for men like him on the other side.

She did.

Bethany had said that the beyond was what you made of it.

What some people made was worse than any Hell they could imagine.

"Agh . . . Ahnj," he said. Pleading. Frightened.

She thought again about forgiveness, absolution, mercy.

Then she fixed her gaze on him, and the pressure began to increase, the air pushing down with crushing weight. He lifted his left hand, the only one he still had some movement in, and grasped at his throat. His breathing, already labored, turned to frantic choking gasps.

The monitors signaled his distress, but before the first nurse rushed into the room, Brad Thornton was dead.

Angela held on a moment longer, just a moment, long enough to move to the room where Jerry Forrester slept. She leaned down and brushed an insubstantial kiss on his forehead, and then raised her face and arms to the light that poured down, and let herself go.

* * *

Epilogue

Two weeks after the burning, a small group gathered in the oldest section of Trinity Bay's cemetery to say a final good-bye.

The clouds overhead were a heavy purple-grey, but a golden sun peered under them from the west, spangling the sea with rhinestones. All of the colors, from the rich green of the trees to the stunning pink of the hydrangeas that surrounded the cemetery, seemed bright, vivid, renewed.

Flanked by his dad and sister, Jerry Forrester was still on crutches. His knee was mending well and the doctors expected him to manage without a limp by the holidays, though whether he'd be up for the strenuous role of Peter Pan in January remained to be seen. His eyes were shadowed, not the eyes of a teenage drama star but of a veteran who had toured the darkest regions of Hell.

Theresa knew just how he felt. But in her case, there was a bittersweet light in that shadow. As she stood in her simple black dress with her head bowed, listening to Reverend Carmody offer a prayer for a child who had died long before any of them were born, she was very conscious of the small, warm hand clasping hers in trust and love.

Lora wore the same deep blue knit dress she'd worn to her father's funeral. She stayed close to Theresa, quiet and withdrawn.

As Reverend Carmody finished, Theresa reassuringly hugged Lora and then transferred the girl's grip to Travis. She stepped forward and laid a single white carnation on Glory's grave.

"Rest well, little one," she murmured.

A soft rain began to fall, touching the plain grey headstone with droplets that sparkled like jewels in the slanting sunlight.

Damon came up behind Theresa and put his hands on her shoulders. "Time to go."

She nodded.

The Forresters left, followed by Scott James and Reverend Carmody. Kel McGuire came over to Theresa and Damon while Dani Kensington, her bruises faded to a dull yellow, waited a few yards away.

"How are you two doing? Really?" he asked.

"Better," Damon said. "Almost back to normal."

Kel looked pointedly at Damon's hair, then at Theresa's. She touched it self-consciously.

"Yes, I know," she said. "It . . . it aged us a little. Five years, maybe ten. But I can deal with a few strands of grey. We feel all right, that's the important thing."

"What about Lora?"

Theresa sighed and glanced at Lora, who had towed Travis over to examine the bouquet-sized hydrangea blossoms. "It's been rough on her, of course it has. I'm just glad Mrs. Lowenstein, their neighbor, was able to take care of her until I got to Phoenix. Cheryl was in hysterics, the police were crawling all over the house. I didn't want Lora to have to see any of that."

"I hope she's not going to put you through a big custody fight," Kel said.

"Far from it. When I told Cheryl I wanted to bring Lora here for a while, she insisted that I just have her move in with me. She wasn't able to handle her own grief and help Lora too."

"She needs some time," Damon said. "Time and attention. It won't be easy, but she'll get past it." He put an arm around Theresa's waist. "And remember, like I keep telling you, you're not alone."

"That's the best thing," Kel said. "Not being alone." He turned from them and went to Dani, and they walked toward his car.

"In fact, if you'd like," Damon said, "you'll never have to be alone again."

She smiled up at him. "Is that an offer or a promise?"

He winked. "Whatever you make of it, ma'am."

* * *

Captain Torres picked up her pen, and Mark Gladstone watched attentively to see what she did with it. That pen was the best clue to what was going on in her mind.

When she held it in one hand and twiddled it, she was deciding how best to give her approval. When she tapped it against her lips or chin, she was trying to come up with the best way to politely disagree.

Mark was hoping for either of those, but when she pinched the ends of the pen between her thumbs and forefingers, held it in front of her face, and fixed him with a steely glare over the dividing length of it, his spirits sank.

"Now how about telling me what *really* happened that night, Gladstone?" she ordered in the form of a question.

"Heh . . ." he grinned weakly. "It's all in my report, Captain."

"Yes. I've read your report. I practically have your report memorized, Gladstone, because I've been called upon to present it to the mayor's office, the FBI, Internal Affairs, and the press. According to your report, while you and Blake were on stakeout, the killer broke into Monatella's apartment through the kitchen window, freaked out on PCP and strong as ten weightlifters, wearing a monster suit with claw-gloves. This nutcase knocked Monatella's father down and broke his hip, then went after Monatella."

"That's right."

"You and Blake went in through the kitchen, ordered him to surrender, and when he didn't comply, you had to open fire."

"Yes, Captain."

"But the perp was wearing a vest under his monster costume."

"Uh . . . yeah."

"The investigators later found three bullets embedded in the wall, two from Blake's gun and one from yours. Every other shot, to the tune of three clips, struck the perp. But because of the vest, because he was hopped up on drugs, it didn't take him down. He proceeded to tear Monatella apart like a roast chicken."

"I didn't use those words in my report."

"Then, after *ripping his fucking sternum out*, pardon my French –"

"I didn't use at least one of *those* words in my report either."

She leaned forward sharply, and the pen bent into an arc, only millimeters away from snapping in a spray of ink. "I'm paraphrasing, Gladstone, shut your trap."

He did.

"Then, hearing the sirens, he decided to make a run for it, and went back out the kitchen window. You saw him going up the fire escape, onto the roof. And after that, we lost him. The other officers arriving on the scene saw nothing, never found a trace of this guy."

Mark nodded, still keeping his trap shut.

"Now, are you *sure* he went up the fire escape?" Torres said, dripping sarcasm. "He didn't use his Bat-grapnel?"

"Captain, I know how it sounds –"

"It sounds like a load of crap, Gladstone. I know invention on short notice is your strong point, and I want the truth." Her tone brooked no further nonsense.

He sighed. "Captain, if I tell you what really happened, you'll think I'm crazy."

"And that'd be a new thing?"

"You've already got us both signed up for extra sessions with the head-peepers."

She set down the pen with a click. "Mark . . . I'm going to let your report stand. I'm going to let that be the official story. But this is turning into a media circus, and if I'm going to help cover this, I need to know everything. *Everything*. No matter how outlandish. I want to know what I'm putting my ass on the line for."

"Thanks, Captain." Taking a deep breath, he started talking.

* * *

Theresa tucked Lora into the bed that had once been hers. "Good night, honey."

"Mommy?"

"Yes, Lora?"

"Am I going to stay here for always?"

 291

"Well, until you grow up and want to move out into your own house." She stroked a few errant strands back from Lora's brow, and kissed her. "But that's not for a long, long time."

Jack strolled in, giving Ruff a wide berth. After a harum-scarum first week, the two of them had reached a tentative truce. Ruff raised his head from his forepaws and watched the cat jump up onto the windowseat, then exhaled in a doggy snort and stretched out on his side on the floor beside the bed.

On the dresser, Pikachu the hamster rattled his water bottle as he got a drink, and Lizzy the lizard was hidden from sight but for the tip of a green tail poking from beneath a piece of driftwood. These two were both new additions since the divorce, and Travis had given Theresa a bemused look when he found out that he would be sharing his home with such a menagerie.

"I miss Daddy . . ." Lora's eyes brimmed and she wiped them on the corner of the blanket.

"I know, honey. I know. It's okay to be sad."

"You know what, Mommy?"

"What?" Theresa asked, though she suspected she already knew.

"I had a dream about you. You came in my room and sang to me."

"Did I?"

Lora nodded sleepily. "Will you sing to me again?"

Before Theresa got to the part about asking the grinning bobcat why he grinned, Lora was asleep. Theresa kissed her again, softly, on the forehead, and left the door partway open.

She went downstairs, where she found her dad, Damon Blake, and Scott James sitting around the table. They'd made a pretty good dent in the cookies she'd baked that afternoon.

" . . . guess the board is pushing him to retire," Travis was saying.

"But the investigation cleared him," Damon said. "There's no proof he did anything to worsen Thornton's condition. My God, it's amazing he lived as long as he did!"

"It does look bad, from the hospital's standpoint," Scott said. "Doc Kensington shouldn't have performed any of the surgeries. Not when he had a personal stake in the matter."

Theresa helped herself to a cookie. Oatmeal-raisin-walnut-white-chocolate-chip. "I don't believe even he would stoop to giving someone inadequate care out of revenge."

"I don't know, he was pretty pissed when he saw Dani." Scott shrugged. "Who can say what they'd do in that sort of situation? If she were my daughter, and I was standing with a scalpel over the son of a bitch who beat her up, I'd be tempted."

"So who's suing who?" Theresa wondered.

Damon rolled his eyes. "Thornton's estate is such a godawful mess. He hadn't updated his will after Angela died. Guys like him think they're going to live forever. He's got no family to speak of. So it's looking like things might revert to the terms of April's will. Which left everything to Angela, with Thornton as her guardian until her eighteenth birthday."

"But Angela's dead," Travis said. "And I'd be willing to bet *she* didn't leave one. Who'd expect a sixteen-year-old girl to have a will of her own?"

Theresa gave him an arch look. "Of course you intend to re-phrase that . . ."

He chuckled abashedly. "You know what I meant."

"So right now," Damon continued, "the lawyers are looking at the wording of April Cliffwood's will. April stipulated that should Thornton die before Angela's eighteenth birthday, a new guardian would take care of her and the estate. *Before Angela's eighteenth birthday*. Not until she *turned* eighteen. See the difference?"

"And her birthday is when?" Theresa asked.

"February nineteenth."

"Did she name another guardian?" Travis asked.

"That's the really fun part." Damon took another cookie. "She named her best childhood friend. Sandy Forrester."

"Oh, God," Theresa groaned.

"And Sandy's been declared legally incompetent," Scott said. "What a balls-up! Who gets it then? Charlie? Holy crow, can you see Charlie Forrester trying to handle Seacliff and the mill?"

"Not the mill," Damon cut in. "There was a separate codicil about that. The mill goes to the Employee's Association. It's up to them to decide to sell it or keep it running, and they all share in the profits."

"Charlie Forrester." Travis shook his head in amazement. "The man can't even balance a checkbook."

"A fact of which he's well aware," Damon said dryly. "He doesn't want it. Doesn't want the house, the money, the responsibility. He's planning to sell Seacliff, liquidate everything, keep back enough to make sure Sandy has the best care for as long as she needs it, give huge settlements to Dani Kensington and his own son Jerry, and donate the rest to the town."

"The town managers must be doing cartwheels," Travis observed.

Damon nodded. "But he wants to make sure it goes to good causes. The school, the parks, repaving the streets, Silver Grove –"

"Anything but the pot patrol, right?" Scott interrupted, laughing.

"Well, he did mention environmental causes, but I don't know as that applies," Damon grinned. "The point is, some good will come out of all of this."

"What *about* Sandy?" Theresa asked. "Everyone else seems to have gotten over their . . . their dreams. Embarrassed, yes. Unwilling to talk about it, yes. But the others have all put it behind them. Hasn't she shown *any* improvement?"

"I don't think it's the dream anymore," Damon said. "I think it's a breakdown caused by what the dream made her do. Attack her own son. That's the guilt that's got her. She won't be at Blue Lake State forever."

* * *

Later that night, Theresa slipped quietly from the house.

The rain that had pounded Trinity Bay all evening had finally rained itself out, leaving the October night as clear as glass.

"Taking a stroll, ma'am?"

"Damon!" she laughed as he came from the shadows. "Sneaking up on me again?"

"Couldn't sleep," he admitted. "It's been two weeks, but it's still hard for me to believe it's over."

"It is," she said. "He's gone. They're all gone. No more killings. No more nightmares." She stuffed her hands deep in the pockets of her jacket. "What's going to happen with the investigations? What if someone figures out the link?"

"There's no way they could try to pin it on you," he assured her. "You've been right here the whole time. Besides, the last two took place hundreds of miles and only an hour apart. Not even a Lear jet could have got someone there that fast. The press is all over it right now – tell you the truth, I'm surprised it took them as long as it did – but eventually, the Black Rose murders will get shoved to the back of the line by new cases. They'll go in the unsolved file, and there they'll stay."

"I feel bad about that. The families. Never knowing. And everyone else, always thinking the killer is still out there."

"We both know it's got to be that way. What about you? Are you going to be all right?"

She lifted her chin. "We soiled doves do just fine, Sheriff. We're tough. But it helps if we're not alone, like you said."

He leaned close. "I did say that."

"I know something that might help you sleep," she whispered, lowering her eyelashes to gaze up at him through their fringe.

"And what might that be?"

Theresa slid her arms around his neck, pressed her body against him. "Take me home, and I'll show you."

"With pleasure, ma'am."

They turned away from dark, silent Seacliff, and toward a warm, bright future of their own.

* * *

The End.

About the Author

Christine Morgan lives in the Pacific Northwest with her husband, daughter, and trio of cats. She is a graduate of California's Humboldt State University, with a B.A. in Psychology. Her overnight-shift job as a residential counselor in a psychiatric facility allows her ample time to write as well as the occasional flash of inspiration.

She divides her writing time among a variety of genres – horror, fantasy, childrens' fiction, and erotica among them. Her previous works include the *MageLore* and *ElfLore* fantasy trilogies, the Origins Award nominated short story "Dawn of the Living-Impaired," and various other works appearing in anthologies, magazines, and in several online forums. She and her husband Tim co-edit an online 'zine, *Sabledrake Magazine*.

A longtime gamer, Christine can often be found at regional conventions, running games as well as promoting books. She has a fond relationship with the folks at Steve Jackson Games and other names in the gaming industry, all of whom have been incredibly supportive and helpful.

Her other interests span a wide gamut – robotic combat, British comedy, documentaries, and reality game shows make up the majority of her television viewing habits; horror, mysteries, and thrillers dominate her bookshelves; and she enjoys cooking and crafts.

Christine welcomes and appreciates feedback from readers. She can be reached by e-mail at christine@sabledrake.com and invites visitors to her website, www.sabledrake.com.

Also by Christine Morgan:

The *MageLore* Trilogy

Curse of the Shadow Beasts
MageLore Book One

Arien Mirida, elven wizard in exile, hopes to find an end to the curse that has plagued his family for generations. His only hope is a young thief, and a forbidden love that will either save, or destroy him.

Dark of the Elvenwood
MageLore Book Two

A sinister plot is taking shape in the mysterious southern reaches of the Emerin, in the home of elves who serve a bloodthirsty god. To combat this menace, Arien Mirida must abandon his peaceful life and be reunited with the one woman he cannot forget.

Archmage of the Universe
MageLore Book Three

With the city of Thanis and the impressionable young Highlord under the control of the evil minotaur mage, Solarrin, Arien and his friends embark on a dangerous mission. Their objective is to find Talus Yor, the only wizard whose powers rival Solarrin's. But they face one great obstacle: Talus Yor is dead.

The *ElfLore* Trilogy

Silversilk
ElfLore Book One

Ariana Mirida, sorceress and swordswoman, answers the call to adventure when she travels to her ancestral homeland seeking to clear her father's name. Little does she know how her quest will affect an entire kingdom . . .

Knight of the Basilisk
ElfLore Book Two

She was not always a warrior-priestess of the dark elven god. Once, she was only Tilanne, granted an unexpected destiny by a dying knight. To attain it, she had to defy convention and give up her dreams. This is her story.

Truegold
ElfLore Book Three

The future of the elves and the fate of all humanity hang in the balance. A renegade knight plans to make a deal with a dragon, a sacred jewel in exchange for a deadly poison. As the rightful king of the Emerin races to stop him, the counts and wizards of the elves scheme to fill his vacant throne.

Coming Soon by Christine Morgan:

***The Silver Doorway* Series,
a set of fantasy books for children and pre-teens**

The Broderick kids – twins Kevin and Katie, and their little brother Sam – always thought there was something strange about their Aunt Ellie. When they discover a secret room in her basement, and a magical silver doorway that takes them to another world, they find out for sure.

**Silver Doorway #1 – A Gnome Away From Home
Silver Doorway #2 – Dwarves in the Dark
Silver Doorway #3 – An Elf's Adventure
Silver Doorway #4 – (title TBA)
Silver Doorway #5 – (title TBA)
Silver Doorway #6 – (title TBA)**

**Find out more online:
www.silverdoorway.com**